ILARIO:
THE LION'S
EYE

Also by Mary Gentle

ILARIO:
THE LION'S
EYE

A Story of the First History

Book One

Mary Gentle

An Imprint of HarperCollins*Publishers*

The first part of *Ilario* appeared in a slightly different form as *Under the Penitence*. Copyright © 2004 by Mary Gentle, published by PS Publishing Limited. All rights reserved. An extract titled 'The Logistics of Carthage' was first published in *Worlds that Weren't,* by ROC, in 2002.

This book was originally published in Great Britain in 2006 by Gollancz, an imprint of the Orion Publishing Group, London.

HarperCollins books may be purchased for educational, business, or sales promotional use. For information please write: Special Markets Department, HarperCollins Publishers, 10 East 53rd Street, New York, NY 10022.

FIRST U.S. EDITION

Library of Congress Cataloging-in-Publication Data is available upon request.

ISBN: 978-0-06-082183-8
ISBN-10: 0-06-082183-3

07 08 09 10 11 ❖/RRD 10 9 8 7 6 5 4 3 2 1

A legend of Classical times says that, so strong is the eye of the lion, that its sight does not die with its owner. And here, by the lion's eye, we see prefigured the art of the true maker of images: the painter whose vision remains long after he himself is dead.

Leon Battista Alberti, fragment, in the rough drafts of *De Pictura* ('On Painting'); not included in published verson AD 1435

Contents

Part One
Under the Penitence

1

We are so often a disappointment to the parents who abandon us.

A male voice interrupted my thoughts, speaking the language of Carthage. 'Papers, freeman—'

The man broke off as I turned to face him, as people sporadically do.

For a moment he stood staring at me in the flaring naphtha lights of the harbour hall.

'—freewoman?' he speculated.

People shoved past us, shouting at other harbour guards; keen to be free of the docks and away into the city of Carthage beyond. I had yet to become accustomed to the hissing chemical lights in this red and ivory stone hall, bright at what would be midday anywhere else but here. I blinked at the guard.

'Your documents, freeman,' he finished, more definitely.

The clothes decided him, I thought. Doublet and hose make the man.

The guard himself – one of many customs officers – wore a belted robe of undyed wool. It clung to him in a way that I could have used in painting, to show a lean, muscular body beneath. He gave me a smile that was at least embarrassed. His teeth were white, and he had all of them still. I thought him not more than twenty-five: a year or so older than I.

If I could get into Carthage without showing documents of passage, I would not give my true name. But having chosen to come here, I have no further choice about that.

The Carthaginian customs officer examined the grubby, wax-sealed document that I reluctantly handed over. '"Painter", Freeman . . . Ilario?'

King Rodrigo Sanguerra had not been angry enough to refuse me travelling papers, now he had freed me, but he left me to fill in my own profession – furious that I would not consent to the one he wanted. But I am done with being the King's Freak. Nor will I be the King's engineer for machines of war.

'My name is Ilario, yes. Painter. Statues; funeral portraits,' I said, and added, 'by the encaustic technique.'

Show me a statue and I'll give the skin the colour of life, the stone draperies the shadows and highlights of bright silks; ask me for a funeral portrait, and I'll paint you a formal icon with every distinguishing symbol of grief. I thought it likely that people in Carthage would want their statues coloured and their bereavements commemorated, as they do elsewhere.

'It's a good trade.' The man nodded absently, running his wide thumb over the seal of King Rodrigo of Taraconensis. 'We get a lot of you people over from Iberia. Not surprising. You shouldn't have any trouble getting Carthaginian citizenship—'

'I'm not here to apply for citizenship.'

He stared at me as if I had taken a live mouse out of my mouth. 'But you're immigrating.'

'I'm not immigrating.'

The Visigoth Lords of Carthage tend to assume that every man and woman would be one of them if they could. Evidently the assumption extends to their bureaucracy.

'I'm *visiting* here. On my way to Rome,' I said, using the Iberian term for that city that the Europeans call 'the Empty Chair', since St Peter's Seat has stood unoccupied these many generations. 'There are new things happening—'

They are putting aside painting the iconic meaning of a thing, and merely painting *the thing itself*: a face, or a piece of countryside, as it would appear to any man's naked eye. Which is appalling, shameful, fascinating.

'—and I intend to apprentice myself under a master painter there. I've come here, first' . . . I pointed . . . 'to paint that.'

This hall is the sole available route between the Foreigners' Dock and Carthage itself. Through the great arched doorway in front of me, the black city stood stark under a black sky, streets outlined by naphtha lamps. Stars blazed in the lower parts of the heavens, as clearly as I have ever seen them above the infertile hills behind Taraco city.

Stars should not be visible at noon!

In the high arch of the sky, there hung that great wing of copper-shadowed blackness that men call the Penitence – and where there should have been the sun, I could see only darkness.

I glanced back towards the Maltese ship from which I'd disembarked. Beyond it and the harbour, on the horizon, the last edge of the sun's light feathered the sea. Green, gold, ochre, and a shimmering unnatural blue that made me itch to blend ultramarine and glair, or gum arabic, and try to reproduce it . . .

And yet it is midday.

Even when the ship first encountered a deeper colour in the waves, I had not truly believed we'd come to the edge of the Darkness that has shrouded Carthage and the African coast around it for time out of mind. Did not believe, shivering in fear and wonder, that no man has seen sunlight on this land in centuries. But it is so.

It alters everything. The unseasonal constellations above; the naphtha

4

light on ships' furled sails at the quayside; the tincture of men's skin. If I had my bronze palette box heated, now, and the colours melted – how I could paint!

'You're a painter.' The man stared, bemused. ' . . . And you've come here where it's *dark*.'

A sudden clear smile lit up his face.

'Have you got a place to stay? I'm Marcomir. My mother runs a rooming-house. She's cheap!'

My mother is a noblewoman of Taraconensis.

And she will attempt to kill me again, if she ever finds me.

Marcomir looked down at me (by a couple of inches), slightly satisfied with himself. I thought there was a puzzled frown not far behind his smile. *This short, slight man* – he is thinking – *this man Ilario, with the soft black hair past his shoulders; is he a woman in disguise, or a man of a particular kind?*

The latter will be more welcome to this Marcomir, I realised.

The brilliance of his dark eyes would be difficult but not impossible to capture in pigments. And the city of Taraco, while only across the tideless sea, beyond the Balearic Islands, seems very far away.

'Yes,' I said, automatically using the deeper tones in my voice.

There'll be trouble, accepting such an invitation, since I'm not what he thinks I am, but that kind of trouble is inevitable with me.

I shouldered my baggage and followed him away from the harbour, into narrow streets between tall and completely windowless houses. And steep! The road was cut into steps, more often than not; we climbed high above the harbour; and it had me – I, who have hunted the high hills inland of Taraco, and habitually joust in day-long tourneys – breathing hard.

'Here.' Marcomir pointed.

I halted outside a heavy iron door set into a granite wall. 'You do know I'm . . . not like most men?'

Marcomir's eyes gleamed bright as his smile when he flashed them at me. 'Was sure of that, soon as I looked at you. You got that look. Wiry. Tough guy. But . . . elegant, you know?'

I know. It's one of the two ways that men look at me.

He used my name without the honorific. 'Come inside, Ilario.'

He hastened me past his mother, Donata, a white-haired elderly woman with the hawk-face that would be Marcomir's too, some day, and I didn't protest the brief introduction. The walls inside the cool house were swathed in baked clay, the light of oil-lamps turning them Samian red, and our shadows moved ink-black on the wall behind Marcomir's wooden-framed truckle bed.

'You ought to know this, at least.' I sighed, having undone the ties of my hose; reaching to strip off doublet and shirt together.

Marcomir's response was lost in the rush of cloth past my ears.

I have, occasionally, concealed what I am, under circumstances like these. I have no desire to attempt it again. I wriggled the knit cloth of the hose down my thighs and off my feet, and stood naked, with the faint chill of the room prickling my skin.

'Not what you were expecting?' I said wryly.

The Carthaginian Visigoth sat down on the edge of the bed. 'You're . . . '

His gaze went from my rounded breasts – not quite large enough to dimple the front of an Iberian doublet – down to the phallus already standing up with desire.

Standing no taller than my clenched fist. God was not generous when He made me.

I watched for either a sneer or amusement on this man's face.

'Are you—' Marcomir stood, and stepped close.

He touched a finger to my chin, feeling the soft, ephemeral scatter of hairs which I had let grow for travelling. His wide, capable hands slid down my side, feeling the curve of my hips. The tension of his not touching my penis made me shiver. And – as ever – my penis curved over as my stiffness grew, pointing somewhat downwards.

I searched his expression for something – something – I didn't know what.

He put his hands between my thighs, fingers going up into the wet cleft of my female parts.

'You're a man-woman.' His voice sounded ragged.

An hermaphrodite. Hermaphroditus, the offspring of Hermes and Aphrodite. I didn't bother Marcomir with that.

I said, 'You don't need to have any part of me that you don't like.'

There is little else I *can* say, and it took me all the years between fifteen and twenty to devise that particular remark.

His face altered. I steadied myself. I have been put out onto the street before now. I guessed him not the kind of man who uses violence in an uncontrolled manner. But I can be wrong. There was a knife close to my hand, in my discarded clothes.

The height of him hid the lamp's flame. The close warmth of his body made every hair on my skin stand up.

His frown emerged. 'I thought you were a man like me. Not a ladyboy.'

'Marcomir . . . ' I sighed, reaching for my shirt.

His skin was shadowed ochre- and soot-coloured as he stood with his back to the lamp. Despite the keen sensation of my body, satisfaction is not always worth what one must go through to gain it.

Marcomir sounded uncertain. 'Do you want this? Are you sure?'

'Being a slave,' I said, 'I have not, until recently, been able to take decisions for myself. And now that I can . . . I intend to take every decision I can get!'

He lifted his hand, closing it on my right breast so tightly that a pang of desire shot from there to my groin.

He took my down-curving phallus in his hand.

I could dimly feel that he fingered for balls. There is a lump in the lips of my flesh, there, that sometimes deceives men into thinking I have them. The desire to spend came over me with such force that I barely noticed his investigations.

'Come here!' He urged me at the bed. Not expecting it, I stumbled; fell on my knees on the padded-cloth mattress and wool bedding.

His hands arranged me firmly, belly down on the bed so my breasts couldn't be seen; head to one side, so that we might look at each other in the face. His weight came down on the bed with me as he knelt between my thighs, pushing them together, urging me up onto my knees so that he could get at my buttocks. I felt the position absurd; it still made my heart thump, and my penis become harder.

His hand rubbed flat against my spine, sliding over the breadth of my shoulders. As his palm cupped my hip again, the heat and weight making me shiver, he abruptly took it away. 'I'm rider, not horse. And I don't fuck women.'

I could barely catch my breath. 'Then don't!'

He leaned forward and stroked my wispy stubble. For the first time, I allowed myself to hold his gaze. His pupils were wide and black.

With a rush of relief, I realised, *He wants me.*

Just – not all of me.

Passion fires passion like nothing else. Face-down on the rough wool of his bedding, I spent into it with my male parts before he was fairly in the saddle.

Towards the middle of what I could not keep in mind was the dark afternoon, when he had slept for a short time, Marcomir took me between sleeping and waking as a man takes a woman. I spent as a woman does. He sank asleep again. He won't recall this, later, I thought, as my body shed his seed.

The relaxation of flesh after sexual congress is an infrequent joy for me. I dressed myself, looking down at him stretched out naked and sleeping.

Can it be possible – might I stay all my time in Carthage here?

I didn't dare hope.

Will this man Marcomir be willing to look me in the face when he wakes? Can we do this more than the once?

I have learned, from others unlike this man, that afterwards is always the more dangerous time. I went downstairs. Even if he comes to regret what we did, he is less likely to hit me in front of his mother, I think.

In the warm, fire-lit kitchen, Donata got up from the floor-carpets as I entered. She crossed to the hob, and took the lid off a pot.

'You'll be hungry.' She said it so plainly that either there was no innuendo, or she was used to her son bringing home men for the occupation we had been about. 'Here.'

I seated myself on the cushions beside the hearth. In Taraco, we would be sitting around a wooden table, on wooden benches; here . . . even the house-door had been iron, and not iron-studded oak, I reflected.

Because nothing grows here, under the Penitence. It must all be shipped in. Corn for bread, olive oil for lamps, charcoal for fires, timber for construction. Brought by sail and caravan from Iberia and Egypt, to this great city, so rich . . .

'I can make you meals of an evening, as well as hire you a room.' Donata handed over a full pottery bowl, and sat down as limberly as a woman half her age. I decided there was a glimmer of amusement in her bird-of-prey gaze. Some indulgence of her favoured son?

'I don't know how long I'll stay.' The crushed grain porridge tasted unfamiliar, but was pleasantly filling – *And I haven't eaten since the ship!* I thought.

And since then, I've had . . . physical exercise.

That made me smile. Shovelling up the thick porridge, I scraped the bowl empty within minutes. The old woman Donata gave an amused snort, and went to a capped well in the corner of the room to draw up water.

I realised I was more tired than I thought: the room swayed about me.

My body thinks, because it's dark, I should be asleep.

I miss the light.

'A drink will be welcome – is the water safe, here?'

'Safe as anything else.' The old woman scooped water from the metal pail with something that flashed silver; I couldn't see what it was. A cup, a ladle?

The walls swooped up. I felt sick and dizzy.

The carpeted floor filled my vision as I floated down among the cushions. I felt the thud of my body falling as if muffled by more than eiderdown. A wave of heat and dizziness mounted up into my head.

In Taraco, the court once thought it amusing to give the King's Freak opium.

And this is how I felt then—!

Marcomir's feet came into my field of view, bare on the dusty floor.

He rumbled something to his mother. Not surprise. Not a complaint. My baggage appeared in my field of vision; he must have carried it down from 'my' room.

I wondered muzzily, Will they cut my throat when they've finished going through it?

The last conscious thought I had was *How many strangers have they done this to?* and *How could I fall for it!*

8

2

'Who's "Rosamunda"?'

I ignored the voice at my ear and fumbled at my face. What I touched was smoother skin than I am used to, unless I use depilatories, or pluck out hairs painfully as the ancient Romans used to. It stung.

'Oi! *Girl!* Shut up about Rosamunda, *whoever* she is!'

My throat felt sore. There were cold, cracked tiles under my hands. I pushed myself up into a sitting position.

The man squatting in front of me said something over his shoulder. I didn't catch it. He stood and walked away, his robe's hem flicking me painfully in the eye. The same style robe as Marcomir's.

I am in Carthage, still? – Or at least in lands of the Carthaginian Empire—?

I heard him say, 'Probably shrieking for her mother. Shut her up if she does it again.'

She?

Nausea rolled through me. My sight focused.

Along the granite wall beside me, men and women sat with heavy leather collars around their necks. Chains ran from the collars to ring-bolts. The stink of old sweat and piss haunted the air. Beyond a grille, a few yards off, men walked up and down. Naphtha lights hissed.

I am in a slaver's hall.

And Marcomir and his Hell-damned mother have shaved me, because I won't sell as a skinny man with no strength for manual labour.

The urge to shut my eyes and shut out the world was strong. I didn't follow it – my opium dreams are detailed, precise, and lengthy, and I had indeed been calling for the mother who bore me: Rosamunda.

Calling for her not to stab me.

My fingers felt fine skin at my jaw-line. The next man along from me dropped his gaze, leaning away. The man on his far side muttered; I heard '—woman built like a *stonemason!*'

Oblivious of their cynical laughter, I blurted, 'I can't be a slave again!'

Once, when I was sixteen, King Rodrigo and his court thought it amusing to hold mock-marriage ceremonies for me, to a woman the first night, and to a man the second night. After that, my bride and my husband got to tell the assembled nobles the particulars of the 'wedding night'.

9

That gained me two things. Firstly, the friendship and sympathy of Father Felix, a priest of the Green Christ who disapproved of such blasphemies. And secondly, the irrevocable knowledge that when my foster father and foster mother gave me to the King, they gave me soul and body with the legal deed of sale.

I glimpsed, down the hall and outside a stone archway, the identifiable skyline of Carthage.

A sweat of relief soaked my robe.

'Where's my papers?' I staggered up onto my feet. Bare feet on cold tile. 'I have King Rodrigo's writ of manumission; I'm a free—'

A moment of split-second decision.

'—woman; I can prove it! If you try to sell me, I'll appeal to the King-Caliph!'

The man who had shaken me awake put a hand on the whip at his belt. The chiaroscuro of his face gave him one gleaming eye and one empty socket.

He stepped towards me, and the shadows shifted. I saw he did indeed have but the one eye.

'You think the King-Caliph here's going to care about some poxy little Spaniard king over in the border states?' He chuckled. 'You might have been free then. And you might be free in the future. You're not free *now*. So shut up while I get a good price for you – although Christ-Emperor Himself alone knows, I couldn't sell you to a halfway decent whorehouse! Look at you! Damned cart-horse of a woman, you are.'

My hands touched wool. I looked down. I wore a much-darned robe, almost long enough to be women's skirts in Taraconensis; a belt pulled it in to show the shape of my breasts beneath.

The shock felt like cold water.

Not to see my baggage here – *well, Marcomir and his mother are thieves, yes*. Not to have concealing clothing; to know they must have undressed and dressed me again while I lay drugged . . .

And King Rodrigo's papers will have gone in their fire.

'Was anything brought in to be sold with me?' I asked the one-eyed man. He was not particularly tall; I stood on a level with him.

'What?'

'My tools, my equipment.'

He stared at me.

'I'm *literate*.' It was no more than the truth. 'I'm apprenticed to a master painter's workshop—' The truth, stretched. '—and I shouldn't be sold as unskilled labour! You can get four times the price for what I can do.'

He gave a thoughtful nod.

Part of his thought, I knew, would be the realisation that I had not always been free, since I knew so much.

But then, that's not uncommon: even in the kingdoms of Iberia, there's many a general, or chancellor, or powerful merchant, who either began life in a slave's collar, or wore it at some time in their career. They tell me it's different with the Franks in Europe; that even serfdom is gone a millennium, there.

Another reason for going to Rome.

Sell me; I'll be gone within the hour.

One-Eye could likely guess that too. I found I didn't care. That Marcomir and Donata must have a habit of drugging and selling unwary travellers – that didn't rouse my fury like the thought of my pigments and Punic wax, my scapulas and heating-irons, tossed on the trash somewhere, or sold off piecemeal for a tenth their value.

For all that Federico and Valdamerca (I wasn't invited to call them 'foster father' and 'foster mother' to their faces) picked me up as a foundling, I have all the skills of a noble soldier of Taraconensis. I was taught well, so as to be their gift for the King. Taught the arts of embroidery and the harp, and singing, as a woman; taught to joust with the lance, and fight with the sword, as a man.

Marcomir isn't worthy of a sword. A wooden cudgel will do for him, once I'm free.

'There were some old metal boxes and knives in a sack.' One-Eye gave me a shrewd look. 'They dumped them with you. I'm not letting you have anything sharp. Now shut up, before I have to mark you and make you worth even less.'

Abruptly, I found my gaze drawn by something – someone – over his shoulder.

Drawn by stillness, I realised. The man had been standing, an uncounted shadow in the background, for a little time. He stepped forward to the grille as I made eye-contact with him.

'You are literate, you claim?' He spoke directly to me, across One-Eye as the slaver turned around. 'More than merely to write your name?'

'I'm a painter; I can both draw and write.' Possibly I sounded stubborn. 'My name is Ilario. Give me parchment and a pen, and I'll show you how literate I am!'

Once out of the shadow, the newcomer was a large man, with a shaven head and naked broad shoulders. In the naphtha light, his reddish-tan skin shone very smooth. A woven reed and cloth headband kept sweat from running off his shaved skull into his eyes.

I noticed that his hands, crossed at his chest, were too large to be proportionate. *Also his feet*, I thought, as I glanced down at his sandals. The white cloth kilt that wrapped his waist was not wool, but some weave of flax; and not a Carthaginian garment, either.

To be sold to a foreigner . . . who may take me *anywhere* . . .

'She's special, is Ilario.' One-Eye picked my name out of the air without a stumble. 'And not cheap, because of that. Now—'

I folded my arms and stood watching them. Something about the

11

stranger's body made me want to sketch him, to see where those odd proportions of hands and feet would lead me. He carried his head high, almost daintily; I wondered if he had made the same error that Marcomir had, and took me for an effeminate man.

'No more than one hundred,' he said mildly, his large, lustrous eyes turning towards me. His voice was resonant, because of his depth of chest, but I thought he would sing tenor if he sang. Possibly higher.

I was so lost in speculation about where his people might live that I didn't pay attention to the negotiations. A clatter of metal startled me into alertness as a bag landed at my feet.

'Don't *drop* that!' I instantly knew, by the sound; and fell to my knees to yank open the hessian sack.

The pigments had gone, being saleable. Likewise the small sculpted heads, and the acacia and lime-wood boards I'd prepared with size for painting icons. No surprise. As for my battered tools . . .

One-Eye caught me with hands full of rush-stalk *calami* and reeds, spatulas and scrapers; bent close over my bronze box and *cestrum* and *cauterium*-iron, scrutinising them for damage. Before I realised, he had unlocked the chain from the ring-bolt, and put it in the stranger's hand.

'My name is Rekhmire'.' The foreign man spoke to me gravely, in barely-accented Iberian – as, indeed, he had spoken barely-accented Carthaginian to the slave-owner. He had a rounded aspect to his chin and nose that should have made him appear soft, but only added to his gravitas, given how tall and broad he stood. 'I have need of a literate slave, here. I don't need one that will run away. You,' to One-Eye, 'will therefore fix a name-collar around this one's neck, large enough to be visible in public.'

'You—' *can't!*, I bit off.

So much for being sold to a fool and a quick escape.

Rekhmire' said, 'The other alternative is a brand. You would prefer your face not spoiled, I suppose?'

Dumb, I nodded.

I stood dumb as the slave-owner and his handlers took the leather collar off me, and knelt dumbly beside the anvil as one of them deafeningly riveted an engraved iron collar closed beside my ear.

I have not often worn a slave's collar, but I was a royal slave from fifteen to twenty-four; I have no illusions that there is any difference.

'Let me have my sack,' I said as I stood up.

Rekhmire' said, 'You won't need—'

I took the risk of interrupting him.

'What am I, your slave all twelve hours of the day and all twelve hours of the night? I came to Carthage to paint. When I'm not working, I *will* paint.'

He met my gaze, calmly staring down at me. The bones of his brows were pronounced, under the roundness. The set of his mouth was strong. He held an authority all the more effective because he seemed to be at pains to hide it.

Behind me, One-Eye chuckled nervously. 'I should have charged you double for her; she's feisty.'

'Provided she can read and copy, she may be as "feisty" as she wishes.'

I wondered, seeing the gaze that went between them, whether the slave-owner had himself been in a collar once, and likewise this foreign man.

Rekhmire' gave a nod towards the sack of my belongings. I picked them up, careful not to pull against the chain.

I can paint; the rest is a problem to be solved.

With my leash in his hand, he walked towards the exit, and I hurriedly followed, the bronze box in the sack banging against my shin.

'"Ilario". An Iberian name?'

I grunted assent, matching my pace through the hallway to his with a little difficulty, being shorter. 'Where's "Rekhmire'" a name from?'

I did not call him 'master'.

He gave a light sigh.

'Alexandria-in-Exile.' He gazed down at me. 'You would call the city "Constantinople", I expect. I come from all there is now of Egypt, under the reign of Pharaoh-Queen Ti-ameny; I am,' he said, 'a royal book-buyer, for the Library. And when I cannot persuade a man to let me buy his scrolls, I can sometimes persuade him to lease me the right to copy them. Hence what you will be doing, Ilario.'

Constantinople: that great city of the east, that has stood as the last remnant of the Egyptian empire for more than a millennium, while Carthage and the Turks debate with war their old lands around the Nile. That great city, that stands as a bulwark against the Turks, with its Queen, and its bureaucracy that – that—

I stopped as we came out between iron-grille doors into a dark street. The chain yanked my neck painfully, but I only stared at him. 'You're a eunuch!'

Rekhmire' halted, giving a gracious, if cynical, bow. 'And you, too, are something of the sort, and not a woman.'

I ignored that. 'I thought eunuchs were fat! I thought eunuchs all spoke in high voices.'

'They do, if gelded as children. I was an adult man before I applied.'

His tone gave me to understand that more trespass would be rudeness, but still he did not speak as a man does to a slave.

Astonished – appalled – I said, 'You had yourself castrated *deliberately*?'

His narrow, plucked black brows came down. 'And you did not? No . . . No, I am wrong. You are no gelded boy. What are you? Is this—'

He made a gesture that took me in from head to heels.

'—this the reason why you left the Iberian kingdoms?'

The shock of waking as a slave again, and the shuddering kinship I felt for this mutilated man, moved me to speak honestly.

'I left because my mother tried to kill me with a poisoned dagger. And . . . she plans to follow me, and try again. But – yes. It is because of what I am. Everything is because of what I am.'

3

Above the roof-garden of Rekhmire''s hired house, the North African constellations shone clear.

By night, I saw, the correct season's stars shone visible; evidently not shrouded by whatever hides the sun by day. On the western horizon, a tinge of brown and gold marked the last of the unseen sun's setting. Above my head, veils of aurora-light rippled in the black sky: blue and green and gold.

Past sunset now. It gave me a sudden ache. *I haven't seen the sun since we entered Carthaginian waters.*

The Egyptian Rekhmire' rested his head on his hand, and his elbow on the couch, watching me as we ate. 'You are too ready to be a slave to be someone who has been free long. You say your King Rodrigo manumitted you?'

I looked up from the carpet on the tiles, where he had told me to sit.

'On the feast of St Tanitta, this year. For "long service". Truthfully . . . ' It hurt to say it. 'I think he was bored. Pension the freak off – after a decade at court, its tricks are all well-known.'

The small smoked fish were a delicacy not to be found in rooming-houses. I crunched them, bones and all, while my stomach settled from the poppy-drug.

'And besides, some other nobleman had given him a married pair of Frankish dwarfs. Cheaper for the King if I have to support myself. He pensioned some of the others off, too; and half his menagerie.'

Rekhmire' gave me a glance that made me feel a dangerous willingness to confide further in him.

Shock, I thought. And the disorientation of opium.

He said, 'And you are a danger to someone at the court of Taraconensis? Or was your mother acting for private reasons?'

That made me blink. I drank water from a silver bowl, to give myself time to consider – and waited while the house-slave refilled it. There is rank among slaves, as in everything else.

The castrated man Rekhmire' said, 'What *are* you, Ilario?'

'Why don't you just order me to pull my skirts up!'

It is not a tone for a slave to take to his or her master. But this man . . .

'*How could you do it?*' I burst out, before he could speak again. 'How could you be born perfect and ruin it!'

His shaped strong brows went up. '"Perfect"?'

His voice, when not speaking to the Carthaginians inside the complex of rooms below, sounded lighter to my ear. Not like mine – which is too husky for a woman and too feminine for a man – but still different from the normal run of men.

'Manhood is hardly perfect. I find it a relief to be castrati.' He also drank from a silver bowl, I saw. 'Not to be always thinking of women, when I should be thinking of books. Not to be—' Here he gave me a swift smile, almost a grin. '—seeking relief by my own hand, twice or thrice a day, or more. I was a brawler, as a young man. I find myself very serene now.'

He looked not more than a few years past thirty, to my eye. I wondered when he'd gone under the knife. The thought made me shudder.

' . . . And besides, it is often a condition of employment in the Pharaoh's bureaucracy.'

'You needed to cut your balls off so that you can go wandering around, searching for books for Queen Ty-ameny's library.'

He smiled equably. 'It does sound a little ridiculous, when you put it like that.'

There was nothing keeping him from beating me, or putting heated irons to the soles of my feet, except what looked like a certain natural decency. As well as it being prudent to tell him what he wanted to know, I thought I should repay that.

I said, 'All of it comes from this – I'm a freak. A true man-woman. I bleed. Oh, not often; two or three times a year. And I shed seed, though not as much of it as a true man does. I've never got a maid with child. I've not birthed one, either.'

Rekhmire' met my gaze. 'If what I've read is true, you should take care not to. It is either the operation which birthed great Caesar from the womb, or the man-mother dies in childbed.'

My stomach felt as if it had a sudden lump of ice in it. I thought of the feel of Marcomir's seed.

Mouth dry, I added, 'I was a foundling. Until I was thirteen, I thought I would never know my true mother or father. Hardly surprising, is it, to expose a baby such as I was? I was taken in by a family who, although impoverished, nonetheless had a claim to nobility; they trained me to be a suitable present for King Rodrigo, and Queen Cixila, who was alive then. By the time they brought me to court, there was only Rodrigo. He was . . . amiable to me. I was his favourite freak for a time.'

Rekhmire' swung his legs down from the couch. I saw the ever-burning street-lights of Carthage on the Bursa-hill behind him. For a long moment he sat staring at me.

I shifted uncomfortably. 'What?'

The house-slaves re-lit burned-out torches, in the warm evening. His long lashes shaded his eyes, and I thought I saw a smudge of soot-black at the corners, accenting them as the Alexandrine Egyptians do. His shaven head accentuated all his clean-cut facial features.

His lips pressed together in a thin line. 'There is no anger in your voice. That you should be trained like an *animal*—'

'It wasn't so bad. 'Nilda and 'Nalda were good to me – Sunilda and Reinalda, Federico's youngest daughters.' I smiled. 'I think they liked having a baby they could dress up as girl or boy. And Matasuntha was married before I grew old enough to get under her feet. With three dowries to find . . . I can understand why Federico acted as he did.'

'And this Rosamunda, this mother the slaver said you speak of; she is Federico's wife?'

'No,' I said reluctantly. 'Federico's married to Valdamerca, my foster mother.'

Rekhmire' stood, and shook out the folds of his linen kilt. He lifted an eyebrow at me.

I rose to my feet, as much to give myself time to think as to seem polite.

'Federico and Valdamerca raised me. It was Valdamerca who found me on the stone outside the Green Chapel. They acted as my foster parents . . . '

Whether it was the shock of slavery, or opium, or this man's unjudgmental face – or Rosamunda's actions the last time I had stood in her company – I found myself speaking of things I had never intended:

'My mother, the woman who gave birth to me, is called Rosamunda. My father is Videric, her husband.'

'And they are?'

'The Aldra . . . the "Elder"—' I stumbled for the word. 'The "Lord" Videric is King Rodrigo's closest councillor. Chancellor, you might say. And Aldro – "Lady" – Rosamunda is his wife, his hostess; the cynosure of the Court of Ladies. You begin to understand,' I said bitterly, 'why they would expose a baby born a freak?'

He nodded, but I went on:

'It's not just that a hermaphrodite couldn't inherit their estate, any more than a cripple or a feeble-witted heir can. It's the scandal of Aldra Videric having fathered such a thing! Aldro Rosamunda having given birth to it!'

Rekhmire' absently rested his oddly-large hand on my shoulder. 'I see, I think – this Lady Rosamunda has just discovered who Ilario truly is. And to avoid the scandal if it was realised that their unacknowledged child lives at court, the butt of their noble friends' jokes, scorn, contempt . . . '

The Egyptian spoke clinically, evidently familiar with kings' menageries and jesters. I felt my face heat.

' . . . No,' he corrected himself. '*That* can't be right! How long has Aldro Rosamunda known you were her child?'

'I came to court at fifteen. Since then.' I shrugged. 'How many other hermaphrodite children of my age would have been abandoned? It was obvious to her, who I must be.'

Rekhmire''s gaze sharpened. 'And her husband, a powerful man at court; he can easily have traced back your upbringing, found in what part of the country you were abandoned – yes, I see it. But . . . this same danger will have been in existence a long time: ever since you came to court. You are dangerous to Aldro Rosamunda now? Why now?'

'I've *never* been a danger to her! I've never wanted to bring scandal down on her; why would I? She's my mother!'

His hand dropped from my shoulder and he snapped his large fingers. 'You said – the King freed you! They might think you couldn't raise a scandal as a slave, but once freed—'

'*I would never have hurt her.*'

The Egyptian looked down at me. I begrudged him the height that lent him an illicit moral authority.

I said, 'She first came to me when I'd been at court half a year. We've spoken together, I don't know, six or seven times after that? Over the years. I knew what a scandal there'd be if gossip got hold of the story that she'd given birth to a freak. I would never tell that secret. She *knows* I won't say anything.'

'Clearly, not. Or she would not have attempted to kill you.'

I've watched stonemasons work; how with one tap of a hammer, and the correct wedge, they can sheer off a great slab of stone. I felt tears well up in my eyes, and I had to grit my teeth to keep my breathing even.

This Egyptian bureaucrat knows far too much about the right wedges to split people apart.

'She's afraid.' I managed to keep my voice steady, although I heard it croak like a half-grown boy's. 'She's mistaken. Since I couldn't make her understand that, I left Taraco.'

'Kek and Keket!' he muttered, as if it were some oath.

'And,' I added with a shrug, it being so much less painful than other matters, 'I'm hardly likely to be in favour enough with King Rodrigo to gossip with him. He wanted me to go north, to crusade against the Franks around Poitiers, as his siege engineer. A builder of trebuchets is more valuable than a painter of statues. I would have had to leave the court in any case.'

Rekhmire' looked me up and down. For all the wool of the robe covering my chest, I felt as if my breasts were exposed. He brought a finger up and stroked my hair back from my cheek.

'By the Company of the Eight!' he said softly. 'What a mess. And a puzzle. I don't understand it all . . . '

The fear that rushed through me – at having trusted; having told things I should never have told – made me curt. 'You don't need to. All you need to do is let me paint, in the hours when I'm not doing copy-work for you. I'll earn enough money to buy my freedom, and you can buy another slave when you get to the next city you're going to!'

In a tone that robbed the comment of offensiveness, Rekhmire' said, 'You're remarkably attractive, too. I didn't buy you as a bed-slave, but I'm open to amending the contract, if you're willing?'

Evidently slavery is different in Alexandria.

Startled, I embarrassed myself by saying aloud, 'Can you – I mean . . . *Can* you?'

'It may take me a little concentration to begin,' Rekhmire' said – mildly, for a man who must have been asked too many times before. 'But the only thing I can't do is procreate.'

His smile shone; I thought him honestly amused.

'The Sublime Porte's eunuch guards, let's say, would hardly be so popular among his thousand wives if they couldn't adequately entertain them. Believe me more than capable of making this offer to you. But answer me as *you* wish.'

Meeting his gaze, I saw such a lack of coercion that I was not, at first, inclined to believe it.

A slave's word is worth less than the wind that stirs the torch-flames, of course. And this man might be cruel enough to sell me, if rejected; worst of all, sell me to Aldro Rosamunda, if he could get word to Taraconensis.

But I am tired of being the whore I was sometimes made to be, as the King's Freak. And this . . . would be two freaks in sexual congress.

'I'm not willing.'

He gave an acknowledging nod. 'I'll show you some of the scrolls I have here, indoors, that need copying. And tomorrow we must go to one of the Lords-Amir's houses, to copy a parchment he won't let me take out of his library.'

Will this man forget rejection – and scandal – so easily? No. I should not have spoken . . .

At the moment, even this early in the evening, the black sky and the sickness of my body insisted that what I needed more than thought was sleep.

The tall Egyptian bent to pick up the bowl I had been drinking from, and absently placed it with his own on the rim of the roof, where it would be easier for the house-slaves to clear it away.

'I could make a few inquiries,' Rekhmire' said, glancing back. 'I meet a number of people in this city, while I'm buying books; I could tactfully find out if they know of any Iberian noblewomen travelling in this area.'

It may have been the mixture of diffidence and confidence in his bearing, or his subtle interrogation of me – or simply the realisation that an Egyptian civil servant travelling for the Royal Library will visit many places . . .

I blurted out, 'You're not a *spy*, are you?'

Rekhmire' grinned. It made him look unlined and twenty, instead of the thirty I suspected him to be.

'I get a lot of that. No. I'm not a spy. Go and make them find you a bed, Ilario. Amun and Amunet! You're falling asleep on your feet!'

I slept. But sleeping or waking, what stayed in my mind was my mother.

4

The next day, I bettered my acquaintance with Carthage – or at least, the part of it that lies indoors, in the rich closed mansions of the Bursa-hill district.

'That,' the Alexandrine Egyptian's voice said beside me, 'will be your *rough* copy, one assumes?'

I frowned. Naphtha gas-lamps hissed and sputtered in this scriptorium belonging to one of Carthage's 'philosopher-lords', or 'Lords-Amir', as they call themselves. A close stare at my papyrus showed me perfectly adequate lettering, by that harsh light, even if the subject itself was capable of boring the most pedantic scholar. I opened my mouth to protest – and shut it again.

Three separate oak-gall ink drawings adorned the margin. Two were approximations of diagrams in the original manuscript. The third . . .

. . . Was half-a-dozen sketched lines that caused me to lift my head and look at the Lord-Amir's cat, asleep on the window-ledge overlooking the courtyard, one front leg hanging bonelessly down against the inner wall.

My hand has a mind of its own in absent moments.

'You have to admit,' I looked back from the dark window at my doodle, 'it's not bad.'

'It's a *cat.*'

The Egyptian might or might not have been suppressing a smile.

'At least you can recognise it! This is my rough copy,' I agreed hastily, knowing that meant extra work by lamp-light, or naphtha gas-lamps. Nothing by daylight here.

And yet I'll *draw* without complaint, until my eyes feel like sand.

Rekhmire' murmured, 'How far have you got?'

The Carthaginians do their writing at a high desk at which the copyist stands, the manuscript held open in a frame. The tall Egyptian bent his head to read over my shoulder.

'"Hasdrubal lies between life and death, tended by his brother-in-law Hannibal",' I read. 'There's a page of Hasdrubal recovering from his wound after a local tribesman attacks him, then, "Hasdrubal, after much speech, persuades Hannibal to abandon his childhood oath of vengeance on Rome; they sign the Treaty of Seguntum with Scipio" . . . Then it's all diplomacy between Rome and Carthage until Hannibal and Scipio –

different Scipio – lead the Roman-Punic Alliance to wipe out the Persians at the battle of Zama . . . '

I thumbed several pages ahead. History bores me. I'd hoped to be copying something like Hero of Alexandria's *Pneumatics* – which, if it *is* Greek, at least has drawings of his steam-driven aeolipile, and a couple of books on engines of war and ballistics that King Rodrigo had me read in translation in Taraco.

' . . . Aaaand . . . Much later, there's the Visigoths defeating the Carthaginians in Iberia. No Roman help; the Great Alliance is breaking down by then. And the great *re*-invasion of Iberia from Carthage, starting in the year Anno Domini seven hundred and eleven. Are you sure you *want* all this? I've seen a far better history of the Classical era in the royal library at Taraco—'

My hand clenched, splaying the split tip of my quill against the papyrus. *Christus Imperator! Can't I keep my mouth shut?*

The Egyptian Rekhmire' nodded, and made the reply I might have expected from a book-buyer. 'It may be necessary to travel to Taraco, in that case.'

'I will have bought myself free before you do.'

It came out, not speculative, but as a flat statement. *I will not go back to Taraco.*

The cat landed on the sanded wooden floorboards with a soft, plump sound, and strolled over to wind between Rekhmire''s ankles. My hand sketched the hoop of the cat's back as it arched up against the eunuch's shin. The Egyptian's brows lifted.

'Why must cats always approach those who can't endure their presence?' He sniffled, watery-eyed, edging it away with his sandal. 'Go, daughter of Bast.'

I added two small relevant curves.

'"Son of Bast", I think. Master,' I added, with the look that slave-owners commonly identify as 'dumb insolence'.

To my surprise, Rekhmire' gave me a look he might have given any freeman or freewoman.

'Balls aren't everything, Ilario.'

I didn't know whether to laugh or cry. Or for which of us. 'No, indeed . . . '

'Theologically speaking, all Bast's children are daughters, female or male—'

An elderly white-bearded Lord-Amir bustled in at that point, to converse with the Egyptian. I took out my pen knife – sharp enough to shave the hairs from my arm, or slice through a slave-owner's throat – and re-cut the quill's nib.

Forget Rosamunda, this Alexandrine Egyptian, these Carthaginian Lords!, I thought doggedly, with a glance out at the roiling waves of light that edged the Penitence today in green and gold. I came here to paint. Everything else is behind me now: forgotten and gone.

5

The tophet in Carthage is a place of child-sacrifice.

I walked there to paint, towards the end of the first week or ten days after I entered Rekhmire''s household.

Shake the nightmares out of my head, I thought. Even if what I put in place of them is true horror.

Every man knows rumours of Carthage's 'tophet'. That is not a Carthaginian word. I managed to find the place, after much wandering about the hill of the Bursa and down into the suburbs, by asking for directions to the 'child-garden'.

That made me shudder.

The light . . . remained the light Under the Penitence, and I began to wonder how Carthage's citizens bore it.

I wondered, too, what Messer Tommaso Cassai – nicknamed in Rome 'Mastro Masaccio' – might after all make of an apprentice who offered him not the formal faces of saints and the dead, nor statues with ivory-rose cheeks and brown eyes, but only the mundane landscape of the world. Even if it is the world under Carthage's constant darkness.

Must it not say something about a painter, if they can paint this unique light? He'll *have* to accept me!

The way to the tophet was up a street steep enough to make me regret the wooden easel under my arm, and the metal box of tools with me. I carried also a small iron brazier, to heat the hot coals inside the bronze palette. Unlikely I could paint here unless I could heat my instruments.

The naphtha gas-lamps that lit the street became more widely spaced, and stopped as I reached the crest of the hill. Stepping past the last tall building, I could see, beyond a vast rampart, the great five-fingered harbour below me. The shape of the circular ship-construction docks stood out clearly, outlined by lanterns.

A step or two along the rampart-wall brought me to stunted juniper trees, and I stepped down in among them, onto shed twigs, and into impenetrable blackness. I stopped, for my eyes to adjust.

Low, crabbed junipers. Trees I've seen grow in the desert rock behind Taraco, that thrive without rain. Now Carthage's only surviving trees. For all their small size, junipers grow slow enough that these must have rooted here centuries ago, before the Penitence fell on the city.

My eyes accustomed themselves rapidly to the shadow. Perhaps, I thought wryly, more used to Carthage now than I am.

I picked a way over roots, between gnarled low branches. The empty space that opened ahead of me had the smell of sacrifice on the air. That's recognisable wherever one goes, from prayers to Saint Tanitta in some goat-herds' village in the Taraconian hills, to the spilling of the Bull's blood in the Mass of the Green Christ.

But this will be infants' blood, if the stories speak right.

I was in the tophet before I properly knew it.

Squared-off short pillars of stone jutted up from the earth, and I had to step back sharply from the grave-monuments before I barked my knees.

Allowing the afternoon's starlight to guide me, I put my gear down and used flint and steel to light a torch. Far away, across the tophet, I thought I saw a cave-entrance – an associated sanctuary? – but its torches were too distant to help.

My flickering light spread out, there being little enough wind to make it flare, and let me see the carvings on the truncated oblong pillars.

Not saints' faces, these.

I let my fingers trace the mask-faces on the stone. The up-curved mouths were carved deep enough in the bas-relief that my fingers couldn't find the back of the hole. So, also, the down-turned curves of the hollow eyes. Their expressions were grinning mockery.

All the ages, under the names on the stones, were between birth and three years of age.

I puzzled out the unfamiliar inscriptions: 'here is . . . sacred and dedicated to . . . ' My torch drizzled smoke across the masks' hollowed gazes. I straightened up again.

Rumour spoke of fire: I could smell no smoke or burnt meat. What do they call their god? The one that swallows the children whose bones are buried under these stones . . . ? Travellers' tales speak only of 'Baal' – 'God'.

Rekhmire' would know, he being a man who picks up information like an ant carrying away a leaf. I didn't want to ask him.

The carved god's-heads were as bald as Rekhmire''s. I could see an ironic similarity in their prominent stone ears, too.

I lifted my head and looked at the juniper trees silhouetted against the sky. The tophet moved me to shudder and smile wryly, both.

And now we come to the problem of how we shall paint in the dark.

Even if I can use flint and tinder on my brazier . . .

Carthage's darkness was not homogeneous. I realised that, now – I had thought it a freak of the weather, sailing in. But the Penitence swelled into sooty blackness at times, and at other times shrank up the dome of the sky so that all the horizon quivered and swayed with curtains of light.

Unlike statues or icons in the workshop, to paint here, to attempt a sample of the colours, I needed to wait.

Tommaso Cassai was rumoured to paint the ordinary countryside around the city of Rome. So he might have his own experiences of waiting for weather to clear. If not weather like this.

The wood under the brazier's coals began to take fire from the tinder, glowing red and orange. I scented burning on the air. At this rate it would take a long time for my bronze palette box to warm enough to melt the colours.

Every coin the Egyptian had so far given me, I spent on pigments, wax, willow-twig charcoal (since no man was selling the better-quality vine-twig, under the Penitence), and the materials for size, and different grounds. *So this is not a time to waste them.* If I took out a prepared, properly-sized sheet of parchment and a metal stylus, I might sketch in silver-point – *But colour – the eternal problem is mixing raw pigments to match the colour of reality . . .*

Memory washed over me while I knelt, wondering, in that unnoticed corner of the tophet. There was no connection. Indeed, it felt as if the lack of connection was itself the reason: I have spent a month and more putting this out of my mind, and as soon as I relax—

I had been relaxed in Taraco, if slightly concerned about Rosamunda. I take after my mother more than I do after my father, but – understandably, with a freak offspring – there's little physical resemblance even between she and I. Left to myself, it would have been a long time before I knew Aldro Rosamunda for the woman who bore me.

Five weeks ago to the day, now.

And, as on the very first occasion when she and I spoke at court, it was the Aldra Videric who brought me to her.

As he led me past arches that opened onto fountain-courtyards, sunlight burnt white into the corridor, and cast the shadows of fretwork-cut alabaster back on the flagstones. The fragmentary light picked out the few white hairs in his neatly-trimmed yellow beard, and the blue of his eyes in his sun-burned face as he turned his head to speak to me – Frankish ancestry, somewhere in the bloodline.

'She's upset.' Videric sounded embarrassed. 'She wants to speak to you. I don't know why, Ilario. Be kind to her.'

At the doorway, he held back the linen curtain as if to a lady of King Rodrigo's court, although I was today in men's clothes. He would often joke awkwardly with me about women, or discuss duelling skills. My father, this burly, richly-dressed man; who does not know what to make of his son-daughter – except to know what a scandal it would be if the freak Ilario's parentage were attached to the great Aldra who is King Rodrigo's confidant and long-time First Adviser.

'She's there. Be kind,' Videric repeated.

He turned and walked quickly back down the corridor. The wide blue and white stripes on his linen gown – made with hanging sleeves, as the Franks do, but in light material for our hot weather – billowed up as he walked; I glimpsed his silk hose, and his war-sandals. His hand, where it swung at his side, clenched into a fist.

I entered the room, and let the linen drapes fall closed behind me.

Silver flashed in the air.

The fountains of Taraco are a permanent pleasure, in this arid land that is the first and oldest of the Visigoth sub-kingdoms of Iberia. Warriors coming from the north, after crusade, relax with a welcoming sigh when they see the arcs of water in the sun. The ladies of the court sit in the shade of ferns that grow only in those great stone basins.

Of course, the fountains often smell sour, as I noted this one did; and they take hundreds of servants and slaves to maintain. As King's Freak, I was unlikely ever to be put to cleaning out clogged pipes or pumping water through drains, but that doesn't mean I'm not aware of such things.

'Ilario!' Rosamunda turned her head, looking up from the ripples on the fountain-pool's surface. She smiled – nervously, with a quick stretch of her lips.

'The lord Videric said you wished to see me?' Even in privacy, I do not call her *mother* : it's wise to be discreet. 'Are you well, lady?'

Her eyes flicked back and forwards, under half-lowered lids, and she didn't turn, continuing to look at me over her shoulder.

What has she to tell me? I wondered, suddenly.

The times that we had met before, with the awkwardness of her abandoning me as an infant between us, it seemed to me that she wanted to reach out to me. A year might go by, between such meetings. We had drawn close. Now . . .

'What is it?' I said.

Rosamunda glanced down; I saw her in profile. I suppose her forty-five or so. There is no grey in her black hair, and her brows are clean sweeping lines, without needing to be plucked. I would have painted her portrait, if not that I thought the love between us would show in it for all to see.

'I wanted to tell you . . . ' Her mouth has a perfect fullness to the lower lip. She lifted her dark eyes to me, and I forgot to look at her; could see only the pain in her gaze. 'How it was, when you were born. Your father – Aldra Videric gave me a choice. When he saw you, what you were. I could leave, taking you with me. Or I could . . . give you up, and stay. I had nothing of my own. *Nothing*. How would we have lived? We would have starved!'

Gently, moving forward, I said, 'You hinted as much, before. You don't think I blame you?'

'Don't you?'

I am the taller, and I wanted to kneel down, in that pale alabaster room, and hide my head in her skirts, just as a child would do.

She muttered: I realised she had said, 'I left you where I *knew* you would be found—'

The swirl of green silk, that ran in a sweep from her deep bodice to the wide hem, flew out as she spun around; the golden girdle around her hips clinked as her Aldro's keys-of-the-house jingled.

'Ahh!' she cried out, but not loudly. As if stifled.

Silver flashed in the air.

I acted without thought. It was instinct to step back, and slap her knife out of her hand—

Her knife.

The dagger clattered to the flagstones—

The woman who is my mother stared at me, frozen; translucent flax-linen veil floating across, draping over her mouth. Both her empty hands extended forward, the fingers closing into claws.

The dagger on the tiles was a foot long, the blade triangular, all three edges sharp. Something blackened the steel, and the point itself was all black. Poison.

'What . . . ' I stared.

Her eyes, wide and frantic, stared back at me. The noise of the falling knife echoed in my mind—

Will have echoed down the palace corridors. Far off, I heard a sound of sandals slapping against stone floors. Coming closer?

If Videric is still near . . . He will have heard!

Rosamunda caught her lower lip between her teeth.

My mind replayed her action. The dagger as she had been holding it, point-down, clenched in her hand. Flat against her belly, as she turned. Her quick, panicky movement.

'You tried to stab me.'

My words did not dent the silence.

A voice shouted urgently from the corridor. I heard a clatter of feet. My mother's gaze still locked with mine.

'You *stabbed*—'

Rosamunda whispered, '*Run.*'

'—RUN!'

Jolted out of memory, I stumbled up onto my feet; ducking as something flew past my face.

A man's voice shouted again, in thick Carthaginian Latin; I couldn't understand him. *Did he shout that word? Is it just my memory?*

He ran towards me, from the rock-face where torches shimmered; halted at the edge of the stone pillars, screamed in fury—

I had easel and box scrabbled up under my arm in a second, as his robe flapped white in the darkness and he ran to and fro, not coming within the stones.

He'll be a priest, a priest of Baal; I'll be executed for coming in here, a foreigner!

I kicked the torch over and stamped it out. Sparks stung my ankle above my sandal. I ignored that, and snatched at the brazier; jerked my hand back from burning-hot iron.

'*You!*' The priest's ferocity cut through the pitch-black afternoon.

I sucked at my blistered hand for a moment, caught in indecision – and ran, box and wooden stand clasped to me, abandoning the brazier and the coals.

I can earn another iron brazier – more days copying histories—

The Baal-priest's shouts died down behind me.

By the time I found Rekhmire''s hired house again and staggered in, the skirts of my robe blackened with dirt to the knee, I was in no mood to be spoken to. Only the knowledge of how expensive they would be to replace kept me from dropping my box of instruments and kicking them across the floor.

I placed them, very carefully, at the foot of the mattress that served me as a bed; slammed my fists against the clay-plastered walls of the tiny cubicle room, and swore out loud.

Rekhmire''s voice, amused and blasphemous, came from the doorway. 'I must teach you better gods to appeal to.'

I wiped earthy hands down my woollen gown as I turned and glared at him.

He added, 'You may swear by the Hermopolitan Ogdoad. They permit unbelievers to worship.'

'The which-*what*-how?'

'The Company of Eight.'

I was baptised Christian in the faith of Christ the Emperor; but that doesn't mean enough for me to feel inclined to argue with this lunatic Egyptian pagan. God has never helped me, why should I champion God?

Rekhmire''s smooth, monumental face changed to seriousness. 'I've been awaiting your return. I . . . have heard a rumour, from one of the secretaries of a Lord-Amir whose scrolls I'm paying an exorbitant price for, and I went down to check it at the docks—'

'*What?*' I snapped.

He scratched a hand over his shining head, where a faint fine stubble began to rasp at the end of every other day.

'There is news of an Iberian noblewoman having arrived here. Which means nothing in itself. But this woman is searching—'

'For her—' I stopped, helpless with hope. '—"Daughter"? "Son"?'

'For a young man . . . *And* a young woman.' Rekhmire' rested his broad hand on my shoulder. 'For her twin male and female slaves.'

'Twins!'

'You could be dressed as man or woman, now. How *else* could she look for you and not give away what it is she's searching for?'

'Who', not 'what'!

I bit my tongue to keep from yelling it at him.

He had taken me up to the roof garden again, and had the slaves serve wine where we sat in the chilling air. I didn't drink. Anger was too pure in me to muddy it with that.

'Slaves! Twins!'

I asked Father Felix, once, whether he thought it was possible to be born with two souls within one body. That might explain me, I thought. I bleed like a woman, I spend seed like a man; is that because there's a male soul *and* a female soul in me?

Father Felix explained gently enough that there could not be.

'God has afflicted you. Either you are a woman, afflicted grievously with the ambitions of a man as well as the curse of Eve, or else you are a man forced for some sin to bear the shameful signs of a woman.' He had shaken his tonsured head, in the shadow of his green robe's hood. 'Not *your* sin, Ilario. What have you done, after all? It's the sin of your unknown father and mother, I would judge.'

Rosamunda's here, I thought, stunned.

Is Aldra Videric? He *must* know what she did—

'She won't find you.' Rekhmire''s voice broke the comparative silence of Carthage in the evening. Men's voices called to each other down in the street below; greased cart-wheels screeched. I heard the yelp of an urban hyena come in from the desert to scavenge.

The Egyptian, my master, looked at me speculatively over the top of a glass goblet made in La Serenissima. 'There's no reason you two should meet. I'll keep you busy enough copying books. You will not be addressed by the name "Ilario". But . . . I'm concerned. If this Iberian noblewoman should happen to speak with the man who sold you to me—'

'You *will* this, you *won't* that!' All common sense left me. I glared at Rekhmire' as if he were not my legal owner. '*I* get no say in the matter?'

'You say she's tried to kill you once already.'

'*Run!*' Rosamunda's voice whispered in my memory.

Her expression, if I could have caught it in pigments, would have made my fortune. Torn between fear for herself and ruin, fear for her daughter-son.

But not so much fear for me that she didn't try to hurt me.

'*Where is she?*' I demanded.

'Ilario . . . ' The Egyptian put his glass down beside him on the green ceramic roof-tiles. Their colour echoed the curtains of light flickering inland, where the desert creeps close to the city.

His glance at me was sharp.

'Ilario, she's travelling alone, with very few servants, but those that she does have are armed soldiers.'

I put a finger between the slave collar and the flesh of my neck, lifting up the iron. 'You can chain me up all day and all night from now on, or you can tell me where she is.'

He shook his head. 'Nun and Naunet and the sun-god's *egg!*, but you're stubborn!'

'If you're a foreigner and you can go around asking questions, I'm a foreigner and so can I! I'll find her!'

The iron felt cold, now the evening fell. I let the collar slip down again. If I missed the sun, I missed the changeable light of the moon fully as much, and that would not be new for several days yet.

Under the stars and aurora-curtain of Carthage's Darkness, I couldn't read Rekhmire''s expression clearly.

'You write a neat hand. You cost me an appropriate sum.' His eyes caught the shifting green and gold light as he glanced at me. 'And, sooner or later, your mother will think to send one of her men around the slavers' halls. If you must hear it . . . She's not with the King-Caliph's court; she came in off the *Christus Viridianus* out of Mallorca, and hired rooms anonymously, overlooking the dockyard—'

I scrambled up, interrupting; gathering my skirts around me. I gave him a sudden queasy look. 'I'm sorry – I'll have to hear it in a moment!'

I saw him glance at the edge of the roof, off which it would have been most natural for a man to void his guts were he ill. His expression altered. Thinking of my woman's modesty in such matters.

He gave a curt nod of dismissal.

I stumbled down the inner stairs, into the house – and on, through the intricately tiled hallway, and out of the slaves' door into the street.

It wasn't difficult – if she was not with King-Caliph Ammianus's Carthaginian nobility up at the palace, even a necessity to travel discreetly wouldn't put Aldro Rosamunda, wife of Aldra Videric, in a poor rooming-house of the kind Donata kept.

There were only two establishments rich enough in that particular district; I watched until I saw a man wearing a mail hauberk and cloth-wrapped steel helm, whose face I recognised even if he was not wearing Videric's livery at the moment . . . *Amalaric? Agustin?* Names tugged at my memory.

I followed the soldier in through the crowded eating-area, catching up an unattended jar and carrying it on my shoulder. With the belt of my robe yanked in tight, and my hair loose about my shoulders . . . nobody notices a woman carrying water.

At the top of the stairs I put down the jar, and called her name past him.

'*Rosamunda!*'

The guard spun around, grabbing at me; I saw, past him, my mother standing in the room's doorway—

I snapped, 'She *wants* to speak to me, you idiot!'

The bearded soldier glared, his hands biting into my shoulders. I could see him register my robe and think *a woman, therefore harmless*, even though I was sure I'd fought him a time or two in the training-halls.

Her voice said, 'I do. I want to speak to . . . Ilario. Amalaric, you may go.'

The grip of his hands loosed. He stood back. There was no sound for a long moment but his war-sandals scraping the stone floor, departing.

The striped cloak she wore with the hood back – she had been on the point of going out, evidently – was blue and white silk: Videric's colours, if not the family livery. The richness of the self-lined fabric made her face look the more ill. There were pinch-lines around her mouth. Her skin was crepe-like; more white than white lead could account for.

I saw nothing but women's gear in the rooms beyond her.

She lifted a gloved hand and beckoned me inside, not taking her eyes off me – flinching as the metal door thumped home into the expensive wood-padded door frame.

'Ilario . . . '

There was a window, a striped stone arch looking down into the rooming-house's inner courtyard. Metal-grille shutters had been flung open, flat back against the wall.

A slave drew water at the well in the courtyard. It looked to be a good fifteen feet below the sill of the arch to the flagstones.

No windows at all in the outer wall, where the narrow streets are. This is Carthage.

I said, 'Why did you try to kill me?'

A perceptible, almost-comic trembling made her jaw quiver. I saw the bone-hinge clench, under her skin, hollowing her cheeks for a moment.

'Yes.' Her voice sounded thin. Harsh. No hesitation in that admission, I saw – seeing, also, the strength of this woman who is my mother. 'Yes, I did do that . . . '

'*Why?*'

'Scandal. Ruin. No one must know. *The King would be forced to send us away.*'

The chill that went through me, I felt mostly in my hands. With my fingers this stiff and cold, I could never paint.

Her gaze dropped to my throat. 'You're a slave. Again.'

She seemed unconcerned. I shrugged that minor hurt off.

'So King Rodrigo would have sent you back to your estates.' I know the Aldra Videric's rich lands. Anger began to break the crust of the chill in me. 'And that – would be a *hardship.*'

Men say the faces of the shocked or fearful turn white. To paint them, green and saffron would need to be subtly suggested. Staring at her, I thought, No wonder we paint icons for sorrow and worship. Men's true faces are too complex.

'There'd be scandal!' Her hand clenched. 'Don't you understand? People would see. People would *know*. My child: the King's Freak! My child: born – what you are. *My* baby, abandoned—'

'You need not have abandoned me,' I said, feeling distant enough that I sounded numbly polite. 'It was your choice.'

'Videric made me!'

I realised only then how badly I had wanted not to hear her say that.

'And yet, you didn't kill me.' I sighed and walked further across the room, staring aimlessly down at the courtyard. The slave had gone. 'Why did you tell me to run?'

'Because you're my child.'

I turned about, facing her. There is no one close enough below the window to hear us; the door is solid enough to block all sound. I looked into her eyes, that are green flecked with ochre, and are the same eyes that look at me out of mirrors.

Speaking hastily, Rosamunda protested, 'I couldn't kill you when you were born. Anyone else *would* have done.'

On the last words, her tone came close to a whine.

I blinked. My fingers were cold enough that I wrapped them in the loose volume of my wool robe. They didn't warm. 'So why are you here now? If you haven't come to kill me.'

'I have to take you home.'

Now that you see the collar, why not buy me? – but, no, that will mean disclosing her presence here. Proof of a foreigner's identity is needed for the legal contract.

The wind from the city sifted in through the window, past me. The flames of the oil-lamps wavered. I needed to see her closely. I stepped forward.

She flinched.

Her chin lifted, almost instantly. You could see how little the flesh blurred there, despite her age; she is still the most beautiful of the Court of Ladies. 'I have to take you back to Taraco! Videric told me to.'

If I could see regret on her face, I'd weep. Seeing only desperation, fury, resentment, panic—

Nothing existed to give me proof. But, looking down at her expression, a wash of horror went through me – a sudden picture, in my mind's eye, of how far down it is off deck and dock, how dark and impenetrable to the eye the sea-water down there is. I stopped breathing, for a moment: felt how lungs burn and burst, when the heavy water closes a man in.

'Why are you still going to kill me?'

Rosamunda looked at me.

With shame, I thought. *Her expression shows shame.*

She can at least feel that.

If I were to go with her . . . some way between here and the Balearic Islands, her soldiers – or she herself – will drown me.

Turning, tugging at the gauntlet-cuffs of her gloves, Rosamunda spoke without looking at me. 'Blame Videric. He says I have to do this. Ilario, he's always thought that *something* would happen.'

Her head lifted from the tiny stitching on the gloves. Her gaze flicked briefly towards me.

'When you came to court as a young . . . ' Her lashes blinked down. 'It was *his* idea I should speak to you. Talk with you. Befriend you. Then, if the need came, I would be – close to you. Close enough to do what was necessary.'

I would be close to you.

This – thing – has been planned since I was fifteen.

My legs felt as if they were the lead weights which fishermen tie to their nets. I couldn't walk out of the room; I could barely stand.

This face, of which I know every line – of which, in all honesty, I have sketches which I have never shown any man. My mother's face. Looking at me with . . . impatience?

Murder. And all she feels is impatient?

My mouth dry, I managed to say calmly, 'Why does my father want to kill me?'

Rosamunda switched her head from side to side, as a horse does, troubled with flies. Her gaze avoided me. 'He's not your father. But you *must* see the power and riches we'll lose, if King Rodrigo sends him away!'

'Not my father.'

Her tumbling sentences stopped. She looked at me with tired, frank eyes. I thought she seemed relieved, if only by her own honesty.

'Ilario . . . Videric is only my husband. He's no relation to you.'

Foundlings are bastards, slaves' children, or both. Since fifteen, I have treasured the idea that I am neither. Now . . .

I moved before I intended it, crossing the room, flinging open the iron door.

I found myself staring at Amalaric's solid, mail-covered back.

The soldier stood facing down the corridor towards the steps, hands clasped before him, sword in its scabbard at his side.

Behind me, Rosamunda said, 'Ilario—'

I wrenched the iron door inwards, slammed it towards the room's wall, and it crashed hard against the metal door-stop.

Amalaric, beginning to turn, flinched. I ducked past him as he startled and grabbed.

'No! No disturbance!' Rosamunda's voice whispered, shrill. 'We can't steal a slave in public!'

Her footsteps; his; all sounded behind me in the corridor. A door opened behind me; I heard another man in war-gear clatter out; didn't spare a look back.

'Ramaz!' she hissed. '*Ilario!*'

I raised my voice as I clattered down the steps, not able to avoid the obvious, ironic, bitter thought. 'Oh, you must feel very much at home here – in this city of *child-killers*!'

'Ilario!'

The rooming-house eatery was a blur, an unfocused gallery of faces; I registered nothing as I strode through and out.

8

The two men and one woman dogged my footsteps, as a group; I deliberately pushed them from my mind. I walked the crowded naphtha-lamp-lit streets, arms huddled about myself, hands tucked into my armpits. The windowless houses rose up in four or five-storey tenements to either side.

Videric . . . He . . . Not my father?

How many lies have I been told?

'Ilario!' Rosamunda's steps speeded up. I felt her try to put her silk cloak around my shoulders.

I shrugged it off into the dirt.

The two soldiers stayed back from me at her gesture. As if escorted, as if I led the way, I strode between the blank dark walls, my mother gasping at my heels:

'You'll come with us – we can go to the docks – I've a ship – I can send a slave, get the luggage sent on—'

I ignored her.

The desire to get away ate up ground. I know neither how far I walked, nor for how long. I did know, shortly, in which direction my feet naturally turned.

It was perhaps a quarter-hour, by the city's horns, before I found myself treading on earth and the discarded twigs of juniper trees.

Rosamunda's sudden voice in the dark startled me. 'Where is this?'

'Don't you know? I'd thought you'd know.'

A glance back showed me the black silhouettes of the soldiers, against the stars.

I said, 'This is the tophet. It's where they kill their children. As sacrifices.'

If the light had been better, I could have seen her reaction. The faint torches over at the sanctuary hardly cast illumination here.

I turned my back on her, walking to the sanctuary entrance. Torches stood in cressets at the mouth of the cave. Without looking back, I went in.

All three of them followed me over the dry, tamped-down earth.

Many footsteps are needed to make earth this rock-hard.

I saw no priests as I entered. I was no longer sure what I expected to find, beyond this cave-mouth I had only glimpsed before. Rows of

36

round-bellied urns stood silent on shelves carved out of the rock wall. Above them were rows of expensive beeswax candles. And at the cave's far end, a great mask was carved: the stone mouth of the bald laughing god Baal. The lip had been cut so that anything placed on it would slide down, into the darkness.

Towards fire?

Staring, I stopped. I didn't look at my mother.

'Videric . . . Lord Videric's not my father.'

I could believe, now. Or in some way begin to.

Her tone was nominally apologetic. 'Perhaps I shouldn't have told you. But you'd find out.'

'If he's not – who *is*?'

Rosamunda walked up beside me, moving cautiously. Not because of the smooth earth, or the jars that must contain the bones of children. The movements of her body spoke both of fear and threat.

I don't doubt she intends to kill me, or have me killed. But I am no child, now; I am a man-woman grown.

'Honorius.'

Her voice was barely a sigh. She stood beside me, staring at the hairless, mocking stone face that stood taller than she.

'His name was Honorius. He was a soldier. Videric . . . gave me the chance to go with him, after you were born. Videric's a good man – he was willing to keep you, bring you up with his name. You would have been Ilario Videric Valdevieso . . . '

She pronounced it mellifluously, almost absent-minded, that binding of patronymic and matronymic that I have so often, so privately, longed to have as mine.

'Until you were born. And that became impossible.'

She made a gesture, as if that movement could explain everything.

Perhaps it could: she pointed at me.

'Honorius was *poor*. I told you: you would have had nothing. *We* would have had nothing!' I saw her glance back – checking that the soldiers were not within hearing distance.

They did not hang back far. Absently, I acknowledged that good practice: for all they knew, this cave had other exits.

I could see none.

'Honorius.' I tried the name. 'My father.'

She shot me a glance. 'He went north, afterwards, to the Crusades.'

'And you exposed your baby, at the wolf's hour, in late winter.'

One of the first things Rosamunda told me, when we secretly met, was the day and hour of my birth. Valdamerca had only ever been able to say that I had been a good size. And cold enough to the touch that she was unsure I was alive.

Rosamunda's voice echoed in the shrine. 'Videric sent soldiers with me. I *couldn't* do anything else!'

A thought briefly crossed my mind: to wonder if the midwife had been paid off richly, or lay buried in some grave scraped in the snow-hardened earth. Nearly twenty-five years, those bones might have lain hidden there.

It numbed me. 'And the man I've privately called "father" . . . Videric has been preparing for – nearly ten years? To kill me?'

To make a second attempt. After my birth.

Rosamunda's voice came quietly. 'I couldn't refuse to speak with you when you came to court. Not once I saw you; not once I knew who you were! You were my child. I *made* him permit me. He's always done what I've asked, until . . . I thought it would never happen, never be necessary; he'd never say to me that you . . . '

Beneath the numbness, I felt myself flooding with disgust and pity.

Disgust for this long betrayal. But pity because, do what she might for the best, this woman has still found herself caught in the position where she must harm what she loves.

'Blame your *father*!' she spat, shrilly. 'If Honorius hadn't come back, now – you're as like him as a painted image! You and he, you've only once to stand in the same room together, and all's lost! He's visibly your father. And you and he may both point to me as your mother!'

The sense of it only came to me slowly. 'This soldier, this Honorius, he's alive?' Twenty-five years on from my birth. 'And . . . come back from the Crusades?'

'Oh, he's back! *Alive.*' She stepped in front of me, her face pinched and spiteful. 'He has new lands near his damned goat-hut of an ancestral estate. I rode out there with your fa— with Videric. To look. No, Honorius hasn't come to court in Taraco yet, but that's only a matter of time!'

Realisation crept slowly in. It is not merely King Rodrigo manumitting me as a freedman, a freedwoman, that has panicked Lord Videric and Rosamunda, but the *visible* proof of what I am to them—

I caught the movement of her hand.

A signal.

Shock held me still for a heartbeat.

Armoured up, there was little visible difference between the two soldiers. Amalaric, taller, and with scuffs on his sandals and the chape of his scabbard, looked awkwardly at my mother, and then at the other guard.

The man Ramaz, speaking for the first time, said, 'All right then. Come on.'

His glance also touched on Rosamunda.

Videric has told them he wants *her* to do this.

The two men stepped forward. Amalaric's sword flew out of its scabbard with the soft hiss of steel against wood-veneer; Ramaz's followed.

Torches and candles don't light themselves.

The flaring torches in cressets, outside these caves, will be thrown away when they burn down to charcoal stubs. The beeswax candles in holders, on the other hand, above those high shelves of urns – those will be extinguished when the shrine needs to be in darkness, and afterwards re-lit, because they're too expensive to waste.

In Taraconensis, only the bell-end of a candle-snuffer would be made of metal. It would be mounted on a wooden pole. Here, leaning casually up against the wall, a black iron pole had a snuffer welded to one end. A pole long enough to reach the high candle-holders.

Amalaric carried his naked sword stupidly loose in his hand. Because he is only arresting a woman.

'Come on, now—' He reached out with the evident intention of putting his other hand on my shoulder.

They've decided Rosamunda won't do this.

Videric will have told them: *If she won't, you must.*

I caught up the six-foot length of iron pole in a quarterstaff grip; shifted my hands on the shaft; slammed the butt of it forward into Amalaric's stomach, full force.

Mail stops edge and point. Blunt impact, now—

Amalaric dropped to his knees as if I were a priest he knelt before. His mouth opened; his chest not able to get in air.

Two swift changes of hand-grip on the iron staff, the weight of it swinging it around. I held it by a quartered grip and one end. What I hold travels in a short arc – and the free end comes around with correspondingly greater speed.

The iron vibrated through my hands on impact.

Ramaz staggered into my mother, knocking her sideways, his sword-arm either bruised or broken, his sword clattering off among the grave-urns.

Rosamunda stumbled up against the rock shelves, sending a jar rocking. She clung, staring at me.

Folk-wisdom speaks of men's jaws dropping open in shock. The little sudden opening of her mouth, followed by no words, let me see Rosamunda come the closest I have ever seen anyone come.

I am man and woman both: is it *so* easy to forget to remind them I've been trained as a soldier?

Evidently.

I wiped sweaty hair back out of my eyes. 'I'm *not* going to claim you as mother. Or him – Videric – as father—'

The iron candle-snuffer, as I rested it down on the beaten earth of the shrine's floor, became a suddenly-welcome support.

'—as – stepfather. I never was! This is all *unnecessary.*'

The two men knelt, crouching, groaning.

She put her hand up to her complexly-braided hair, as if her fingers

39

touching her veil and pearls reassured her. 'How can we believe that? And now you're a slave again, you'll tell, just to be freed! You'll claim Honorius, to be judged freeborn! You will!'

Amalaric choked and heaved in a gulp of air; Ramaz began to scrabble in an uncoordinated way in the dust among the urns.

Rosamunda is a courtier's wife, Aldra Videric not being best fond of the battlefield. Will she see how easily I can kill these two men?

And how quickly I will have to decide, and act, before they recover?

'Tell them to disarm!'

'You *have* to be silenced!' Her shrill tone echoed through the sanctuary-cave.

I swung the wrought-iron pole, bringing it up into a guard position. In the seconds while they remain stunned, I can kill both of them, provided the brittle iron doesn't shatter. But—

I looked Rosamunda in the face. Wanting to see relief. Belief that this need not happen. The flickering candle-flames illuminated only frustration, and greater fear.

'I'd never harm you!' I shouted. '*You have to believe me!*'

A sudden rush of footsteps thudded on the earth at the cave entrance.

Candle-light caught mail aventails, white surcoats, pointed helms; sword-edges, bearded faces – ten, twelve or more armed men running; pouring into the sanctuary—

'In the name of the Lord-Amir Hanno Anagastes, every man and woman here is under arrest!' a better-dressed soldier called out, curtly.

Past his shoulder, in linen kilt and hooded cloak against the night air, I saw Rekhmire'.

9

'You can't *do* this!' I snarled.

Rekhmire' snorted. 'Of course I can. I own you!'

My grip on the cold iron pole would not loosen.

The soldier Ramaz straightened up, swearing. He shot a glance at Aldro Rosamunda – and at the Carthaginian troops, since her face remained white and stark.

At a nod from the commander, Ramaz left his sword, limped across the cave, and picked up Amalaric with his uninjured hand under the other man's arm. Stronger than he looks.

The Carthaginian guard commander marched up to Rekhmire' and nodded casually in my direction. 'This your ladyboy slave?'

Rosamunda's face coloured a stained red that I could see even by this light. She glared at the Egyptian. '*How could you tell him that?*'

'I have no reason to be afraid of disclosing the description.' Rekhmire''s smile was small but complex. 'It is, merely, a description.'

'Enough of this here, sir.' The commander raised his voice from the respect with which he spoke to Rekhmire', giving orders to his men. 'Back to the house. Keep it tight. You and you – bring the slave!'

Not thinking, not feeling, I let one of the Carthaginian soldiers take the iron candle-snuffer from my hand. He had to unwrap my fingers to do it. He was not harsh.

It was not until I found myself walking Carthage's dark, unidentifiable streets among the squad of soldiers, the Egyptian pacing beside my guards, that I began to grab at one solid thing, an anchor in my shock.

I spoke to Rekhmire', across one guard. 'How could you bring these men? You didn't know where I was!'

His expression remained mild in the starlight. 'I thought that I did.'

'You did?'

Rekhmire' gave me an oddly companionable smile. 'I realised you'd just heard where the Lady Rosamunda was. I thought I had only to call out the Lord-Amir's guards and make my way there. And if not the rooming-houses, then you'd have left there and be on your way to the docks.'

'I wasn't.'

'No.'

The paved steps of the street took me by surprise, catching my sandals against the lips of stone. I was not just disorientated – I realised I hadn't been in this part of the city before. And if not for these soldiers, I would be gone.

'So how?'

'I guessed.' Rekhmire''s voice came out of the shadows. 'By two means. The first being that a Lord-Amir's guards have remarkable powers of interrogation – I think there's no man, woman, nor slave they didn't round up and question at the rooming-house. And, second – I remembered where you had been to paint, and one man recalled overhearing a foreign slave shout "child-killers".'

His tone had a shrug in it.

' . . . It's the kind of slur they remember.'

The soldiers' sandals thudded on stone. Taller walls rose up about us. The basalt and steel doors we passed had naphtha lights above them, painfully brilliant to a dark-adjusted eye.

We are among the rich of the city here.

'Of course,' Rekhmire' murmured, with that mildness that I suspected hid humour, 'I had envisaged myself arriving in time to save you from a dog's death. Instead of which, I arrive too late and find you've saved yourself.'

I ignored his irony. 'I'll never "save myself". She'll come after me again. I know that, now. She won't give up. And I do not – do *not* – want to be forced into killing her. Even in self-defence—'

'Is it that way? Yes, I feared—'

The commander's voice overrode Rekhmire''s: the squad turned and marched down a long tunnel that led through the solid walls of a building, sandals clashing on rock, and emerged into more bright naphtha-light and the inner courtyard of a mansion.

The light confused me. I stumbled with the group, guided here and there by a shove. The house was a blur of naphtha-lit corridors, and deep burgundy paint on plastered walls, and slaves peering around archways as we passed. I saw rich oak furniture. The more-than-life-size statue of a man carved in yellow marble, with his joints outlined in brass or gold . . .

We entered a room, and each man went down on his knees like a wind going over corn, except for Aldro Rosamunda, and Rekhmire'.

An elderly small man in a maroon-and-ivory striped robe entered from a different archway, easing himself across the flagstones with the help of a stick. He gestured as he walked; the soldiers rose; and he sank down into a wooden chair with a grunt of effort and satisfaction.

A few servants entered and stood behind him. The room seemed empty enough, apart from the chair, that it must be an audience chamber or justice hall.

I noted the man to have the features of Visigoth Carthaginians. Pale skin. Blue-grey eyes in a wrinkled face; his hair an equal mixture of yellow and silver.

His beard was clipped short and neat. My hand went automatically to my chin, and the soft down that was beginning to re-grow.

Rekhmire' bowed. 'Lord Anagastes; may the eight-fold gods protect the House of Hanno!'

'One will be quite sufficient,' the Carthaginian Lord-Amir said dryly. 'Well, Freeman Egyptian – this is what you disturb my dinner for?'

Rekhmire' bowed again, with no appearance of undue respect. 'This woman is attempting to kill my slave. I paid good money for Ilario; I see no reason why Carthage would allow a poor man to be robbed of his scribe. I therefore appeal to Carthaginian justice.'

The Lord Hanno Anagastes grumbled something to the effect that no man had ever seen a poor Alexandrine yet, and that he, Rekhmire', might have waited until the morrow, and that local magistrates got no rest.

Their tone was one I have often heard between patron and client in the court of Taraco, when not too much obligation separates the social ranks.

Does this house also have a library in which I would have found myself copying scrolls?

'Lord Rekhmire'!' I called sharply. 'May I speak to you?'

Rekhmire' glanced at Hanno Anagastes, received a nod, and crossed the room to loom close over me. In an undertone, he said, 'Unless you wish to be running from your murderous parent for ever—'

'Why should *Carthage* care if a Lady of Taraconensis wants to kill her—' I broke off. '—her offspring?'

Rekhmire's luminous dark eyes met mine. 'You're a slave. Carthage's justice can be invoked purely because killing another man's property is illegal. And because Lord Hanno Anagastes here is a fellow collector of scrolls. Do you want to spend your life looking for hired murderers at every corner? Because the pot *will* eventually be carried too often to the well!'

Stunned, I could only mutter, 'You're trying to *rescue* me? But – you don't know what—'

'I know more than I did before I questioned your mother's servants,' Rekhmire' remarked, expression bland. 'Trust slaves and soldiers for gossip.'

'But – *wait!*' I protested.

One of the Lord-Amir's servants called out in Carthaginian.

Rekhmire' turned his back on me, crossing the room and bowing in front of Hanno Anagastes again.

The Lord-Amir nodded. 'Command the Iberian noblewoman to come forward.'

She is my mother. Whatever Videric may have tried to force her into, she is my mother.

Videric, who, I think, I must accept is not my father. Because there is truth in her when she speaks of that.

Twelve or fifteen armed men in a room are a powerful inducement. I could see, between their surcoats and mailed shoulders, how very little Rosamunda wanted to come forward. She reluctantly allowed herself to be led by the guard commander into the clear space before the Lord-Amir's chair.

I took a step forward; one of the guards looped his fingers into my iron collar.

Air hissed in my throat as I choked. I could neither move properly, nor speak; the collar allowing the exercise of such control.

Hanno Anagastes demanded, in an exasperated tone, 'Why did your husband not offer Freeman Rekhmire' money for his slave?'

Husband. Oh that will please her! Aldro Rosamunda, from a country where noblewomen handle at least some of their own business affairs.

'My husband's not here.' She flushed. 'Lord-Amir – I had no idea who owned this slave. If I let it go, how would I have found it again? If my men had disarmed Ilario, then I would have been able to find this Rekhmire', and . . . ' She paused. ' . . . ask my husband to pay him money.'

I caught the Carthaginian Amir flick a glance to his guard commander. The commander shook his head.

Hanno Anagastes' thin voice filled the chamber. 'Carthage is a city composed of one hundred thousand people, and four times that many slaves. Skilled as this "Ilario" may be, I find it hard to think you could not have found another who would be as good a scribe. And you are a noblewoman, are you not, at your home in – Zaragoza? Taraco? And therefore not poor.'

Rosamunda flinched. 'My lord . . . '

Rekhmire' spoke up. 'She is Aldro Rosamunda Valdevieso Sandino de Videric. Wife of that Aldra Pirro Videric Galindo who is chief councillor to King Rodrigo Sanguerra of Taraconensis.'

That his poking into my business should have led him to get even their matronymic names correct . . . I twisted against the hand on my collar; could not get air to speak. I saw Rosamunda's tight face. There can be no hiding this – Hanno Anagastes would need only to send word to some diplomat up at the King-Caliph's palace for the same information. *But she doesn't want it said.*

Rosamunda carried her chin up, and her spine straight; she did not look at me. 'Is it not permissible, here, to kill a slave who is treacherous, or otherwise dangerous?'

'I'm neither treacherous nor dangerous!' The guard's sharp yank on the iron collar cut me off. I reached to get both my hands under the metal and release the choking pressure; the soldier next to him grabbed my wrists.

It was as if I hadn't spoken.

I am a slave. If slaves are questioned, it's under torture, because it's taken for granted we'll lie.

Hanno Anagastes frowned at Rosamunda, indicating me with his liver-spotted hand. 'This is just a slave: why should a noble lady desire to kill her?' He peered back at me. 'Or "him", is it?'

Rosamunda went utterly still.

Rekhmire's voice broke the silence. 'My lord, it is both.'

'"Both"?'

'Both male and female. The noble lady Rosamunda knows this. Four-and-twenty years ago, Ilario was born her child.'

'Shut your mouth!' I strained to throw myself forward as much as I could; reach the Egyptian.

The guard commander nodded: three of his men seized me under the arms; the flagstones bruised my feet as I tried to jam my toes into crevices, so as not to be forced bodily from the room.

The wall of the corridor hit my shoulder, hip, thigh; caught the side of my head.

The impact was enough that I slid down to sit on the flagstones among the soldiers' sandals. Half a dozen yards away, murmurous voices came from the justice-room.

'Let me go back in! I have to speak!'

The Carthaginian guard nearest to me drew his foot back; I dodged, and caught the well-practised swipe to the head from his companion.

I sagged against the plaster wall, its intricate geometric patterns blurring in my sight, and put my head in my hands. Pain throbbed. I saw Rosamunda's face in my mind's eye.

What else is the Egyptian saying?

Sick in my stomach, I realised I was feeling a cauterising pleasure in hearing these things said aloud. Or it might only be relief—

How could I keep such secrets? Nine years, ten years; how could I go without saying a word of the truth of it?

No, not relief. Nor pleasure. *I can keep secrets; could do it longer, if she will only trust me!* If my blood-father so closely resembles me that it's a scandal – let him go back to the wars in Castile and Aragon!

I suppose that it lasted no longer than a quarter or third of an hour; it seemed to go on all night. Rekhmire"s soft voice recounting, inaudible. My mother's tones rising in protest.

'There's the signal,' one of the guards said.

'Come on.' The nearer soldier reached down and hauled me up, hand under my arm; his fingers closing briefly over the side of my breast.

I glanced up at his impassive face, caught his hand as he moved it, and pressed it to the front of my robe, at my groin.

45

His stunned reaction let me walk back into the Lord-Amir's chamber without being held.

I looked forward, over the shoulders of the guards in front of me. Rosamunda's expression gave nothing away; Rekhmire' looked urbane. The Lord-Amir Hanno Anagastes didn't cast a glance in my direction.

'Here's my verdict.' Hanno leaned back in his chair, sparing no glance for me, his tone that of a man who has come to his decision.

'Aldro Rosamunda. You are a woman, and not responsible. It is, therefore, your husband, Lord Videric, who is responsible for this attempted theft and killing. And although it is only a slave, we take the sanctity of property seriously, here in Carthage. Therefore, I will tomorrow petition the King-Caliph to send a diplomatic envoy to the court of your King . . . Rodrigo, is it? To give a formal rebuke, that will bid him keep his noble councillor Videric under better control.'

'*No!*' Rosamunda's voice came softer than a whisper. If I hadn't had an agonised gaze on her, I would not have known that she spoke.

Hanno Anagastes stood up from the justice chair, and laughed at some remark of Rekhmire''s.

The soldiers relaxed, talking with each other as if I were not there.

I wiped my hands down the front of my gown, and realised that I was leaving sweat-marks on the white wool. The subtle difference in colour filled my vision.

A voice said, 'May I speak to you?'

I raised my head and looked at Rosamunda.

10

'Think about it before you do this,' Rekhmire''s voice unexpectedly interrupted.

A glance across the room showed me the Lord-Amir speaking to his guard commander, ignoring the fact that Rekhmire' had left his side. Soldiers still surrounded me. I echoed: '"Think about it"?'

Rosamunda glared up at Rekhmire'. The soldiers might have been furniture for all the attention she paid them. 'What business is this of *yours*?'

He spoke not to her, but to me. 'Ilario – *think*, for once!'

'Why do you speak to a slave that way?' Rosamunda's lips pursed together. She slitted her eyes, looking up at him. 'Fellow-feeling, is it?'

Rekhmire''s voice took on an urbane, slightly higher-pitched quality. The voice he used back at the house – and at home in Constantinople, I guessed, where there was no need to hide his being a eunuch. Where it's a signifier of high status.

'Ilario is an excellent scribe. Perhaps a painter, too – if Ilario ever stops thinking of your scorpion's nest of a family before all else!'

I opened my mouth to protest – and thought: He's *noticed* enough to make judgements about my family?

I hesitated; he spoke again before I could.

'And, yes . . . perhaps.' Rekhmire' sounded embarrassed. 'Fellow-feeling. Friendship.'

I couldn't listen to that. I looked at Rosamunda, small beside him. She made me notice not just the breadth of his shoulders and chest, but his height – the cloak he wore, with the hood pushed back, would have been ankle-length on another man; it fell in one clean line on him, barely to his calves.

All her clothing – the wispy veil pinned to her piled braids, the long gown with hanging sleeves – seemed fussy. No clean lines anywhere.

'What would *you* know?' she snapped at him. 'You're not a real man.'

It hurt, even if I knew she only spoke carelessly aloud what most people think.

Nor am *I* a real man. Nor a real woman either.

Rekhmire' turned to me. 'Think before you do this!'

I looked at him, helplessly searching for a response and not finding one.

'How long did you wait after hearing that she might be in Carthage, before you went chasing off after her?' he demanded.

I scowled.

Rekhmire''s shaped brows came down. 'How long was it after she tried to stab you, that you got on a ship out of Taraco? How long?'

'I don't know.' I shrugged. 'A few hours. Perhaps. There was a ship.'

'Ilario—'

'*She's my mother.*'

I took a breath, to steady myself. It might have occurred to me that I needed to speak as slave does to a master, but with Rekhmire' that thought didn't come.

'It was Videric, he was making her, influencing her – and now I find he's not even my father—'

I broke off. Thinking of Videric, showing me into the room of fountains, claiming Rosamunda wanted to speak to me . . . but he didn't know why. Lying. Lying, and with a perfect imitation of true feeling. Aldra Videric, the politician.

I let myself look at Rosamunda.

Pain broke something in me.

'Why did you never stop him? Why did you *let him* make you do these things? Try to stab me? Expose me when I was born? Are you *that* afraid of him?'

An unwelcome pang of sympathy defused my anger.

'Were you so much afraid of him that you couldn't go with this Honorius – my father?'

She gave a sardonic snort, much more the Aldro Rosamunda of the Taraconian court than the humble petitioner to a Carthaginian Lord-Amir.

'Why would I go with Honorius? He gave me a deformed baby!' She made an apologetic movement with her mouth. 'Ilario, I'm sorry. It was hard enough giving you up. The thought of such a birth happening again . . . And he had *nothing*. One of those ancient family titles that goes back to the Visigoth invasion of Iberia, with a tiny hunting lodge in the hills, and rents from a pair of goat-farms. I couldn't have stayed at court.'

She extended a hand to me, the glove off, her fingers pink and free of calluses.

'*You* would have had nothing.'

'I had Federico and Valdamerca and no "hunting lodge".' The words came out flatly; I could hardly believe I said them. 'I had winters where I went barefoot, because the shoe-money went to Matasuntha – she had to be married before 'Nalda and 'Nilda could. This Honorius – You said "nothing". I thought you meant he was just a soldier, like . . . '

I nodded across the burgundy room at Ramaz, who was wincing every time Amalaric leaned heavily on his shoulder, even if it was the other shoulder from his broken arm.

'A nobleman? That's not "nothing"!'

'A *poor* nobleman. *I couldn't have stayed at court!*' Her breasts rose and fell rapidly, under the laced top of her gown. She glared at me. 'I would have had to go north, to the border, to the Crusade. There would have been nothing for me but mud and Franks screaming down out of the hills and—'

'—no influence.' Rekhmire' cut in. He added, into her silence, 'No influence with a king, albeit through a husband. No playing the game of courtiers. "Nothing."'

Rosamunda's head moved fractionally. A nod of agreement, or a shudder of apprehension; it could be taken for either.

'*You could have told me!*' A few of the soldiers were evidently listening; I could take no notice of that, other than to attempt to speak lower, and I could not tell whether or not I succeeded: 'Told me that Videric's not my father! About this Honorius who could stand beside me and be visibly my father – point to you as my mother—'

I shook my head, feeling hot and cold under my skin at the same time.

'*Videric* could have told me. Or – no, that doesn't matter, does it? If you're my mother, and his wife, it'll be assumed I'm his.'

I blinked.

'Either way . . . I see it. It doesn't matter which way the scandal goes. If I'm said *not* to be his child – then you conceived a bastard by some man, and therefore Videric's been cuckolded, and looks a public fool. Or if Videric *is* thought to be my father, then he fathered a hermaphrodite. And in the public eye, that makes him a monster as well as a fool.'

If I had been chilled, speaking to Rosamunda in the room of the fountains, now I was boiling hot. I felt as if I might dissolve in it. Everything I am, melting away.

'*Why* did you tell me to run? Not because I was yours. Not because you didn't want me dead.' As a blow in combat can crush with numbness, before it hurts, saying these things out loud numbed me. 'Because . . . you wanted me to leave Taraco? No matter what?'

She looked at me with no appearance of shame.

I repeated what I had thought was only spite, on my part. 'Child-killer.'

'Evidently not. Here you are, alive.'

'I thought he forced you. Videric. You said he *made* you do it.'

'I never said I didn't agree with him – that it was necessary.' Her face altered. 'And I was right! See what's happened. If there's a diplomatic rebuke from the King-Caliph, it will all come out! King Rodrigo will know! The envoy . . . He will *say* that I'm your mother. Videric will be sent away from court. I— You have to stop this happening!'

Nine years at court has taught me politics enough. The King-Caliph will send his envoy to slap King Rodrigo's wrist. That in itself wouldn't be enough to put Videric out of favour. But if what comes out in public is the parentage of the recently freed King's Freak . . .

If no man knows, yet, about the adultery of my mother, then Videric will be thought the father of a freak hermaphrodite child – whom he has allowed to grow up as a slave in the King's court. Without a word of acknowledgement.

And sent his wife to kill.

Because Taraco is sometimes no more capable than Carthage of thinking a woman responsible for her own actions.

'Videric may have to put you aside. Divorce you. Disassociate himself—' Dizzyingly, my mind swung around. 'You lied. You *would* have killed me when I was born. Valdamerca found me by pure accident. How could you expect anyone to find a foundling, in the dark and the snow?'

This is obvious, now; how can it not have been obvious before?

'I thought you'd been forced into a position where you had to hurt what you loved.' The boiling liquidity of rage threatened to drown me. 'But that's not true.'

'I was! I did . . . need to see you.' She locked gazes with me. 'I did need to speak to you. You were mine. I couldn't . . . '

'You could.'

'You have to stop this happening, Ilario!'

Rage almost choked me. 'Even if I wanted to, there's nothing I can do!'

Rekhmire', his voice lowered so that the guards should not hear more than they had, said, 'Oh, there is a way.'

I looked at him.

'This is a court case over *property*.' He gently put his too-large hand on my shoulder. 'Tell me that you want it, and I'll free you. Formally. Manumit you here and now. And then it's merely a squabble between two freewomen of Taraconensis, and no business of a Carthaginian magistrate. This all becomes mere hearsay. The Lord-Amir will drop the case, I think, rather than bother King-Caliph Ammianus with a witness who can't be tortured into confessing the necessary truth.'

Rosamunda's face, filled with everything from fury to love, anguish to regret, stared at me.

With a wisp of what I thought of as Rekhmire''s own humour, I said to the Egyptian, 'You had to *tell* me this?'

'You would have thought of it yourself, afterwards, and asked me why I didn't.'

I glanced to one side. The soldiers still talked among themselves. I realised we'd fallen into an Iberian dialect of Visigothic – even Rekhmire'. *This must seem a local squabble, natives; nothing to concern Carthaginians* . . .

The Lord-Amir signalled to one of his slaves, turning away from us.

Through the arches of the mansion, I could glimpse other slaves. There would be couches in another room, where Hanno Anagastes' food waited for him.

A bare second, to decide. To speak.

Rosamunda's voice creaked, 'You must want to be freed . . . '

I looked at her.

'I'm done with protecting you. And with protecting him.' I turned towards Rekhmire'. 'I'll earn the money to pay you for my freedom, like I said. Bit by bit. Don't free me now.'

11

A month or more after Rosamunda left the city, I sat in the tophet, my wooden resting-frame in front of me; hot wax and pigments steaming in the cool air.

She has no real compassion or love, but I am not free of her yet.

It's been less than a season: why would I expect it, in that short time?

The sky above me was a black that defied words, containing, as it seemed to, an orange reflection that did not brighten the dark. The shadows of the junipers held a metallic green like the carapaces of beetles.

The desire for sunlight – for the yellow glow of sunlight on old stone – was a gnawing desire. A craving. I want blue skies, deep and shining, with the band of milk-blue haze at the horizon . . .

Instantaneously with my looking up at the viridian line of the sea, a man's voice remarked, 'The weather changes remarkably little, under the Penitence. I dare say high summer is no hotter than the spring you get in Iberia.'

A priest? A man bringing a sacrifice?

Neither.

'Lord-Amir.' I put my irons down and stood, avoiding kicking over my bronze palette box by a minute margin.

Hanno Anagastes leaned on his stick. 'Your master gave me leave to speak to you. He tells me he allows you to paint.'

The little wizened Carthaginian wore white silk, over layers of robes; the two men behind him were less noticeable in the dark, and maroon livery. He took no notice of his armed guards' presence. He leaned forward, peering at the lime-wood board I had been painting on.

'Not an icon,' he said, at last. 'You paint no face except Lord Baal's, and the picture is not focused on him.'

The wax would cool in my palette box soon, if I didn't add more coals. I squatted down by my brazier, picking up tongs, and replenished it, all the while feeling the Carthaginian's displeasure.

'It's all *background*.' His pepper-and-salt brows dipped down. 'All decoration and no subject!'

Straightening, I spared a glance at the painting. The truncated stone pillars that bore Baal's face were not the focus, no. I would not expect such a man as Hanno Anagastes to notice. The outline of the junipers beyond, and the two-thirds of the flat board that was sky – and from which I had scraped off the wax twice, completely, this morning – might seem background, to an eye not educated to new things.

Tempted to say *How I waste my pigments is my own affair!* I gave him a brief court bow. Not a time to show disrespect, with his soldiers there ready for disciplining a slave.

But, I thought, again, I might be immune from normal treatment. He wouldn't come here and speak unless he wanted something.

I shrugged. 'I thought I would paint it to show people what it's like.'

'*Paint* it.'

'As Messer Tommaso paints the hills of Rome, now he paints Rome, not generic hills that *symbolise* the city of the Empty Chair.'

'Freeman Rekhmire' said you were mad.' The Lord-Amir Hanno Anagastes spoke as if he had no concept that he could be either rude, or contradicted. 'Can you paint funeral portraits?'

I can charge him fifteen; twenty, perhaps. More money for me to save towards freedom. Or perhaps buy one of those poplar- and acacia-wood boards I saw in the market, priced as high as bronze.

'Yes,' I said.

'Good. Freeman Rekhmire' said you have a neat hand.' He stared at the painting again, shook his head, and visibly dismissed it. 'I want a funeral icon for my granddaughter.'

The thought is always sobering. I bowed again, Taraco-fashion. 'How old was she, lord?'

'She would have been three, in the autumn . . . ' He lifted the tip of his stick from the hard-packed earth, and gestured away towards the sanctuary entrance. 'She's there. Her name was—'

'*There?*'

Surprise all but choked it back; I blurted it out, nonetheless:

'Do you expect me to paint a formal funeral portrait for a child you *sacrificed?*'

His stick hit the earth sharply. 'Don't blaspheme!'

For a long moment we stared, each at the other, under the shifting light of Carthage's Penitence.

Finally, I spoke. 'Lord-Amir, at home, many say the Penitence is a penalty for your child-sacrifice. Although indeed some say not – instead, that the people of Carthage killed some prophet, or sold him to his enemies and *they* killed him, and the Dark came here . . . But most say it is the dead children.'

'Ah. Ah, *that* story.'

He did not condescend to sound as if he explained, but Hanno Anagastes spoke while he stared away towards the sanctuary of Baal.

'When a child dies at birth, or soon after, we give them back to God. They haven't been alive long enough to have forgotten His presence, or

53

truly left it . . . so they come here, to His sanctuary. Stillbirths, early miscarriages, children whose spirits die in the night for no cause.'

His pale eyes moved as he looked at me.

'Hanno Tesha is there. You will paint her.'

'I thought—' Saying the words aloud would cause him pain. *I thought those were the bones of children that you people killed!*

Stunned, I muttered, 'There are animals' bones in there too.'

Because sometimes you try to cheat the god; sacrifice a goat instead of a child—

'Children have pets.' Hanno's shoulders, under his layers of robes, were thin; so much became visible when he put great weight on his walking stick. 'Tesha's little marmoset will come here when it dies. I dare say she misses it.'

'They're *all* . . . ?'

He seemed to catch himself, as if becoming newly aware that he spoke to a slave. 'I desire it done within the week. A portrait for my grandchild. You may inform Freeman Rekhmire' I have given you this commission.'

'It's a graveyard?'

'Do you think we're *savages*?' His shrewd eyes fixed on me. 'I don't care what you do up in your Taraconian hills, goat-boy. Goat-*girl*. Bury your still-births outside consecrated ground, like as not! This is the children's garden. Think yourself lucky your master allows you this trade. I would have your head on the Palace gate, otherwise.'

Dumb, I bowed. I thought him momentarily on the verge of giving up his desire for a funeral icon, or his desire for one from me; ordering his soldiers to beat me, breaking fingers and wrist-bones.

Fury. I had seen no priests here since the day that one chased me. And it occurred to me, now: *perhaps he was no priest, but only a parent.*

The anger transmuted in Hanno Anagastes. He shook his head.

'They do say we gave the Prophet Gundobad over to be killed.' He spoke as if we stood in an academy of formal debate, and not a crematorium of the unborn. 'Centuries ago. Who knows? Who knows how long the darkness has covered us, or if this Penitence was even imposed for that, if we did? You will not be a slave for ever, I think.'

That startled me into looking into his face.

'If I were to buy you,' Hanno Anagastes observed, 'I should certainly manumit you in my will, and I am old and cannot expect to live long. An artist's talent should be used. You are wasted as a slave scribe. Shall I ask your master to sell you to me?'

This man wants to *buy* me?

I bowed my head with a sudden show of respect. That let me hide my face before he saw shock on it – where he would expect joy.

'I'll . . . ask him to speak to you, Aldra Hanno; thank you.'

He didn't move for a moment. His stick finally tapped the shadowed earth.

As if I had made a quite different statement, he said reluctantly, 'Very well.'

He knows I won't ask Rekhmire'.

I think he knows I find this offer suspicious.

Hanno Anagastes looked around at the graveyard. He said quietly, 'You should remember that punishments do not need a reason.'

It might have been philosophy; it might have been threat. I could tell nothing from his tone. He turned without farewell, and walked away between his soldiers, into the darkness.

I found my palette box cold, the waxes congealed; I dropped brushes and a smoothing-spoon, from sheer clumsiness.

This place should feel less bloody, less savage, less sad, if it is a graveyard – and it does, but I find it no less disturbing.

Disturbing, too, that a man wishes to buy a slave he doesn't want. Apart from one or two pieces of indifferent quality, I'd seen no paintings in the House of Anagastes. Certainly nothing of the New School.

This morning I'd let the house-slaves know (as I must) that I might paint at one of two places; an urge woke in me to move to the other. The hollow eyes of Baal's face would need to be repainted . . . *No, cannot be*, I thought, looking at the half-finished board.

To paint them with knowledge I'll need to paint them again, from the beginning.

It took me a while to cool my instruments, and pack all away; and a while longer than that to make my way down past the Bursa, to where guides shadow the rich merchants' houses, and offer to show their foreign guests the sights of Carthage.

A small sum to a man whose name Rekhmire' had given me as trustworthy would provide both a guide, and assistance in not being knocked over the head and robbed when I was lost in laying the wax and blending the colours.

'We can walk,' the man Sarus said, shouldering my easel. 'The first of the pyramids are close to the city.'

He was correct. We walked for no more than twenty minutes outside the walls before we came up from a gully, and I felt the dry tingle of the desert wind. My hair stood up on that part of my neck which in dogs is the scruff.

The daytime darkness of the Penitence shivered in the sky, veils of crimson and blue twisting away on the southern horizon.

A mile away, the first of the tombs of the King-Caliphs stood. *And I will need to be this far from it, to paint*, I realised. Or else how can I get the size of it in?

The pagan ancestors of Carthage built pyramids of brick, covering the sides with plaster facing. Great masses of colour shrouded the sloping walls, hues distorted by the auroral light – a hundred thousand men had been set to painting images so huge as to be properly visible only from a distance. Even under the Penitence, the pyramid facing me clearly showed a rearing lioness, the crescent moon visible on her brow: the image itself taller than Carthage's walls.

I found I couldn't paint.

Sometimes it's so. This new form of painting isn't a mechanical skill. With the panorama of light and darkness in front of me, I sat cross-legged on the rock; tinkering with the *cera Punica*, and letting colours impinge on my mind as I fruitlessly mixed them. Rubica, sinopis, orpiment, caeruleum: red, brown, yellow, blue. Nothing I can match to the real colours in front of my eye. The chill wind, and Sarus's sandals kicking up sand as he trod the immediate area, faded from my perception.

To paint an icon to represent the city of Carthage will be easy. Crenellated walls, blue-tiled towers, men in robes and pointed helms. And in a corner, indicating distance and heraldic importance, a tiny triangular shape.

To make Carthage resemble its unique self . . . to make that corner into the foreground . . .

I ate Carthage's fish-biscuit (which the poor eat); shifted a corner of my cloak under myself on the chill rock; and found I was thinking not of Taraco, but about Marcomir.

I'd walked down to the docks once to look at Donata's rooming-house – still open for business – and caught sight of Marcomir on his way to work at the customs hall. It would be no great hardship to wait between the windowless walls of some alley and hit him with a cudgel, and kick him until I ceased to feel pain.

The turn of his head, as I saw it, reminded me of the attraction of bodies. Which had been genuine, and mutual.

Gazing now at the plain prepared board on the easel – calcium sulphate and egg-white; tinted with blue to add darkness to the Penitence's colours – I wondered whether it would be revenge if I beat him. Or merely the prejudice of the normal man against the man who is effeminate?

But then, I am the last to think of myself as normal.

And I would have to know whether it was the woman-part of me that desired Marcomir, or the man-soul, or both.

The idea of leaving Donata and Marcomir to prey on travellers felt distasteful. Rekhmire' might be persuaded to speak unofficially to someone in his wide circle of acquaintances in Carthage, I thought. It could be hinted to Marcomir that his customs job depended on his mother's rooming-house sticking to legal ways of fleecing foreigners . . .

I doubt there'll be more penalty – it's not Carthaginian citizens they've been robbing, after all.

Focusing again, I realised that the veils of light picked out two men in the sweep of land, coming up by a roundabout way from the city. Trudging figures made minuscule by the pyramids.

I hitched my cloak up around my shoulders, aware that Sarus squinted into the dim distance with me.

The men forged closer, across rock and sand.

'It's the Egyptian.' The lines of Sarus's shoulders loosened. 'He don't look *worried* by the man with him.'

I suspected Sarus, with his worn sandals and habit of standing with his hands relaxed at his sides, had seen service in one of Carthage's many legions. Certainly he thought easily in terms of hostility and acquiescence.

The man with Rekhmire', as he came close enough to be seen by the torches I had put up to help me paint, I thought also to be a soldier.

And not a Carthaginian soldier: he wore a Frankish brigandine, and hose.

The sight of clothing potentially from home brought me up onto my feet. My cloak fell down behind, onto the rock.

'Ilario!' Rekhmire' raised a large hand in greeting, and finished with an authoritative gesture that sent Sarus off to patrol a perimeter out of earshot.

The walk had daubed the Egyptian with dust to the knee. Rekhmire' swatted sand from his linen kilt, and glanced at me from the sides of his eyes. 'I've brought someone to see you. This is Honorius.'

I managed the single word. 'Honorius.'

The man with Rekhmire' looked me in the eye.

'Honorius, your father. Hello, Ilario.'

12

Wind-flickering torches showed me the newcomer standing almost as tall as Rekhmire'. Thinner, though; bare-headed, and dressed as a common soldier – under the blue velvet shell of his brigandine I could see the outline of the riveted iron plates.

This Honorius had hooked the buckled strap of his helmet over the pommel of his sword, so that the steel sallet hung, if not conveniently, at least usefully inverted at his hip: his mail gauntlets stuffed into it for safe-keeping. His uncovered head showed hair cropped short in a Frankish cut, as often adopted by Iberian crusaders in the north. If his hair had been black once, it was grey now.

I heard myself sound ungracious. 'What do *you* want?'

I saw no likeness in his eyes, under the torches and the aurora's dim light. I have Rosamunda's eyes.

Everything else of his face – chin, cheek, broad forehead, prominent nose – was a more masculine form of my own.

If I sketched myself, I would need only a few lines to change it to Honorius's face. That, and age. Stand us together in the same room, and—

Father.

'*Well?*' I demanded.

Honorius grinned, not taking his eyes off me, but speaking to Rekhmire'. 'You were right. There's no doubt!'

I demanded of the Egyptian eunuch, 'Did *you* bring him here? From – Iberia?'

I couldn't help staring at Honorius. Plainly a knight. He seemed to draw himself up, but not stiffly; his body kept the lanky, relaxed attitude of a cavalry soldier. And he must be close on fifty.

'I was in Taraco.' Honorius's voice held a rasp under the surface: years of shouting to be heard over the scream of edged iron, and the hollow percussion of guns. 'I've been buying new estates in the west. This – man – sent me word that you were here. My daughter-son.'

He said *that* without hesitation.

I stooped, catching my board as a gust of desert wind would have taken it off the easel. 'And . . . what do you want?'

'I want to adopt you.'

Slowly, I replaced the board and straightened up.

'As an adult. Formally legitimise you.'

Standing this close to him, I could see a shining quality to his eyes, despite the poor light. As if there was water there, and it might overflow.

'You're joking.' I glanced at Rekhmire', who said nothing. 'He's joking, isn't he?'

Honorius forged on. 'I have no heir.' The grin broke out on his face again. 'Except that I do! I've spent nearly thirty years cursed; I could give no wife of mine a child that lived. And – here you are.'

'I was here all the time.' I stared at him. 'In Taraco.'

'My career's been in the north. I'd planned to come home to retire.' His hands, by his side, clenched. I realised that he wanted to embrace me – and that it was not revulsion which held him back.

'You were there all the time. If that woman had told me—' He broke off. 'All this is too soon! It'll take time to get used to. For both of us. What do you want, Ilario?'

I turned away from that demand, glaring up in a blind rage at the Egyptian. 'You sent him a message? To King Rodrigo's court? With all that's happened!'

Rekhmire', who had gazed off with every aspect of politeness at the distant pyramids, turned back to me. His light voice was calm.

'As you can imagine, there's been considerable gossip among the trading houses. I listened while I was buying scrolls. I heard that the King-Caliph's diplomatic envoy did arrive in Taraconensis – and heard that the court is duly in an uproar. And I heard about Messer Honorius, here, and how he had indeed returned from the north to estates near Taraco. I thought it a good thing to send word to him. That's all.'

Honorius narrowed his eyes, staring at the Egyptian as if he reassessed him. 'You "heard" much, it seems. You're not a *spy*, are you?'

I couldn't help but laugh. Tension dissolved out of me.

'He gets a lot of that,' I said gravely, at Honorius's questioning look. 'Messer Honorius—'

Honorius interrupted. 'Is it too soon for you to call me "Father"?'

He put up a sun-browned hand, covered with old white scars, and corrected himself:

'Of course it is. Ilario . . . I'd planned to stay a few weeks in Carthage; I'd hoped we could learn to know each other.'

He pointed a scarred finger at Rekhmire'.

'This man, your owner. Should he desire to stay here – or leave Carthage for somewhere you do not wish to go? – you need not be with him. I can buy your contract and free you.'

The offer brought me up short, although Rekhmire' didn't look offended.

There are sound legal reasons to be a slave at the moment, but that was not why I bristled. My spine stiffened. 'This collar comes off when *I* say it comes off!'

The man who is my father and the eunuch who owns me exchanged a look that, in the midst of our tension, was nothing less than thoroughly amused.

Rekhmire' shook his head. '"You try". I said that, didn't I? "*You* try!"'

'Oh yes . . . '

I stared from one man to the other. 'I'll earn my freedom. And when I've paid off my debt, then nobody owns me except me. Is that clear?'

Honorius nodded. 'That's clear. And I'm proud to hear my son-daughter say it.'

I blinked at that.

Buying my contract.

Buying new estates? I suddenly thought.

'Rosamunda told me you were poor!'

Hearing my own exclamation made my face heat.

'Not that I wish to know anything of your private business—'

'It's *our* business. Family business,' Honorius interrupted firmly. He rested his hand down against his scabbard. 'I was poor, when I knew Rosamunda. I've been quite successful as a soldier, since.'

'You don't dress like it.' I grew still hotter. *Why is my foot firmly in my mouth?* 'That is . . . '

Honorius smiled, openly amused.

'Master Rekhmire' advised me to travel as a commoner – and with a small household. Apparently drawing attention to myself is a bad idea.'

If he was willing to discuss household affairs in front of the Egyptian, that argued he either thought Rekhmire' had a right to be there as my purchaser – which I frankly doubted – or else, in the time he had evidently spent getting to know the Egyptian, he recognised Rekhmire' for my only ally here, and would not rob me of that reassurance.

Which says something about both his judgement of character – if he hires soldiers, he should be accomplished at that! – and his own character.

Rekhmire' observed, 'Master Honorius is, in fact, a Captain-General.'

Honorius's voice took on instant military authority. 'I've retired!'

'A man doesn't retire from his reputation.'

Rekhmire' bowed his head, self-possessed, and addressed me without taking his eyes from the older man's face.

'Ilario, your father recently resigned from leading the royal armies of the House of Trastamara against the Franks. He is credited with keeping the borders of Castile-and-Leon intact. This is that Captain-General Honorius Licinus, known as *il leone di Castiglia*: the Lion of Castile.'

Despite the dark light, I could see my father visibly shifting from foot to foot. His embarrassment in front of a son-daughter he never thought to have was touching.

Honorius shoved his hand abruptly through his cropped greying hair. 'Ilario. Go where you wish. With this Egyptian if that's what you want, so long as you're safe. I've no desire to interfere. You're my only living heir: everything will come to you in the end. But I hope that you'll come home to see the estates, when this scandal dies away.' He coughed, clearly embarrassed. 'I have a house in the city, too; I need not disturb you while you paint.'

Despite appearances, he may be no different to the rest.

'You don't want to be seen with a man-woman?'

His lips pressed together; his head nodded very slightly.

I had a lurch of cold sweat before I realised it was not agreement – only an acknowledgement.

'Frankly, Ilario, I'm too old and too influential to have to care!' Honorius appeared to catch a look from Rekhmire'. He stiffened, and rode over what the Egyptian began to say: 'I would be proud to be seen with you, Ilario. Whatever you decide, I hope you'll visit me, at the least, even if living with an old man would be too tedious.'

Rekhmire' interrupted my muttered rebuttal. 'I doubt Ilario's life will be *tedious*, no matter where he – she – lives . . . '

'Rome,' I put in firmly.

I caught Honorius's questioning glance.

As well to get this mentioned before any other plans are made.

'Rome is where Mastro Masaccio has his workshop – Tommaso Cassai, the painter of the New School! – I don't suppose you have much acquaintance with painters—?'

The lean, tall man showed an infectious grin. 'Had a few of them designing banners and siege equipment for me, in some of my companies.'

It stopped me dead for a moment.

'This – this is different.' I found I was waving my hands, gesturing at the board on my easel. 'Masaccio and the other new artists in Florence – they paint nothing except how the world *looks* to the human eye!' It was difficult not to pace on the uneven rock. 'Mastro Cassai must have a hundred men in a week asking to be his apprentice – but I've studied drawings of his frescoes, I've been using his techniques in my own work, I can show him; he'll see that *I'm* the one he should teach!'

Honorius unfolded his arms with a creak of the brigandine. Unexpectedly, he reached out and ruffled at my hair, despite my lacking only half a head of his height. I suppose he had missed the chance when I was seven.

If I didn't manage to conceal affront, it only made him smile.

'So, this Masaccio – that's who you want this scribe to sell you to?'

Not for the first time, I regretted my papers lost in Donata's hearth-fire. 'An apprenticeship will do just as well.'

Honorius looked apologetic. 'Excuse a soldier's rough humour. Messer Rekhmire' here told me something of your skills as a painter; I only intended to make a jest.'

This is my father! I realised anew; the shock of it seeming to come in distinct waves of surprise, joy, shock, and distrust.

I squatted down to pack up paints, brushes, bowls, pestles, charcoal, and all the other paraphernalia, giving me time to think. Because I must think, for once.

Abandoning the mussel shells containing my mixed pigments, I stood up again.

With a cold clarity, I realised, *Rekhmire' thinks I have a need for allies.*

Sarus's sandals crunched on the gritty rock, approaching. I signalled, sending the guide patrolling back off towards the north-west. He was used to me acting in Rekhmire''s name: he obeyed a slave's orders without question.

Carthage's naphtha glow whitened the black horizon.

I faced the Egyptian.

'You haven't told all of what you heard from Taraco. And you didn't go to the trouble of getting messages all the way to Taraco without a good reason. What else has gone wrong?'

Honorius folded his arms, nodding to himself. I didn't have opportunity or time to enquire into his look of satisfaction.

'Pessimist that you are, Ilario!' Rekhmire' snorted, but I thought he looked relieved. 'It seemed to me that I *should* search out news from Taraco . . . '

He hesitated.

' . . . If only because there have been several offers made to me, in these last few weeks. Very casual, but genuine offers – to buy my slave-scribe. And much as I admire your cursive script, Ilario . . . you're not that good.'

The grey-haired soldier Honorius looked massively affronted.

I realised it was on my behalf.

Despite the dread I felt at hearing the news, Honorius's reaction was oddly warming. If his newly-discovered son-daughter is a slave – well, then; he'll have me be the best slave possible!

'Lord Hanno!' I blurted.

The memory coming back vividly, I recounted how Hanno Anagastes had found me at the tophet in the morning hours, and what he had said.

'Four offers to buy, then,' I concluded, momentarily cheered by Rekhmire''s failure to conceal his surprise.

'And they've taken to approaching you directly . . . '

The two vertical pleats in the skin between Rekhmire''s eyebrows deepened, the fineness of the shadow's gradation so unlike the conventions of funeral portraits.

A look passed between him and the man who was my father.

'Damn Carthaginians,' Honorius grunted.

The Egyptian inclined his head, acknowledging the point. 'As I confessed to you when you arrived, Master Honorius, I believe I may have made an error of judgement.'

'What error?' I looked from Rekhmire' to Honorius. 'What's happening at home?'

The soldier shrugged. 'Doubtless the usual nonsensical court business, no different to Castile or any other kingdom—'

'It was my intention—' Rekhmire' looked uncharacteristically as if he hadn't realised he was interrupting.

Honorius waved a hand. 'Go on. Tell the boy. Girl.'

Honorius looked openly embarrassed by his confusion, which reassured me. He admits me hermaphrodite, without pretending I'm man or woman.

'It was my intention,' Rekhmire' repeated quietly, 'in Lord Hanno's court, with the Aldro Rosamunda, that I would break the threat to Ilario's life by breaking the silence about Ilario.'

Honorius gave a slow nod of acknowledgement.

'If more people knew of the secret than Ilario alone . . . then, I thought, there could be no point in murder to ensure Ilario's silence.' Rekhmire' folded his arms across his bare chest. 'Truthfully, I didn't expect the matter to travel very far, or make more than a small fuss. I thought Aldro Rosamunda hysterical in her insistence that disclosure would be disastrous for her. The dust would soon settle, I thought. It's possible that . . . Recent developments suggest . . . '

He looked increasingly embarrassed.

' . . . It's possible that I was not entirely correct in my supposition of what would result from Lord Hanno Anagastes' judgement.'

I cocked an eyebrow.

'Aldra Videric's a powerful man!' the Egyptian snapped. 'Aldro Rosamunda is his wife! How could she fear a scandal, and her husband the richest man in Taraconensis apart from the King? I assumed the end of it would be what normally occurs with the rich and powerful – any scandal concerning them would be hushed up afterwards; silenced, disposed of!'

I stared at him as he sliced the air with his large hand. 'You might have told *me*!'

'Yes, I might – and I would have been wrong!'

He drew a harsh breath.

'There are so many rumours now, in Taraco . . . If the scandal hasn't been squashed . . . Ilario, I may have ignored the way in which spite would be a motive for attacking you. Or there may be something else behind this—'

Fear and impatience made me rude. 'What *else* did you get wrong!'

The Egyptian took out a finely-woven cotton kerchief and dusted fastidiously at his hands. 'I underestimated the use Carthage would wish to make of a scandal.'

Honorius's narrowed gaze, that I saw returned regularly to our surroundings, scanned rock and desert and desolate valley as if the Egyptian's words didn't come as news to him. In the distance, Sarus lifted a reassuring hand.

Rekhmire' went on quietly, 'The diplomatic rebuke in Taraco seems to have been . . . more effective than one would ever have imagined. It is enabling them to make demands of Taraco. And as long as you're available to be questioned, Ilario – or for producing to order – Carthage can keep this scandal alive. Hence their wish to buy you.'

'I thought you said it would be hushed up!' I know the machinery of gossip in Taraco: I have no wish to take another turn as its focus. 'What does Carthage want?'

'To take advantage of the Aldro Rosamunda's stupidity.'

I must have looked as if I would interrupt him with another question: he gestured to me to keep quiet.

'The Carthaginians want grain,' he said shortly. 'Need grain. Look around you! Iberia is their grain-basket. The King-Caliph here rules over Granada and the south, with legions and a "governor" friendly to North Africa – Taraconensis would be a valuable addition to their lands.'

I stared, taken aback. *This is not the scale at which I have been thinking.*

Rekhmire' shrugged. 'The Carthaginians can't be seen to destabilise Taraconensis too openly. Not if they hope to send in their legions and a local governor in the future, to save it, when the kingdom is obviously too weak to stand against a Frankish invasion and needs the protection of Carthage.'

Cold in the desert darkness and sputtering torches, I asked, 'What do I have to do with this?'

'This is the confidential part of the letter I received, which I share with you because it concerns you.' His gaze weighed and judged Honorius. 'And your father. The Carthaginian diplomatic interview with King Rodrigo Sanguerra took place in private. The King-Caliph's envoy, one Stilicho by name, began by requesting that Lord Videric be extradited back to North Africa, to be put on trial for his crimes – since, obviously, Aldro Rosamunda had been acting on his orders.'

'They *what*?'

Rekhmire' faintly smiled.

'Oh, I doubt the envoy expected any agreement. And that demand met the reception it deserved! The next request was – that in view of the scandal, Videric should step down, and resign his position as First Minister.'

'He wouldn't.' I was sure of nothing so much in my life. 'Videric would never do that.'

'It seems your King Rodrigo pointed out that any responsibility was in fact Aldro Rosamunda's, not Aldra Videric's. To which the envoy replied that in such a case, where the woman had attempted murder, if only of a slave—'

Rekhmire''s amused gaze met mine, over Honorius's scowl; I thought that part of his information had come verbatim.

'—in that case,' Rekhmire' emphasised, 'the Lord Videric would certainly put his wife aside – the envoy said – and divorce her. To prove his own honesty. She ruins and dishonours Videric's own reputation. She's a murderess. And, after all, she's a barren woman; any bishop would give him an annulment.'

The ironies of that were not lost on me. Nor, I thought, on the Carthaginian diplomat they had seen fit to send to Taraco, and who doubtless had heard from Hanno Anagastes that I was Rosamunda's child.

Honorius had his arms folded, an impatient expression on his face. 'And? He was told he might take a shite on his request, I assume?'

Rekhmire''s smile slowly faded.

'My colleague from Zaragoza has no account of what passed between them then. Or, indeed, between Lord Videric and King Rodrigo, when they met privately, afterwards. But – the upshot is, Aldra Videric has returned to his country estates, leaving the capital, and taking Rosamunda with him. The post of First Minister is – unoccupied.'

'*What?*'

In the silence, I heard only the desert wind.

It seemed too much to take in. Videric has been First Minister at court all the years I was there – for all the years I've been alive, if I thought about it. No man would expect to see him leave. Any more than they'd expect the great palace at Taraco to fly away.

'Are you sure you've been told the truth?'

'As sure as I can be. It seems, incredibly enough, as if the King of Taraconensis gave Aldra Videric an ultimatum. To rid himself of a dangerously volatile wife – or to leave the court. And that Lord Videric chose, not power, but his wife.'

Slowly, reason began to penetrate my shock.

'King Rodrigo can't have scandal near him.' I pieced it together, the mentality of years as court fool returning to me. 'Especially if it's true that Carthage threatens him. Videric looking as if he ordered my death – is too much. The only acceptable choice would be blaming it on my mother Rosamunda . . . And Videric won't put her aside? What hold does she have over him!'

'You would know more than I.' Rekhmire' shrugged broad shoulders. '*We* know the Aldro Rosamunda bore one child, but as far as the world is concerned, it's she who can't give Videric an heir. Any other lord would have had the marriage annulled as soon as he could. And, if for some reason he couldn't do that, he would have taken mistresses and legitimised his bastards.'

The family of Lady Rosamunda, the Valdeviesos and the Sandinos, are not particularly powerful; that much I discovered for myself over the years. Videric need not keep in with them. That he should choose to let Carthage manipulate him in this way, that he should reject his King's express order . . .

This is not how I am used to thinking of Videric.

Rekhmire''s voice took on a musing quality. 'He has already shown more than common bias by remaining married to a woman perceived as barren, and living without an acknowledged heir.'

I caught a look on Honorius's face. Evidently he feels he has unfinished business with my mother

The Egyptian scowled. 'I should have realised he'd be reluctant to put her aside, whatever the true reason for it is. And now, what I had expected to be a two-day wonder and then die away . . . does not.'

'She has some political hold on him.' It was a sure conviction, deep as the chill making itself felt down my spine. 'But that isn't the immediate concern, is it? What happens now?'

'It . . . may be wise if I take my scroll-buying business out of Carthage for a time.'

Rekhmire' smiled, evidently intending reassurance.

'I doubt that I'll be knocked over the head in a dark alley and have my slave stolen! It's not considered at all wise to offend the Pharaoh-Queen. However . . . I mistrust the spite of the powerful.'

'Ilario.' Honorius surveyed me shrewdly. 'Is it safe for you to come back to Taraco if you're under my protection? I know you don't know me well, but would you trust me that far?'

The impulse to agree instantly was strong.

I suppressed it.

Wryly, I thought, *Seeking fathers and mothers miscellaneously has not yet helped improve my life.*

'You've been away in Castile,' I said. 'Pardon me, Master Honorius, but I may well know Taraco more recently than you do. I don't think any of us should go there until it's known what's going on.'

Honorius did not look insulted. He gave a slow, considering nod. I thought him torn between desiring my immediate trust, and being pleased by a lack of impulsiveness on my part.

The wind blew dust across us in a skein. I'd find fine sand embedded in the drying surfaces of my pigments, I realised. Nothing to be done about it now.

I thought this was over!

Rekhmire' swore by a pair of gods, and busied himself cleaning grit out of his eye.

In the preoccupied tone men assume on such occasions, he murmured, 'What would you yourself suggest, Ilario?'

I offered him my water bottle. A shiver of realisation suggested to me that I might be being tested, here, by being asked that unemphatic question in the presence of more experienced men.

And that makes the difference between being treated as a freeman or a slave more surely than this iron collar.

'Your book-buying trade, Master Rekhmire'.' My mouth was drier than the desert air could account for. 'I'd suppose you can go to more or less any large city and still be working for the Pharaoh-Queen – ah – the Pharaoh-Queen's Library?'

Rekhmire' rinsed his eye, dabbing at the lid with his kerchief. The corner of his mouth twitched. 'I'd suppose that, too.'

He handed me the leather water bottle, and folded his now-wet and muddy cloth. Monumental and grave, but not quite restraining a smile, he added, 'Why do I have the impression that you're coming up with a reason for your master to go somewhere to your advantage?'

'Because that's how you taught me to think . . . '

It conjured a smile out of him, but that didn't last long. I squinted against the wind, conscious of Sarus distantly turning and beginning to head back to us. Clearly, he saw nothing hostile nearby.

We are the half of an hour's walk from any city streets.

I have not thought of this place as a wilderness before. Or even as an empty place suitable for an ambush. With Rosamunda out of Carthage, I assumed this would be at an end. Now – I do not even begin to see the end of it. Or the end of my connection with her.

But I'm done with letting her control my life.

The wind blew out of the south. A wind that will take ships out of the harbour here.

I crouched down, under the daytime darkness and the aurora that swept from blue to crimson, and set about finishing packing up my tools and brushes. As I worked, I glanced up at my father. 'Where will you go, Master Honorius?'

Flesh creased at the corners of his eyes. I couldn't see if he narrowed his gaze against the now-brilliant purple of a rolling aurora, or if he smiled.

'I sailed with only a few men, as Master Rekhmire' recommended – but I can send word north fast enough. I dare say a good number of my household guard would be happy to accompany us – since they've by now found out that farm-work has to be done every day . . . '

His tone made me smile, rather than his weak joke.

And – he's just offered me an armed escort. Because he's worried about my safety.

This man is concerned on my behalf.

On top of that realisation came another:

Rekhmire' . . . Rekhmire' sending a message to Honorius was not the act of a slave-master.

One outsider to another, perhaps?

Carefully wrapping boards in prepared cloth, I said, 'Messer Honorius, I'm sorry I can't call you "Father" yet. I would like that time together. But I'll go nowhere near Taraco.'

The soldier hid it exceptionally well. I know the shape of that face in disappointment, however, since it's my own.

Conscious of a tight feeling in my stomach, I continued. 'But, since you're willing, and if Master Rekhmire' agrees – would you send word to your household, and travel with us?'

Honorius grinned, and I could see what he'd been like as a boy. The cheerfulness informed the posture of his whole body.

'You're a scribe, aren't you? I'll pay your master, here, and *you* can write the letters to my people! Ah – if we're leaving Carthage . . . where are we going?' Honorius demanded. 'Where am I about to be dragged off to in my old age?'

It would have seemed crass to crush his optimism by saying *Let's succeed in leaving Carthage first.*

And now I get to see in what state *I* leave this place.

My bag stood packed, ready for me to sling on my shoulders. The pale ghosts of painted pyramids will haunt my canvases and boards. I glanced back and up at Rekhmire', to see if he would merely issue orders.

In the shifting crimson light, and with his self-control, he was unreadable. He said nothing.

He's waiting. Judging.

I straightened up, brushing dirt from my knees under the hem of my slave's tunic. 'Being a pawn in Carthage isn't safe. So we should leave. Why *not* take refuge in Rome?'

Rekhmire''s head tilted, chin jutting with an air of challenge, and Honorius gave me a watchful stare. Both men with their arms folded, they resembled a pair of gateway statues. I let neither of them get out an objection.

'Master Rekhmire – you can buy scrolls in any city. Your colleagues will write to you, I expect, or visit if you ask, so we'll discover what's happening in Taraco. Perhaps even before Carthage realises we're gone. I know that Rome's a backwater—'

It will not remain a backwater, not with Mastro Masaccio down from Florence to paint frescoes, and who knows what other painters of the New Art being commissioned to join him. But this is not the time to mention that.

'—no one ever travels to the Empty Chair, but that's what makes it safe for us! Or safer than anywhere else I can think of. Messer Honorius ought not to go back to Taraco just now. And, yes, you yourself could go home to Constantinople – to Alexandria, sorry – but that'll be expected. Those roads and shipping routes are the first places Carthage would look.'

Rekhmire''s brow creased. He exchanged a glance with Honorius. Both men relaxed, slightly.

'Safer!' Honorius grumbled good-naturedly, looking as if he quite liked the prospect of adventure.

The Egyptian nodded. 'Well, certainly safer than Taraco or Alexandria, which are the first two places any agent of Carthage would go looking for us . . . '

I caught up the bag of tools and slung it across my shoulder. 'So, then, if trouble is coming, we'll be out of the way of it! We'll leave Carthage, travel to the Empty Chair, stay there – I can seek out Master Masaccio, and you can make sure we're better informed. We'll have Master Honorius's soldiers. What do you say?'

I couldn't help a crooked grin.

'What could possibly go wrong?'

Part Two
The Empty Chair

1

'All of these paintings are rubbish!'

Master Masaccio swiped me a sharp tap across the back of my head. 'What's *this*?'

Slave reflexes stopped me hitting back.

'My head? Mastro?' I added, somewhat bewildered.

'Exactly. Your head. And how big is it?'

I could only stare, confused. *Is he saying that I'm conceited?*

'Eyes. Nose.' Masaccio pointed at my most-prized painting – done not face-on, as encaustic wax funeral portraits are, or profile as bas-reliefs are shown, but in a three-quarter profile: a woman sitting with her head turned as if to the life.

'Ear,' he continued, pointing. 'Mouth. Chin, even. Where's the *head*?'

He swatted the back of my head again. It stung.

'Do you even *know* how large the skull is, compared to the face? How much head there is above the eyes and behind the ears? *No!* None of you amateurs do! Because you think the *face* is important, and you don't paint what you *see*.'

I had chosen my study of Rekhmire''s cook, back in Carthage, to first show to Mastro Masaccio, because I was abominably proud of that portrait. I wondered why, given the stiff lines and lack of any proportion – her head now appeared to be cut off flat not far above her eyebrows, and there was no swell of skull behind her ears.

Why was this not *apparent to me while I painted?*

'Rubbish!' He flicked casually through my stacked boards. 'Complete rubbish!'

The voice of Tommaso Cassai, nicknamed 'Masaccio', sounded completely certain.

'Masaccio' in the Florentine tongue can mean 'clumsy, bad Thomas', 'Thomas the blunt', or 'Thomas who is rude' – but not 'Thomas who is a liar'.

'They can't be!' Shocked, I reached to grab the portrait, set out on his wooden easel-frame. My peripheral vision caught Rekhmire' holding out his hand – and pulling it back, evidently thinking better of assisting a collared slave in public.

The dizziness that went through me threatened to make me fall or puke.

Doing either will be bad.

I swallowed, hard.

Masaccio snorted. 'Complete trash.'

I could only stare.

'You have not even *promise!* See, here—' He rapped his knuckles against the heat-glazed wax of my painted acacia boards. I winced as the sound echoed around his high, cluttered workshop. 'This "city wall with tower". Straight out of a pattern book! And these figures. You've painted men on tiptoe!'

'Like every fresco I see in a church!'

The colours swam in front of my eyes. I ignored the doe-eyed faces and jewelled belts and robes and looked at these my images of men.

Flat, facing out at the viewer, lined around with black. The tips of their feet pointed down in front of them.

'How else?' I said, bewildered. 'The body and face painted as if a man faces them straight on. And the feet are painted as if seen looking down from above. Everybody understands that! How else is it to be done!'

The bearded Florentine painter shook his head, looking up at me. 'You are an untutored barbarian. Perspective. Perspective, boy!'

I bristled at that but couldn't bring myself to say *I am no boy.* I'd intend *I am full-grown, adult,* but it would bring the truth too forcibly to my mind – here in this city where I am determined, now, to pass for male.

'What about the light?' I demanded. 'The . . . '

Words deserted my mind. I pulled out and stuck at the front a treated lime-wood board. Colours shone, encased in wax. Behind the painted masonry walls, I'd coloured the skies of Carthage under the Penitence. *I wasn't thinking of men, but of landscape—*

I stared at the painted city walls.

It's true.

These might be the walls of any fortified town in Iberia. Pattern-book style: 'this icon signifies a city'. At best, the architecture is a little in the Visigothic style. But as for it being specific – being Carthage, that great city of the King-Caliphs, rather than Zaragoza in Aragon, or Taraco, or—

No. There's nothing.

Why haven't I seen this myself!

The skies outside the workshop's great clerestory windows showed autumn grey. Brighter by far than the Penitence, but I felt as if the cloud's weight settled into me. The colour washed out light, energy, hope.

'Well . . . *this* is not without some merit.' Mastro Masaccio held at arm's length a small board I had left half-done. 'This is what you saw, no?'

Above the desert, above the regular sides of a small triangular pyramid, veils of green light rippled. The aurora. I remembered standing with the scent of the heated bronze pallet and liquid wax in my nostrils, staring up, feeling as if the curtains of Heaven were about to be drawn back.

'But—' Masaccio pointed at the triangle. 'No! *This* is not what was in front of you!'

The walls of the pyramid outside Carthage had been too large and detailed to cram into that small area.

'But it's what I know is there. The tombs of the King-Caliphs—'

'But you could not see all of it. Not with all this sky!'

'How can I paint what I see, if I don't paint what it means?'

The small, dark man nodded, as if I had finally said something of note. 'And that is the question of the New Art. Come. See. Here.'

Ignoring my supposed 'master' Rekhmire', he led me past the work-benches where the pestles and porphyry slabs for grinding colours stood interrupted in their cleaning. It was a large workshop: it was, nonetheless, crowded to the oak-beam rafters with the gear of a painter – rods of thin silver, for drawings that would oxidise brown on prepared paper; stoppered bottles of pigment after pigment, colours so rich that I all but tasted them; a squirrel-hair brush in the process of careful construction; a hundred differently shaped brushes hanging from their hooks; pots of bone-dust, size, and every type of varnish you might imagine . . .

Ranks of stacked paintings stood against the room's far wall. He pulled one out – surprisingly, painted on gesso on canvas, I realised, rather than on wood.

'This is a study for a fresco. I've done many for chapels – sermons on walls . . . This one, this is in Pisa.'

I caught a glance from the side of his eye which didn't match his emphatic tone. As if waiting to be judged, even by a slave who's asking to be his apprentice.

The painting's background was a flat gold, like any church icon. Likewise the discs of haloes, behind the heads of saints and angels. But the Empress-Mother in her green robes, and Her Divine Child . . .

'You've painted statues!' I blurted out.

It was true enough: the painting's flesh had the look of glossy pearl-white stone. Round enough to be tangible.

'They're . . . ' I realised I was making vague hand-gestures, as if I could capture the nature of the woman and naked child more easily that way than in words. 'They're . . . weighty.'

He frowned – but not from anger. Concentration, perhaps. 'I'm making mass out of value changes . . . Yes, it's too heavy here; flesh might indeed be marble. But once edge is abandoned, then depth or lightness of tone must take the place of outline . . . eh!'

He made hand-gestures of his own. It felt as if we both sought a vocabulary not yet created, or one *being* created, here in his workshop, and back in Florence; hammered out on the anvil of the New School's art.

The light and shadow of the Empress-Mother's face was as if I looked through the board at a real woman sitting on the other side of it. If this is done only by varying tone, hue, brilliance . . .

'I can't see how you do it!'

Masaccio grinned. 'Look, boy, I understand why you have come to Rome. I see you have the exact same ambition that I do: to be the best painter in the city of the Empty Chair, at the centre of the civilised world. But the difference is, *I* am Tommaso Cassai. And you are not.'

Rekhmire' raised an eloquent eyebrow, which I thought might query Masaccio's location of the civilised world's centre. I didn't allow the Egyptian the time to speak.

'If those—' I gestured briefly at my stacked boards, carried so carefully from Carthage to Rome. 'If those are trash, teach me otherwise.'

'No,' Masaccio returned instantly. 'You have not the talent. Look at you, how old?'

'Twenty-four.'

'Twenty-four, and what have you done?' He spoke arrogantly for a man who looked only three or four years my senior. 'These are mediocre. It would be better if you had done nothing. You've spoiled what little talent you had on mundane, trivial work. Do you even draw?'

The abrupt question startled me. 'Yes.'

'How long since? When did you start?'

I shrugged. 'I don't know. Always, I think. My foster-father used to hit me for wasting time drawing with a stone on the walls, when I was a small child.'

The sharp points of flints had been good for scoring lines into the crumbling plaster walls of Aldra Federico's villa; I could still feel the sensation in my fingertips.

'I drew the horses that the men unsaddled in the stables.' I added, 'It wasn't until I came to King Rodrigo's court that I learned the encaustic technique for pigments in wax.'

Masaccio grunted. I thought he sounded surprised, as if it was not what he expected to hear. Hope pierced clear through me; I felt my fingertips prickle and go cold with it.

'Still,' he said thoughtfully, as if holding a conversation with himself, 'you have all the old dross embedded in your technique. How could you unlearn that?'

'You did!' I burst out.

He stared at me.

'*You* must have unlearned the old school of painting,' I emphasised. My chest hurt with the tightness of my breathing, as well as the bandaging that flattened my small breasts under the Frankish fashion of thin, tight doublets. Holding the gaze of his black eyes, I added, 'If you can do it, so can I!'

'You're too old, now.' He turned aside, dismissively. 'You should have been drawing each day, every day, since you were ten.'

'I did – from before age ten—'

'I would have you spend six years grinding colours; then you would learn mixing, and it would be another ten years before you would be allowed to work on any painting to come from my workshop. No.'

Rekhmire' made a quiet interruption behind us. 'I've said that I can pay sufficiently for an apprenticeship. But is there no other work my slave might do here?'

His level tone made my temper flare. I clamped down on it. Masaccio turned back from the workshop tables. His eye had a look of interest in it – but not for me.

The planes of the tall Egyptian's face, and his disproportionate hands and feet, made him an automatic object of interest. His linen kilt looked not so out of place here as I'd imagined it would – and I realised why. Rekhmire' might be one of the Old Testament patriarchs scattered about the place in Masaccio's sketches. His size and height gave him the same gravity.

'You are a man of Egypt-in-exile. Castrato?' Masaccio hazarded.

Rekhmire' gave a social bow. 'We are not here to speak of me. In the matter of my slave here . . . might he begin as a servant?'

'I have all the servants I need.'

'Then, some other way in which he might aid you here, and meanwhile learn from what he sees—'

The Florentine interrupted with an over-loud laugh. 'I couldn't even use him as a model! His hips are wide enough for a woman!'

Another man wouldn't have noticed it. To the untutored eye, I look wiry: a man of medium height. I saw Mastro Masaccio looking at me in the way that a painter looks at the body and bones of men. His gaze lingered on my crotch, where the Frankish fashion for tight hose necessitated a cod-flap covering the bulge of my male genitalia. His gaze lifted to my chest.

He gave an absent nod. ' . . . And the shoulders of a man.'

I found my hand going up to smooth the fine down of hair on my cheek, sparse as it still was after my unshaven travelling. *I am a man, see: how could I be otherwise?*

Rekhmire' caught my eye, his gaze disapproving. I set my mouth.

Masaccio shook his head at me. 'You could model for neither man nor woman. Or both!'

I stared at him. Frustration kept me rigid. No use to plead. Nor bluster – not with a slave's name-collar resting around my neck.

I need him to teach me how he paints.

I need him to teach me how he *sees*.

'Wait!' the Italian said.

He approached me where I stood between the work-benches and easels. He squinted with the practised gaze of one used to perception by north light. I fisted my hands to stop them shaking.

'You have a Spanish colouring,' he said.

I nodded, stiffly. 'I'm from Taraconensis, in Iberia.'

'That would be well. A touch swarthy. And the rest of you . . . '

His head rose and fell as he studied me. I sweated. Any moment now he'll see – because he is a man who sees – what I am: hermaphrodite passing as male. And then I'll be beaten, hunted through the streets; perhaps burned at the public bonfires the Franks love so much—

'Cardinal Valente has paid for a painting of the Betrayal in the Garden.' Masaccio's black eyes closed to slits; sprang open again. 'I have no model for Judas.'

He smiled up at me with white teeth.

'Until now. A man who looks neither a man nor a woman – or looks like both! What could be more monstrous? Or more fitting? Mastro Rekhmire', I'll take your slave on as a model for the Great Traitor. Is that a deal?'

2

Rekhmire' took a deep breath as we stepped into the narrow street outside the workshop. 'There is a man who deserves his name!'

The control Rekhmire' could exercise amazed me. My hands were vibrating. I took an equal breath, to see if it would calm me too. 'You were happy to stand there and have your slave insulted!'

His mouth twisted as I mentioned the subject of slavery. It might have been amusement, or some other thought in his mind.

Not able to hold back, I spat out, '"Judas!" The Franks think of Gaius Judas as a villain! It's adding insult to injury – I'm a bad painter *and* their Great Traitor!'

Rekhmire' laughed ruefully. He glanced down at me as he shook out his Frankish woollen cloak, and swung it around his bare shoulders. The garment sat oddly with his kilt and sandals, and the reed head-band around his brow.

'Ilario. He was testing you. To see what mettle you have.'

'I know.'

'Yes.' This time Rekhmire' inclined his shaven head as he put up his cloak-hood. An acknowledgement?

Stepping out into the fine rain, he added, 'I haven't seen you – restraining your impulses in that manner, before.'

I threw my own cloak across my shoulders and followed Rekhmire' between the heavy, high buildings. 'He wanted to see if he could drive me out.'

'I congratulate you for the realisation of that.'

In the chill air and the failing rain, I could feel my face burn. To assure myself, privately, that I need to be less impulsive is one thing. To hear it from another—!

Rekhmire' gave me a disarmingly friendly look. My temper subsided.

We walked back towards our lodgings. I glanced up at the narrow sky. In the twelve interminable days it had taken to get an interview with Master Masaccio, I'd slogged morning and evening around every column and temple and atrium, bath and forum and amphitheatre, of ruined Imperial Rome. My eyes dazzled at first with the proportions of thousand-year-old architecture. Now—

I miss Taraco's heat. And Rome is failing.

'Well.' I stretched my arms to the rain, feeling spine and tendons realign. 'It puts off considering how I would live here for the seven years of an apprenticeship, as things stand now.'

Rekhmire' answered my look with one of his own, that was particularly reassuring.

'Master Honorius has twenty-five years he wishes to make up for: he would pay your apprenticeship unhesitatingly.' The Egyptian shrugged. 'And I did not lie: I would pay to have a slave trained. Although the painter would treat a freedman better.'

'All of it leaves me indebted,' I remarked.

The upper floors of most Roman buildings have crumbled away. Leaves dropped past my face with the rain, falling from shrubs embedded high in the brickwork. There was not one high wall without a tracery of weeds, or tiny rooted saplings. My fingers ached to draw the rotted shutters showing the sky through empty window-frames. And reproduce the texture of skin-tight moss on fallen monuments. Or attempt to.

Neither of these men would regard it as a debt, but – and then there is Carthage—

The moment's inattention cost me my balance. The surface of the street was in no less disrepair than the buildings: cobblestones out of their holes like teeth out of an old man's jaw, and slippery in the wet. I stumbled out of the way of a two-wheeled *cisia*-cart, lurching into the Roman men and matrons crowding the narrow streets, and found myself shoved back against Rekhmire' with curses.

Rekhmire' steadied me, his sandalled feet padding between dips and puddles with a flawless certainty that in another mood would have made me grin.

'You may be certain,' the Egyptian remarked. 'The Mastro would not have given you a job of any kind if he had not seen something in you.'

'*Ahh!*' I came to a dead halt in the street and slapped my hand against my forehead. The crowds parted, not amiably; and flowed around us.

Rekhmire' looked genuinely alarmed. 'What is it?'

'Sculpture! I should have told him! *I paint statues!* Instead of being a model, I could . . . '

Rekhmire' shrugged as he met my gaze. In that moment I saw it had both occurred to him as a choice and been dismissed.

'"Old art." Would it impress Master Masaccio, do you think, that you can practise that skill? Or would he think it merely something else on which your time is wasted?'

I grunted.

The Egyptian didn't press for an admission that he was correct.

Which would have been less irritating had I not realised quite how correct he was.

'This place is *shabby*,' I complained, as we began to walk again. '"Holy city." "Centre of the civilised world!" There's nothing here but – but – an empty chair. There's no centre of power here.'

The Egyptian looked silently down the several inches between our heights, and raised his eyebrow. He won a grin out of me.

'All *right*. I'm *in* Masaccio's workshop. Even if only as a model.'

I can watch. I can *learn*.

'Carthage's curse is darkness,' Rekhmire' murmured, slowing at the end of the street, next to the Tiber River. Looking for the entrance to the alley that led to our lodgings. 'Rome's curse is an empty Papal chair. History can lay a heavy hand on the present.'

'Yes, I know.'

He shot me a glance. I wondered what had come back to him, in that moment. I see Rosamunda's face: the face of my mother when I tell her that I *know* she planned to kill me when she abandoned me as a baby.

I have acknowledged that it happened. And now it has no influence over me. No, none.

'Messer Egyptian?' a voice called.

Rekhmire' turned with a smooth power in his movement. He didn't carry a sword, any more than I did; Frankish religious law not permitting it within the city walls. As a eunuch bureaucrat, I realised, he might not be trained in arms.

In a brawl, his tall, powerful body would go a long way to defending him. *And I have been trained to be a man.*

There seemed nothing to justify apprehension. No bandit or Carthaginian spy was visible. Only a small, elderly man in clerical robes, his hands tucked under his arms against the chill. He looked as though he had been waiting.

I moved my hand away from my dagger.

'A message from Cardinal Corradeo, Messer Egyptian,' the elderly man said in a squeak, wiping moisture from his nose. 'He will see you tomorrow, when it's convenient to you; an hour past noon, perhaps?'

Rekhmire' bowed with his hands crossed over his chest. 'My compliments to your master. I will attend on him at that time.'

His hands came down and out, and with that movement acquired something in them. I saw him palm a coin into the secretary's hand, and the little man bobbed his head and hurried off.

I cocked a brow at Rekhmire', in much the Egyptian's own fashion.

He smiled. 'There are forbidden books here, that the Franks themselves may not read. I hope to copy some for the Royal Library, at home. Being already a heathen, how can I be harmed by the sight of them?'

The look of innocence accompanying his last words made me grin.

'A Cardinal—' I stumbled over the unfamiliar church title. '—is truly prepared to let you into forbidden archives?'

The Egyptian began to pick his way down the street with the delicacy of a cat that dislikes getting its feet wet, incongruous in such a large man.

'On the one condition. That if I find anything relating to lifting the curse on St Peter's Chair, I turn it over to him. Corradeo is hoping I'll see something he won't, because he supposes I have knowledge from the Royal Library. I doubt that will happen.' Rekhmire''s expression under his shielding hood took on a faux innocence. 'Oh, and I must let him take the credit for whatever I find.'

That made me chuckle.

A thought wiped amusement out.

'Will you need me as a copyist?'

'No. I think it will take quite enough to persuade them to let one man in. I'll have to do my own copying.'

I was unsure whether that was generosity on his part, so that I might go to Masaccio's workshop, or useful truth; and while I frowned over it, he stopped, and pointed me towards our lodgings.

'You go on, Ilario. I realise I intended to pass by the Alexandrine house again, and see if there are letters for me.'

Which would make once every two days that he had gone to his embassy in this city, I calculated. Regular as a water-clock.

'You think your "colleague from Zaragoza" will have written to you yet? Or anyone else?'

'I have hopes.' Rekhmire' pulled his hood further down, against the rain and men seeing his face. 'I don't otherwise know whether to take this lack of news to be reassuring – or a silence before a storm.'

3

Outside the tenement lodgings, the scent of sweating beasts filled the rainy air. The horses of a *carrucas* snorted – the four-wheeled cart which men use to carry baggage and cargo to the sea-coast at Ostia Antica. Beyond them, similar muscles straining, men wrestling with roped boxes. I felt the shapes of the thick arched necks in my fingers.

One deep voice pierced the noise:

'*That* one first! Then these crates here. It shouldn't take you fifteen minutes!' Honorius's gaze shifted from the work-crew to me. He beamed. 'Ilario!'

The boxes had the marks of the small artisans' workshops, up behind the cathedral that housed the Empty Chair itself. Rosaries, for the most part: made in light materials like pearl-shell, attractive in Iberia for their foreignness, and usefully no different in structure whether one worships *Christus Imperator* or the Frankish heresy.

'You got everything packed up in time?'

'Yes. Get 'em taken down to the warehouses in Ostia and stored.' He spoke with satisfaction, stepping back to eye the cart with the vision of a man used to calculating bombard and baggage loads. 'Old mercenary company habit: trade light items . . . When the Egyptian gives me word it's safe, I can start exporting back to Taraconensis. All his letters from "book-buyers" in Iberia – if he's not a spy, he damn well *should* be!'

I gave my father the best innocent-slave look I could muster. 'He gets a lot of that, too . . . '

Honorius snorted, and turned back to settling payments with the carters, still laughing. I went into the house, hugging my secret news to me since I would not tell him in company; stumbling on the tiles in the inner rooms, blinking in the indoor twilight.

I set about igniting oil-lamps, the light blossoming up the plaster walls, and returned to some of the tasks I had left half-done before going out.

'Casserole?' Honorius remarked hopefully as he bustled through the low door, shaking rain from himself, and looking over my shoulder with ease. He frowned as I pressed the last of the clay seal around the edges of the pot.

'Not unless you plan on eating charcoal . . . '

'Spent my life in military camps, remember?'

Through a laugh, I explained, 'Charcoal for drawing,' and shifted the heavy pot over to the oven, where it could sit in the banked embers through the night. There were twelve of the small wired bundles in the pot; I thought that should last me my first month in Masaccio's workshop. 'By morning, I'll either have my own willow-twig charcoal, or . . . '

'Or—?'

'Or lots of crumbly little bits of wood.' I straightened up, one hand in the small of my back. 'Used to take a pot down to the baker's in the square at home, at the end of the day when he'd finished working. He'd always let me put it in his ovens overnight. That was vine charcoal, though. Better for drawing.'

About to leap from that to Masaccio, and my news, I saw my father looked distant. As if he remembered those few of the Taraconensis hills that will bear terraced vines, and the taste of the grape.

'I never know . . . ' Honorius frowned. 'Whether I should *expect* to see you play the housewife and bake meats. Or whether you don't cook when you're dressed as a man. Or whether you don't cook at all. I don't know what your nature is. Are you determined to keep up this charade?'

He jerked his thumb at me.

At my clothing, rather.

Frankish doublet and hose, in the Italian style, and not the slave tunic of North Africa's climate, which is worn equally by male and female.

I couldn't keep asperity out of my tone. 'I would have thought you'd prefer a son. Don't men want that?'

Finding your long-unknown, long-lost son-daughter is one thing. Travelling together can be another. For some reason, while it didn't bother him who turned my head in the street, how I dressed was an abrasive matter between us.

Honorius spoke bluntly. 'I'm not ashamed to have a ladyboy as my heir. But *you* seem to be ashamed, here. Is that why you pass as something you're not?'

I sat down at the table, leaving him standing over me.

'I have to be man *or* woman. It's not safe to be both in Frankish lands.'

Or in most other lands, outside of specific roles such as Taraco's court.

I strained my neck looking up at my father. His blue eyes were pale enough to be grey indoors, even with the room's shutters still open. I would need a highlight on the cornea, and a catch-light in the white, to make his eyes stand out emphatically enough in a painting.

'As a woman, I wouldn't be permitted to paint. And to be a woman and a slave . . . Legally, that makes me an animal. So I keep part of me hidden and play all the man.'

Normally he would have sat down companionably with me; I knew by this how disturbed he felt. He scratched at his hair, leaving himself with the curled short tuft on the crown of his head that everything – removing his linen-lined helmet; standing at a wind-ridden ship's rail – appeared to give him.

'A woman . . . It's not *that* bad, their life.'

I couldn't help giving him a raised brow. 'You would know?'

'Ximena – my late wife—'

I said nothing more. No man – or no man like Honorius – desires to listen to anything that would make him think his wife unhappy. Less so when there's no mending it after death. She might have been happier than most women, but that was based on supposing him as good a husband as father.

'I try to think of you as a son and a daughter in the same body,' he said earnestly. 'Is that not what you'd have me do?'

I wanted to say *You're doing well*; what fell out of my mouth was, 'You don't need to try so hard!'

Nothing on his face showed him affronted, but I saw it in the lessening curve of his spine and the movement of his shoulders.

Biting off each syllable, he said, 'I have missed twenty-four years.'

And I. Bitterly frustrated by not finding the right words, I managed all that I could put into speech. 'I'm – very glad you answered Rekhmire''s message.'

The line of his shoulders released itself. He dropped down onto the opposite bench, smiling across the table. 'So am I.'

I had rested my hands on the table to feel the grain, where much scrubbing clean had raised it above the surrounding soft wood. I registered my fingers in peripheral vision, stained with wax and umber and red lead, and looked up to meet Honorius's eyes.

I couldn't help beaming. 'I didn't tell you yet – Masaccio accepted me into his workshop. *Only* as a model. But—'

'Ilario!' He slapped his open palm on his thigh. 'I didn't like to ask when you came in; I thought . . . But this is wonderful! A beginning—'

'*Eightfold GODS!*'

The street and inner doors slammed, so close on each other that it was one blast of sound and cold air. Rekhmire' ducked to miss the low beams of the tenement-house ceiling. He threw himself down on the wooden bench beside Honorius, hurling an armful of scroll cases to the table-top.

I caught two before they could skitter to the floor. 'Good news, then?'

Rekhmire' gave me a look that would have melted glass in a Murano workshop.

One of Honorius's fists banged a ceramic bowl down in front of him, and the other a bottle of wine.

The Egyptian inclined his head in a way that told me, at least, that he was both pleased and surprised.

'*Finally*, news,' he corrected, untying his cloak at the throat, and wiping his hand over his shaven head.

'From home?'

I should have stood to serve him, but found I couldn't.

'Some of it.' Rekhmire' poured himself a bowl of wine. 'Sahathor sends me every whisper, rumour, and gossip; but of hard facts—! Heh and Hehet of the infinite spaces! How much *rubbish* the man writes!'

His large hands twisted the tops from cases and swept scrolls open, anchoring them that way with ceramic pots and jugs. Honorius gave me a glance. I gathered my father to be much amused by the bureaucrat's unbureaucratic swearing.

And to be waiting with as much apprehension as I felt.

Rekhmire' sat back, resting his large hands on the heap of papers. He looked from my father to me.

'There has been no time to write to Alexandria and get a reply, but I have consulted with some colleagues in the embassy here. I have not told more there than I thought any man should know, nor mentioned your names. Simply put, it isn't in Alexandria's interests to have Taraconensis destabilised, and Carthage made stronger. I would be no man's favourite if I said my error in Hanno's court might lead to that.' He flicked a gaze to me. 'Including you, I know.'

Any resentment had gone, I found, startled. 'You did the best you could at the time, with the knowledge you had.'

Rekhmire' reached across the table. His hand closed briefly and surprisingly over mine before he leaned back again. 'In the event that the Pharaoh-Queen communicates personally with me through the embassy, I think that the message will scrape the ears off the side of my head . . . '

'Let me write back to her.' I couldn't help smiling at him. 'I'll tell her it wasn't your fault. And my marvellous cursive hand will win her over.'

Since I knew that monumental gravity well by now, I could see how much humour he hid.

'I can only hope the autumn weather prevents a too-speedy delivery of post . . . '

'So.' Honorius indicated the scrolls with a wave of his hand. 'Where do we stand?'

I reached out for the last crumbs of cheese on one plate, although I could barely swallow. If I could paint their faces, in this remarkable mix of day-lit oil-lamps and rain-light coming in through half-shuttered windows . . . My master, the bureaucrat; my father, the soldier; myself, the artist. Because I will be an artist, I reminded myself. No matter what word comes from home.

From outside I heard the shouts of the *carrucas*-drivers. And the spatter of rain.

'Videric *is* gone from office. It's confirmed from many sources.' Rekhmire' traced a line of hieroglyphs on one sheet. 'There are no public rumours about Aldro Rosamunda's attempt to kill you, Ilario. The Lord Videric is supposed caught with his hand in the treasury chest, or in some other way under the King's displeasure. The Carthaginian envoy has taken ship back to Carthage . . . '

Honorius grunted, picking up a heel of loaf and tearing shreds of crust off it. 'Putting some distance in, so that if the King's tree falls, they're not caught shaking the trunk.'

Rekhmire''s smile was a rictus twitch. His oval eyelids were stained blue, I realised; with a lack of sleep that I thought only I had suffered these last few weeks. He rubbed hard with his thumb along the ridge of his brow.

'Ilario . . . Like it or not, you're still the key to this. These, here, these are the stories that are being spread around by Lord Videric's supporters. You'll see they all say, one way or another, that he's retired to his estates because he's *ill*. Not thrown out of his position as First Minister, but in bad health. Why would he claim sickness?'

I shook my head.

'Because,' Honorius rumbled, scowling, 'a man recovers from sickness.'

The Egyptian gave a swift nod. 'Quicker than from scandal. Videric's men are evidently preparing the ground so that he *can* return, in the future, without his dismissal or resignation ever having to be acknowledged. Why would King Rodrigo be willing to have Aldra Videric back as his First Minister?'

Grudgingly, I admitted, 'Because he's good at what he does?'

'That, too. And also, other kings and princes *believe* Taraconensis stronger while Videric is Rodrigo Sanguerra's minister. But, no.' Rekhmire' picked up a knife and began doodling the point under certain of the written glyphs. 'No, I think what has happened . . . is that Aldra Videric has found it possible to promise King Rodrigo something.'

I knew I would not like what I next heard. 'What?'

'A word overheard here, a whisper there . . . One can make a supposition from them. Suppose,' Rekhmire' leaned forward, lowering his voice. 'Suppose that this difficulty went away? Suppose that Lord Videric was able to say, "It's all lies, my wife did nothing, *I* did nothing: look at where this story comes from? Carthage would make any ridiculous claim, if it enables them to weaken this kingdom." How many men in Taraconensis would believe it a scandal cooked up by the King-Caliph, to make the King distrust his most necessary minister?'

I shrugged. 'Knowing the court, and given that men believe what they want to believe – most of them.'

Honorius downed a mug of wine, and wiped his sleeve across his mouth with a rasp of stubble. 'But the problem with that is – oh.'

Rekhmire''s chiselled lips soundlessly and satirically mimicked the *oh*, but I thought his smile more self-mocking. 'Yes. The problem for Videric is that Carthage has a witness. He may or may not know that witness is not in Carthage, now. But . . . '

Rekhmire' put his hand down flat on one letter. The unrolled end of the scroll was in cipher, and not one of the basic ones that every scribe learns.

'But, for reasons contained in these letters, I think that what Videric has promised the King is the life of Ilario.'

His gaze moved to me.

'Or, more specifically, the death of Ilario. If Aldra Videric can make this problem go away, then in a few months he can come back and take over his position again, and blame it all on Carthaginian rumour. But for that to work . . . Ilario, I believe he needs your death very urgently, now. Because he sees in it his way back to power.'

4

There was a coldness in my stomach. A round wooden bowl nudged my hand: I looked up to see Honorius offering it to me, filled with red wine.

The taste was only superficially warming.

'What I can gather from *Carthage*, on the other hand . . . ' Rekhmire' tapped his fingertips together, and I guessed that he changed direction to give me time to gain composure. ' . . . From Carthage, we have little enough to fear as regards harming you, Ilario. They have reason to wish you alive and well and in their hands, so they can keep the scandal-pot boiling nicely; all you have to fear from *them* is abduction. That way they keep the muck-raking alive, keep Videric out of office, keep King Rodrigo off-balance, and begin to convince the Frankish kingdoms that Taraconensis is ripe for a crusade.'

Honorius nodded. I realised he would be used to this scope of discussion, from his life in the north.

He reached to top my wine-bowl up, and said gruffly, 'He's right. The worst they'd do is kidnap you.'

The surface of the wine rippled. I realised I shuddered. *The shit and piss of the slaver's hall briefly real in my nostrils again.*

As if he could read my mind, Rekhmire' said, 'You have men who would seek you out, now, and free you.'

If it had not been Rekhmire' standing in the shadows. If I had not been reckless enough to demand to be taken seriously as a scribe . . .

I stood up from the table, crossing to the window, leaning between the open shutters. The rain felt cool on my scalding face. Twilight comes early among these tall Roman tenements. The wetness brought out the stink of dung, ripe fruit, sour sweat, horses.

My urge to pull back from the reassurance of these men comes because a slave can never trust anybody, and far too many will pretend to be a friend in fair weather.

You trust them or you don't. And if you have not known your father more than two months, well, the Egyptian has proved himself to feel – what was it he said in Hanno's court? – fellow-feeling. Friendship.

I wiped rain off my face and turned back, groping my way to the table since the waning day blinded me to the lamp's softer light. Shadows leapt up as I sat down, banging table and bench, and I clearly saw both men watching me.

Rekhmire' interlinked his large fingers in front of him. 'There's nothing to say it's known where we are. Believe me, I've sought to be sure of that! Because whereas I could safely refuse to sell you in Carthage, as a cousin of Ty-ameny—'

Catching the question in Honorius's eye, he added:

'We in the bureaucratic service are customarily called "cousins of the Lioness Throne". And in Carthage, that carries influence. But if they should discover us in Rome ... I think Ilario should not go out unaccompanied, if we ever have reason to think any man from Carthage has succeeded in finding us.'

Honorius jerked a thumb at the door to the side rooms, and looked questioningly at me. 'You want me to send the lads out with you?'

I could hear some of them at dinner; even recognise a few voices. I had sketched the small grizzled sergeant called 'Orazi' (none of the household guard being able to pronounce his proper Armenian name), and Attila and Tottola: twin hulking Germanic peasants become expert men-at-arms. Also a man named Berenguer, who stuck in my mind for how deeply he appeared to resent the company of an Alexandrine eunuch; one Saverico, an ensign who resembled one of the cathedral's boy-singers at home in Taraco, but must surely have more martial qualities somewhere about him; a handful of others ... All making cheerful conversation in the room beyond, which they had adopted as their barracks, as if it did not concern them that their captain would drag them halfway across the Mediterranean on an apparent whim.

The majority of Honorius's thirty or so men were faces to me, whose names I tended to confuse. Coming to the Empty Chair, only one name had had my attention: *Masaccio*.

'I think Ilario would be better off without an escort.' Rekhmire' sounded bland. 'Wiser not to draw attention to ourselves if we can avoid it.'

Bland, I thought, and nothing at all like a man protesting, *Mercenary Frankish soldiers, out from under their captain-general's thumb: I give it two days at best before all of them end in jail as drunken sots and Ilario with them!*

I couldn't imitate Rekhmire''s smooth insincerity without a give-away grin. 'I can just see that lot masquerading as body-servants! And fellow-slaves. And scribes.'

'All *right*.' Honorius glared. He failed to conceal a smile, and shook his head. 'But, damn it, I'd feel safer if you had armed men in attendance to protect you.'

'Anonymity is a good defence.' Rekhmire' spoke with the sound of long experience.

'Bloody big sword's a *better* one!'

I couldn't restrain laughter. Apart from his being my father, Honorius is an easily likeable man.

Concern abruptly chilled me. 'Aldra Videric. If he finds out I'm in Rome. He might know *you're* here. You won't be his favourite, either.'

Honorius snorted an obscenity.

'The Lord General Honorius won't be in great danger.' Rekhmire' looked over at me as he emphasised my father's title. 'Even his word and facial resemblance mean nothing if you're dead, Ilario. It would be Lord Honorius's word against Lord Videric's. And I suspect your father counts as a foreigner after having been gone for so long. The story's hearsay. Ilario . . . you're the only living proof that Videric's wife attempted to kill a slave who is her own offspring.'

He shot an apologetic look at me, as if his chess-master weighing of the pieces might have offended.

'In a way, removing himself from court is a wise thing for Aldra Videric to do. Until the King of Taraconensis names a new First Minister – and none of my correspondents say he seems ready to do that – there's nothing to say that Videric doesn't *still* hold that position. But if, now, he were to go to his King and say that all can be blamed on Carthage – then King Rodrigo would refuse the idea, because Ilario can arrive at any time out of the blue, and prove Videric a liar.'

'I could talk with Videric.' The expectation of being in his presence again made my stomach twist, both with fear and rage. 'Tell him . . . '

Tell him what?

Rekhmire' spoke while Honorius was still visibly weighing his words.

'If things are as we see them, then Aldra Videric is in circumstances where he *must* desire your death, leaving aside any personal vindictiveness. When the dust settles, he can take up the reins as chancellor of Taraconensis – *if* there's no possibility of a witness to Aldro Rosamunda's actions. With no witnesses, men will believe him if he says it's all Carthaginian propaganda. Is there an Iberian who doesn't know that Carthage wants to re-conquer the Peninsula? But that relies on no witness ever appearing to prove Carthage's accusations. It's in Lord Videric's interests now for you to be dead, Ilario. For you to be dead, and as soon as possible.'

'*Turds!*'

Had there been anything inexpensive and breakable, it would have been very relieving to throw it. Since there was neither, I settled for fetching one of the empty benches a kick. The oak left a throbbing bruise on the ball of my foot.

'I just want to *paint!*'

I held up both hands, stopping dual interruptions.

'I *know*. I am aware of the circumstances! But King Rodrigo knows me. Videric knows me. God's burning Hellfire, *Rosamunda knows me!* All of them know I have no intention of being used as a tool, by Carthage or anyone else; I – just – want – to – paint.'

Rekhmire' and Honorius exchanged looks.

'They can't afford to think they know you.' Honorius shrugged. 'It's like that in battle. Doesn't matter if the enemy's a man you've known for years. To achieve your objective, you have to take *all* precautions. If the Egyptian here's right, Videric thinks it's necessary for you to be dead.' His forehead corrugated. 'I still can't credit that Rosamunda would try to kill you.'

'You knew her twenty-five years ago—'

I didn't remark that she had done her best to make sure I died then, too, albeit without actually killing me.

'—That doesn't mean you know what she's capable of now.'

Honorius broke his bread into smaller and smaller pieces, eventually chewing and swallowing one. There was silence in the room except for the tearing of the crust.

It was broken so suddenly by a rap on the outer door that all three of us visibly startled.

One of the men-at-arms exchanged inaudible words outside the house; the door opened, and a rain-soaked soldier entered, removing papers from the breast of his cloak and laying them down on the table beside Honorius. I thought they might be bills of lading from the carts, but Honorius frowned, and began immediately to unfold them.

Rekhmire' caught my gaze, and stood. I joined him at the window, affording my father privacy. I watched the torch-lighter failing to ignite the pitch-torches on the taverna wall opposite, as the last light faded from the drizzling sky.

The Egyptian murmured, 'Rome is likely safe for a few months. Perhaps longer. If you ever spoke of Mastro Masaccio to Lord Videric or Lady Rosamunda—'

I nodded, mutely, seeing the expectation in his expression. Is there any man or woman to whom I *haven't* extolled the New Art?

'—Then they'll expect you to be travelling to Florence. Although I suppose they'll eventually receive news that he's staying in Rome, now. I don't know how to manage your apprenticeship under these circumstances.'

'*Dismissed.*'

Honorius didn't raise his voice, behind me, but the intensity of it brought me swinging around, away from the window. The inner door closed behind his lieutenant's back, and the man-at-arms who had been lighting further oil-lamps scurried out after him.

The lean man was on his feet beside the table. A bundle of untied papers covered the planks before him. He cocked his head in my direction: a grey-feathered raven.

'Message for me,' he grunted. 'Just had my aide take my token to the bank for funds – *this* was there for me—'

He threw down a scroll, with its red wax seal cracked open.

'"Message"?' Rekhmire' scowled, shoving his way back to the table. 'You surely left no word of where you were travelling!'

I thought my father might hit him.

Hastily joining them, I as hastily interrupted:

'How could any man know to send you a letter in Rome?'

'Read it if you like—' Honorius gulped his wine messily, wiped his hand down his doublet, and jerked his chin in the direction of the scroll. 'Wasn't sent to me in Rome. Didn't write to me *here*. Seems there's a copy gone out to every major branch of the Fugger moneylenders. I would have found the letter wherever I went, whenever I next drew on my funds.'

The Egyptian choked off a laugh, his eyes bright. 'Clever!'

I demanded, 'Who's it from?'

Honorius scratched at his cropped hair as if lice troubled him, and snapped a glance at me. 'Ask yourself, who can afford to do a thing like that?'

Videric might think of it. But if it were Videric, Honorius would have said.

'The King!' I said, simultaneously with Rekhmire''s reading aloud of the superscription:

'His Grace, Rodrigo Sanguerra Covarrubias, Lord of Taraconensis.'

5

Rodrigo's wise to use bankers, I thought. Taraconensis maintains ambassa-
dors living at foreign courts, rather than having embassies like the
Alexandrines, and the King wouldn't want every ambassador knowing
his business if it concerned Carthage.

'But . . . ' I frowned. 'The King doesn't have any reason to connect
you with me! Unless Videric's told him.'

'For once, it's not about *you*.'

Honorius gave me a grin that was both sardonic and reassuring. It
melted away as he scowled down at the parchment scroll.

'It's about me. When I have the time, I'm cordially requested to come
to court – and reading between the lines, he suggests I have the time right
now.'

'To court? To *Taraco*?'

'Exactly. And why would King Rodrigo want to see me so badly?'
Honorius turned his head, giving Rekhmire' a suspicious glare, clearly
supposing him to have the answer, I think for no other reason than the
book-buyer's general fluency with politics.

Rekhmire' sat down abruptly on his bench.

'I . . . imagine he thinks you're conspiring with the King-Caliph
against his throne.'

'*What!*'

My father's indignation rang off the plaster walls. Despite the
seriousness of the situation, I couldn't help smiling. His sharp glare made
me drop the expression as rapidly as any of his new recruits.

Rekhmire' glanced up from the document, his lustrous eyes soot-dark
in the lamp-light. 'I confess, I . . . well, at first, *I* had expected you to be a
political rival of Aldra Videric, Lord General.'

'You gave me my son-daughter: enough of the "Lord General"!'
Honorius's fist struck the flat of one of the oak beams above his head,
loud enough to make a man-at-arms look around the inner door.
Honorius gestured without looking and the soldier vanished. No man
would argue with him in this mood.

'Why on God's earth would I rival Videric? It's been five-and-twenty
years since I've seen Rosamunda—'

'*Political* rival,' Rekhmire' emphasised, his voice gentle. 'Why would it
be so surprising? You've made yourself rich in foreign wars. You can

expect to live to a fine old age. Why not come home to be – First Minister, even, in Aldra Videric's place?'

Honorius gave a startled bark that I recognised, after a second, as laughter.

'True enough,' Rekhmire' agreed, 'and I knew it within forty minutes of meeting you face to face. But King Rodrigo can't be expected to know that. Has he even seen you?'

Honorius slowly seated himself. 'As a young man, at court.'

'Then look at it from the King's position. Licinus Honorius. A rich man, with a considerable reputation—'

The Egyptian bowed his head respectfully; Honorius snorted.

'A considerable *military* reputation,' Rekhmire' emphasised. 'And a man who's been gone from his country for upwards of a generation. The King will only remember you as a young man, if at all. Say you sit on the throne of Taraconensis, you hear a man is coming home and buying land, and therefore means to stay in your kingdom; he has wealth, therefore can have influence, and his reputation will draw men to him. And having been – how many months had you been home?'

Honorius sounded reluctant. 'Three. Four, perhaps.'

'Having been a quarter of a year in Taraconensis, has not yet come to make his formal submission to his King—'

'I was buying an estate! And getting it in order! And sorting my men out; the ones who wanted to come back from the crusades and settle – parcelling land out to them, sorting out cattle and horses, arranging a monthly justice-meet for—' Honorius heaved a great sigh and slumped forward onto his elbows, on the table. 'I put it off. I don't like courts. Bunch of back-stabbing, lying, shit-eating toadies – it's why I preferred being on campaign to being in Alfonso's court. I kept thinking I could ride over to Taraco in the spring . . . '

Rekhmire' raised an eloquent eyebrow. 'And yet you sail to Carthage.'

'*You* know why I did that!'

'*King Rodrigo Sanguerra doesn't!*'

'I have never given my King any reason to doubt my loyalty!' Honorius thumped his fist down on the table, making every green-glazed jug and wooden spoon jump up. Over the clatter, he snarled, 'Ask the Kings of Aragon and Castile and Leon, ask His Royal Majesty Alfonso: I have *never* broken my word once given; why should I conspire against the lord of the kingdom in which I was *born*!'

I found myself wincing. Not as a slave does, from fear of a beating, but with the stunned appreciation with which one watches a mountain storm, or the great waves crashing on Taraco's shores in winter. Such primal loyalty is overwhelming.

'"Chancellor Honorius"!' Honorius snarled. '*Ha!*'

Rekhmire' had warmth in his gaze, I saw: amusement, and affection, as if the older man were a protégé of his, whom Rekhmire' was proud to see justify himself.

Christus Imperator! Rekhmire' found my father for me; I believe he feels a responsibility for Honorius being a good man.

There was something in that that spoke to friendship between the Egyptian and myself, but I put it aside to consider later, concentrating on Honorius where he sat and fumed:

'Who could imagine *me* wanting to be First Minister!'

'A lot of men want to.' I vividly recalled life at court. 'Most men, possibly. And I spent long enough in Taraco to know that no one's considered above suspicion.'

Honorius shot me a scorching glare from glass-grey eyes. 'I suppose *you* think I'm conspiring with the King-Caliph!'

It was possible. As a thing that some other man might do. *I'm not fool enough to think I know all fifty years of Honorius after two months in his company.* But having held Honorius's sallet while he puked over the ship's rail off Sardinia (which he assured me was commonly how bad weather took him), and having seen how he nonetheless cared for his household down to the youngest squire and kitchen-boy – and, more significantly, how little his mind ever turns from battle tactics to political power – I know this is not a possible thing for Licinus Honorius to do.

Honorius looked at me with a plain appeal on his face.

'I believe you!' I couldn't find words to explain what I knew he would see as cold rationality, and not faith in my father.

Rekhmire' came to my rescue. He tapped the paper. 'At worst, King Rodrigo Sanguerra suspects that, when the Carthaginian legions march up from Granada to offer their "protection" against crusading Franks, riding at their head will be Aldra Licinus Honorius – either as "adviser" to the King . . . or as a Carthaginian puppet-governor.'

'Rubbish!' Honorius sounded almost imploring. 'Ridiculous!'

'I've known you these past weeks; I suspect you have fewer political ambitions than any man alive—'

'Damn *right*! I just want to live in peace, on my estate, breeding my blood-line of horses.' He lifted his head, gazing intently at me. 'Looking after Ilario, if my son-daughter will let me.'

Rekhmire' upended the last of the Frankish wine into Honorius's bowl and pushed it at him. 'But you're not commanding the kingdom of Taraconensis. And if you were you'd look at it differently.'

Creases indented Honorius's forehead. The word *commanding* had been carefully chosen, I realised. Seeing the intent expression on my father's face, I realised that he knew it too.

'I've had my own problems with under-officers.' Honorius stared down into the reflections of his wine, and back at me before I had time to hide my expression. 'Surely a man who's been king as long as Rodrigo Sanguerra will *know* this is not what it seems?'

'No. He won't.' It was not news I wanted to give. 'His Majesty Rodrigo will tell you that endless suspicion is how any man stays king. Whether that's right or not, I don't know – it's certainly what *he* thinks.' I calculated the time that Honorius must have first arrived in Taraconensis. 'I think if I hadn't been busy with being kicked out as the King's Freak, and planning my voyage to Carthage, I would have heard rumours about this myself.'

Honorius looked torn between rage, anger at himself, and sorrow. Incised lines made his creased face seem older: a premonition of how we would both look at sixty.

'If I'd known you were there, Ilario, I would have come if I'd had to walk barefoot.'

'Well, that might have convinced Rodrigo you weren't rich and a problem.' I grinned. 'Except that, as my mother told me, you and I would have been seen together, and the gossips and rumour-mongers would have rung the cathedral bells in celebration!'

It cheered him a little, evidently. He set to prodding the letter with his forefinger, as if the royal seal would change into something less troublesome.

'My mind isn't made up.' He frowned. 'As to whether the bank will inform King Rodrigo Sanguerra where his letter was collected, because he's a king . . . or whether that makes it certain they'll refuse to say, because they bow their heads to no king. With the money they handle, they don't need to.'

The Egyptian moved his large hands as if they were the balance of a pair of scales. 'Could go either way.'

Honorius wiped his upper lip free of wine, where silver stubble already began to show after his shave.

'I think my way is clear, in any case.'

I didn't want to ask, but couldn't keep silent. 'What will you do?'

Honorius pushed his bench back as he rose, with a squeal of wood against floorboard. Circling the table, he sat beside me and rested his hand on my shoulder. 'I have to go back to Taraco and set the King straight on this.'

'I—'

Rekhmire' leaned towards us, cutting in as if he thought I would explode: 'He's his own best witness, Ilario.'

The Egyptian is a swift and good judge of character. I grimly reminded myself of that. Honorius's fingers dug into the fleshy part of my shoulder. As I have often done in court, I set a curb on my reactions.

'In that case – I'm going back to Taraco with you. As for Mastro Cassai . . . there'll be other Masters.'

'You are *not*!'

Rekhmire''s voice echoed simultaneously: '—not!'

Honorius's other hand closed on my arm. 'If the Egyptian here can make *me* see why Videric needs you dead, the argument has to be convincing to anybody. Even you, Ilario!'

Frustrated as I was, I had to smile at him. 'You're not as much of a blunt soldier as you make out.'

'I'm not a politician. However—' Honorius smiled somewhat grimly. 'I survived twenty-five years of the Frankish armies trying to kill me in Navarra and Leon. More to the point, I survived Castile's court! I'm not familiar with Rodrigo's courtiers after all this time, but I can take enough men to protect myself until I can see the King and clear up all this nonsense! But if you think I'm taking you back to Iberia, where Videric has every reason to *need* you dead—! And you can't even trust Rosamunda—'

I had shown Honorius my sketch-books on the voyage to Rome, pointing out my foster parents Federico and Valdamerca, and my stepsisters, and Father Felix. He wanted to know if he would recognise Rosamunda's face after so many years, but I could not show him. Every drawing I made of her, I burned in Carthage.

'No, I can't trust my mother. I can't trust Videric either. But I want to come with you.'

He gave me a small shake, as if he knew how much a slave gets used to being beaten, and would not wake such memories. 'Let me watch my back without having to look out for yours.'

He must have seen me look half-convinced.

'If you were killed, so soon after we've met, and the fault was mine—'

'All right!' I gave consent ungraciously, not able to help it. 'I'll feel the same. All of this is my fault.'

Rekhmire' had moved to rummage among boxes and baskets on the shelf beyond the hearth. His voice came clearly back. 'No.'

He straightened up with a differently shaped bottle. I recognised brandy. The Egyptian snagged wooden drinking bowls no smaller than we had used for wine, and rejoined us at the table.

'No,' he repeated, pouring the spirits. 'Aldra Videric's fault, in fact. Perhaps the Lady Rosamunda's, for her adultery. Just possibly, the Lord Commander Honorius here, for being a foolish young man in love, and helping her break her marriage vows. But everything that was done to cause this was done long before you were born, Ilario.'

I caught Honorius giving Rekhmire' a grateful look.

'I'll go back by land,' he muttered to me. 'Damned autumn storms are too much for my gullet. You stay here, study with Tommaso Cassai, and I'll leave some of my men with you—'

'Not unless you *want* to mark me as a target. Having a private army will draw unwanted attention and wrong conclusions.'

From his glare, I deduced we would have that argument again before his departure.

Before he could continue to wrangle, I said soberly, 'Unless you're planning to sell your estates and settle in another kingdom, you need to make peace with Rodrigo. I don't like it any better than you do, I don't suppose. As to Videric, I'm safe enough here at the moment. I . . . What else can I say? I wish you could stay? I don't know you well enough yet, after a lifetime apart?'

Honorius blinked fiercely. Of my three fathers – Federico and his commercial foster care; Videric, who, deep as he may be embedded in my life, is only a murderous step-father; and my blood-father Honorius – Honorius is the one I am least used to and feel I might understand best.

I wish I could say, *Stay a while longer.*

'But you're right,' I concluded, and said what I immediately realised he hadn't voiced, but had run in my reasoning in tandem. 'If the money-lenders do tell King Rodrigo where you picked up your letter, then Videric will hear about it. I don't care if he's on his estates, in Ethiopia with Prester John, or sailing the seas of the Moon – he'll hear the information. And he may, he just *may*, hear who's with you.'

Honorius was nodding as I spoke.

'Lectured by my own damned son-daughter! On politics!'

I opened my mouth to protest *Father!* and caught the glimmer of humour and aching sadness combined in his expression.

'*Somebody* evidently has to,' I remarked.

He closed with me, ruffled my hair into complete disarray, and embraced me as the Franks do, his lean muscles corded with strength. Unlike most, he touched my flesh as if there were no difference between it and anyone else's.

He stood back, grinning at how he'd dishevelled me. 'I don't plan to waste time. If it goes well, I'll be back by December.'

'Back?' I was suddenly and surprisingly light. 'You won't winter over in Taraco?'

'As far as that whoreson mule-fucker Videric is concerned—' Honorius spoke in a surprisingly even tone. '—I'll be travelling to my estates, to winter over, after I've visited the court and King Rodrigo. Fortunately, this lot of bone-headed layabouts who sponge off me are used to campaigning in bad weather, so we'll just take the Via Augusta straight back to Italy.'

He grinned like a soldier, relief under the surface. It took me a minute to realise that it must be because I looked pleased at the prospect.

'I don't seem to have lost the habit of travel, retired as I am. Of course, it's always easier without five thousand armed men along for the ride, not to mention a baggage train . . . '

In one of which I might have ridden as King Rodrigo's siege engineer, had my past decisions been different. *Would I ever have stood in my father's presence and known him?*

Honorius switched his gaze to Rekhmire'. 'If you're not here, leave word in that embassy of yours, and make sure they know who to pass it on to. I'll find you.'

Rekhmire' raised a hand, palm out, in a placating gesture. 'I swear, if I think there is the slightest danger, I will ask for asylum in the Alexandrine embassy.' He raised the drinking bowl of brandy in my direction. 'I may even take my slave with me . . . '

Honorius relaxed into a grin. I made a mental note to thank Rekhmire' for the diplomatic skills of a book-buyer.

'I *may* even go,' I observed. 'Assuming I'm not busy being Judas.'

'Judas – oh. A model.' Honorius rested his hip against the table and raised his brow at me, doubtless considering his son-daughter and heir ornamenting a chapel wall in fresco.

'I suppose if I'd had the raising of you,' he said wistfully, 'you'd do as you were told.'

He intercepted Rekhmire''s stare.

'Ah. Silly of me . . . '

Between them they raised my mood sufficiently that I could put Videric and Rosamunda to the back of my mind, treading firmly on any cold chill of fear that prodded my belly.

Honorius returned to the subject of Gaius Judas the following noon, when his men-at-arms – entirely unlike the layabouts he cheerfully called them to their faces – had four more *carrucas*-carts packed with their baggage, ready to leave Rome.

Rekhmire' made his own negotiations with a junior officer I recognised from his particularly wide-set eyes, and handed over a sealed scroll-case. Honorius drew me into the shadow of an awning on the far side of the street.

He rested his hand on my shoulder, the sun glinting off his articulated metal gauntlet. 'Convince this Bad Thomas he needs an apprentice, won't you? Think you'll do it before I get back?'

It's easy to take anything as rejection under such circumstances. Harshly attempting humour, I said, 'You mean you don't want me home for seven years?'

He cuffed my ear with the very tips of his fingers, so the gauntlet didn't catch me. 'Idiot! Nothing to say *I* can't stay in Rome a few years, is there? If – you'd want that?'

I nodded. After Rosamunda, Videric, Valdamerca, Rodrigo, silent assent was all I could manage.

'I want you with this Thomas Cassai, or some man as good.' Honorius absently rested his hand down on his sword-pommel as if it were part of him, his tone blunt. 'You need a trade. You tell me you don't want to be King Rodrigo's siege-engineer – I don't blame you. Battle's sickening enough. But I'd like to see you succeed at something. A man-woman needs a trade other than Court Freak, if they're to retain any self-respect.'

I blinked against the sunlight. Honesty, even without malice, is painful.

But not all pain is bad.

'That's what I *like* about you.' I smiled at my father. 'Your tact. December?'

Honorius hugged me as if I were a boy, and kissed me squarely on the brow as if I were a daughter.

'December!'

6

Mastro Masaccio burst out in a great guffaw.

I stepped away from his wooden painting-frame fast enough to lock one heel back against the other. I came to an abrupt halt.

Gasping, all but overbalancing, I shot a look from him to the drawing – *Is it damaged? I was only—*

'I didn't mean to touch it!' I protested. 'I was just brushing . . . away . . . brushing off . . . '

'Brushing off a fly.' His grin was wide and white, he having most of his teeth still. He walked briskly forward to stand beside me, gazing at the sketch of Judas, seated, in which the head and hands were now mostly complete.

Four fingers of space away from his rendition of my hair on my shoulder, the blow-fly sat motionless on the canvas.

I stared at it, more closely.

'It's . . . '

I looked back at him. Masaccio had the rough-skinned knuckles of his fist pushed into his mouth. He bit down, spluttered, dropped his hand away, and went off into peals of laughter.

' . . . *smudged*,' I said grimly.

While the Mastro finished his fit, I peered closely again. At such a small distance it was coal-dust and white pigment, and charcoal spotted in as the shadow the beast would cast.

And if I move here, then the shadow will be wrong . . .

But to a man standing before the easel, in the way that a man stands to view a picture, the illusion is absolute.

Wiping at his eyes, the Florentine said, 'The one great master, Giotto, played that trick eighty years ago. It still works. If a master plays it.'

Masaccio is an arse.

But – I understand his ambition. He's come to Rome to be the best. How can I *not* understand that?

More stiff and suspicious than I wished to sound, I said, 'It only works if you stand in the right place.'

'Ah.' His black eyes glinted. 'Ah, you see that, do you?'

I had no hope of him answering, but I scooped Judas's blood-red cloak up around me and asked, regardless. 'How do you *do* that?'

He glanced around the workshop – emptier at the moment than I'd seen it in two weeks, with his brother Giovanni gone back to Florence, and yet another assistant sacked – and stroked his hand over his tight curly beard.

'Go and sit for me again. I'm not done.'

'*I* am.' I bent down to catch my ankle as I lifted my foot, balancing like a heron, and stretched the muscles of my leg in tension against my arm. 'I have cramp, Mastro. You may as well tell me while I rest.'

'"Rest"? What are you doing but *sitting*?' He shook his head and snorted. 'And not half an hour by the clock at St Martin's, either. Every man and woman I ask to model is the same!'

I eyed him stubbornly.

He wants to tell me!

Fifteen days of being St Gaius *Tradditore* (as these Franks occasionally call their Judas), in twenty-odd positions. Masaccio's looking for a way to do this fresco in the style of the New Art, and he wants to tell another man who will understand him . . .

I attempted to look like just such a man.

Masaccio's finger stabbed out at the study on canvas. 'Tell me what's there.'

The air in the workshop was cool enough that sitting made my flesh freeze. I rubbed at my arms under the centurion's cloak while I moved around the sketch. The knowledge that I was being tested would have made me sweat on a less cold day.

When this is made into a fresco on a church wall, it will look more like a real man you'll see in the streets than any usual icon. *Why?*

'Here.' I pointed at the flurry of fine lines where he had drawn the figure of the Betrayer. 'It follows those, somehow . . . I don't know why.'

I got the confession out with difficulty, my fingertip close to the canvas, almost marking the canvas. There is nothing like those lines in nature: I wasn't sitting as Judas among converging wires in the air.

'But something about them,' I finished my thought, 'something means you can . . . distort things, so that they look more real. I don't understand! How can a distortion represent things more truly?'

Masaccio smiled, reaching past me; prodding with his fingertip at a central point that was perhaps one-third of the way up the canvas. 'Perspective.'

'It all . . . it . . . ' I drew with my finger in the air, inwards. 'All . . . points.'

'Comes down to that one point. And ends. That is the vanishing point. Simple one-point perspective, here. You may *know* what's beyond it – the other side of that box, or the far side of Judas's arm – but you can't *see* it. So I don't paint it.'

'And the distortion—'

'You see the world distorted.' He waved his hands. 'Every man does! Foreshortened, shrunk, extended, compressed. Every man sees the world from his own perspective. Two ends of a building measure the same, but the one that's far off, you see small. And I, I don't paint what you know must be there, I paint what you see!'

'What *you* see.' Meeting his angry gaze, I shrugged. 'Don't you choose the point I'm looking from?'

'As much as I can.' He nodded. 'I know where my paintings will be seen from. I know when the light will be best. If I put the point in the right place, every man will see the painting correctly.'

Experimentally, I took a pace to the side; then back. 'What happens if I don't stand here?'

'Then it's incorrect. I can do only what I can.' He scowled and nodded, as if, I thought, he would happily have nailed men's feet to the floor if it meant he could control their gaze. He reminded me in that moment of Aldra Videric.

'But I don't see how you . . . ' I leaned in. Where my sketched hands clasped together over the hilt of the Roman gladius, he had drawn only parts of my fingers and hands, and those parts curved and distorted.

This is a fingernail – although I can't see all of it. How is it that I know what it's *intended* to be?

'Go, walk!' Masaccio waved one hand extensively in circles above his head, which meant (judging by the last fortnight): walk around the workshop, don't knock over the bowls of ground bone-dust, or steeping parchment glue, or untreated canvas; don't step on the packing-crates, don't disturb the brushes in soak, do *not* spoil the expensive pigments.

He had taken my complaints of needing a break seriously since the third day, when cramp knocked me off the wooden box doing duty for the Tree, and spasmed me far enough along the floorboards to knock over his easel.

'Mastro—'

'Ach! Go, while I think!'

I caught the tip of my tongue between my teeth. The small pain reminded me: controlling my impatience got me here. Wait until he's willing to tell me more—

Cramp snagged a ball of muscle in my calf. 'Ah!'

I pressed the sole of my foot down against the floor, pushed at the knot of pain, and swore under my breath. Remembering to swear quietly, because swearing by the proper Christian saints will call attention in this heretic country—

Foreshortened, I thought, out of nowhere.

The nails on the hand are drawn foreshortened.

In the same way that if you look up at Rome's crumbling roofs, the wall and pillars of the building beside you are foreshortened. So, when a man looks at the hand from this one perspective, from the front, the nail appears distorted in that way.

And . . . *that's* what you do with feet. Not shown from above, so that you look down on the man's feet at the same time that you look face-on at his body. All parts, everything, shown from the artist's sole viewpoint. And so the feet are foreshortened, *also* seen from the front.

It's not merely perspective. Men often draw naturalistically – as the Egyptians do when they draw a torso seen full on, but a face in profile. It's perspective seen not from many places in the same painting, but consistently from one—

A glance across the benches showed me Masaccio bent over his steel engraving tools, talking under his breath.

Not a moment to interrupt. *But I can tell him I understand; I understand at least the beginning of his principles!*

I grinned wildly. I could have jumped and danced, if not for the cramp. Bending and rubbing at the muscle, I made my way to the back of the workshop, stamping on the wooden floorboards only when I was far enough off not to disturb the Florentine.

Digging my fingers into my locked flesh brought my head upside down, into odd positions. I gazed at objects – at boxes, at poles, at flat boards and canvases; at statues standing at the back of the workshop; at the slant of the half-open door to the courtyard.

Each one has its own distortion of its actual measurements and dimensions. Seen from each man's eyes.

Realisation filled up my vision. As if things rounded out before me, I saw how a man might draw lines converging to a single point, and place on them a simple regular object like a packing-case, or as complex an object as the statue of a man. They will appear larger or smaller, in themselves *or in their parts*, according to how close or distant they are!

I am no provincial amateur; I can *see*—

The cramp had been gone for some minutes by the time I stopped standing with my lowered head cocked sideways. I straightened up, feeling a heat in my cheeks not entirely due to bending over. If any man sees me, he'd think me mad!

Any man but one.

I turned, sweeping the rubbed velvet cloak around me, to look for Masaccio.

I had assumed that he would be anxiously waiting for me to get back into position. I was shocked to see him still bent close to the wooden frame, fractionally altering charcoal lines.

Perhaps he's nearly done with Judas?

Suppose this is the version he wants? Supposing it's right? Then he won't need me any more.

The chill of apprehension didn't paralyse me. Galvanised, instead, I moved forward to the middle of the workshop, waiting for Mastro Masaccio to notice me.

His head lifted.

I said, 'You have statues here.'

His oval lids blinked over his black eyes.

Masaccio remained blank-faced for all of a minute before his lines of concentration relaxed. His gaze swept the cluttered rear of the workshop, where indeed unpainted stone stood.

He gave me a very Florentine shrug.

'Oh, well, what will you? This is Rome; this is a new market for me. Some things I must do to bring immediate money in, for pigments and the rest—'

I knelt, with the Judas cloak sliding off my shoulders, and pulled at my leather travelling bag with half-numb fingers. I sprang up in time to interrupt him:

'*I* can paint them. Look. These are samples, that I did in Carthage. I could ... if I painted the statues, *you'd* have the time to do the real painting!'

I felt the weight lift as he took one of the miniature busts from my outspread hands. It was the head and shoulders of a man of Carthage, carved in the local fashion. I had shaded the folds at the neck of his gown, and put tints of light into his curled hair and beard.

'Adequate.'

Masaccio nodded, as if his praise were nothing remarkable.

'All right. I have other work to do. Yes. Start tomorrow.'

'I – *Mastro!*'

He interrupted. 'Don't spoil the stonework. I'll take the cost of the pigments you use out of your wages.'

He gave me a level look as I was about to open my mouth and protest *But you don't pay me!*

The money will go to Rekhmire'. At least in the first instance. As will any losses.

That was a less welcome thought, but it couldn't sadden me at the moment.

'I'll need wax. *Cera Punica.* I can bring my own tools!' Suppressing the urge to dance on the spot, I said, 'Which statue shall I start on?'

'Any.' He shrugged carelessly. 'They're all overdue. But don't hurry so much you spoil the work.'

I thanked him, stumbling over the words, growing redder and hotter at the ears, hearing myself sound like a fool.

Am I in fact *thanking* this man for a chance to do what I'm weary of – old-style painting of monuments, graveyard statues, garden ornaments?

Yes. I am. Because it means I can stay on here!

Masaccio turned to his easel again. My heart hammering in my chest, I walked around to the back of the workshop.

The statues stood unpainted, although some had been treated with an undercoat of plaster and egg-white. Many were copies of Classical works. Sculptors mostly do not have the skill, now, to make them as fluid and lifelike as a millennium and a half ago – men and women stood flat-footed, carved face-on, stiff in the shoulders. I walked between them, reaching out. The unforgiving hardness of marble bruised my fingertips, and I had no care for it.

Side-stepping round a badly proportioned gladiator, I turned my head and found myself looking into the face of the most beautiful woman in the world.

'Oh . . . '

Someone is doing for stone what Masaccio is doing for paint!

She stood out for her workmanship from among the crowd of statues – saints, hermits, cardinals, and the occasional bust of Gaius Julius Caesar, Hannibal Barca, or Platon. I doubted the statue's model could be more than fifteen or sixteen years old. The Carrara marble was of such high quality, and the workmanship so good, that it had caught the heaviness in her oval eyelids without drowning out the sparkle of liveliness in her eye.

I ran my finger over the cold smoothness where the corner of her sculpted mouth turned up delicately, and her lips were just parted.

'That's a bride-piece.' Masaccio's voice came from behind me. He ignored how I jumped. Something showed in his expression; I couldn't put a name to it.

I stuttered, 'Should I start here? With this one? Or—'

'Why not? Yes.' He gave a curt nod and turned away.

Have I displeased him?

The thought faded away. I ran a finger along the icy stone of her rounded shoulder. She had been carved naked, as was common in the Antique past. The statue already had draped over it a long, light pleated tunic, which it would wear when displayed in public. Flimsy white linen, caught in around the stone waist with a knotted cord . . .

The hem had caught under the cord at one side. The rucked-up material left unclothed the curve of her lower thigh, and the soft, baby-fat contours of her knee, and her lower leg.

I crouched down, to gaze up at her. As Masaccio was inadvertently teaching me: *look at what you are to paint from all angles.*

If wax and paint could only make stone live! *Look* at her . . .

She gazed over her turned-back shoulder, as if to speak to someone behind her. I got up and walked around to her right side, to look her full in the face. Her eyes were stone-blind, as the eyes of unpainted statues are.

But wax and colours will give her the most exact copy of a young girl's eye, focusing on the world. *If* I have sufficient skill.

I *must* work on her first!

A striped linen cloak or mantle had been draped from one of her hands, so that it fell to pool and gather around her feet.

I stepped back, getting all of her in view.

The mantle she held didn't drape both her feet. It fell to the floor beside one foot.

Something about the proportions made me frown.

I don't know what I'm seeing. Is she not complete?

I knelt down.

The carving of her foot was not unfinished.

Down to her ankle, she was a young woman. But, from her ankle down, the sculptor had given her skin the texture of hair.

Smooth, silky – the pelt of an animal.

Beneath her ankle, she had no human foot. She had the carved hock, the beast's foot, and the split hoof that belongs to a goat.

7

If Rome was shabby, the Vatican palace was shabbiest of all. I made a habit of meeting Rekhmire' outside it in the late afternoons, after siesta, when the light became too bad for painting or reading or copying, and there was no hope of a messenger or letter arriving from Taraco that day. Although I knew it soon yet, even if my father Honorius had changed his mind and gone all the way from Ostia Antica by ship, rather than joining the land road.

The Egyptian's eyes showed red-rimmed as he lifted his hand in greeting. His clothes stank of lamp-oil. 'Ilario. How does your colouring of the bride-piece statue go?'

He habitually copies from so many libraries that he must be as much a scholar as bookseller. Having worked up courage enough with that thought, I asked him the question I badly needed answered:

'Master Rekhmire' – am I painting a demon?'

'The statue itself?' His brows shot up. 'I'd imagined that a Phoenician superstition, not an Iberian one—'

'No, *not* the statue itself!'

With the goat-foot explained, his large, lined face relaxed into a smile.

'No demon. A god, perhaps.' Rekhmire' shrugged at my expression. 'The temples at home are filled with animal-headed gods. A foot would not be unusual. And one of the Attic gods has a goat-foot, no?'

'Pan.'

'But, Attic work here . . . '

Rekhmire' pointed up, with a finger that showed ground-in ink to the second knuckle. Stumps of sculpture stood along the roof of this great cathedral, next to the Vatican. Rome's Classical gods shared a minimal presence with the many saints of the Green Christ.

The Egyptian snorted. 'They're not a people who love their Classical heritage. I'm finding scrolls by Homer and Sappho stuffed in damp corners, sole surviving copies eaten by rot – but the hagiographies of their Frankish saints are preserved under crystal, and copied and *re-*copied. A god's hoof on a statue would be . . . odd.'

I frowned. 'Then . . . could it be symbolism?'

He arched his plucked brow at me.

'Symbolising something physically monstrous,' I continued the thought. 'A club-foot, perhaps.'

'Being lame is hardly monstrous!'

'Not to you. Or in Iberia. The Franks are different. And if this statue is to advertise a bride ... They wouldn't copy a physical deformity in stone. They might symbolise that something *is* there. As a warning.'

'A warning.' Rekhmire''s expression held distaste.

'Just as well they're not making one for me.' I didn't add: *Or you.*

He smiled sardonically. '*Does* the work go well?'

I thought for a moment, and nodded.

'Good.'

Rekhmire' didn't say more, perhaps for fear of unnerving me, but I knew what was in his mind. Masaccio won't want anything coming out of his workshop to be done badly. His name will be on it. So he must trust me to do this. And – I must do it well. Do it better than I've done any work before now.

'This isn't difficult.' I could feel her icy marble texture in my fingers. 'She's the most beautiful thing I've ever seen. I swear she tells me herself how she ought to be painted.'

'Despite the club-foot?'

'Despite the club-foot.'

Rekhmire' smiled. 'I should be careful if I were you, Ilario. None of the Classical stories of men in love with images end well.'

I blushed red.

He laughed out loud. 'My slave *is* infatuated!'

'My master can go fornicate with a three-legged donkey!'

Men of the Egyptian's mass and bulk shouldn't snicker; it leads to a perceptible loss of dignity on their part. Even if they do appear unmoved by that.

The following day I had a loss of nerve and ground up no pigments, merely taking up some of my old lime-wood boards and using the backs for drawing exercises – something I could be sure Masaccio would never reprove me for.

The Florentine merely grunted when he saw me. 'When you've finished there, you may as well do something useful.'

Matching size and angle and inclination of line can only be done for so long before the eye tires. At last I set down the boards and charcoal, and wandered over to Masaccio's other bench.

'You can do the cheese glue for the panel work,' he observed. 'You mix the cheese with powdered lime ... '

He pushed a plate of decidedly rotten Roman pale cheese across the workbench.

'It works better if you crumble it with your fingers.'

'Cheese glue.'

I looked at him.

'If I were a younger apprentice—' I stifled choking and the urge to gag, as I fully smelled the cheese. '—I *might* be taken in by that one!'

I'd had enough in the scriptorium at Taraco, as the youngest apprentice, being sent down to the vellum store for a long stand and other traditional red herrings.

Masaccio hefted a piece of painted board up from where it was propped against the side of the bench. Covered in plaster dust, it had obviously been removed from some altar wall.

'Got this out of a chapel at Pavia . . . '

It was an ordinary altar painting of St Lawrence roasting on his griddle, done in the ancient style. There being few pieces of suitable flat wood large enough for such an altar panel, it was made of six separate boards glued together, and then covered over with linen as a ground for the pigment.

Masaccio rested the edge of the board on the lip of the workbench, holding it there as he stroked his beard with his free hand. 'Been up in the chapel three centuries, according to the monastery records – but who trusts them? A long time, certainly . . . '

He picked up a mallet, hefted it, and abruptly lifted his arm and smashed it down with all his strength.

The mallet-head sounded loud as a gun exploding. It landed squarely on a visible ridge in the painting that marked a join in the planks. I winced and stepped back from an anticipated fragmentation of splinters.

The wooden panel didn't break.

Masaccio stared down at it, rubbing his thumb over the small dent in the shiny surface. He scratched at it with his nail.

'Cheese glue,' he remarked. 'Once it's well set.'

Wordlessly, I reached for the plate and began crumbling the sticky wet cheese into the lime-dust, taking great care to get neither close to my eyes, and leaning back as the mess began to bubble and minutely sputter.

At the short afternoon's end, Masaccio invited me down to the taverna at the end of the street.

I accepted with no hesitation.

Technically, Master Tommaso Cassai's people are at war with mine. The Crusades still grind on, somewhere in the north of Iberia, on the Navarra-Castile border where Honorius fought: he had told me stories. But it still seems more than a world away, here in Masaccio's Roman workshop – which, Masaccio let slip, had taken only a bare month to become as cluttered as it was; he having come down from Florence just at the beginning of the autumn.

I finishing tidying and sweeping up and found him waiting impatiently at the door. But for all that, he was the first to open his purse at the tavern.

'You've got bad news for me.' I looked up from the bench where I sat, and then back at the leather jack of ale. 'You must have!'

His black eyes glinted. He drank, wiped his mouth on his sleeve, and lowered his voice below the chatter from the packed tavern-room.

'On the contrary, Spaniard. I'm impressed with your work on stone.'

He didn't pause long enough to let me take that in.

Shooting a sharp glance my way, he said, 'That's why I'm going to include you on the work I'm doing now – it's suddenly become a rush job, and I need another set of hands. Think you can work at the Egyptian embassy?'

If I'd drunk any ale, I'd have choked.

The ridiculous thought came instantly into my mind: *Rekhmire' has arranged this!*

I couldn't help asking. 'It's nothing to do with my master, is it?'

Masaccio looked bewildered.

'Your . . . ' His expression cleared. 'Oh, the Egyptian castrato-bureaucrat. No; this is a contract from before I met your master. They have a statue they need painted before it's shipped out; suddenly it must be shipped in three weeks' time . . . ' He shrugged. 'That's patrons for you.'

I looked down. Drawn in ale, the wet lines of a man's face glistened on the grain of the wood – one of the soldiers sitting by the hearth in ragged jack and hose, half his jaw gone to a combat wound. I rubbed my hand across the absent work of my fingers. 'Mastro, my drawing exercises. Are they well, in your estimation?'

'You're progressing.'

'I . . . ' A refusal wouldn't come out: my throat constricted too tightly. I breathed deep. 'I think I'm just *beginning* to learn perspective. Mastro, if you want me to do another statue—'

I couldn't hold it back.

'I don't want to be left doing nothing but stone-work! I want to learn more of the *real* art!'

In the dark curls of his beard, the white glint of a smile showed. 'This statue's different, Spaniard. You'll see.'

I took up the jack, drained it, and got to my feet, gazing down at Masaccio.

He gave a brief nod and led me out into the dark afternoon.

The streets of Rome aren't lit as Carthage's are; they don't have the use of naphtha. Nothing is so black as city streets between monumental buildings. I stumbled in Masaccio's wake, treading wetly in dung and less reputable rubbish. He walked as if it were clear daylight. But that was merely an excess of self-confidence.

Past one more bend in the Tiber, an island lay in the middle of the river. Mastro Masaccio spoke to the guards on the bridge, who let us across, and he strode on without looking back at me, up the steps of a Doric-pillared Roman mansion, and knocked without hesitation.

The hen-tracks and pictograms inscribed on one side of the door read (if I had it correctly from Rekhmire''s teaching), *Embassy of Alexandria-*

in-exile. And on the other side, in Latin letters, the city's name from before the conquest: *Embassy of Constantinople.*

I wondered if I might see Rekhmire' at this outpost of Egypt-in-Europe. *I must tell him I've been here.*

Light blazed unexpectedly into my eyes as the doors opened. Inside, the mansion was full of brilliance. Masaccio talked, laughing, to ruddy-skinned men in linen kilts. I rubbed at my streaming eyes as we went inside.

Lamps and candle-stands stood every few feet along the corridor, and, in the room they took us to, stood side-by-side. The heat and sweet scent of beeswax stunned me into a faintly nauseous state.

'It's not natural light,' I protested, when Masaccio came back from ushering our guides out through the square-pilastered doorway. 'The colours won't be right!'

'Apparently, this is the light they're to be seen by in Constantinople.' He shrugged, walking towards a sheet-covered monolith standing among pots, brushes, and pallets. I was pleased to see a brazier-box and slabs of Punic wax. The sheet would no doubt come off to show the statue in question.

Masaccio grinned lopsidedly. 'Behold!'

The white cloth fell away. I found myself gazing up at a statue of a man seven or eight feet high, made of fine white marble – and of brass.

'I've—' *seen one of these before,* I stopped myself saying.

In Carthage.

Rekhmire' is prone to lecture me about tact. It was hardly tact that allowed Mastro Masaccio to present me with his 'surprise'; I stood stunned by more than the statue's presence. Remembering Hanno Anagastes' house, and a glimpse of a similar metal-jointed statue that stood head-and-shoulders taller than an average man. Although Hanno's had been of yellow sandstone, not marble; and unpainted, rather than decorated as this one would be.

If there are any men from Carthage here – if they know of Rekhmire' – of me—

Desperately desiring to speak to Rekhmire', I examined the stonework, stumbling to make suitable exclamations. The statue towered taller than me by four-and-twenty inches; stood carved naked, and with its arms posed hanging at its sides.

Masaccio pointed at the legs and lower torso. 'Much of the flesh, I've done.'

Ruddy Egyptian flesh colours made it seem as if the lower part of a man indeed stood there, rounded out into life from the white stone.

'It will take many hours of skilful work to complete it well.' He gave me an uncompromising look. 'And I will have it done well.'

The arms and head and upper chest remained not coloured as yet, and I found myself sizing up the job as he talked, and nodding agreement.

The sculptor had carved every muscle, tendon-cord, and bone under the surface of the stone skin, and the brass-smith had chiselled the arm- and shoulder- and knee-joints with the same skill.

Masaccio broke what I realised had become a silence. He stroked his hand over his mouth, barely hiding a grin. 'They shipped it here to be painted by the world's best painter.'

Is that – can this be coincidence?

'Is it going back to Carthage, after?'

He shot me a look that suggested I ought not to hazard guesses about the origins of such statues.

'No. It's going on to Constantinople. A gift for the Pharaoh-Queen, Ty-ameny. With the name of my workshop on it, *and* the master's brush. So if you mess it up, Spaniard, I'll have your bollocks!'

I stifled a grin at what I knew in that last respect and he didn't.

And . . . If Carthage *knew* I'd come here, I would have walked into this embassy at Masaccio's heels and found Carthaginians ready to arrest me.

Not everything in the world concerning Carthage can revolve around Taraco. Or even me. They must have their business with powerful kingdoms such as New Alexandria . . .

Exhilarated, I squatted down by the boxes where my brushes and other tools were set out. *Calami* rush-stalks; the *rhabdion* that is spatulate at one end and round at the other; large and small brushes; different heating-irons. I reached forward to rake up the brazier that was heating coals for the pallet box.

Squinting up, I saw how foreshortened my view of the statue in fact was; the thighs and hands enormous, the neck and chin tiny . . .

The Florentine painter said, 'And you must make certain to do the details under the arms perfectly.'

Mastro Masaccio smiled when I looked at him.

'What for?'

'Because it'll show!' His tone implied *Obviously, you idiot!*

I stood up and touched the immense, chill marble. I couldn't push my fingertips between the statue's torso and the inside of its arm.

'I don't think—'

'You can't reach there?' Masaccio gave a short nod, and then lifted his chin, looking up into the carved marble face of the statue. '*Golem, lift up your arm.*'

The stone statue's arm noiselessly swivelled at the shoulder-joint and elbow-joint, and lifted up and forward from its body.

8

Masaccio's laughter peeled out loud enough that half the embassy bureaucrats came to peek round the door, before he ushered them away.

Obstruction blotting out the candle-light – a soundless, heavy motion passing my face—

I stood up from where I had ended, crouched against the room's far wall.

I dimly remembered muscles that flexed and sprang by instinct, putting me with my back to the masonry; and instinct and training also had a reed-cutting knife clenched in my hand.

Little enough good *that* would have done me.

I gazed up at the more than life-size statue, breathing heavily. 'So! It's a joke. I don't see ropes, or pulleys – is there a man inside?'

It looked solid marble, but it might be no thicker than a running-bird's eggshell; I have seen men who can carve stone or ivory to such thin perfection.

Masaccio rapped his knuckles against the polished smoothness of the statue's biceps. 'No one inside. You *are* a barbarian, boy! Have you never heard of Hero of Alexandria, who made a walking statue of a man? Now, evidently, someone has re-discovered that Classical science—'

'A *walking* statue?' Every muscle, as I relaxed it, shivered with cramp. I flexed my fingers. 'A walking *statue?*'

'—And re-discovered it in Carthage, by my best guess.' Masaccio frowned, concentrating, clearly not realising I'd interrupted. 'Although these Alexandrines are none too keen to talk about who shipped it from there; it might have been made elsewhere . . . What? Do you call me a liar? Look at it!'

I had not the slightest desire to approach the now-motionless carved shape of a man.

Except that I'll still be expected to lay colour onto the surface of that marble.

There being tools about the place, I picked up a mallet of soft wood as I approached, and – poised to spring away in an instant – rapped it against the statue's pectoral muscles.

The *thunk* of solid marble echoed through the low-roofed room.

The statue did not move.

Masaccio spoke loudly but calmly, as if to a deaf but only slightly dangerous animal. '*Golem, pour a drink of wine into the cup for me.*'

Its joints moved.

Soundlessly, it lifted a knee, flexed at ankle and toe – with a flash of light from the yellow brass gears – and it was walking.

A soft grating of stone against tile became the only noise in the room while a man might count a hundred.

The golem-statue stalked to the niche where the wine jug stood, lifted it, and poured liquid from the jug into an alabaster cup.

Surely the strength of that hand will crush—

The statue swivelled about, stopped; then moved with the same unchanging pace to Mastro Masaccio, and halted with an arm stretched out.

He took the cup.

I saw Masaccio's fingers were not steady.

The carved features of the statue's over-large face did not move: neither stone brows, nor mouth, nor eyes.

'How does it see?' I breathed. And flushed, not thinking to have spoken aloud.

'How indeed? There is some secret science of the ancient peoples, here.' Masaccio suddenly dipped his head, and threw back all the wine at a gulp. He stared up into the stone man's face. 'Which you cannot tell us, friend, can you? It can't speak,' he added to me.

The Egyptians had gone some way to decorating this Roman mansion in their own style. The house of the Lord-Amir of Carthage Hanno Anagastes was not too unlike this one: striped stone at the door arches, and red-and-yellow friezes along the walls. I thanked Christ the Emperor for that slight familiarity, disoriented as I felt.

There again, if I'd been longer in the house of Hanno Anagastes – would I have seen *his* statue move?

'Am I expected to touch that?' My voice sounded high, womanish. I made an effort to force it low. 'Paint it?'

Masaccio's glance was impatient. 'Unless you wish me to hire another assistant?'

'No!'

What else can I say? No matter if it belongs to Carthage, and I should stay away from anything belonging to the King-Caliph's people – I can't miss this!

Masaccio said, 'It obeys a man's commands, if told to by the Alexandrines here. That means my voice will be heeded, but yours not. If you need to paint where you cannot reach, you must ask me.'

'And I should say nothing of this, outside the workshop?' I pre-empted his speech.

His brilliant dark eyes summed me up. 'You'll take the formal oath as my apprentice.'

All I could do was stare.

'Your master'll permit it,' Masaccio added. 'He was anxious enough to get you apprenticed. Are you Frankish Christian?'

This not being a time to lie, I admitted, 'I was brought up in the faith of Christ Emperor.'

He dismissed a thousand years of religious schism and warfare with a wave of his hand. 'Same thing.'

I put the flat of my hand up against his palm as he raised it, feeling the heat of his paint-marked skin.

'Swear by Jesus Christ and the Holy Mother to give me your fidelity as my apprentice.'

'I swear by Christus Imperator and the Wise Holy Mother to be your true apprentice.'

'Good. I'll have you on the executioner's block if you fail me.' Masaccio nodded. 'Are you ready to begin?'

The reality of judicial punishment made me startle; only then did I think, *But I haven't asked Honorius.* Not for the first time, I wished him present to advise me. And Rekhmire'. Cold with apprehension, I thought, Should I have taken this step without consulting them?

Masaccio brought me to see this: he had no intention of letting me escape without an oath.

My gaze fell from the statue's face – but to look at its shoulders was no more reassuring. Reckoning by eye, now, I made it seven feet and two hands high. Carved proportionate to a man, it was almost a giant.

'Three weeks,' I said.

'I likely could finish it myself.' Masaccio's brows dipped in concentration. 'But I want no part of it hurried. And they're not paying me enough to have all of it *pel suo pennello*: from the master's brush alone. You'll still sit for me as Judas in the meanwhile. Cardinal Valente won't wait while I finish this.'

That momentarily took my attention from the golem-statue. In most Frankish church icons they represent Judas as he was in his Hebrew robes, before he joined the army and gained Roman citizenship. Robes would have suited me. But this Cardinal had chosen a depiction much closer to our own: Judas, under his Roman legionary name of Gaius, debating with the priests of Mithras. And wearing his military cloak, *lorica segmentata*, and a centurion's 'skirt' of leather straps.

Modelling that made me uneasy. Even changing to baggier hose in defiance of fashion hadn't rid me of a feeling that my hips and belly *must* show broad as a woman's. And there are no women in Masaccio's workshop.

I shifted, casually now, to a stance that I thought more concealed my feminine arse.

Masaccio lifted his chin confrontationally. 'You won't mind working night and day, will you?'

I couldn't help but smile through my fright. Monstrous the golem might be, but such a challenge to an artist's skill—! 'Where do you want me to start?'

He had me begin with fingernails, oddly enough. No foreshortening. Merely the laying of ground-work colour, where he had prepared the surface: then shading and wash, onto a solid surface; highlights to be brushed on when dry.

I pushed dry-mouthed apprehensiveness away. *The statue doesn't move, save at command.*

After a day or two of touching it without harm, fear gave way to sheer exhilaration. Fascination – how can such things be?

I found myself working at all hours of the night. Since the golem-statue could be painted during the evenings, the shortening daylight hours of autumn could be spent on other remunerative work. Judas. And the statue of the goat-foot girl.

Masaccio had not yet approached Rekhmire' to countersign the apprentice's contract – I would have had the Egyptian shouting at me if he had. I desired urgently to talk to Rekhmire' about the stone golem, but I thought that he would also regard my verbal oath as binding. Which meant I could not.

I bit my tongue, and concluded at the end of two days that Rekhmire' – in and out of the embassy as he eternally was! – must by now have found out all there was to know about the stone golem. He said nothing. *But that need only mean he respects my oath.*

Carthage had passed the golem straight to the Alexandrine embassy, it appeared, with orders to get it painted and sent on to Constantinople. I had merely to be careful of meeting stray Carthaginians before the statue was shipped out. I thought one or two times that I might have been followed in the street, but nothing came of it – and hermaphrodites are sometimes followed for reasons unconnected with politics, even when disguised as men.

Or, I thought, it might be Rekhmire' keeping a watchful eye open.

My opportunity to speak came when we were both all but asleep in the pungent Roman night, and Rekhmire' got up to open a shutter, and stare for some minutes at the waxing moon.

'In Lord Hanno Anagastes' house,' I got up on one elbow, 'I saw a statue – a man, done larger than life-size. I meant to ask you. There were rumours among the other slaves, that it moved. Walked. Like a man, I mean.'

The moonlight showed me Rekhmire''s expression: the lift of his brows, and faint amusement.

'That's the Lord-Amirs of Carthage for you. The Royal Library has had Lords arrive in person, to study the scrolls of Hero of ancient Alexandria-that-was. If they could match his engineering feats, the

Franks and the Turks would indeed have cause to fear Carthage's armies . . . '

'You think Lord Hanno's statue moves?'

'Single wonders of such a nature are . . . not unknown.' His face fell half into shadow. 'Although "not unknown" does not mean "not dangerous".'

I kept my satisfaction concealed. *I have managed to say nothing that breaks my promise of secrecy.*

'And on the subject of the Turks . . . ' Rekhmire' turned back to gazing out of the window, changing the subject more clumsily than he customarily did. 'I have found a document in the Vatican library that I think has been lost – mis-filed – these two hundred years.'

Monochrome light reflected from the dome of his shaven head; the planes of his cheeks. I reached for the board beside my pallet and, for all my sleepiness, began to sketch him in that profile. 'Document?'

'A Turkish traveller's account. I presume, ignored because written by a foreigner. But, depending on whether it is a forgery or not . . . it is an eye-witness testimony of the Prophet Gundobad's death.' Rekhmire''s brows came down. 'And it contains the actual words of the curse that Gundobad spoke. Those were unknown until now. Whether the cardinals might at last begin to break the curse on the Papal Chair, if they knew . . . '

'*Is* it genuine?'

His massive shoulders shrugged. 'I am attempting to find other supporting evidence. So far, there's none. Then again, the Vatican has a library half the size of ours, and with no competent custodians whatsoever. It is a task of years!'

I lay back down. Rekhmire' continued to gaze from the unshuttered window, frustration plain on his large face.

After I had slumped asleep as Judas a time or two, Mastro Masaccio took to letting me doze on a couch at the back of the workshop. My eyes shut, often, gazing up at the face of the marble girl. I had the preparation of her body done, ready to paint, colour, shade and highlight. But for that rest—

'I need to ask you a favour,' I said that dawn, as Masaccio and I returned from the embassy; he holding up a flaring pitch torch to scare off street toughs. The shadows in the hollows of his cheeks and eye-sockets danced with the torch and wind.

'And that is?'

'I've prepared all the stonework for pigment, and sewn the bride-piece's clothing . . . ' I had, to his sardonic amusement, also brought in a goat from a woman living in the next street, so that I could adequately paint the symbolic foot from life. ' . . . But I can't go on with the painting yet.'

His chin came up combatively. 'Why? Aren't I paying your master enough?'

'I need to see her face.'

'*I* need you not to waste time on that piece of . . . '

When he said nothing more, I added cautiously, 'If it's a bride-piece, does it not need to look like *her*? So far, according to instruction, I know her fair-skinned and fair-haired—'

'Yellow.'

I stared as he unlocked the heavy wooden gates of the workshop. '"Yellow"?'

'Her hair is yellow as a marsh buttercup.'

His back spoke a volume or two as he stalked in ahead of me, but I hadn't the language to read it.

Direct, I demanded, 'Who *is* she?'

'A whore.'

That startled me. The sun was not yet risen: I'd picked up and lit a candle-stump, preparatory to lighting the shop's oil-lamps; I all but burned my hand as he spoke. 'A *whore*?'

Masaccio's expression was hidden by darkness. He spoke quietly.

'A woman who *said* she loved me – she got me the commission on the strength of it. After the bride-piece statue was painted, I was to go to her father and . . . But before it was even carved, she told me she'd changed her mind. No marriage for Tommaso Cassai. A painter wasn't rich enough for her. The whore! For *her*. And *her* family!'

If we had been outside in the street, he would have spat.

'Perhaps her family stopped her,' I said. 'Women have little enough choice, commonly.'

Masaccio's laugh, in the closed-up workshop, was harsh and ugly. 'Defending her, boy? You don't know her! Why – you're in love with her yourself!'

'No—'

'You're red, boy!'

'I'm not!'

'Just from her image!' He laughed the more at my denial. I stifled protest.

'Well.' He shrugged. 'All I want is the money for a job done. If you need to see the bitch's face for that, well, see her. It's nothing to me.'

From his tone, money was far from all that concerned him. And evidently he could see that thought in my face, bad light notwithstanding.

'Here!' He scrawled quickly in charcoal, on a splinter of lath. 'Here's the address; I've drawn you where she lives. But mind, I can't spare you more than an hour from Judas – and the Egyptian embassy.'

9

I ran all the way.

The Paziathe mansion stood solid, dark, and grim, for all the gilding the morning sun attempted to lay on its masonry. It looked startlingly well-built for such a shabby district. Iron bars were set into the stone, covering the lower and upper windows.

What have they to lock up? They don't look rich.

I smiled wryly at that. They're well enough off to hire a sculptor and a painter to advertise their daughter for sale.

Who'd be a woman, in the Empty Chair? Thank God – Rekhmire''s eight of Them! – that I can pass as a man.

A sleepless night had left me gritty-eyed. The sprint across Rome, past the Forum and the amazingly narrow Via Sacra, to this outlying district, woke me fully. The mansion stood near a park, if the oak trees ahead of me were any guide. Clean, chill air hissed in my lungs. I felt the palms of my hands hot and wet.

I am Mastro Tommaso Cassai's apprentice, I rehearsed in my head. Come to make colour sketches for your daughter's statue.

'Old Aranthur's more likely to let *you* in than me,' Masaccio had called after me as daylight cleared his head, temper making him scowl.

Rekhmire', when I diverted my way past our lodgings, was out; gone already to the Vatican library. It would have eased my mind to talk to him, although I could not say why.

An elderly servant came out of a side door of the mansion, pulling a cloak around his shoulders.

I let him walk off before I went to the same door and rapped, using their bronze door-hammer cast in the shape of a Sacred Boar.

The iron-studded door was made from thick enough wood that I heard no footsteps approaching. It swung suddenly open, startling me.

'What did you forget?' In the doorway, a girl put her hand up to her face, shading her eyes from the sun; hiding her features from me. '*Oh!* I'm sorry! I thought you were Father, come back! I shouldn't have answered the door!'

Her voice sounded musical, textured, distressed.

I do not need to see her face.

I watched the curve of those fingers into her palm as she shaded her eyes. I have seen them beside me for days on end. And the fold of her elbow, the curl of her hair.

Masaccio had given me her name, unwillingly enough. My voice half-broke in a boyish squeak. 'Madonna Sulva Paziathe?'

She took a step back. The movement had all grace in it. Both her bodice and her skirts were dark enough brocade to look black in the house's shadow. A hood or veil covered all but the edges of her braided bright hair.

She glanced around, as if looking for her servants.

'Don't be afraid!' I stuttered it out. She might as well have said it to me.

'I'm not supposed to—'

'I'm a painter; I come from Masaccio – I mean, Master Tommaso—'

She lowered her hand and glared at me. 'Tommaso Cassai?'

Now I could see inside the taffeta-cloth veil that framed her face. Her hair had been pinned up beside her temples in a myriad small braids. Enough of it was left unbound to flow over her shoulders. An unmarried woman's style, I guessed, even among the Franks.

And it is not the colour of buttercups, but the exact colour of the outer part of a candle's flame.

Her face. I'd need to use every skill I possessed to make that cream-pale face glow, as it did in the eastern sun. Shadow the faintest violet under her eyes; touch the crisp line of her lip with pink—

'Tell Messer Cassai to leave me alone!'

'He will! It's ... I'm painting your statue. I needed to ... ' A thunderstroke would have left me more articulate. 'To see you.'

Another woman might have blushed, pretending modesty. I was myself trained to behave that way, from time to time, at the court of King Rodrigo. She only opened her lips in a soundless *oh* of realisation.

'I'm Ilario,' I added, and hesitated too long over giving a family name for it to be natural. 'You don't have to be afraid. Mastro Cassai doesn't intend to come here. And I only need to make sketches.' I burbled. 'Match colours.'

She glanced back over her shoulder into the depths of the mansion. 'Father won't allow me to ask a stranger into the house.'

I was about to swear I would come back – any day; every day; whenever it would be convenient to see her – when she reached back into the darkness, and brought out a silk-fringed mantle to put around her narrow shoulders.

'We'll go into the garden.' A tiny curve of mischief lifted her lip, just as the sculptor had caught it. 'My maid can chaperone us. Hathli! *Hathli!*'

A dark-featured round woman with an incipient goitre came to the door with remarkable speed. She said nothing, only nodding at her mistress's commands, but her lips folded together, and I had no doubt what she was thinking.

'Madonna Sulva.' I followed them inside. 'I know Frankish women are more free in their behaviour than my people, but—'

'You're not Frankish?' Her eyes widened. 'That's exciting. I never travel. Tell me! Tell me what it's like where you're from.'

I told her of King Rodrigo's court as the maid accompanied us through corridors – to which my eyes were night-blind – and out into a central courtyard. Frail sun gleamed. Bay and basil grew in pots. A walled pool held the glint and flicker of carp. The girl gazed up at me from under her hood.

I let the leather sack of my tools fall at my feet, on the flagstones. *How can I ever reproduce you in pigments!*

'Messer . . . Ilario?'

'Ilario Honorius,' I finally managed. I will not use *Valdevieso*.

Sulva Paziathe had that heavy curve of flesh under her lower eyelids that was the plumpness of girlhood vanishing. It ought to have been ugly. All of her face *should* be ugly: her brows are too heavy, her lids too wide and oval; the philtrum under her nose too long, so that she doesn't show her teeth when she smiles.

But all these things together in her are . . . beautiful. She's rich as cream.

'This way,' Sulva Paziathe said. 'Here.'

She walked on, out across the courtyard. The woman Hathli hooked her arm under Sulva's, as if it were a thing of common use and no moment.

The girl is limping. Lame.

Sulva Paziathe pointed to the stone surround of the pond, and a marble bench beside it. 'We'll sit down. Hathli, you can walk over *that* way for a while.'

They exchanged a look. I guessed at history between them. There would be other servants about here, I could surmise that much. Men-servants. Men-at-arms, if the house still hid wealth under its shabbiness.

The older woman shrugged her own mantle about her swollen neck, toga-like. Her skirts swept ochre and umber leaves as she crossed the courtyard to be out of ear-shot.

'Now.' Sulva's eyes as she looked up had a mischievous gleam that it would defeat me to put into marble. 'You can tell me the things I shouldn't hear! What's it like, to travel from Iberia? And from – Carthage, was it? North Africa?'

She named it as if she named the Moon.

Numbed, I did as court usage had taught me; held out my hand to the young woman, so that she could steady herself as she sat down on the stone bench. Her flesh felt warm enough to be almost hot. At the touch of smooth skin, I felt as if that heat went through me in needles – and, simultaneously, as if I couldn't bear *not* to have the contact of her hand.

Marcomir had been planes and angles and male sweat: this girl was tactile beauty.

She stumbled, sat awkwardly down, and lifted up her head to gaze at me; her fingers still resting on mine. The brocade of her dress was woven with bronze thread, and oyster-shell black, and deep blue. Her skirts were rucked up where she had sat clumsily.

I couldn't help but look. And blushed bright red. *She'll think I'm looking to see her lame foot. She'll be embarrassed by her deformity—*

On her right foot, her silk slipper was strapped into a wooden patten, three or four inches high, to keep her out of mud or damp.

Her left foot had neither slipper nor patten; they could not have fitted. Only a sock-like silk cloth wrapped round it.

The fabric could not conceal the underlying shape from me; not now that I'm used to drawing the skin, muscle, tendon and bone that lies under men's clothes. Her foot was a twisted ball of clubbed flesh. It had folded back on itself, into a stump. I guessed she had either no toes at all, or else only vestigial ones. Her ankle was knobbled, under the concealing silk.

I looked up, meeting her gaze.

With a heartbreaking gentleness, she said, 'I'm . . . not allowed to go out into the city. People would . . . Tell me what it's like, far away?'

For all her brave words, she stared at me, terrified; as if my silence judged her. And as if one word of judgement could shatter her.

How alone, how isolated, she must feel, to invite a stranger in. To risk scandal, insult, mirth, disrespect.

Regardless of the wet leaves on the flagstones, I went down on one knee beside her, gripping her chilled hand tightly.

'Sulva . . . ' I watched her expression. 'Let me tell you how it's been for you. There is no more than one of you in the world. You are unique. Men think you something monstrous, but you're not; you're a soul like any other. All your life, you've been alone, finding no other like you. No one has ever spoken to you normally, as men speak to one another.' I took a breath. 'You are— As you *are*, you're more beautiful than anything I've ever seen. But they keep you here. Hide you away, for fear.'

Sulva put her free hand up to her face, gazing at me over the tips of her fingers. I saw her biting at her full lower lip as she hid it.

I said, 'Your father thought it right to commission a bride-piece. If you will have me, I'll speak to your father. If you will have me, I'll marry you.'

10

On my way back to Masaccio's workshop I stepped aside to our lodgings, hoping to bring the news to my Egyptian master.

'*You've done what?*'

Looking up at Rekhmire''s aghast face, I spoke doggedly.

'I've told Madonna Sulva Paziathe that I'll marry her. And she's agreed.'

He opened and shut his mouth soundlessly. Under other circumstances – when it didn't incise a sudden line of fire through my belly – I would have found it comic.

Rekhmire' caught his breath. 'And did you tell her that you're *not a man*!'

Now is not the moment to explain why Sulva Paziathe so desperately needs to be rescued.

I slammed the lodging-house door behind me as I left.

The door to Masaccio's workshop opened a quarter-hour after I'd got back, and let Rekhmire' in.

Masaccio didn't look up, being fixated by how the light fell on Judas's hands, where the Betrayer held the Spanish sword that drew no blood.

Rekhmire''s voice echoed up to the rafters. '*And* have you told her family that you're a *slave?*'

Masaccio looked up, startled. He grinned in the anticipation of scandal.

'I need a rest-break!' Hurriedly, I dropped the prop-sword, draped the velvet cloak in folds over the box, and strode across the room to herd the Egyptian back out.

I closed the workshop door on the painter's outraged complaints.

'Have you?' Rekhmire' demanded, voice echoing across the cobbled street.

'No!'

I was breathless with striding after him through Roman alleys.

Twenty feet below, the Tiber sluggishly flowed. I stared down off the bridge. Hadrian's fortress-crowned burial mound reflected here and there in the water, wherever the currents beneath let it appear still enough on the surface.

'As your owner—' Rekhmire' came to a sudden halt. '—I can easily refuse permission for you to get married!'

'*I* was hoping you'd come to the wedding.'

Rekhmire''s fist thumped down on the sandstone coping of the bridge parapet. '*Are you mad?*'

Now is not the time to tell him that I'll tell her, when the time's right.

Leaning on the coping-stones with my chest heaving, I managed an equable reply. 'Her father finds my proposal acceptable.'

Silence.

'It seems he thinks a fine upstanding young painter – *apprentice* to a painter – is completely suitable for his daughter.'

I shrugged.

'Of course, if she wasn't deformed, he wouldn't accept it. He's probably been wondering since she was born how the Hell he's going to get her married off.'

Aranthur Paziathe's face came back to me. My fingers ached to sketch the deep lines at the corners of his mouth, and those etched across his forehead. Small, dark, contained: I had no idea how such a fair acorn could drop from that oak.

'Her father may wonder, too,' I said aloud. And, at Rekhmire''s bemused look, explained, 'Whether her mother played him false . . . '

'Ilario—'

'I can let her stay locked up in that, that *prison*, crippled, until she grows old. Or I can get her out of there.' I watched emotion shift in Rekhmire''s dark eyes. 'And you know what? The club-foot isn't ugly. It's the thing that makes her beautiful.'

'You *are* mad.' He muttered something under his breath: a string of Alexandrine god-names. He began to pace, on the dusty surface of the bridge, turning with a sharp twist every three or four steps.

He stopped, facing me. 'You haven't thought about this.'

'Yes. This time I have.'

'If nothing else, *your* father's permission—'

'No need; I've long been of age. And Honorius isn't here. Besides . . . ' I remembered Honorius's creased face, seeing me for the first time. The joy in his eyes uncontaminated by disgust. 'I think he'd approve.'

'And back at the court of Taraco—!' He gestured with his large hands, as if he presented every incident between Carthage and Taraconensis, and my part in it, for my inspection. 'A wife is a hostage to fortune!'

'So are you! So is Honorius! So is any friend I might make, or my Mastro!'

I know well enough that, once out of Rome, my company might be dangerous.

'You're—' Rekhmire' cut off whatever he had been about to say. 'And

126

her father, he'll be happy to have you marry her by the Arian Christian rite, will he?'

That made me frown. 'I don't suppose they *are* worshippers of Christ-the-Emperor, here. No . . . That doesn't matter. I can marry her by the Frankish rite.'

'Amun and Amunet! *How can you marry her when you're half a woman yourself!* You're—'

'—A freak? And what's she, Rekhmire'? What's she!' I hauled in breath. 'She's the same as *I* am—'

'You're property. My property. You're a slave!'

'You think you're going to stop me doing this? Have me arrested! Because you're going to have to put chains on me to stop me helping her!'

Rekhmire' threw up his hands. In the purest dialect of Rome, audible to every man within fifty feet, he exclaimed, '*You stupid bitch*—!'

I brought my bags, the rest of my tools for the encaustic wax technique, and my bedroll, and put them on the couch at the back of the workshop.

Masaccio raised no eyebrow; he only harried me harder with modelling for the Franks' Great Betrayer, and painting the Alexandrine's miraculous moving golem-statue. He asked no questions about the Paziathe family.

It was twelve long hours, well into the evening, before I could get away to meet Sulva again – and then it was her father I found myself speaking with, not her.

That didn't come until the following morning.

'You haven't changed your mind?' I hardly dared look down into her face, that held the round newness of youth and too much knowledge of suffering.

Sulva gripped my arm for support as we walked. She lifted her head, pretending a wicked glint in her smile. 'No – not if you promise to take me travelling after we're married!'

Not only is Rekhmire' legally paid my wages for working in Masaccio's shop, not only will those wages be the only way to pay passage on a ship, but by law his permission is needed for me to travel anywhere.

We'll reconcile him to the idea, I thought, grimly determined, and smiled down at Sulva Paziathe. 'You can travel wherever you like. As far as Constantinople! As far as the lapis lazuli mine in Persia!'

She stifled her laughter with her fingers, for all we were outdoors.

A walled park lay behind their mansion. Grassed paths wound among ancient oak trees. Aranthur Paziathe and one of his middle-aged sons walked twenty yards ahead of us; Hathli and another maid dogged our footsteps, half that distance behind. The only respectable way in which a betrothed couple may meet and talk.

I am not under the illusion that she sees in me anything but escape from her prison of a mansion. How can she? But does that matter? Once she has her marriage lines, she's free; a woman can have greater freedom posing as a respectable widow than she can as wife or daughter.

She can make her choices, then. And if she *does* decide she'll stay with me . . .

I pushed muddy oak-leaves aside with my foot, hotly aware of the pressure of her hand on my sleeve. All the wealth of the household went into her brocade bodice and skirts. I had been excusably mistaken when I thought her father a servant: he dressed the part, at least. The family was not rich.

Sulva broke the silence. 'Which is your local church, here?'

'My local—?'

'For reading the banns.'

In the cathedral of Taraco, the King's Freak prayed by the King's side. Now, I pray less often than a man ought. I didn't desire to explain why.

I said, 'I haven't been in Rome long enough to have a local parish. Won't your father speak to your family priest?'

'No.' Sulva looked up. I suppose my face showed surprise. She spoke hesitantly. 'Father said I had to tell you. I hope you won't . . . We're not followers of the Christ of the Frankish people. You and I will have a private ceremony later, and be married as my family custom is.'

I glanced ahead, at Aranthur's rigid spine. 'Later?'

'First, we should be married properly, in public.' Her eyes were serious and sad. 'So no gossip gets about. Believe me, it's best.'

My suspicion became a sudden certainty.

'You don't worship the Green Christ at all, do you? Not as Christ-the-Emperor, or Christus Viridianus, or any other way?'

She glanced ahead and behind, as if looking for help from Aranthur or Hathli.

'I don't care who a man prays to,' I added.

I caught the tiny movement of her head. Assent.

'We're Etruscan,' she whispered. 'We were here long before the Romans! We have our own gods. People don't . . . It isn't good to be a heretic here. But it's worse to be a heathen. Outside the city, we have a place to celebrate ceremonies: the villa in the trees . . . You look *relieved*,' she exclaimed.

I let out an explosive breath. 'It explains why your father's willing to let you marry *me*. I suppose local families know you are – what you are.'

Her face hid expression no better than glass hides sunlight. I watched wonder and realisation and desperate hope go across her features. If I could take her to Masaccio's shop, now; work on the statue—

No. Not with how he still speaks of her as a whore, because she didn't return his desire.

'Heresy doesn't worry me.' I shrugged. 'Let men pray to what they will. And if your people are, what is it, "Etruscan"?'

'Yes. The Rasenna. I did pray to the Frankish Christ, once! For a small miracle. For a healing.' She looked down at her foot as she walked.

'That doesn't worry me either,' I said. 'But – wasn't your father willing to let you marry Tommaso Cassai?'

Into her silence, I added, 'I know how poor I am. I suppose I do look . . . respectable.'

The word almost choked me with irony.

'But so is Masaccio,' I completed. 'And more so. He has the reputation of being a fine painter, a friend to the architects and painters of Florence – Brunelleschi, Donatello. A man with an abbot for a patron. Wasn't he a better prospect for your father to approve?'

Sulva's lips pressed together at the centre, and turned up at the corners, giving her exactly the smile of her statue. 'My father thought Tommaso Cassai a respectable man. But . . . after I knew him better . . . *Mas accio!*'

She emphasised the sounds of his nickname: the pejorative *-accio* ending. *Bad Thomas*.

'He was rough, and rude, and spiteful sometimes, and I told my father I wouldn't marry him!' Sulva watched me, her expression anxious. 'You think badly of me, now?'

'I was just thinking . . . ' I let her wait. 'Of how we can find a priest here who'll let us into his church to marry.'

'Oh!' She swatted lightly at my arm, and this time she didn't stifle her laughter.

The old man glanced back at us. I saw his concern fade into a disgust at youthful horse-play.

Sulva's light-heartedness ceased, abruptly. Her eyes, under her oval lids and long lashes, lowered with doubt.

'This is Rome.' I wrapped Sulva's hand more securely over my arm, steadying her on the slick leaves. 'It contains the most worldly priests on earth. You arrange your ceremony at the – villa?'

'The villa in the trees.'

'And I'll see there's a marriage here first. Is that what you would like?'

Her smile was painfully raw in its joy.

11

Restlessness swarmed inside me, needing wind on my face to disperse it.

Masaccio swore and sent me off for an hour, for fidgeting as I sat.

I walked around as much of the ancient parts of Rome as I could encompass. Because who knows how much longer I shall be able to stay in this city? *I have plans to make.*

Must I leave Masaccio's workshop. How *can* I? There must be a way to manage it all!

At the bottom of one green valley, a great white marble arch stood – a gate to and from nowhere, covered with the triumphs of a general whose name no man remembers. I walked to the domed chapel of the Vestal Virgins: so small it seems impossible any woman could ever have lived inside. And I walked uphill – all Rome seems to be up a steep hill, or else down one – to an amphitheatre half-buried in the ground.

Row upon row of empty windows pierced the oval surrounding walls. Inside the roofless amphitheatre, and around an equally half-buried column (carved with Roman soldiers overcoming long-haired barbarians), all the earth was covered over with cob-walled, thatch-roofed houses; crammed up against each other, chickens and children running in the dust between them.

The sun burned down on my head. Even in the late months of the year, the high hours after noon are not well spent outdoors. I put away my charcoal and the board I always took with me to sketch on – put them away without regret; nothing of the monuments I had drawn was of any merit. In one corner of the board, I had managed a line or two that gave a hint how Sulva's cheek and shoulder looked when she turned her head. *This, only, I will keep.*

Closer to the Vatican, the buildings were mostly of ancient stone or brick. I welcomed the shade in the narrow passages. Seeing an open taverna, I ducked inside. The sun-blindness cleared from my gaze and I thought; *Luck is with me.* Sitting over my wine, I watched half a dozen clerics drinking and talking.

Over the next hour, two left, and a number more came in. It was strange to see no man in the robes belonging to a bishop's staff, but after a while I saw the green cloth robes of friars. And a friar would be sufficient.

'Where might a man go for a special marriage licence?' I asked my man, after I had chosen him and spent some time in drinking and conversation.

The priest, a Friar Sebastian, as he had introduced himself, looked at me shrewdly and wiped his finger across his upper lip. 'Time is too short for banns?'

He sketched a curve with his hand. I understood him to intend a woman's great belly, when she is about to have her child.

'I must leave Rome on business,' I improvised, the words coming fluently. 'My master, who is a painter, is sending me to Venice to buy blue pigment.'

Friar Sebastian nodded at that. In Rome, one evidently finds priests who understand the painting trade: how the colour blue is made solely from lapis lazuli, and how lapis-stone can only be bought at its one port of import from the East, Venice. He can probably quote me how many ducats the ounce – four for the good, and two ducats for the inferior stuff!

'I don't know how long I'll be gone,' I added, 'and my betrothed's father is anxious that I wed before I leave.'

His lip quirked up. My hands itched to draw that worldly smile. Let him conclude what he will: scandal is nothing to me. But I should encourage him towards silence, I thought. In case Sulva ever desires to return to Rome.

'A licence might be acquired,' Friar Sebastian remarked. 'By, let us say, tomorrow morning? I don't see how it can be done earlier. There will be fees, of course.'

'Of course,' I said flatly. I put down on the taverna bench between us the sole silver coin I had. It had been sewn into my cloak-hem since Carthage. But he need not know that. 'There is a down-payment. What church shall I come to?'

'To St Mithras Viridianus. By the Catacombs,' he added, seeing me look blank. 'You've not been long in the Empty Chair, have you? There again, so few people move into the city these days.'

He did not add, *in our ruin*, but the sigh that followed his words clearly implied it. Among the things I had seen in my walks were the great number of permanently closed churches.

'I consider Rome beautiful beyond all cities,' I flattered him, 'having found a bride in it. What hour shall I come to the church? There will be myself, and the bride, and her father and family.'

And no family of mine.

Nothing I do here can get me into *more* trouble with Aldra Videric, since he already needs me dead—

I jerked my thoughts away from Videric – and Rosamunda – and found my mind momentarily turning to Honorius. And Rekhmire'. Who before this I had imagined would stand in for family, were there the need.

'Tomorrow morning, before Matins.' Friar Sebastian reached across the ancient stained wood of the table. 'Now, let us finish this wine, shall we?'

12

I suppose every man asks himself on his wedding day, *How did I come to be here?*

Not so many will be confused about whether they ought to be the bride or the groom.

My confusion was not aided by a night spent largely sleepless – Masaccio had not thought it odd I should stay in the workshop when we returned from more hours spent covering square inches of stone golem with the accurate colours of skin. I lay awake, watching slivers of the moon's light cross the floor.

Rekhmire' did not send a message.

Nor did I.

How *did* I come to be here? I thought, walking in the pre-dawn mist through the wet, clean streets of the Empty Chair. It made me smile to myself – if wryly. Had I known the ship from Carthage would bring me to Mastro Masaccio, and sitting endless stiff hours as model for a man he thinks a traitor . . . That might have amused me, given what names the Aldra Videric must be calling me now. Had I known it would bring me wonders: a statue that moves of itself, a club-footed girl with a beauty so much greater for its imperfections . . .

I looked up as I reached the lodgings that had been mine and Rekhmire''s.

'Your master's already left for his work!' the woman from the next floor up remarked as she came down the stairs. She gave me a grin. 'Late night, was it?'

'Yes . . . ' Thinking rapidly, I improvised the look of a man frustrated in some effort. 'And I need to get my things, and I haven't his key—'

'Oh, that don't matter; I can let you in. Quintilla leaves the key with me most mornings.'

It was that easy to make an entry into the familiar low-roofed rooms, with the bustling woman at my back.

She nodded, as if to signal I should get on. I began grabbing at random among the men's clothes I still had here. *If she won't leave—*

Another woman came down the tenement stairs, carrying a slop-bucket; the two of them leaned either side of the door, and entered into conversation. Neither looking at a harmless slave.

I reached under his mattress, lifted the loose floorboard that Rekhmire' had indicated to me – 'Should we ever be in need of help, either of us' – and took, by feel, a handful of the coins that I knew were there.

No matter that he told me they were there to take – *Now I am a thief.*

Even worn baggy, I was finding Italian hose too close-fitting for pockets. I dropped the coins into my shirt-sleeve and tightened the draw-string; nodded to the two women, and left.

Friar Sebastian greeted me at the very door of St Mithras Viridianus. The coins vanished into his robe as if I had never stolen them.

His hand came out again.

'I had not appreciated the particular nature of the family,' he murmured.

I fumbled again in my sleeve, counting tiny ducat-coins into his hand until his face showed agreement. He nodded and led me in. I barely noticed the ornamental stonework, struck through with a sudden panic fear of poverty.

The back of the church was part of the catacombs themselves. Each wall I passed as he led me towards the altar was hollowed out into an ossuary. Morning's light through the round-arched windows couldn't combat the sticky darkness clinging to piles of bones, behind stone bars. Brown and yellow skulls stared out at me from their empty orbits.

'Ilario?' a soft voice said.

I had arrived before the rood-screen. Sulva stood to my right side, a veil covering her face. The bleached flax was transparent enough that I could see her eyes. Her irises the colour of turquoise-stone.

I smiled at her.

I can pass as a man; I can work; if I paint, I can sell my canvases and boards. Somehow, we'll contrive.

The rood-screen was not made of carved wood as they commonly are in Iberia. Like half the churches in the Empty Chair, it was built of brick or masonry, covered over and decorated with mosaic. On the other side of me, Aranthur Paziathe glared at the mosaics of the Bull and the Tree; barely hiding his affront.

I could not help studying the mosaic's antique style. Do men still know, now, how to make that blue, that green, that gold?

The crowd of men with Aranthur, who I took to be relatives, stood in a tight fearful group.

'Will we go to your country?' Sulva whispered to me, hardly audible. 'When we're truly married? I should like that.'

I would not, I thought grimly. Matters will have to be safer before that can happen.

And there will have to be a mending of fences before I can bring her to Rekhmire'. Or to Honorius, if the Egyptian won't be reconciled. This will take some thinking out . . .

Heated flesh touched mine; Sulva's fingers crept into my hand. Startled, I gripped her tightly. She gave me a tremulous smile.

'They say,' Aranthur emphasised the word enough to hint at complete disbelief, 'that the heretic Gundobad would have devastated the whole Frankish world, if Saint Heito hadn't stopped him. By which I suppose they mean, *his* heresy would have supplanted *their* heresy.'

It was a Frankish name I had not heard. '"Heito"?'

Aranthur Paziathe stepped forward, stabbing a walnut-coloured finger at the mosaic panels that hid the altar and Friar Sebastian praying.

Beside a figure burning on a bonfire – which must be Gundobad the Prophet – another man was depicted. His dress was antique, and white deer's horns sprang from his brow. That was enough to make me raise my own brows. What superstitions *do* the Franks believe?

'That's Saint Heito,' Aranthur's voice rumbled. 'And this man, burning, this is the Carthaginian's Prophet Gundobad, who cursed Rome and brought about the Empty Chair . . . They say Heito prevented him doing worse. Here is Pope Leo, whom the mob tore to pieces, and blinded and castrated. Pope Stephen the Fifth, whose horse trampled him, three days after he took the Papal Keys. Pope Paschal the First, who was struck by a levin-bolt. Pope Eugene, killed by a bust of St Thomas the Doubter falling from the front of St Peter's in a storm. All in the space of three months.'

Beside me, Sulva whispered, 'Father!'

Aranthur grunted, staring down at a patch of sunlight on the miniature glass tiles. 'Valentine, Gregory, Sergius, the second Paschal. They haven't room enough here to show all their dead popes! And they blame it on this Gundobad, when they must *know* that the true Gods find Frankish priests an abomination! . . . It didn't take long for the cardinals to become fearful. Their conclave has sat these two hundred years; it will never elect another pope – or not one who will consent to serve.'

'*Father!*'

Sulva's embarrassed whisper got his attention just in time for him to step back, and be standing beside me as Friar Sebastian arrived from the altar. I recovered my expression as best I might. The true Gods?

'Who,' Friar Sebastian enquired, 'gives possession of this woman?'

I glanced at Sulva – and found her looking back at me; her expression finally an exact copy of what I thought my own must be.

I paid little attention to the rest of the ceremony, only speaking in the right places, and signing my name where it was desired. Sulva Paziathe, now of the family Honorius, made an ink-mark with her thumb in the registry book. I had a hard job not to flinch every time a door opened somewhere in the church.

I wouldn't put it past Rekhmire' to walk in and proclaim: 'This ceremony is void: this slave has no permission to be married!'

Not until we walked out into the still-cool morning air did I draw an unrestricted breath.

'Sulva—'

A two-wheeled *cisia*-carriage stood waiting: Aranthur swung himself up into the seat, and peremptorily gestured for her to follow.

She put her hand up to my cheek in evident farewell. 'It won't be long now.'

'"Won't be long"?' I was bewildered.

'I have to be . . . ' She searched for a word. 'Purified. After *that*.'

She nodded at the front of the church. Friar Sebastian waved at us, cheerfully, too far away to hear what she said.

'You come to me in three nights' time.' She put her veil down, her gaze still on me through the translucent cloth. 'It's outside the walls. You'll have to travel secretly. Etruscans aren't supposed to leave the city without a permit, but one of my cousins will come and bring you to the villa in the trees on the third night—'

'"On the third night"?' I stared. 'Why didn't you tell me this!'

'Wasn't it obvious?' Her brows dipped down, a little vertical fold of flesh between them. 'I thought you'd know! You're a heretic too!'

How old is she, sixteen?

Hardly surprising if she forgets, or makes assumptions . . .

Gently, I touched my thumb to her forehead, smoothing the skin. Hathli gave me a sour look. I smiled down at Sulva. She smelled of musk; I supposed her veil to have been perfumed.

'A different kind of heretic,' I said softly. 'No matter. I'll come to you.'

Her skin flushed with a colour that I could never have caught in marble, not to make it lifelike.

'The custom is . . . that there are no lamps,' she said, in a hurry. Her gaze dropped. 'All will be in the dark. For the . . . wedding night.'

Quickly, she turned away, took Hathli's hand, and made an ungainly jerking movement that got her up into the *cisia* vehicle. The driver touched the horses with a whip and it moved away – no faster than walking-pace; the relatives and servants hurrying behind it, leaving me alone. Sunlight dazzled my eyes as I stared after them.

The sound of wheels on cobbles clattered into the distance, fading under street cries and the sounds of two men having an argument, and a barking dog. All the morning noises of the Empty Chair.

I smiled. *I am a married man.*

I stopped smiling.

I am a married *man*.

It will be in the dark. She desires it because of her foot, but *I*—

It was not until that moment that I realised. A wedding is not legal until consummated. And, until now . . .

Until *now*, I haven't thought to wonder what will happen when I come to her bed.

136

Standing alone in the street, I realised: I've become so used to passing as a man that I never once thought about the danger of discovery!

What have I done?

What have I become?

13

I strode back through the early morning to Masaccio's workshop.

I felt the pull of the lodging-house – a desperate need to speak with Rekhmire'.

But I doubt I'll get good advice from a man who calls me *bitch on heat*, I reflected, face burning at the memory of the tall Egyptian shouting just that across the bridge at Castel San' Angelo.

If she does not desire it, I will not touch her. We can lie about the fornication that legally seals a marriage.

The Egyptian thinks me besotted. He has no idea of the world a woman finds herself inhabiting.

'Your master's been here for you,' Mastro Tommaso Cassai greeted me as I came in. He jerked a thumb at the couch where I'd left my belongings. 'Took your bag back with him.'

Rage flared through me. 'Why didn't you stop him?'

For once, Masaccio didn't answer in words; he pointed. At me. I stared, for a moment; then reached up to touch my neck.

My fingers encountered my iron collar. I have grown so used to it resting there that I forget it. The engraved words would be plainly visible to him:

I am ::ILARIO:: owned by ::REKHMIRE'::

In Carthage, they only need to fill in the name-blanks; the collars come ready-chiselled with the remaining form of words. Now I had taken my cloak off, any man might see it. I wondered if Friar Sebastian would have objected in the slightest, had he noticed it in church. Perhaps he would have charged me more.

'I'm sleeping here tonight,' I said, in a tone that let Masaccio know I was not inclined to listen to joke or reason.

He shrugged. 'Sleep in the street if you like, boy. It's all one to me. What have you done to upset the Alexandrine?'

The tension brought truth out of me. I pointed at her statue: the goat-foot coloured like life, the face a white marble blank.

'I've married Sulva Paziathe. My master doesn't approve.'

'You've married— You've *married*—?'

The Florentine shook his head furiously, as if he cleared a bee out of his ear. His black eyes glinted at me.

'Did I hear you right? You, you are speaking of – you *married that bitch*?'

Had I been at Rodrigo's court (and had it been a day there that I was dressed as a male), I should have thrown a steel gauntlet in his face, or simply found a sword and stuck it through his belly.

Having only a dagger, and an immense respect for Masaccio as a painter, if not as a man, the red blur had washed through and past me by the time my hand touched my belt.

Masaccio noticed none of that. He grated incredulously, 'How is it she'd marry *you*?'

I shrugged lightly, and walked past him to throw the cloak I carried onto the couch. 'Perhaps because you only saw a pretty face?'

His voice dropped; he sounded like a man in a taverna ready to begin a fight. '*I loved her.*'

That stopped me. I looked back at him. 'I'm sorry.'

He blinked.

'Married you?' he repeated, after a moment.

Yes, me: is that so strange?

Well . . . yes.

'When are you – when did you—?' He stopped, and looked at me. 'Is the ceremony done?'

'This morning. Just now. At dawn.' I intended him to hear the finality of that.

'Dawn?' He echoed me, stupidly. The pupils of his black eyes altered in the light of an oil-lamp left burning on the table. 'But – you want to sleep here *tonight*?'

Flustered, I said, 'Yes. But—'

'So you're lying. Or else – eh, she's *using* you, isn't she? The bitch! You fall in love with a pretty stone face. And she sees a fool who'll marry a whore! And be fooled into not sticking his prick in her!'

'*She is not a whore!*'

The bearded man straightened, chin coming up. 'I know more about her than you do. Boy. All you see is a pretty face, you know *nothing* of her—'

'Then how is it *you* don't know why I have to sleep here until the third night? Or don't you know the customs of the Etruscan people?'

The workshop echoed my defiance.

Silence succeeded it.

My back ran with sudden cold sweat.

'Etruscan?' Masaccio stared in shock. 'That . . . would explain much.'

He gazed at me, his expression shuttling through unreadable emotions and settling on disgust.

'One of those people. And the whole family—? Yes, of course. Of course. I always *knew* there was something wrong about the Paziathe.'

Bewildered, I watched the Florentine shaking his head. I wanted to ask: If you still loved her, as indeed it seems you do, how can you go from that to this, in a matter of moments?

And – what have I said?

'It's a good thing your baggage is gone,' Masaccio said with harsh contempt. 'Model for Judas! *Judas!* Go. Leave! Get out of here!'

'What?' I said stupidly.

'You're fired. Go. I don't want to see your face again. Out of my workshop, now!'

He made flapping gestures at me, like an old woman shooing hens, that made me burst out into shocked laughter.

'*Out!*' His hand dipped down: he caught up a pestle from a mortar on the bench, and threw it.

The heavy porphyry implement hit the door-frame beside me in a shower of red pigment; thudded down onto the floorboards; left a dent in the wood.

I stopped laughing.

His hand scrabbled for another missile.

'I'm going!' I slid my foot back, pushing the door open; caught it and swung it closed behind me as I darted through.

Something solid hit the inside, hard enough to dent the planks.

Masaccio's voice raised in incoherent rage. I couldn't make out what he yelled; I could hear the raw fury. I took a pace or two back into the narrow cobbled street.

The threat of violence faded from my muscles and tendons.

'Mastro, you *won't* fire me.' I realised that I found myself not so bereft as I might have expected. 'Not until Judas is finished and on the church wall.'

Give him a day or two . . .

Should I try to warn Sulva? That I've said she's . . . Warn her of what? What can he do?

Like the Jews in Taraco, I guessed, it would be no real secret which families in the city were Etruscan.

Masaccio can only spread gossip. But words are a dangerous enough poison.

The impossible-to-paint blue of mist and sunlight grew in the sky overheard.

Thirty paces down the narrow street, I realised: I am still left with nowhere to sleep tonight. Or tomorrow.

'Then again,' I said aloud, 'I don't have to sleep.'

Tonight will be a night or two before the full of the moon. That will give me monochrome light enough to walk the city streets, go from district to district, draw sketches in return for jugs of wine in tavernas. I could do that tonight and tomorrow, and on the third night, share the hours of darkness with Sulva in this 'villa of the trees'.

I looked up from placing my feet between scattered mule-dung, and

recognised where instinct had taken me. The road down to Castel San'
Angelo.

I turned to go back, and stopped.

'No,' I said aloud.

Whether I need to sleep or not, whether I can hide or not . . .
No, I will not hide from anything I've done.

And whatever mess I've made – I'll clear it up.

14

'What are you doing?' I asked.

Rekhmire' looked up from where he sat cross-legged on the tenement room's floorboards. A small box-shrine stood open in front of the Egyptian.

'Praying to the gods of the primordial water, and the gods of invisibility. Heh and Hehet. Amun and Amunet.'

'Oh. Oh . . . I mean – God and Goddess of the primordial water, yes, but a god and goddess of *invisibility*?'

He stared at me, saying nothing.

Uncomfortable, I walked into the room and sat down on the low bed, watching him all the time.

'Your gods are all twin gods, aren't they? Paired. Are they male and female?' I added rapidly, before he could speak: 'Maybe they're hermaphrodites! That would be something, wouldn't it? Hermaphroditic deities. Maybe I should do that. Should I be "Ilario" and "Ilariet", do you think?'

He winced – at the butchery of language, too. 'Ilario. What do you want?'

'I want to apologise.'

His head came up. Without looking, but with a seamless movement, he closed the box-shrine. The click of painted wood sounded loudly in the tenement room.

'"Apologise"?'

'I'm sorry,' I said. 'I'm sorry I stole money from you. I'm sorry I didn't take your advice – although I couldn't, and I know I'm right in what I'm doing. I'm sorry I quarrelled with you. I'm sorry I've done so many things without . . . well, talking it over with you.'

Rekhmire''s face stayed impassive. 'With your master.'

'With my friend.'

'You're in trouble.'

Anger flared in me – but I caught, in time, the almost-imperceptible note of amusement in his voice.

Shakily, I smiled back at him. 'No. Well, yes. But nothing I can't sort out with carefulness and attention.'

'That would be something new . . . '

I spoke in the same tone as he. 'Be careful, Egyptian – I'll be Mastro

Tommaso Cassai's apprentice again in a couple of days; you don't want to speak disrespectfully to someone associated with such a superior man.'

'Threw you out, did he?' Rekhmire''s impassive face slipped into something close to a grin. He recovered himself immediately. I thought I should like to paint him amused: the liveliness of his expression setting off the monumental gravity of his features.

'You might throw me out, too.' I took a deep breath, hoping he didn't notice. 'I have married Madonna Sulva, after all.'

The Egyptian nodded slowly.

'It'll be—' I searched for a word. 'Complete. Three days from now. There's an Etruscan ceremony. I don't know if they allow strangers, but if they do, I'd like you to be there. As groom's man.'

His eyebrows rose up at *Etruscan*; at *groom's man* his eyes widened so much that I momentarily saw white all around the blue-brown irises.

I said, 'I'm sorry.'

His monumental features shifted. He nodded acceptance. 'I, also, apologise. I am sorry to have called you a bitch.'

That startled me; I could only stare at him.

Rekhmire''s lips quirked. 'There are people to whom I am only a man when they're pleased with me. At their *dis*pleasure, I become a gelded thing neither man nor woman; a monster, a freak of the surgeon's knife. I . . . didn't intend to speak to you in that same way. I'm sorry for that.'

I have been given more than was owed to me, I thought, and for a moment couldn't speak.

'It's possible there'll be trouble,' I said, finally. 'Masaccio didn't know her family were Etruscan until I told him. I'm not asking for help. Only to talk things through. When I can see what's right, then I'll do it.'

'I can see we have a lot to discuss.' Rekhmire' got to his feet in one smooth, heavy movement; for a moment reminding me of the stone golem. 'Meanwhile . . . meanwhile, we accept each other's apologies, I see, and – come with me.'

'What?'

He swung up a cloak from the foot of the bed, wrapping it around himself, largely concealing his Alexandrine clothes. One hand checked the purse tied to his belt. He thrust the room's door open. 'This way.'

I walked past him, through the doorway, out onto the staircase; half wondering if he would shut it behind me.

He did shut the door, but with himself on the same side of it as me, pausing only to turn the crude iron key in the lock.

'That won't keep Quintilla from snooping,' he murmured, 'but we shan't be out long. Come on.'

'But – we ought to – *but*—'

I found myself facing his back as he moved away down the stairs.

Out in the street, I must half-run to keep up with his strides. A shower of late morning rain left puddles the length of the alley. Our cloak-hems grew soaked and black. He strode from alley to street, and street to lane, until we crossed a great ancient square, whose wide empty geometry I ached to sketch, and came to a small shop set under an awning. A bald-headed, short Roman man stood with his arms folded, looking out disconsolately at the weather that would keep away customers.

'You are a notary?' Rekhmire' demanded.

The man straightened, and nodded.

Rekhmire' said, 'Good. Somewhere in your shop you will have the form for a deed of manumission. Draw it up. I am formally freeing my slave, here.'

He pointed at me.

'What?' I stuttered.

Coins changed hands.

The man went back into the dimness of his shop. A moment later, I saw the blossoming of lamp-light, and heard the stropping of a quill on paper. Rekhmire' took two steps across the antique pavement, worn into dips by millennia of passing feet, and grabbed me by the upper arm.

'What,' I managed to get out, 'are you *doing*?'

'I'm stopping you pretending to be helpless!'

The grip of his hand was firm, but not painful. I looked up at him, a head taller as he was. This is not so different from how I saw him in Carthage, at the slaver's hall. Only now a Frankish cloak covers the linen kilt and the woven reed head-band, and his sandals are crusted with mud, not dust.

'Pretending.' I couldn't manage to make it a question.

He nodded at that, and loosed his grip. I stood for a moment, feeling the first drops on my face as a heavier rain began to fall. It swept in a veil across the great paved square, and misted the ends of the arcade of shops. I felt, also, the weight of the iron band, resting on the linen at the neck of my shirt. It rubbed, by the day's end. I had seen few enough other slaves in Frankish Rome; most of them with evident foreigners.

Rekhmire' rumbled, 'It's long past time you took off that collar. You're no slave.'

'Alexandrine slavery is different?' I put forward, to see what he would say.

He was unstoppable. 'You and I do not behave as master and slave.'

I met his gaze. 'I don't have the money to pay you for my freedom.'

Recalling where I had got the money to pay Friar Sebastian, I felt my face heat until I must be scarlet to look at.

He shrugged. 'Then owe me a debt, as one free man does to another. The notary here can draw up the terms of that. I am not your conscience, to forbid you to do this or that. I am not master of you in any way. I won't let you hide behind that. You are to be freed, now. Whether you wish it or not.'

I couldn't help smiling at that. He gave a brief smile in answer. For a moment there was no sound but the pricking of the notary's iron pen on vellum.

'I understand why you're doing this,' I said. 'I have decisions to make, to clear up this mess.'

Rekhmire' inclined his head. 'And you must take them, not I for you.'

I touched the cold metal at my throat for the last time.

'Here's my first decision, then. I'm going back to Mastro Masaccio, to apologise to *him*.'

15

It took me more than twenty-four hours to get him to speak to me.

The clock at St Martin's chimed six on the evening of the next day. Masaccio came out of the workshop door, throwing out water from stained bowls he was evidently swilling clean.

I stepped back out of the way.

Instead of *I apologise*, which he had not yet allowed me to get out at all, I said, 'A woman with her poor taste is a fool, Mastro. But you will forgive her for that.'

Framing it so was the sacrifice I made in hope of reconciliation. His lips moved, half-hidden in his beard. I thought I might touch his vanity. Now I saw I had touched his humour.

'You're right,' Masaccio said. 'In both.' He upended the last bowl and watched it drip.

On impulse, I said, 'Would you like a drink at the taverna, Mastro?'

He grinned at me, showing white teeth. 'No drinking until we're done working. Do you know, I actually *fell behind* yesterday, with you not there at the Gyppos' house? There must be some use in an assistant after all!'

If bigoted, it was still a remark that reached out for reconciliation.

He looked the nearest he might come to shame-faced, which was momentary. I bowed acknowledgement, after the fashion of the court at Taraco. If it's work that will reconcile us, I'm willing. Tommaso Cassai is not a man to apologise for anything.

More tools and pigments than three men could carry had been piled on a two-wheeled flat hand-cart.

'You push,' he said, unsurprisingly, with a more relaxed grin, and walked beside me. The cart jolted at every shove. Why I should feel so light-hearted at Tommaso Cassai's fast-ended anger, I wasn't sure – until he began talking, as we walked through the streets to the Alexandrine embassy.

'You *will* be a painter. One day.' He waved his arm in a gesture that brought a tearing-metal bray from a donkey tied up by a pot-shop. 'That's more important than women! That stuff you brought with you from under the Penitence – trash! And who but *I* could have seen the little that wasn't? That showed talent? I do flatter myself I can see promise.'

So blankly it must have been comic, I said, 'You can?'

'You're beginning – just beginning – to learn. Or to know what it is you *don't* know!' Masaccio's smile was dizzying. He nodded to the guards on the embassy door, and talked to them at high speed as I wheeled the loaded hand-cart down through the building, towards the room that we worked in.

He thinks I have talent. He really thinks—

I stopped in the doorway.

Having not seen it for two days, the impact of the stone man on my senses was profound. I could only stand for a moment, and gaze up at it; patchwork flesh and marble as it appeared to be. 'I . . . *really* don't understand this.'

'Why should you?' Masaccio shrugged, seized the handles of the piled-high flat cart, and with a physical strength I had not expected pushed it ahead of himself into the room. He began to untie the tarpaulin that covered it. 'I ask myself: is it a machine, or is it a miracle? But I am not priest-ridden, like most Franks, so I have no doubt. *Men* made this. What I don't know is how!'

I put in: 'Or why.'

'"Why"? It's a servant! What else could it be?'

'When I was in Iberia, the King—'

Whom I need not now, or ever again, call *my master the King*, odd as that feels.

'—King Rodrigo Sanguerra had me trained in the techniques of siege works, thinking I had some talent for that. Mobile assault towers, to be used against walls. Catapults, mangonels, scorpions, trebuchets, ballista . . . cannon. Mastro Masaccio, you say a machine is a servant. I have little enough training. But if *I* can wonder what would be the killing ability of a dart-throwing machine, were it powered in the same way this stone man is – then so can any man wonder.'

'Weapons of war?' He cocked a brow at the golem, his expression thoughtful.

'Stone can't be hurt like flesh.'

'Who knows what hurts it? Is it in pain now, frozen as it stands? What does it feel?' Masaccio tapped his finger against his red lower lip, half-hidden in his curling beard. 'It sees nothing, but is not blind. You will have seen bats after dusk, avoiding nets and traps and walls. Does it see with their blind senses? If I were to carve a whistle that only dogs hear, would it come to that call?'

He shook his head, his gaze as he stared up at the golem's face frighteningly intense.

'Could I paint an image of the world, as this golem perceives it? Perhaps. If I truly understood it . . . But I don't know,' he finished. '*I don't know.*'

'You might go to Carthage.'

It was the obvious suggestion; it might excite suspicion not to make it.

Rekhmire''s Eight grant that he doesn't ask me to come with him!

'To see if I can find out who's making them? And how? That will be kept a secret. Guilds and trades . . . '

Masaccio shook his head. 'I never refuse knowledge to a man unless he's stupid enough that he can't benefit from it. Other men keep their secrets tight to their chests. And, I am weary of that. Very weary.'

'Mastro—'

He lifted a hand and pointed at the golem, interrupting me. 'Which is why I intend to do something about it. You'll see. Now, paint!'

He would say no more while we worked. Egyptian slaves came around two or three times to replenish the lamps with oil. Each time I felt a qualm. Masaccio did not comment on the weight of metal gone from my throat.

Being Masaccio, I thought, it may be because he hasn't noticed.

The sensation of lack was keen, to me. And watching the collared embassy slaves made me frown. Whether or not Alexandrine slavery is less onerous than the Carthaginian kind, they are still slaves.

Then again, they need not take decisions for themselves.

Evening wore on into night; overseers came to the door; Masaccio went to speak to them – to tell them we must continue working, I guessed. There looked to be less painting done than I'd expect since I'd last put brush to the stone.

I wonder if he spent time drunk in a taverna?

It might explain his tolerance of the thought of Sulva married, if wine had numbed him.

There were no windows in the low-ceilinged room. I did not always register the chime of the water-clock, but I guessed it to be past midnight when Masaccio put his brush down with finality. He cocked his head, listening. I could hear nothing move in the mansion. He opened the room doors. There was not even a sound of the guards.

'I had a friend in the Florentine militia,' he said, apparently out of nowhere.

In answer to my stare, he added, 'Who told me a thing that's certain. Soldiers would rather drink than guard! If there's one man on the door, now, I'll be surprised. A gift of wine may work a miracle.'

He grinned, his expression febrile.

'Mastro, what—'

'Didn't I say, I intend to do something about my lack of knowledge?' Masaccio put his hand flat on the unpainted part of the stone man's chest, looking up at it. 'This is the only golem I've ever seen. If I let this chance pass, I think it'll be the only one I *will* ever see.'

He turned to look at me.

'And that's why we're stealing it.'

For a moment, I couldn't speak.

I shot a glance at the unloaded hand-cart.

Masaccio nodded, without my needing to say anything; his lips stretching in an excited, enthusiastic grin.

'You planned this!' I accused.

The Florentine spoke amiably. 'It would be difficult to do it *without* planning.'

'You – you can't—' I put my single brush down with too much care. 'Mastro, I mean, you *really* can't. They'll work out who did it. They'll know where to come!'

'I have a cargo-boat moored down at the Tiber, ready to be rowed to Ostia Antica.' Masaccio shrugged. 'From there – well. Never mind. You shouldn't know more.'

Florence! flashed through my mind with absolute certainty. He'll take it home with him, to the city he calls *Fiorenza.*

'And all we have to do is get it down to the river. Come on.'

He made a beckoning gesture, as if I should fetch the hand-cart to him, and turned his thoughtful stare back to the immense statue.

I don't think the wheels will take it.

I didn't say it aloud. There was no necessity.

I blurted, 'Even if the guards are drinking, they'll still be at the entrances! We won't get as far as the front door!'

'Mother of God, boy! The wine's drugged, of course. Fortified with spirits – and poppy.' He stepped past me, impatiently grabbing the handles of the cart, and pushing it around behind the statue. '*Golem, lie down!* Here! *Golem, lie down here on the cart!*'

Stunned, I realised: This is why we've brought no rope and pulley. He knew it wouldn't be necessary.

I flinched back from the impossible movement of the stone man. Swivelling at the joints of hips and knee, turning about; the great marble hands reaching down to grasp the sides of the cart . . .

The stone man lowered himself carefully – comically carefully – back down onto the flat bed of the hand-cart.

The sound of protesting wood creaked through the room.

Masaccio put his lower lip between his teeth, biting hard enough that blood ran down into his beard.

The wood sang – and held.

He gave a sigh and a nod.

The Franks, in their practise of trades, are very expert at estimating, by eye, weights and volumes – which they must be, since (unlike Carthage) they have no common unit of measurement. A barrel and a bale in Rome are not the same as a barrel and a bale in Venice. Masaccio had judged this weight just bearable by the cart. *And so it is. Just.*

'Now, we push it.' He showed all his teeth in a grin of triumph.

'We—? I—?' By an effort, I stopped myself stuttering. I lowered my voice, every nerve tense against some Alexandrine coming down the corridor, entering the room, finding *this*. 'I'm not going to do it!'

'Afraid, *boy*?' He sounded too jubilant for his insult to sting.

'It's theft.' I found my face heating at his stare. 'I'm not a thief!'

A voice in my thoughts whispered sardonically, *Would that that were true* . . .

'The world needs this,' Masaccio said soberly. He reached out to draw the tarpaulin over the marble man laying flat on the cart.

Its feet lay nearer the floor than its head, because of the way it had placed itself down. As the golem vanished under the oiled cloth, I thought: That foreshortening, that perspective – I could *draw* this, now, and stand some chance of doing it justice.

'Who knows how it works?' Masaccio said, tying off a cord. 'Who knows what else could be done with it, if we *did* know?'

He looked at me, as if for the first time he saw me: Ilario.

'Wouldn't you rather slave-work was done by stone men, than by men of flesh and blood with iron collars around their necks?'

'How can I answer that? Of course I would!'

'Then lend a hand here.'

'But it's not that easy!'

Masaccio ignored me and bent to the cart's handles, half crouching. He got the weight of his body on a line through foot and calf and thigh and hip, and thrust forward.

By some miracle the wheels creaked and began to turn. The cart began moving from that first forward jolt.

Almost automatically, I stepped forward and reached for one of the cart-handles.

Before I could touch it, the end of the cart rolled out of the room. The feet of the stone man passed over the threshold of the room, out into the wide embassy corridor.

Cords snapped. The tarpaulin slid away. Stone grated on wood.

A strut somewhere in the cart gave way. A sharp *crack!* echoed flatly in the room.

The stone golem sat up.

My mouth opened on a breath, a warning shout: '*Ahh*—'

Too swiftly for heavy marble to move, the stone man sprang off the hand-cart, landing with an impact that jerked dust up from between the floor tiles. One of the tiles cracked under the weight.

The body of the stone man swivelled. It took too quick a step forward. Its marble hand shot under Masaccio's bearded chin – and closed.

He made one sound: a wheeze.

His lips stretched in a rictus grin, all his white teeth exposed. The handles of the cart dropped out of his fingers. His hands came up, locking around the golem's stone wrists. He kicked, furiously; slammed a boot at a knee-joint—

The statue lifted him, one-handed, into the air.

150

I sprang forward, grabbed at the painted marble wrist and knuckles, heaved—

And moved nothing.

'Let go! Let go of him! Golem, let go of him! *Golem, let go of his throat!*'

The cold brass joints moved unstoppably under my palms.

Masaccio choked.

His eyes bulged. His lips moved; his jaw worked.

Soundlessly.

Stone fingers clenched around his larynx. He couldn't speak a word.

His skin above his beard darkened, grew dusky blue; his eyes shone red as they filled up with blood. His fingers lost purchase on the stone arms. One flailing hand clawed towards its face. He caught me a sharp, dizzying blow with the other.

I stumbled; scrabbled down on the floor for a weapon.

'Help!' My voice echoed flatly in the room; outside; in the corridor. '*Somebody help us here!*'

The haft of a mallet slotted into my palm. I straightened up. With all my strength, I brought the mallet up and slammed it down on the metal wrist-joint; hit it, hit it again—

The golem's hand flexed closed.

I heard a distinct, sticky, hollow *click*.

I know that noise – it is the noise a hanged man makes, when the rope snaps his vertebrae apart.

Masaccio's feet drummed rapidly, briefly, against the stone man's thighs; and stopped.

His body hung from the statue's hand. Every line of his flesh was drawn down by gravity; limp as a rabbit in a poacher's hand.

I leaned forward, choking, bringing up acid and bile.

Still holding Masaccio's body out at arm's length, the stone golem swivelled around to face me.

Every muscle in my body instantly weakened; my thighs quivered.

The golem stepped lightly forward, arm stretched out. Masaccio swung limply in its grip.

The golem brought its other hand up.

Up and forward.

Towards *me*.

I broke out of the frozen, powerless daze; jolted violently back as the golem's foot came down on pigment-bowls, crushing them flat.

The stone golem's outstretched marble fingertips swung, reaching out for me; brushed past my forehead—

The mere touch slammed my head over to one side. Sharp, solid pain blinded me.

I staggered backwards, spun around, and ran.

16

Masaccio's dead!

Rain and panic froze me.

Grazes stung my knees, through abraded hose. My hands shook, cut where I had fallen on stones. The pitch-dark of the city hemmed me in. Lost. *I am lost.* And Masaccio—

I shook wet hair out of my eyes. A distant glimmer showed the barred, closed door of a taverna. I snatched a torch from its socket under the high awning. The light let me see enough to finally recognise streets as I ran, feet pounding the broken pavements. My head pounded with pain.

He will know; Rekhmire' will know what to do—

Masaccio is dead.

No mistaking that; no hope of a doctor's help.

I have drawn men hanged, by the justice of King Rodrigo's magistrates. They kick; choke. They loose their bowels; they hang, when their necks break, with just such a boneless immobility.

'Masaccio!' I howled, at the freezing rain.

Rekhmire' didn't answer his door; I hammered on it with the butt-end of the torch, yelling. Shutters slammed open over my head

The woman Quintilla bawled something down.

Gasping in a breath, I held up the torch so she might see it was me. '*Rekhmire'!* Wake him! Let me in; *I'll* wake him!'

'He's gone.'

Coldness flooded through me. I stopped – stopped breathing, almost.

'It is you, Ilario?' She leaned out of the window, peering down. 'If you want him, you'll have to follow him. His people came.'

Stupefied, I echoed, 'His people?'

'The other Egyptians. The Gyppies that live in the embassy house? One of them came banging on the shutters and woke everybody up; he's gone with *them*.'

Soaked, winded, I stood in the dark square; staring at the light spilling out through the embassy door.

Cold sent shudders through me. Rain slicked my skin.

I walked forward into the brilliance.

'You!' One of the linen-kilted guards reached towards his sword. 'It's the painter's apprentice; hold her!'

Egyptians see with the eyes of a different culture, I thought numbly. I'd never realised.

The Alexandrines are used to seeing eunuchs. So if they see a Frankish man who's 'wrong', they don't take him for a castrato as Romans do; they think him a woman. Even if that's equally inaccurate.

I didn't move as men rushed up either side of me.

'I want to see Master Rekhmire'. Take me inside, to him.'

Inside, nothing had changed in the time – minutes or hours – since I ran.

The end of the flat-bed cart still projected out into the corridor. Men milled around it; soldiers, diplomats, men whom I didn't recognise. My escort shouldered me through, into the room.

It smelled of dying.

The half-painted marble man stood in the centre of the floor, as motionless as if it was the statue it seemed.

Rekhmire' straightened up from examining its hands.

'*Get away from that!*' I snarled.

The Egyptian looked at the golem, looked at me – and walked across the room to where I stood.

'We're not safe in the same room with it!' My voice shook.

A sheet covered a body on the floor. I hadn't realised Masaccio was so small a man. It was his vital spirit that made him seem taller than he was.

'Ilario?' Rekhmire' glanced from me to the shroud. 'Tell me what happened here.'

I couldn't stop myself looking towards the stone golem. 'It killed him.'

A tenor voice interrupted from behind me, speaking Egyptian-accented Latin. 'The painter's apprentice? That's your slave, is it? Good! I'll have her tortured for information.'

Rekhmire' didn't take his gaze from my face. '*He* is a freedman. – *And* a freedwoman. In any case, free.'

The tall, fat Egyptian man behind him, wrapped in a night-robe evidently snatched up at random, swore in his native language. His voice rose higher than tenor.

'Ilario.' Rekhmire' spoke in a deliberate, soothing voice. 'This is Lord Menmet-Ra. Tell him the truth of what happened here. You will not be punished.'

I must close my eyes to do it, but I told the castrato Menmet-Ra all.

'I didn't know,' I finished, 'what Masaccio planned. Or I would have stopped him. *Somehow.* I would . . . He would still – be alive—'

In the silence, I opened my eyes. The sheet covering Masaccio was rucked. I felt a foolish impulse to smooth it down.

He's beyond discomfort now.

'How could the Florentine *do* that!' Menmet-Ra snarled, thumping one heavy fist into his other hand. He was little shorter than Rekhmire', I now saw, but much broader; and with more of a belly of middle-age on him. His brows were soft and fine below the dome of his shaved head.

He drew his foot back as if to kick the corpse.

I made a jolting movement forward, and an inarticulate sound.

Rekhmire''s hand closed over my shoulder.

The Ambassador swung away from the body, leaving it untouched; spat another string of god-names that must be curses, and glared at Rekhmire'. 'If he hadn't struggled, it wouldn't have killed him!'

Cold sweat covered my skin.

'Who *wouldn't* struggle?' Rekhmire''s mild tone held an acid edge. 'Who wouldn't run? Menmet – Pamiu—'

He spoke the second word in the tone of a nickname. I suddenly understood: They know each other well.

'—How much trouble will this mean?'

Menmet-Ra let out an explosive sigh. 'Precisely as much as you think!'

'Well, then . . . ' Rekhmire''s face altered; I knew him well enough to know he was thinking fast and deeply.

Menmet-Ra glared up at the half-painted marble face of the golem. 'It was a precaution! To stop it being stolen! To stop *itself* being stolen. It should have held onto a thief. Who would have dreamed that the *painter* . . . '

Rekhmire' lifted his head, looking at the Ambassador. 'You go, Pamiu. Send your men away. Nothing was seen; nothing was heard. I'll clear up here myself.'

If I'd had emotion enough left to have been surprised, I would have felt shock. I stared dumbly as Rekhmire' and Menmet-Ra conversed quickly, in low tones, and parted, each with a grip to the forearm of the other.

The servants and soldiers vanished so quietly they might never have existed.

All this Alexandrine-decorated Roman mansion could have been drowned in sleep – except that, stupefied as I was, even I could sense the tension quivering in the air. The haste for the body to be dealt with, a scandal to be averted.

My knees loosened.

I went down on the tiles with a thump, beside Masaccio's body. Reaching out, I drew the improvised shroud more neatly over his face.

That shifted the cloth, exposing his hand.

I took it in mine and sat holding the still-warm flesh.

'Ilario.'

I did not look up. 'I thought . . . I know we joked . . . I thought you were a book-buyer who just carried messages, sometimes, or wrote – observations. You're . . . more, aren't you?'

'I am a man of some experience. And an old friend of Menmet-Ra.' Rekhmire' rested his hand on my shoulder, conveying reassurance, warmth. 'At the university, we called him "Pamiu", "Old Tom-Cat" . . .'

The smile in his voice faded.

'If Pamiu must take official notice of this, there'll be scandal. Who knows what, then, will be uncovered? Better if it's handled out of sight.'

I squeezed Masaccio's cooling fingers hard enough that it would have hurt him, had he lived. These hands, these very hands, with which he painted—

'Because the golem *murdered* him? *That* will be a scandal?'

'Politics.' Rekhmire' spoke with a deliberation that acknowledged grief, while he himself stood aside from it. His heavy lids shrouded his eyes, and lifted again. 'In Carthage, they translate "Lord-Amir" as "scientist-magus". This is a political matter. According to Pamiu, the stone golem is their gift, and it shouldn't be known to have passed through Rome on its way to Alexandria-in-exile.'

'Carthage *again*.' The irony bit hard.

'As matters stand, Rome should not be *seen* to be friendly either to Carthage or to "Constantinople".' Rekhmire' used the foreigners' name for his own city with distaste. 'I have friends in many of the Alexandrine embassies,' he added. 'People gossip. It is not ever difficult to know what must be going on.'

Stunned, dizzy, I said, 'Masaccio's *dead*. That thing murdered him!'

Rekhmire' touched the icy hand of the stone golem. It gave me equal chills.

The Egyptian said, 'If I understand rightly, it has no will of its own. It no more murdered this man than the runaway cart which kills a child in the street.'

'*He was a genius.*'

My voice came back flatly from the walls. I hadn't realised I was shouting.

'There's *never* been a painter like him; now it's all – gone.'

'Painter. Yes.' Rekhmire''s gaze for a moment seemed absent. 'Let me see . . . Mastro Masaccio was painting a triptych, wasn't he? For Cardinal Valente. So one, at least, of the cardinals will be interested in his death.'

His gaze sharpened as he caught my eye.

'It would be – better – if the Conclave of Cardinals weren't drawn towards this embassy. Or towards Alexandria. Or Carthage. It would be *best* if Master Tommaso Cassai had died a natural death.'

A flash of memory put the living Masaccio before my eyes. Lips drawn back. Spine arched. Held out at arm's length, by a stone statue.

I swallowed. Between my hands, his flesh still held tepid warmth. But it felt too soft, with none of the tension of muscle that belongs to a living man.

Carefully, I placed Masaccio's useless hand back down at his side. 'I don't like the idea of hiding this. Masaccio's dead! Someone ought to—'

'Pay?' Rekhmire' prompted gently.

'Why did this happen!'

My cry went unanswered. Rekhmire' shook his head. I had a sudden flash of memory, of Hanno Anagastes, whose house looked so like this one, speaking to me in the graveyard of children. 'You should remember,' he said, 'that punishments do not need a reason.'

Later, I wondered if he had been speaking of the 'punishment' of living in a body that is both man and woman. Some things have no reason, they only are.

And yet Masaccio *did* this, I realised. If ignorance killed him, still, he chose to act.

With the sensation of Masaccio's dead skin still imprinted on mine, I must force myself to be calm. To think. Because something must be done, done now, and what will it be?

Do I stay here with Rekhmire' and his people? Do I run out into the Roman streets and call for the Watchmen? Tell the cardinals?

The golem is only a machine.

And will it do good for men to know that Masaccio died a thief?

I looked down at his motionless fingers.

'What would be true justice here . . . isn't clear to me.' Slowly, feeling all the pain of my bruises, I got to my feet. 'This is too much. Too sudden. But I'll tell you one thing I can think of. Masaccio wouldn't want his name associated with scandal.'

I looked up at the Egyptian who was no longer my master.

'If people heard he was a thief – that Mastro Masaccio had been killed while doing something criminal – that might smear the New Art. I know what he'd think. That patrons might then not want to buy paintings from artists who are following his techniques. Because men are fools. And everything he's worked for; how he tried to reform painting, re-birth it – would be dead. Gone. The New Art would be . . . finished.'

In the periphery of my sight, the golem's blank white eyes stared without knowledge or remorse.

'I'm hardly impartial,' I said. 'But . . . I don't think I can let that happen.'

17

I had no need to uncover Masaccio's face. The blue, crushed, swollen flesh was imprinted in detail in my mind. I glanced around the room; then back at Rekhmire'.

'How can we make *this* look like a natural death!'

Rekhmire' frowned. 'I don't know.'

'You don't *know?*'

His lip twitched. If a man had not lain dead on the floor beside us, I think it would have been a smile, if blackly sardonic.

'You expect much of me, Ilario. This isn't easy . . . Help me put him on that.' Rekhmire' nodded at the flat-bed cart.

'*What?*'

'Would it be the first time a man's been brought home drunk from the taverna like this? On his own cart?' The Egyptian shook his head, answering his own rhetorical questions. 'Whatever we do, first we must take him away from here. Quickly.'

I nodded, and knelt. Masaccio's cheek felt colder. But still soft. Bodies stiffen some time after death.

The water-clock chimed.

It's not an *hour*, yet!

How can I believe he's dead?

It felt almost as if, should I sufficiently refuse to believe it, Masaccio might *not* be dead. All this might yet resolve into some nightmare delusion.

But that false hope often accompanies sudden death.

As if he still breathed, I gently eased my hands under Masaccio's armpits, waiting for Rekhmire' to lift him at the knees.

We put him on the hand-cart. Rekhmire' reached out to shift his limbs. I protested; cut myself off. The Egyptian arranged Masaccio's body on its side, cloak-hood drawn across to shelter the blue, bruised face.

With the macabre humour that comes with death, I felt a terrible grin stretching at my mouth. 'He *does* look dead drunk, not dead.'

'The Eight grant the Watch think so, if we meet them!'

The handles of the cart moved easily as I lifted them. Iron wheel-rims gritted over rush mats laid down on the way out of the room.

I didn't turn my head to look back at the stone golem.

Let it stay half painted: half-statue and half-man. It's all the monument Mastro Tommaso Cassai will have.

There was no rain outside. The air was damp and clear. A swollen moon hung high enough to guide us in the fetid alleys.

The cart makes it too easy, I thought. He should be more of a weight.

This is not how he expected to come home. Nor the burden he expected this cart to bear.

'We *might* claim he died of plague.' Rekhmire' spoke quietly, walking beside me. 'That would keep people from viewing the body . . . But a Roman physician would need to sign the certificate. No physician can look at him. There's no disguising an evident death by violence—'

'Murder.' My bare hands clenched on the cold wood. A sudden jolt went through me. 'Master – Rekhmire' – I've just realised! There'll be witnesses to say that he and I quarrelled. People will say, Masaccio loved the girl first . . . There'll be enough gossip to make us enemies; justify me having battered Masaccio to death. *I* could be accused of his murder. Easily!'

Rekhmire' shot me a glance from those oval, dark eyes. Even by the guttering light of the one embassy torch, I could read his agreement.

'I want to *grieve* for him!' I exclaimed. 'Not to have to think of – of . . . '

'Yes, I understand. But we must think of it all.'

This is all I can do for him now. Save his reputation.

The workshop door was locked.

Masaccio wore his purse tied to his belt. I felt inside for the key. My fingers brushed against his bare wrist as I withdrew my hand. His flesh felt cold as Carrara marble to the touch. Stiff, stuck in one position, undignified, absurd.

Yes, he *is* dead. I don't want to believe it, but he is.

Hot water tracked a single runnel down my cheek.

'All that skill, lost. The first *painter* for eighty years—' I couldn't keep my voice male-sounding, or level. 'He won't paint anything else.'

The workshop doors creaked as Rekhmire' opened them. He came and took the cart handles from my hands, pushing the vehicle quickly inside. I saw how the moon's light cast shadows from each individual cobblestone paving the street. Masaccio might have been able to paint that tenuous, deceptive light.

'His brother!' I exclaimed. I kicked the door closed as I followed Rekhmire' in. 'Giovanni Cassai! He went back to Florence, a few weeks ago. He'll have to be told. He can't get here in time for the funeral, but . . . '

My thoughts outraced my words.

Rekhmire' gave me a keen look and prompted me. 'Yes?'

'Wait . . . '

I looked around the shadowy workshop: at tables, easels, pestles, stacked boards and canvases. The crate upon which I had sat to be Judas negotiating with the traitorous officers of Mithras.

Masaccio didn't know he was leaving all this for the last time tonight.

I pushed the thought aside.

'I think I begin to see . . . It's not important what he died of. Plague, accident. Whatever lie. What's important is that no one *sees* him; that he's buried. Quickly. Yes?'

Rekhmire' nodded. 'But I gather he's not unknown in the city, and without a physician to certify the death—'

'I know a priest who'll bury him without one.'

'You do?' Rekhmire' looked startled. 'How can you be certain this priest won't merely report a murder?'

'Friar Sebastian married me, illegally, to an Etruscan woman.' I shrugged. 'And so he's susceptible to . . . '

The Egyptian had no hesitation in completing the thought bluntly. 'Blackmail.'

18

The smell of newly-turned earth is pleasant in spring, when planting crops. Although life in Rodrigo's court has not led me to have much more experience of it than watching other men strew seeds from their aprons.

In grey autumn, turned earth is merely clammy and cold. And it smells of corpses.

That thought might have been imagination.

The dawn wind blowing across the churchyard would have brought tears to my eyes even had I not had cause to weep.

Friar Sebastian did not gabble. He read with haste, undoubtedly, but still with a gravitas that gave Tommaso Cassai his due. Grave-diggers stood back towards the wall of the church. A scant half-dozen of Mastro Tommaso Cassai's Roman neighbours stood in front of Rekhmire' and I, around the foot of the grave. I did not know how gossip had brought them the early news, but it had. As his apprentice, I had been commiserated with on his sad, accidental death. Rumour differed as to whether it might have been a stroke brought on by drink, a fall in his workshop, or sudden illness.

I let my grief shelter me from any importunate questions.

This burial is just barely in time.

The prayers were unfamiliar in form, although much the same in content as I would have heard in Taraco: Judge this soul mercifully, and let the cold earth lie easily on him.

Under cover of the Frankish priest's intonation, Rekhmire' murmured, 'Your friar would be unwilling to do this, I think, were he not aware that we are about to leave Rome.'

'"Leave"?' I stared blankly.

'What else?' Rekhmire' had his gaze fixed on the coffin. 'Disruptive as that may be, we *must* go.'

'But Honorius is coming back here. We *came* here to hide from Videric and Carthage—'

'We came here because Rome was your painter's Grail-Castle.' Rekhmire' seemed at home with the Frankish metaphor. He kept his tone low. 'And now Rome's a place where Carthage and Alexandria are about to have a quarrel that will spread beyond their embassies, and involve the city authorities. The cardinals know my name. If they hear the name of the painter's apprentice, when they speak to the embassy . . . Too great a likelihood that Carthage will hear that my slave is in Rome.'

Now he did shoot a glance my way, his eyes bright with the cold wind, and his expression a complex mixture of grief, irony, and annoyance.

'Tommaso Cassai was an impetuous fool,' Rekhmire' said, his voice low. 'Which even you won't deny, Ilario. Do you think this friar would give in to threats of exposure *unless* we were leaving? It's that which makes this the easiest way out of the situation for him.'

Rekhmire''s forehead creased in concentration.

'I'll need to pass the Turkish document over to Cardinal Corradeo, or I doubt he'll allow me to go. I'll visit the Vatican immediately after the funeral's over. Can I rely on you to find us a boat for Ostia Antica?'

Leaving Rome?

The thought made me blink against the sliver of unbearable fire that was the rising sun. Shadows fell out of the east. I could have painted three of us about the grave: priest, eunuch, and another who is not a man. For better composition, I would have Friar Sebastian move to *there* . . .

No composition. No Masaccio. No apprenticeship. What is there to keep me in Rome?

Rekhmire' whispered urgently, 'I know you are no longer my slave, but will you pack belongings for both of us?'

The world snapped into focus around me.

'I can't leave.'

'*Can't* leave? When you could be arrested for murder?'

'What about my *wife*?'

Rekhmire' stared at me.

'I can't leave Sulva!' I made a movement somewhere between a shrug and a shiver, in the freezing morning air. 'Maybe . . . She liked the idea of travel. Maybe she'll be willing to leave Rome. But I have no money—'

Rekhmire' waved a dismissive hand. 'This woman. You're not legally married, you said?'

The third night is tonight, I realised.

'No, not until tonight, by their law. But I gave my word; I'm married in my eyes. *Yes,*' I got in, before Rekhmire' could interrupt, 'I have a lot to tell her! I will. She can do what she chooses, then, but— She *needs* to escape that prison of a house. I can't avoid that on a – a legal technicality.'

My heart beat out long, silent moments.

'That would mean not leaving until tonight. That's unwise. But—' Rekhmire' cut himself off.

A smile broke the monumental, forbidding surfaces of his face; out of place at a funeral.

'But that's not my decision, is it? Freedman. Freedwoman. *My* decision is only: will I wait for you, or will I leave now, alone?'

True as it was, I found it disconcerting.

'Ilario?'

I mentally shook myself, and looked up at the tall man by my side. 'What's your decision?'

He shrugged. 'I'll wait. The library will hide me a day longer – or so I must hope. Ilario, we must both stay out of sight. If the authorities arrest either of us, it will be of no use to appeal to the embassy. Pamiu can do nothing but disown me. And, now you are *not* my slave, he can do nothing for you; you're not an Alexandrine. We must be careful. And lucky. Ilario?'

I rubbed at the ridge of bone just under the skin of my brows. It felt tight. I touched the drying scab of blood where the golem's fingers had caught me, and winced.

Rekhmire' turned back to face the end of Friar Sebastian's praying. His murmur came softly to me:

'Inadvisable it may be – but I see that I will risk one more visit to my countrymen in the embassy. Injuries to the head are unpredictable. Potentially dangerous. You're hurt. I trust none of these Frankish butchers. You'll see a proper Alexandrine doctor before we leave.'

'Rekhmire'—'

'*No argument!*'

In the chill of the funeral, it was a moment's warmth.

19

The doctor, as it came about, was a short, round man – an essay in curves – with the confident manner of the professional physician. And while he nodded a greeting to Rekhmire' as to a friend, his eyes lit up when he saw me.

'This is Siamun,' Rekhmire' introduced me, folding his arms and leaning up against the Roman interior wall that some Egyptian hand had covered with cartouches.

'*This* is a professional consultation,' Siamun said, shooing him out through the door.

The physician Siamun prodded, poked; looked into my eyes; had me unlace my doublet and remove my shirt – *and* the bandages that bound my breasts. I did it all with no more than a sigh, rubbing my forehead against the insistent ache. He's a doctor: of course he will want to see this. What physician wouldn't? How many hermaphrodites will he see in his career?

It wouldn't have surprised me to see him taking notes.

'Your facial hair,' he murmured, 'it has been less dark than this, yes?'

I stared at him. 'It's my *head* that hurts.'

'But to answer the question?'

Sitting solely dressed in one's hose doesn't promote recalcitrance. My fingers were touching my cheek, I realised. Only a very little wispy hair. I had hoped it made disguise as a man more convincing. 'Yes, it's darkened, of late. My brows, too. I thought . . . I'm just growing older, yes?'

'And you perhaps have pains, here?' He reached down with a spatulate fingertip and tapped my knee. 'And other joints of the body?'

'Only when Masaccio makes me sit—' I began with a laugh; I ended in a reedy, thin croak. Constriction in my throat made it impossible to complete my words.

When Masaccio, who is *dead*, makes me sit for too long.

The doctor reached forward and took my right breast in his hand. He squeezed, firmly.

I yelped. 'What the hell—!'

'I apologise; I intended no hurt. Take off—' He gestured at my woollen hose, as if he couldn't find the Frankish word. 'Take off these, please.'

Not being laced to my doublet now, my hose were falling around my hips in any case. I finished their removal, and looked away as he felt at my belly, took my small penis in his hand, and then probed in with his fingers to find the cavity that lay behind it. The colours in the cartouches blurred. I stared as bas-reliefs of chariot warfare; winged gods; the fall of Old Alexandria to the Turks . . . Faces painted in profile, to the left or right; men's muscular chests painted face-on. Eyes elongated with kohl . . .

'Are you done yet?' I said harshly, self-conscious with the weight I'd put on eating Roman food. *My arse is truly a woman's, now!* 'Is looking at my belly-button going to tell you what's wrong with my cracked skull?'

Siamun straightened up from palpating my abdomen. His round, brown eyes fixed on me. 'Your skull is not cracked. Fortunately, you're bruised.'

You could have phrased that better!, I thought, grinning despite the pain in my head; but he hadn't finished.

'However,' he added, 'you are pregnant.'

20

The physical effects of shock are inescapable.

I learned that early on, being trained in the arts of hunting and war. A fall from a horse can leave you with more than pain or a cracked skull. The mind itself becomes stunned.

I have to see Sulva.

No lights showed at the barred windows of the Paziathe mansion.

Rekhmire''s hand at my elbow steadied me. Night had come. Clouds covered the full moon. No eye could distinguish detail below the roof-lines. I found myself too numb to realise, except vaguely, how lucky that was.

Rekhmire''s voice spoke in the dark. 'This will conceal us from passers-by.'

From time to time, as we walked here, Rekhmire' had spoken quietly to me; but by the time I worked out what he had said, the moment for answering seemed to have passed. I did not think he mentioned Carthage, or Videric, or the golem, but it might be that I just didn't hear.

How is it I didn't realise that things were worse than I knew?

'It was Marcomir.' I interrupted Rekhmire'. 'If I'm – if it's not far advanced—'

He echoed Siamun's words: 'Four months.'

'Then it has to be Marcomir. There hasn't . . . been . . . anybody . . . '

Rekhmire' touched my arm, his voice a breath. '*Look*. There.'

The darkness gave up a figure holding up a pierced iron lantern.

Rekhmire' murmured, 'Is it the right man?'

Chiaroscuro: a face in light and shadow. Illumination made a hollow darkness of the eye-sockets.

I remembered his features from St Mithras Viridianus. 'It's one of Sulva's cousins.'

Rekhmire' lifted his voice. 'The groom is injured. I am here to help.'

His air of authority quashed any possible question. The cousin gave an uncertain nod, and beckoned. He turned away from the direction of the mansion. Towards 'the villa in the trees'.

The night blurred in my eyes.

We must at some point have passed a gate and left the city of Rome. If there were watchmen, I didn't see how we avoided them. The Etruscans, the 'Rasna'; they must be used to doing this . . .

For a mile or more, I recognised the Via Aemilia: that ancient road that runs north the whole length of the Warring States. Paving stones were cold and slippery under my shoes.

Broken earth. A track.

I lifted my head to find that we walked under trees, off the road.

Sulva's cousin spoke tightly, his voice breaking the long silence. 'Follow that path.'

Where he pointed, a broad, well-trodden trackway went off between mature oaks. In summer, no light could have penetrated the leaf-canopy. Now, as the clouds began to shred, full moonlight shone intermittently down between the bare branches.

The Etruscan man folded his arms. He made no further move to accompany us.

Rekhmire''s hand gripped my forearm. I realised that he had taken the iron lantern; yellow light dazzled in the corner of my eye.

'I don't need help!' It came out more harshly than I intended.

'You are still uncertain, from the wound.' In the lantern's light, I saw him glance at my forehead.

'You needn't worry.' I attempted to sound conciliatory. There is no obligation on Rekhmire' to come here. 'But I need to get there *fast*.'

We walked a distance.

Twigs crackled under my feet.

The noise became submerged by sounds I felt I ought to recognise, but could only find both familiar and unknown. I frowned. Rekhmire' swore under his breath, missing his footing. I thought I heard the faint sound of a reed.

'*Music?*' I blurted out.

Rekhmire' gave a sharp, preoccupied nod. 'It must be the young woman.'

I thrust out of my mind the thought *How shall I tell her?*

Because, now we're near, if I think about that, I shall go back.

Ahead, the trees began to thin. I caught sight of a slope rising up in the distance, out of the wood. On it, something that might be a villa. Bare branches all but hid a sloping roof. Splotched pillars – because painted, I realised, but the moonlight is showing only black and white.

The thread of sound grew strong.

Rekhmire''s voice was no more than a whisper. 'That – I think that is an aulos. An Etruscan flute. What . . . ?'

I stepped between two oaks, and found myself entering a wide clearing. The double melody sounded stronger.

Over it, regular, rhythmic grunts echoed through the frosty air. Deep, echoing sound. Music . . .

Branches creaked behind me in the wind. The remainder of the cloud-cover shredded away from the moon. Silver light splashed every leaf and twig, every bramble, every frost-curled fern. The moon hung full-bellied

166

enough to make me wince, until the sight before me wiped that thought away.

I shuddered to a halt, staring.

'Sulva's come out to meet me . . . '

She is not alone.

'Kek and Keket and all the *Eight*!' Rekhmire' exclaimed.

Sulva stood in the centre of the clearing, perhaps thirty feet away. She held a double-piped flute to her lips. Two strands of melody wove in the moonlight. A mantle draped her shoulders; tiny braids kept her flowing hair back from her eyes.

Ten or twelve giant wild boars clustered around her.

They rootled beside the skirts of her long pleated tunic, their pointed ears flicking each time the melody altered. *Wild boars.* Not the small, black shapes of domestic pigs – what trampled the leaf-mould in the clearing ahead of me was huge, lean, and razor-backed, with curved tusks glinting in the moonlight.

Men call that light deceptive, but it was clear enough for me to see the testicles hanging between their back legs, and the breath rising up from their mouths. As they passed in front of her, their shaggy shoulders stood as high as Sulva's breast.

I breathed out. 'I don't believe . . . '

The boar is the most dangerous beast of the hunt; its ferocity and bad temper make it a favourite among heraldic devices. Here are no horses, no men, no weapons. Here is only a sixteen-year-old girl. And, if we were this close, ordinary boar would attack. They would have attacked *her* before now . . .

Rekhmire' spoke as if we sat in our lodgings over a scroll. 'As I recall, there is a legend attached to the aulos. That the Etruscans could play it skilfully enough to entice wild boar out of the hills, and bring them tame to the huntsman.'

Sulva lowered the flute from her lips. She slid it into a fold of her mantle, and from another fold brought out something white. Bread, I saw.

Her eyes bright, she offered the food in her hands; her gaze fixed on the beasts.

The wild boars gruntled. They reached up their snouts to her, and took old crusts from her fingers with the greatest gentleness.

'Sulva.' My voice came out a squeaky croak.

Her head lifted; her glance went past the Egyptian without pause. '*Ilario!*'

The boar furthest from her – and closest to me – swivelled his head around, staring. The gaze of his tiny wicked eye jolted me.

He turned his head back towards the nearest tree, and took a branch the size of a man's wrist between his jaws. Effortlessly, he bit down.

A sharp *crack!* sounded as the living wood split in two.

I shut my eyes.

The golem's closing hand.

Masaccio's face.

'Ilario . . . '

Sulva stood alone. Silent, but for the suck of mud against sharp trotters, the wild boar were moving away, fading into the moonlit trees at the clearing's edge.

Stumbling on the black, broken earth; pushing my way between the silver arcs of brambles; I closed the distance between she and I.

Sulva smiled.

It was painful; strained; embarrassed.

'What—' I started. 'Why—?'

'This.'

She pointed at moonlit stones I had not noticed buried in the bracken.

'This is the boundary. Beyond here is the villa in the trees. If you pass . . . '

Human feet sucked out of the mud. Rekhmire' came forward to stand by my shoulder, his sandals encrusted with wet churned dirt. He suddenly stilled.

I followed his gaze, downwards.

A flash of white.

Sulva's tunic was kilted up, to be out of the freezing mud. On one foot she wore a patten over her slipper, as before. The other—

The other shone white as an animal's pelt shines in moonlight.

She stepped forward on her perfect goat's foot.

I could only stare.

She ignored the fact that I was not alone. As if she had tensed herself to speak, and could let nothing stop her now, she blurted out, 'I prayed to the Christian priests for healing! They perform small miracles, sometimes. I thought . . . '

Her beautiful voice came clearly through the frost-bitten air:

'But I didn't receive Grace. Only a glamour that makes this seem to be a club-foot when I'm not in the forest.'

The moonlight shone undeniably on her.

Miracles.

Grace.

Glamour.

Frankish superstition!

I shook my head; laughed out loud; clapped my hands over my mouth. Just another strange occurrence – and how can I protest that, when I'm already one myself? As well be born with an animal's foot as the organs of both man and woman—

Rekhmire''s hand closed on my shoulder. 'Ilario.'

'I understand what this is. Sulva's . . . come to give me a choice. Haven't you?'

She gazed up at me. 'We are the Rasna,' she whispered. The people of Etruria. We're *old*. And these things happen in our families. The Christians' legends of satyrs . . . Will it matter to you so much?'

'Sulva . . . ' I could barely speak.

'Only your people consider us married. We have yet to lie together.'

She means we have yet to lie in bed, in bodily communion.

I felt my mouth twist. 'No, there's been lies between us. Believe me!'

Whatever the truth of her disfigurement is, she has come to warn me. To give me a chance to back out of this marriage. Because she is honest. While I . . .

Reaching out, I took her cold, crumb-dusted hands in mine.

They are still warmer than the dead.

'I have to tell you something,' I said.

She parted her lips slightly, as if she would have protested, but said nothing. No man could have painted her.

'No man could paint the moonlight on your face,' I said aloud. 'And I am no man. Sulva, I have to explain, tell you; somehow. I'm not a man. Or, I *am* – but not in the way you think I am.'

Her pupils contracted and expanded as moonlight varied between the clouds. '*Not* a – I don't—'

The confusion in her voice flayed me.

She frowned. 'Are you like your master? Him, there, beside you? A gelded man?'

I glanced back at Rekhmire', and saw in the dim lantern light that his expression was wretched, as if he hurt for me.

I shook my head hurriedly. 'Not my master, my friend. But in any case, no. I'm not a eunuch.'

'You're not a *woman*—'

'No! Yes! Sulva!'

My hold on her hands tightened. She gasped. I loosed her slightly.

'Listen.' I could barely get words out. The shock that numbed me at the Alexandrine embassy thawed – and I regretted it. I would sooner be numb, for this.

I shivered in the cold moonlight and frost.

'This is a night for myths, it seems. Have you heard of Hermaphroditus? The nymph Salmacis loved him, and Zeus answered her prayers by making them one flesh, man and woman joined in the same body. But this isn't a myth. I'm hermaphrodite. I'm both man and woman. I have the body of each.'

Sulva blinked, as if I had dazed her with a blow. 'I don't understand.'

I folded my fingers tightly around Sulva's. Pain coursed through my body.

'There's more. I must tell you it all. Listen to me! You know that I've been travelling. When I was in Carthage . . . In Carthage, I went to bed with a man. A man called Marcomir.'

'You're telling me you're a boy-lover? A sodomite?' She still looked beautiful when she was puzzled.

This is not something I ever wanted to say to my wife.

'Sulva. I'm telling you that I'm pregnant.'

She took her hands out of mine and put them over her face, and wailed like a child.

I did not wail – her grief was not mine to interrupt – but I wept.

21

'Is it true?' Aranthur Paziathe demanded.

The pictures on the walls of the villa were yellow, red, gold. Green ferns. Blue fountain-water. Either painted, or put on in mosaic. Men in primitive togas, dancing with their hands high. Pale naked girls in forests. Augurs before altars. Haruspices painted looking into the entrails of birds. The figures all drawn to depict, not what a man sees, but what a man knows is there.

The feet all pointing down.

'Tell me! *Is it true?*' Aranthur shouted.

'Oh, it's true! I've seen!' Sulva's eyes seemed literally to flash. In another frame of mind, I could have wished to capture the effect in wax and pigment.

'Yes,' I said. She has seen.

It had not been how I had imagined being in her bedchamber would be.

In her painted rooms, in this hidden villa, she assumed a brittle attitude that we were all girls, and so I might as well undress and show what I was.

Sulva frowned deeply, shaking her head. 'She's got a belly on her. *He* has. Not so big, but how he didn't *notice*—' She turned on me. 'Didn't your *bleeding* stop?'

I saw Aranthur wince at the mention of women's mysteries. Rekhmire' told me Etruscan women had freedom, in ancient times; I caught the echo of it in Aranthur's daughter's speech.

'Bleeding has never been a regular occurrence for me.' I felt cold, as if the house's warmth couldn't penetrate the night's frost. 'I thought – the travelling – the change of city – I'm sorry.'

Her hand flashed out. Her small palm cracked across my face.

Rekhmire' stirred, where he leaned against the wall by the door.

I shook my head, warning him back. A bruise on the cheek is hardly sufficient recompense for what I've done to her. It seems there are some hurts I can't cure.

Aranthur grated, 'Monstrous! A man, *pregnant*. A woman who's a man. Sulva, leave the room.'

He stood up from his high-backed oak chair. Simultaneously she stepped away.

Before I could protest what that told me – that, like other fathers now, Etruscans have come to beat their daughters – she noisily began to weep. 'I will *not!*

The room felt oppressive, the ceiling low for a single-storey building. The windows opened only out into the central courtyard. Just outside, folding chairs stood under the colonnade of pillars. I had an urge to walk out there; to find the forest; to run.

He turned on me. '*You.*'

'I lied,' I admitted, before he could choke out anything else. 'I'm sorry. She's still virgin. She can marry—'

His expression stopped me.

'We have to abide by Rome's legal code.' Aranthur began to pace. 'That is the bargain made in Alaric's day. By Rome's law, my daughter is married to you. So it doesn't matter that by Rasna law she's still unmarried and virgin.'

The room was dominated by a long dining table; not polished, but covered in bright embroidered linen. He left his own chair and walked down past the length of the table, and paused with his hands resting on the back of another chair.

Aranthur's own throne-style wooden chair, carved all over with acorns and galls, stood at the head of the table, like the Romans who supplanted them. *Pater familias*, head of the house. All the other chairs were made out of curving slats, with a leather seat.

He rested his brown gnarled hands on the chair-back and gazed at me. 'Do you *know* what would have happened, if you had married Sulva by Roman and Etruscan law?'

All the answers I could think of were mere lists of disaster. I shook my head.

He pulled the chair back towards himself, and looked down at it for a moment.

I noted without in the least wishing to that the interlocking curved slats were beechwood, polished with linseed oil; that the shapes of air between the parts would make an excellent drawing exercise.

'You would have taken her away,' Aranthur said quietly. 'Even if you had never left Rome, you would have taken her away from *us*. That happens so often in this generation . . . She would never have come back. It would have swallowed her. She would have dressed as a Roman matron, not a *puia* – a wife. She would have prayed at a Roman church.'

I started to correct him, and stopped. If the details are here and there inaccurate, the picture is nonetheless true to life.

'She would never have associated with her family, after that,' Aranthur said. 'There would have been an empty chair at this table. It's our custom. We would have kept it for her. To remind us.'

I repeated, inadequately, 'I'm sorry.'

'*That's* what you're sorry for?' His head lifted; his eyes met mine. 'Sulva would have been *safe.*'

I stared.

He jabbed a finger at me. 'Not one of us, not part of this family any longer, no; not part of our people – but *safe*. And we would have honoured that, and sorrowed for it, with an empty chair here. Because I . . .'

His voice broke.

'I would have known that next time there were rumours of Etruscans poisoning wells, or Etruscan merchants cheating their Christian customers, or the city fathers needing a scapegoat and the Inquisition needing bodies for burning – *Sulva would have been safe*. As a Christian wife, a Christian mother. Not Rasna; not part of our *lautun*, our family. Lost to me. But safe.'

His hands slammed palm-down on the back of the chair.

'And in time, I would have added *another* chair, for the Etruscan husband who would never sit at this table! And then *more* chairs, on feast days, for the children she would never bring back here. In time, how many chairs would I put out for grandchildren?'

His torrent left me speechless.

'But you are *not* the young Christian man you made yourself out to be.' Aranthur Paziathe clenched his fists. 'You are not "he". And so she is *not* safe.'

My head felt clear. Pain will do that, sometimes. 'I'm sorry I lied. I will do what I can—'

'What *can* you do?' The old man pointed at my stomach. 'You have a *child* there. And you a man! And it a bastard!'

I let that one pass.

'Sulva can still be safe. It's as I tried to explain. Mastro Masaccio is dead, and I'm leaving Rome. If Sulva comes with me, I'll look after her—'

He slammed both hands down again on the carved back of the chair. 'You? What life can *you* have? You'll always be what you are! Sooner or later, men will know that. What life can she have with a— But no. No. I am not the bad father you think me. Ask her what she wants. Ask Sulva!'

He stamped across the room to his daughter, ignoring how Rekhmire' stepped fluidly back out of his way. He swung Sulva around.

His shout ricocheted off the illustrated walls. 'What do you want out of this?'

Sulva lifted her chin. Her eyes had red rims. Her skin showed pallid in some places, and blotchy in others. No man on earth would pay me to lay those colours on her statue.

That she should look that way, because of me, wrenched at my gut.

Abrupt, Aranthur demanded, 'Do you still wish to marry this man?'

She gazed about the room as if blind – a *lautun* room, I thought, remembering Aranthur's word. Where the family comes together. Where they can be what they are, themselves, instead of hiding, as in Rome.

I spoke to her. 'I'll look after you. As I promised. You – need not be wife in anything but name.'

'In name?'

Sulva swung around, staring.

'I thought you wanted to *marry* me.' Her eyes brimmed over: water ran in quick streaks down her face. 'Don't you love me? I thought you fell in love with me!'

Stupid as wood and fog, I said, 'I thought you wanted to escape. I thought you needed rescue.'

The room held absolute silence.

'"Rescue"!' Aranthur ended his pacing around the table back at his chair. He sat down suddenly, seemingly swallowed by the polished oak throne. 'A man my age has grown too old for the kindness of the gods. "Love". "Escape". "Rescue"!'

'This is my *family*.' Sulva sounded bewildered. 'Why would I need rescue? They love me. Even as I am. Ilario, I thought, you . . . '

Aranthur, brown face pulled by strain, spoke as if to himself. 'You Romans, you call it the *disciplina etrusca*. The sacred books. The *Libri Fatales*. They tell the truth of it! An old man is a body with barely a soul in it. This is my punishment, for having a daughter when I was already old.'

Punishments come for no reason.

With my gaze fixed on Sulva, I said, 'I'm not a Roman. Nor am I a punishment.'

I forced the configuration of my body out of my mind.

'I will do what I can for Sulva and for you: I swear it.'

'What can *you* do!'

Rekhmire''s sonorous tenor broke in. 'More than sit lamenting foolishly about "punishment", for one thing!'

I startled. 'We agreed – this is my business to settle.'

'Oh, so it is, it is.' He waved a large hand, and resumed leaning against a mural of a god springing from a furrow. 'But not for nothing do the Romans call the Rasenna the most superstitious men on earth!'

I turned back to Sulva. 'You're the most beautiful thing I've ever seen. Even with your foot. It seemed such a crime to keep you locked up in that old house.'

I broke off, sick at my stomach, watching how she looked at me.

'And as to love . . . Sulva . . . I knew you wouldn't want me.'

'"Want"? *Want?*'

Her expression changed, features tensing in a scorn that was absolute. 'I *want* a husband. Who loves me! Not some freak—'

'Aren't you a freak, too?'

It was no attack on her, only pain. My heart hammered, and my pulse all but blinded me.

'Your foot— Shouldn't that make you . . . shouldn't you feel *more* sympathetic? Because of that? And because your people are persecuted?'

'"That"?'

She looked down at her skirts, then up at me. 'That's why I want a normal husband! Isn't it all the more reason why I should want someone normal?'

She clenched small fists in front of her.

'I didn't ask to be like born this! I didn't ask to be born Rasna! And you – I wanted *children*—' She cut me off, before I could speak, with biting scorn. '*My* children!'

I followed her gaze, down. I had done, without knowing it, what I have seen women do: put my hand flat over my belly, as if I protected what was inside.

Sulva sounded shrill. 'You'll give birth to monsters. And father monsters on *me*! I'm sick with being called a monster because I'm Etruscan; I don't want a double burden!'

I held up both hands, watching her anger abate a fraction. 'What *do* you want?'

She changed in an instant; as cold as the ice on the brown, dead oak leaves outside. 'I want you to go away, Ilario. If you're missing for seven years, the Romans will have you legally declared dead, and I can re-marry.'

So many emotions crowded her face: spite, malice, hurt, hatred, and grief. I understood every one of them.

'And I don't want to waste time,' she added, caustically. 'The seven years can start now. Tonight. Just *go*. Man-woman!'

This is because she thought I loved her.

And if I were to claim, now, that I *do* love her, this pique would disappear. And she'd think she can forgive me.

Very careful in my words, I said, 'Sulva, we could still appear to be a family. You, I, and the child. You *must* want to get away from this life.'

'You don't understand our ways.' Blurry-eyed, bewildered, she glared at me and wept. Her contorted face seared me. I have put those colours there.

So I will have no family. It seared me. I put the thought of my own body out of my mind, and turned to face the old man. 'I will do *anything* I can. I swear it.'

'You've done enough, girl!' White showed around Aranthur's eyes. I saw the realisation come to him. 'You have! You've brought everything down on us! The painter, dead – questions— All this will come out— They'll trace you to us—'

'Then let me help!'

'No.' Aranthur's hands closed over the ends of the chair-arms, knuckles whitening against the patina of ancient polish. 'We must shut up the villa; move from the Roman house to the one in— And you, you can't help. You can't even help yourself!'

Spite and malice flickered in the deep creases of his expression.

'You're a monster carrying a child. The *Libri ostentaria* talks of such things. Even if you *could* carry the bastard to term, it would kill you when you came to birth it. You leave us to our troubles, she-male! You'll be too busy finding a back-alley abortionist.'

22

Silvery scales collect on unwashed human skin.

I picked with a fingernail at my swollen ankle. The thought surfaced: I should do something about this.

Bathe? The mental comment had something of Rekhmire''s acerbic tone about it. It stirred my sluggish mind.

Footsteps sounded on the dhow's deck, and the flap of the makeshift canvas shelter lifted. For a moment, I didn't look up. The water- and wind-scoured planks held a grain whose pattern I could trace in patches of sunlight, losing thought for hours. Now, only faint light from the outside shifted with the lift and swell of the sea.

A weight settled on the palliasse beside me. 'We're in for ill weather, they tell me.'

Rekhmire' rested his heavy arm around my shoulder.

Whether it was the comfort a man offers a man, or the comfort a man offers a woman . . . Rekhmire''s tenor might have belonged to a deep-voiced woman if I closed my eyes.

After a moment, something unclenched inside me.

I shifted, albeit awkward and ungainly, stared forward, and looked out of the shelter at the Adriatic. The cloth walls made all converging vertical lines, leading the eye towards the small opening. Outside, I saw the dhow's wet rigging. And a ship's rail that rose up above the horizon and fell below it. A sky the colour of a three-day-old bruise.

'How far are we from land?'

The Egyptian shrugged, which movement sent a tremor through me also. 'Too far to reach a port, or so the sailors say. Apparently we may run before this storm.'

Rekhmire''s hand closed loosely over the ball of my shoulder; his fingers large enough to encompass it. Had I been intending to draw anything, the Egyptian's hands would have been a suitable subject.

'Well, then.' He drew a breath. 'You will remember the Turkish document? I took it to Vittorio, Cardinal Corradeo, as we were leaving.'

'What . . . ?'

It was so poorly transparent an attempt to distract me – and from *this* man – that I must respond, despite myself, out of embarrassment and charity.

'What . . . happened? Is the Empty Chair to be cured?'

Rekhmire''s eyelashes flickered. I could all but see the other image form behind the lens of his eye with those words. Aranthur Paziathe, his hands gripping carved oak-wood—

Hurriedly, I said, 'And we can expect another Frankish pope, can we?'

'Not in my lifetime!'

'No?'

I met his gaze for the first time in many days, conscious of something other than numb misery and fog. Roused by his trivialities – by his design. I braced myself for the effort to reply:

'It wasn't true? The Turk wasn't truly there for the Prophet's death? Or . . . his scroll was a forgery? Or . . . knowing the words of the curse . . . doesn't help?'

Rekhmire''s unconscious shifting of body with ship, and the ship moving with the water, seemed soothing.

'If there *is* any such thing as a curse,' he remarked. 'But no, that's not why. Cardinal Corradeo took it away to be prayed over.'

A certain cynicism in his tone implied I ought to know why he phrased that so.

'He's a cardinal,' I objected, almost roused to asperity, had I sufficient strength. 'He's *supposed* to pray about things! What makes you think he isn't going to revoke the curse? And do – whatever the Conclave of Cardinals do when they elect a new pope?'

Rekhmire' smiled whimsically. 'Do you know where the Franks get their cardinals from, now?'

My ankle itched: I scratched at it again.

'From among bishops?'

'No. The death of all those popes discouraged men from Episcopal ambition. Only your Iberian and North African church *has* bishops, now. And the Franks would never elect a heretic bishop as pope . . . '

Rekhmire' held up a long dirty finger:

'The Franks have, these many years, depended on abbots to run their church. I'll tell you where they get their cardinals. Since they have no bishops, they rely on *abbots*, retired from their monasteries – "Cardinal Corradeo" was "Abbot Vittorio", not so many years ago.'

It began to concern me that my thoughts were so fog-ridden.

'Rekhmire', have we got any food?'

Rekhmire' leaned forward and bellowed through the open canvas flap to one of the crew. I felt a sudden and new desire for water. Or ale, or bread. Cheese. Solid plain food.

'So the cardinals used to be abbots. And . . . ' I paused expectantly.

Rekhmire' sat back, and left one hand resting heavily on my shoulder. 'And – they have absolutely *no* interest in putting any man on Peter's Chair who will bring back the bishops! The abbots control the Frankish church. They desire it no other way. As for the College of Cardinals –

electing one of the cardinals pope would mean one of them gaining more power than the others. So they prefer things exactly as they are.'

It had the feel of machinations at the court of Taraconensis. The familiarity was both nostalgic and ironic.

'So "prayed over" means "quietly taken away and lost"?'

'Corradeo has his reasons.' Rekhmire' waved his free hand illustratively. 'Decentralised power is obviously best. Look at Carthage and the Arian heresy. *They* have bishops – and they have the Penitence! Obviously God made a *felix culpa* out of Gundobad's curse, and is protecting the Frankish lands from the evils of Episcopal power . . . Or so the Cardinal says.'

My chest hurt. Wonderingly, I realised I had laughed. 'So, you having unearthed an eye-witness account . . . '

'Corradeo was remarkably happy to hear that I was on my way out of Rome, and not liable to return.'

Rekhmire' shook his head, chuckling.

'He can have a sub-committee of the other cardinals pray confidentially over this. It'll take them years, and the scroll will still be suppressed at the end of it. However, Corradeo did allow me a copy – on the firm understanding that I lose it in some dusty corner of the Royal Library, where no Christian scholar will ever look for it. It's not scholarship as I know it. But it does lead to original sources being preserved, rather than destroyed. Will you eat?'

Startled, I realised one of the Macedonian captain's crew-members squatted outside the deck-tent, balancing on the lifting and falling planks. I nodded thanks, and took the dark bread and ale. My movement disturbed the long shift I wore for warmth, and I realised how much it would benefit from rinsing, even if sea-water would make it scratchy against my skin.

Blackly, I thought, *Who else but I should wear a penitential shirt?*

Not Sulva Paziathe. Not Tommaso Cassai.

'And besides,' Rekhmire' added, pouring ale from a lidded pewter jug, 'Cardinal Corradeo is happy because, in the absolute meaning of the word, he need not lie if someone asks for the document to study. The Vatican library *doesn't* have a copy.'

Through a mouthful of bread, I found myself laughing.

Twice in a half-hour?

The food went swiftly, despite the swell's increase. Rekhmire' got up to claim more, and crept back under the deck-shelter with loaded square wooden plates. His platter cleaned remarkably fast, I noted. He stretched out his arms – no easy task in the combined space – and knocked open the canvas flap.

The salt-heavy wind blew in cold against my face, shocking more than skin and nerve awake.

'Rekhmire'. Where is this ship going?'

He wrapped long arms around his knees, and squinted at the rail and ropes outside. 'Venice.'

'*Venice?*'

Shock further broke the clouds surrounding my mind. I had assumed – beyond questioning – that it must be Alexandrian Constantinople this ship made its heading for.

'Why? Did you get more letters from Iberia? From Carthage? What . . . '

Hot liquid spilled over the lower lids of my eyes: I had not known until then that I would weep.

'Masaccio.' I wiped the back of my hand across my face. 'He said, once, he'd send me on a buying trip to Venice. For *lapis* blue. I made an excuse of it to that heretic priest that married me to Sulva . . . I never expected— Why *Venice?*'

'You were not in a state to give directions.'

The Egyptian shifted to sit closer, cautiously reached out, and combed his fingers through my tangled hair. His delicate touch worried knots undone without causing me pain. He made no other consolatory attempt, speaking with a bureaucrat's dry self-possession:

'In one way, this resembles our leaving Carthage for Rome – no man will expect us to travel anywhere else *but* Alexandria. So they will not look for us in the north. And there were considerable rumours of Carthaginian agents in Rome asking questions, the last week we were there. I left a trail I think will take any astray . . . '

His gaze, surveying something with inner satisfaction, left it and came back to me.

'Truthfully—' His bronze skin was a little darker on the high surfaces of his cheeks. 'Menmet-Ra, old friend that he is, called in a favour I could not honestly refuse him. He desires to stay in Rome, but *some* man must go north and sort out the Alexandrine house in Venice, after the ambassador there died this last autumn. Rather than Menmet-Ra being uprooted from his comfortable nest, he sees no reason why *I* need not return to Alexandria by the longer route . . . '

Much longer, I reflected, with the copied maps of travellers' itineraries in my mind's eye. The port of Venice being at the northern head of the Adriatic waters, and Constantinople way past the Greek Islands to the east.

'I thought it safer. The diversion's not uninteresting.' Rekhmire' absently set forefingers and thumbs to the knottier tangle of hair over my ear. To have his stare so close on me, but not meeting my eyes, felt oddly intimate.

He added, 'There seems to be some confusion with a printer of woodcuts. And whichever of Ty-ameny's book-buyers has been left as caretaker of the embassy. And rumours of a device—'

He cut himself off abruptly.

'No.' His large hand tilted my head back towards him; I hadn't realised I had turned away. '*Not* the golem. That will leave Rome by ship, Menmet-Ra was giving orders as we departed—'

There seemed no way to control the tears that collected inescapably in my eyes, blurring my vision, running hotly down my cheeks and neck. I shrugged out from under Rekhmire''s grasp, crawled unsteadily to the tent-opening, and ducked out under canvas and ropes.

Straightening up on cramped and blood-starved legs sent me staggering to the ship's rail. And not only that: my body's balance of gravity felt altered, as if I carried it in the now-visible curve of my belly.

You will be too busy seeking a back-alley abortionist—

'What "device"? Something else from Carthage?'

Rekhmire' came up beside me, perfectly steady on his bare feet despite the deck's pitch and yaw, a bundle over his arm.

'No. Something from the Frankish North. Burgundy or the Germanies, Menmet says. I have a report to read on it, when I cease the profession of nurse . . . '

He smiled, unwrapped the bundle, and it became a heavy woollen Frankish cloak, which he threw about my shoulders. One of his powerful hands grasped the rail behind me, serving as a brace while I settled the warm swathes of wool around me in toga-fashion.

My own hands were cold enough that this was not unlike clothing a sculpted marble figure. I could think of nothing but Masaccio. *I saw him die.* And now I'll explore the New Art on my own, because from what he told me, none of it has spread to the Venetian state.

In peripheral vision, I saw Rekhmire' frown. *Is that against grief, horror, bereavement?*

The Egyptian turned his head away from the wind, droplets of salt water dampening his shaven head, raising his voice a very little above the wind.

'Ilario – listen to me. Aranthur was not kind in what he said. But there is some truth there. Too much to ignore. If you continue to carry this child . . . But then again, it's very rare for a hermaphrodite *not* to lose any child by miscarriage, long before birth . . . That would be an ill thing to have happen to you, yes. But, forgive me, better than the other. If you *do* carry a child full term, it may rip you apart. You're not made for it.'

If my throat is stiff from disuse and private weeping, it's not for that.

'Your doctor *said* I carry Marcomir's child in my belly.' I wiped sea-spray off my face. 'I have no motherly feeling. If it quickens . . . But I feel no different from before.'

'You might *die* in labour!'

The sea-wind smelled of cold depths. The deck under my feet dipped deeper. Cries came from the crew; the steersman and captain shouting orders.

Rekhmire' bent down so that he could speak close into my ear. His voice sounded high with tension.

'I desire that we find an Alexandrine physician to manage the business. There will surely be one in Venice, attached to the Alexandria house. But it needs to be done sooner, more safely . . . I can order us put ashore at wherever we can get a ship east. The Dalmatian coast, perhaps.' He sounded distracted. '*Soon*. Before – if it is not already too late!'

'I made my decision in Rome.' I hadn't realised until I spoke it aloud.

'Suppose you carry it long enough that you're damaged when— what?' he interrupted himself.

He might have narrowed his eyes against the lashing water, or at me.

I faced him on the swaying deck. 'The doctor may be in error. If I *am* with child . . . If my body sheds this, well then, it's done. If not, then not. There's – what did you call it? – "the operation which birthed great Caesar". And that's my decision.'

'Don't you understand, you stupid—!' Rekhmire' cut himself off, I think caught between epitaphs, and lifted up his large hands. 'Your body is talking, not your mind; your mind is as absent as a woman in child-bed!'

My temper snapped. 'A eunuch gives me advice on procreation, does he!'

Rekhmire' straightened, towering over me. 'I'll speak it slowly. You. Could. Die.'

That he cared both warmed and puzzled me. Who would ever have thought that the man who purchased me would become so close?

'Rekhmire'—'

The deck shifted under me; came back at a slant.

I staggered two steps down the rail; grabbing at it.

One of the square wooden plates slid out of the tent-shelter and skidded across the deck towards the scuppers.

Rekhmire' bent and scooped it up, grabbing my arm with his other hand, and hustled us back towards the canopy. As I fell on my knees on the deck, I began dry-heaving.

Sea-sickness, that I had never suffered from in the seas between Iberia and Carthage, now emptied me and dried me out, until I could barely leave my blanket-roll.

I lost track of time, though I know that at some point the Egyptian demanded and got space for us under hatches with the cargo. In extreme physical misery, two things stood out in my mind. That Rekhmire' tended me, feeding me sips of water when nothing else would stay down. And that my belly remained distended, swelling and thickening even as I grew worn and thin. Once I bled, but it soon stopped, and did not happen again.

I dreamed of each precise fold of the sheet covering Masaccio's dead face. And of having to compulsively touch each one, before practising the charcoal drawing of cloth-folds to improve my use of tone. No more than that, but it made me wake myself crying out with horror.

The dhow *Iskander* ran south before the storm, lost itself among the first of the Greek islands – lost our armed convoy escort with the brass cannon, against pirates – and beat back against the tempests that came down one after another across the Adriatic.

And was driven repeatedly away from coasts and any ports by appalling seas.

'It is at least good we're where no man can search for us,' Rekhmire' observed, sodden from head to foot, and wincing every time the ship yawed. He looked across at me in the faint light leaking into the hold. 'It may be the agents from Carthage investigated the whereabouts of the King-Caliph's golem, rather than one Ilario, but—'

'Carthage won't be a concern if we drown.' *Nor will my belly.*

I wondered if Honorius had settled matters with King Rodrigo yet – and tried not to wonder if I would die before I saw my father again.

Days became a week, two, three.

I crept up on deck from time to time, suffocated by the creaking, shifting dark of the hold. The skies were filled with violet lightning, of a colour that I despaired of ever being able to paint; the crew screamed stories of sea-monsters; and one black noon I saw how such tales begin, with an optical delusion of the kind that men in the deserts call *mirage* – this time of a ship, an apparent sea-mile distant from us, with an impossible number of lateen sails making a tower of triangular shapes above the hull, and the whiskery face of a monster painted on the prow. Some trick of the storm-twilight made it seem immense, ten times the size of any mortal ship: a vessel that could belong only to giants.

I watched the geometric shapes merge into a squall, and remembered enough to sketch a line or two of the 'ghost-ship's' curious painted monster on damp paper with crumbling charcoal, before the next blast of the tempest made that impossible. It was the first time I had picked up charcoal since Masaccio died.

I let the sea take it.

The storms broke.

The clouds clearing, I could see that the stars in the night sky were not those of late autumn, now, but the constellations of deep winter.

The look-out sighted landmarks known to lie south-east of Venice.

I could no longer wear my doublet and hose. The hose would not stretch over my hips, nor the doublet lace up over my abdomen.

The Egyptian vanished into a far crevice of the cargo hold, and emerged with salt-water-stained cloth that unrolled itself and proved to be a shift and over-dress of soft linen and embroidered silk, respectively. As cargo it was ruined. Dried out, I could lace it loosely over my high belly and wear it.

I haven't worn skirts since the King's court in Taraco . . .

We were past the Republic of Venezia's guard and customs ships and the Lido before I came uncertainly up onto the deck.

'There.' Rekhmire' pointed.

Wind blew in my face from the rising sun. I squinted, seeing the sea and a great sky full of light; colours all so close to each other's shades as to be impossible to paint. Haze hid islands, ships' masts, and a glimmer of chimneys, roofs, and *campanile* . . . The lagoon's flat coastline was barely distinguishable from the water or the hazy air.

'Venice,' Rekhmire' said.

Painters, sculptors, architects, scholars . . . But all of the old schools.

I wondered where I might go, now Rome was closed to me, and noticed Rekhmire''s gaze sliding down to my bulge. So, as I came on deck, did that of the ship's captain. And the sailors.

Eavesdropping on gossip allowed me know that they supposed me a young woman who had come on board disguised as a man. The Egyptian, since a eunuch could not beget a bastard, figured as my protector only.

Venice's ships and spires began to solidify out of the dawn mist.

The beauty oppressed me. I went below, called for hot water, and shaved the last wisps of beard off my chin. In the event that Rekhmire''s hypothetical agent of Carthage did find his way to Venice, I wanted him to see nothing of the man who had been in Rome.

As I came back up on deck, Rekhmire' stepped in close, his linen kilt bright in the new sunlight. He towered over me, speaking quietly.

'Ilario. No argument. I'm sending for an Alexandrine physician as soon as we're docked.'

'You're not my master!'

'If I were still your owner, I'd *order* you—' Rekhmire' checked himself, an appalled expression on his face. 'Amun and Amunet! Thank the Eight I *don't* have to order that!'

For all my predicament, I couldn't help but laugh. 'Thank you. But I've dealt with my own problems all my life: I'll do the same now.'

The sun's warmth eased me, in body and temper. Dawn broke red over the islands and the lagoons, the winter geese rising up into the cold air. Hundreds of small ships poled and rowed their way past us as the dhow *Iskander* sailed in towards the mouth of the Grand Canal, and the dock at the steps of St Mark's Square.

Of course, Venice is a navy port, I thought, looking at the bigger trading vessels and the armed galleys. And much larger than Rome—

'But I wonder,' Rekhmire' continued soberly, as sails were furled above us, and small boats rowed out to ferry passengers ashore. 'You were a slave all your life. In your King Rodrigo's court – I know it was worse than you pretend. You have little *experience* of taking decisions.'

I winced, and thought of Marcomir in Carthage. 'I have some experience.'

'Yet you refuse to take responsibility for saving your own life.'

'*I've taken my decision.*'

I scooped up my small roll of belongings and let Rekhmire' offer me his large hand to steady me as I climbed down into a black boat.

From the flat level of the water, everything rose up to tower above me. Islands surrounded us; the sea hidden beyond a distant barrier. The oarsman sang in a thick patois as he poled us towards wide steps. Rekhmire' had the pinched expression of a man who will continue a conversation the moment he is not overheard.

Mooring-posts for boats jutted out of the water all along the quayside, in a clutter of straight lines and diagonals.

Trying to keep my balance as I disembarked, I found my gaze lifting from the murky depths of the lagoon, to steps rising up from the quayside to a piazza, and ancient red-tiled roofs. Chimes from a bell-tower deafened me as much as sheer visual complexity confused my eyes. I stared up at a Classical pillar on which a lion and a saint – San Marco? – wrestled for supremacy against the eggshell-blue sky.

Someone pushed against me. I staggered, shoved away from the moored boat by men's shoulders as they bustled past. Rekhmire' stepped ashore behind me, passing coins to the oarsman.

My share of the voyage will have to be added to the debt I owe for manumission, I thought, blinking at the stench of sweat and still water. Sailors I recognised from the dhow *Iskander* loped ashore and into the crowds. I saw porters, Venetian merchants, men and escorted women, unescorted whores, hand-carts and loaded mules, children running up with their dirty palms extended, bright eyes and teeth feverishly directed at me . . .

The Egyptian scattered a handful of small coins, which they pursued. I rested my hand by habit on my belly. *Orphans beg*, I thought, staring past the Riva steps at the facades of Gothic palaces, rising seemingly directly from the waters of a canal. The funnels of a thousand chimneys filled the skyline. I went to walk forward – and stopped.

In front of me, on the Riva steps, a familiar face resolved itself out of the crowds.

A lean man, on the tall side, his grey hair cropped down almost to baldness. Wearing military boots, and the high-collared cloak of the Iberian nations . . .

I stared at Honorius.

My father Honorius—

His eyes grew wider and wider. He glared at me. At Rekhmire'. At the moored ships—

And back at the Egyptian book-buyer.

'How *dare* you get my *son* PREGNANT!'

Part Three

The Most Serene

1

They call the city of Venice *La Serenissima*: 'the most serene'.

Honorius bellowed again, loudly enough to turn men's heads all the way across the Riva degli Schiavoni.

'*How* could you get her pregnant!'

He hesitated.

' . . . *him* pregnant?'

Rekhmire' gaped, struck speechless.

I snorted, sudden dry laughter overtaking me. 'It's a long story! But don't blame Master Rekhmire'; it's not his fault.'

'Oh.' Honorius looked at me. And back at Rekhmire'. 'Ah. Sorry! Thought you must have lied about—' Honorius grabbed illustratively at the crotch of his hose. '—You know?'

'In fact, no!' Rekhmire' appeared thoroughly flustered. 'Did you get my letter?'

I turned about, to stare at him. 'You wrote a *letter*? To my father?'

The Egyptian looked completely caught out.

Honorius spoke grimly. 'Oh, I got your letter. It caught me up when I'd got as far as Marseilles. *"Ilario and I are travelling from Rome to Venice"*. *"Ilario might welcome a father's company"*. And then I see Ilario like this! How *else* was I to read it, retrospectively, except *"I've got your son-daughter with child"*! *I* didn't know you and Ilario were fornicating—'

I put a hand up. 'I'm not. We're not! If we were, it *still* couldn't be Rekhmire''s child. And this—'

In peripheral vision, I saw many interested faces where the quayside steps went up to San Marco square. Brightly-dressed Venetian crowds, watching the entertaining foreigners shout at each other.

'—This is too public.'

Honorius nodded agreement, took a pace forward, and held out his arms. I stepped into his embrace. He felt solid, muscular; smelling of cassia. Used for a month and more to wind- and wave-noise, his silence made a welcome respite from the sudden human chatter.

Since it warms me to find him here – I believe I must have missed Honorius's company since Rome.

Now I was in skirts, the Captain-General of Castile and Leon seemed taller, although my true height was no less. The wool of his cloak was damp with dew under my hands. *From standing here since dawn?* I wondered. How long has he been waiting here?

How long has he been in *Venice?*

'I understand.' Honorius's voice growled beside my ear. 'It wasn't the Egyptian. How did this happen? Tell me! Were you attacked?'

The picture is all too plausible: a man-woman freak held down and raped by some gang of drunken thugs, just to see what would happen.

'No. The father's in Carthage. I'll explain later.' I stepped back, straightened my own shabby cloak, and managed a smile. 'If you ever visit the baths with Rekhmire', I'm sure he'll convince you of his credentials! As for this pregnancy—'

Honorius's stunned expression made me think he had not yet considered any of the medical aspects.

'—We'll speak about that later. Rekhmire', where's this Alexandrine embassy?'

Honorius spoke before Rekhmire' could, his lean weathered expression turned abruptly grim. 'Wait. The shock put it out of my mind – Master Rekhmire''s letter isn't the only reason I'm here.'

He raised his hand, signalling. Eight or nine men in Frankish helmets and Iberian brigandines shouldered towards us on the crowded steps; others moved in from further away. My heart went straight into my mouth.

No, I *know* them. That, there, is Tottola: the massive one. And that, the Armenian sergeant, Orazi—

I knew the other faces from Rome, also; my fingers having directed charcoal in the shape of a brow here, a nose and eyelid there. Even if most detail was hidden now by burnished steel sallets and the visors of burgonets.

'Your men – they didn't go back to Iberia with you?'

Honorius gave a further motion with his sun-browned hand. The men-at-arms fell into a loose, outward-facing circle about us.

'Those of my men who were weary of travelling, I sent on to Taraco and my estates. They can make my excuses to King Rodrigo. These men – these followed me in the Navarra wars; they'll follow me now, without question.'

'That doesn't answer *my* question!'

Honorius busied himself pulling on his gauntlets. One of the soldiers – a junior ensign; Saverico, if I remembered his name correctly – moved up, holding the Captain-General's sallet.

The mirror-polished curve of the steel reflected all the Doge's palace, and the wooden scaffolding that cloaked the building's walls.

Honorius dipped his head, putting the helmet on, and met my gaze as Saverico buckled the strap under his chin.

'Your foster family, Ilario – Aldra Federico, and his wife Valdamerca, and their daughters, and entourage. They're here, in Venice. They have an assassin with them. I believe he has orders to kill you.'

2

The teeming, shouting crowds of Venetians washed up against us like seas around a reef. I could only stare.

'What?' I managed.

'Ilario—'

'A *what*!'

My foster family: Aldra Federico, who has been a social climber since before he sold me to the King at the age of fifteen; Valdamerca, who rules her husband with iron will. And their daughters: Matasuntha, married and gone before I was of an age to know her, and Reinalda and Sunilda. Who are likely enough, now, to be respectable married women themselves. As I would be, were I wholly a woman.

I put them behind me when it seemed I had found kin in Rosamunda and the Lord Videric. Federico would have exploited my position as King's Freak – had I let him.

'What are they doing in *Venice*?' I turned from Honorius, to meet Rekhmire''s puzzled expression. 'How could they know I was coming here! *I* didn't know I was coming here . . . '

Honorius's eyes narrowed against the fretwork sun, bright even in winter, reflecting up from the lagoon's ripples.

'Your foster father Federico claims he's looking for "the New Art of the Italian city-states", to take back to Taraconensis. Apparently it's become the latest court fashion.'

The weight of irony in his tone could have sunk the *Iskander*, and several other ships beside.

'The assassin isn't Federico's own man,' Honorius added briskly. 'As far as I can discover, he's one of Aldra Videric's hired murderers.'

That made better sense of the matter. I nodded in understanding.

My father added, 'Videric got the man into your foster father's entourage. With Aldra Federico's knowledge, or without it; I don't know. I ran into them at Marseilles—'

'Marseilles?' Fear and realisation struck hard. 'Christus! You haven't answered the King's summons, have you? You came *here*, instead of going home to Rodrigo!'

Exasperated, Honorius declared, 'King Rodrigo Sanguerra can *wait*. When I left Rome, I had no idea that the Aldra Videric might employ others of your family against you. Now I know, matters are changed.

Your foster father sees himself as some kind of ally – lackey, more like! –
to ex-First Minister Videric?'

'Very likely.' I agreed, dazed.

Familiar armed men jostled close to us, Honorius's badge sewn to their
sleeves. Swords in scabbards; some of them carrying bows, and poleaxes.
Fully-armed mercenaries . . . I looked at Honorius. At Rekhmire' –
plainly as stunned as I. Back at the soldiers.

'An *assassin?*'

A sigh came from beside me. Rekhmire' observed, 'It appears this isn't
to be the restful stay in Venice that I had hoped for . . . '

'JESÚ CHRISTUS IMPERATOR!'

Heads turned all along the quay, and on the nearer small boats in the
lagoon.

'*Gaius Judas Tradditore!*' I added, neatly merging both sides of the
Green religious schism. 'An assassin!'

Rekhmire''s smile covered a degree of concern. He touched my arm.

'I apologise,' I said, more stiffly than I intended. 'Clearly, you'll be
better off lodging in a different part of the city—'

'Conceivably in a different city.'

His tone was light; steel underneath.

And if he's that determined to keep it a joke, I can't talk sense into him
here.

I glanced about, questioning our destination now. The opening of the
Canal Grande immediately took my eye – as it draws every man's gaze
on entering La Serenissima. A prospect of red roof-tiles, funnel-shaped
chimneys, and plastered brick walls rising directly out of the canal water
. . . plaster the colour of oatmeal and mustard, red chalk and pale sand.

I have only ever seen one painting of Florence: a fresco done on the
walls of a chapel in Zaragoza.

Venice is the same, only taller.

Some of the stone-fronted palaces stood five and six storeys tall, not
counting their attics and dovecotes. I saw bridges, innumerable bridges;
and the sea omnipresent in harbour-basin and canal . . .

Turning away from the laden boats, and men bustling everywhere, I
found Rekhmire' sending an unobtrusive stare around the San Marco
steps. I trusted him to see anything out of place that Honorius's plain
soldiers might miss.

Videric is sending hired murderers to Italy.

With my foster parents.

And I thought I had nothing to do but come here and die in childbirth . . .

'"Alexandrine Embassy"?' my father queried.

Rekhmire' raised the hood of his cloak, and gave me a glance that was
evidently my cue to do likewise.

'My intention is to take Ilario to the Alexandrine house here, at the
Campo San Barnaba, in the Dorsodura quarter. The late Ambassador

Pakharu died of cholera last autumn; the embassy's closed for ambassadorial business, but I have the Pharaoh-Queen's permission to stay there while I go about my own affairs.'

Rekhmire' regarded the soldiers.

'Being closed up, it may be safe. I think no man will willingly risk attacking us under the protection of the Pharaoh-Queen.'

'I'm not so sure.' Honorius grimaced. 'But, better than my lodgings. Videric's man isn't a fool. He's been watching. He knows where I stay.'

The same anger against pursuit that I had felt in Carthage rose hot in my throat. 'You know who it is?'

'I've been travelling with your foster father. I have an educated guess.'

'*Travelling* with Aldra Federico—!'

'I'll explain all when we're safe.'

The mass of people looked thickest towards the square of San Marco. Any man might approach us there covertly.

But in deserted streets, we'll be vulnerable. And in skirts, I doubt any man will lend me a weapon.

'Perhaps I should have disguised myself as a man again,' I remarked acerbically. 'A very *fat* man. I suppose the sole advantage is, your assassin won't be expecting to kill a woman.'

Honorius gave a snort at once sardonic and approving. 'Glad to see you taking it so well!'

'If you're watched, we should go,' Rekhmire' cut in. 'I advise walking – if we take a boat, we'll pay four times on the Riva what we should elsewhere, and the gondoliers will be bribed to say where we went.'

Honorius gave a shrug and a nod, of the kind indicating trust. 'Lead the way, then.'

The Egyptian strode off; the armed escort breaking our way with him, cresting the crowd. I stumbled after, feet coming down awkwardly among trash on the trampled mud and stone.

It was not the common feeling after being on board a ship. Even considering the month or five weeks it had been since I last trod land. There, the earth seems at once too rocking and too solid, and strikes hard up under the soles of the feet.

Now, my balance felt different; I no longer walked from the shoulder, but from the hip. The centre of my weight carried lower. I could neither achieve the female glide I had been taught in Taraco, nor walk like a man.

An assassin.

There have been the usual 'hunting accidents' and badly-disguised bandit-raids among Taraco's nobility; I'm used to the idea that not all accidental deaths might be natural. But that I should be followed by a man, or men, ordered to kill *me* . . .

At least Rosamunda's motive was personal.

The shadow of a tall brick tower fell across me – a beacon, or lighthouse, I thought at first, and then realised it was a bell-tower, facing the sea – and the vast expanse of the San Marco square opened up. Sun blazed back from marble and ornamental facades; from the gilding on the Green Basilica. Before I could memorise more than a dozen astounding architectural details (since Honorius scowled at my groping in my baggage roll for my drawing-book), we were through the crowds, and striding briskly into alleys, between tall houses where plaster fell from the underlying brickwork. Weeds rooted in the crumbling mortar.

The black canal at my left hand reflected a series of windows rising up on either side, all shutters thrown open. Loud conversations in the Venezia dialect passed across the gap above our heads. I caught a balance and strode fast enough to catch up with Honorius.

'Where *is* my foster father?'

Honorius glanced about so casually that any man not much around soldiers might have been deceived into thinking him relaxed.

'In a hired palazzo, halfway down the Canal Grande. Little weasel keeps saying how regrettable it is that Chancellor Videric had to "give up" his position! There's a formidable woman with him who I take to be your foster mother.'

'*Formidable.*' I couldn't help a snort. 'This from the Captain-General of the House of Trastamara! Yes, that will be Valdamerca.'

My father grinned, and then looked grim. 'Two girls – young women. One of whom has your assassin with her.'

'Not Matasuntha, she'll be at home with her babies. It must be 'Nilda and 'Nalda.'

Who, to be truthful, I have not expected to encounter again, after being sold to King Rodrigo.

'Why would one of my sisters have a hired killer with her?' I persisted. 'And *do* you know who it is?'

'One Ramiro Carrasco de Luis, by name. He's here as their secretary.'

Honorius gave the name the familiar accents of Taraconensis. Nostalgia and homesickness unexpectedly stabbed through me.

Honorius walked as men of the sword do, all the weight loose from his shoulders, all the balance in the column of his spine. I ached to draw him. A rush of chill in my belly reminded me of other business.

'I doubt either young woman knows what Secretary Carrasco is . . . and I believe Carrasco's the last possible candidate. I've taken care to err on the *generous* side while getting rid of agents of Videric,' Honorius added, with a smile at the lift of my eyebrows.

His expression faded to seriousness.

'I'm a soldier, I know when the enemy's about – and I'm not the only man who's spent his every morning here watching the ships dock.'

A brick hurtled past my head, smashing into the building two yards ahead of me.

I brought up my baggage-roll, protecting my head. Chunks of plaster ricocheted from the cloth-wrapped wood and down across the earth, knocked free from the wall by the impact. Rekhmire' jumped in front of me. Honorius gave a harsh bark.

The soldiers skidded to a halt just on the canal's edge.

Out across the filthy green water, in the crepuscular light, two men stood in a knife-pointed black boat. Its covered central section seemed empty. One of the men, standing at the boat's rear, rapidly poled it towards a side canal.

'Hey! *You're* not a girl!' The other, shorter man lowered his hand from the throw. I saw his chest expand, breath punching a self-righteous tone across the increasing gap of the canal: 'You're a skinny ugly *boy* in a *dress*! With a pot belly! Who the fuck let *you* out into the streets?'

The German soldier Tottola raised a crossbow.

I saw the Venetian man's face change colour even across twelve yards of plague-ridden canal water – which will protect from swords and poleaxes, but not from the bolt of a bow.

I grabbed Honorius's wrist. 'Wait!'

He closed his mouth without giving an order. The boat silently glided on, moving only by impetus now; the boatman frozen. The shorter man stared blankly at me, no regret on his face.

I sighed. 'I *do* make an ugly woman. If you're planning to shoot every man who yells at me in the street, you should stock up on crossbow bolts.'

'This has happened to you before?'

'*Woman built like a stonemason!*', I remember from Carthage.

'Try asking Rekhmire' what it's like being a eunuch inside Frankish territory . . . Yes. It happens all the time. Or it's "whoreson catamite", when I'm wearing doublet and hose.'

Honorius wrinkled his nose, either at the smell of the water or his thoughts. He gestured with his free hand. Tottola removed his bolt, lowered the crossbow to uncrank it, and unhitched the bow-string.

The black boat vanished with rapidity into the side-canal. Distant voices raised in something unintelligible: relief, anger, or further insult.

'If I didn't want to keep us out of sight of the Council of Ten, I'd have both of them up here for the lads to beat bloody.' Honorius consolingly placed my hand on his arm and patted it.

Having come to know him somewhat, I thought he would do exactly the same if I were in male dress.

My heart hammered unusually hard. *Too much talk of assassins: I'm unnerved!*

It took until we had crossed the Canal Grande by a most splendid bridge, and passed into Venice's southernmost quarter, for me to steady myself. *Dorsodura*, they call the area, for the hard rock under it. It seemed poorer than San Marco: tall dank beam-and-plaster houses surrounding us. Swallows might nest under those eaves in the spring. For now, the water breathed off pure chill.

Rekhmire' strolled a few yards, hands clasped behind his back, frowning at a junction of three side-canals and streets. 'Yes . . . This way.'

He led us, rapidly, over two high-humped canal bridges. I gripped Honorius's elbow, assisting my balance on the slick cobblestones and mud, cursing skirts and pattens and the balance of my body.

It was easy to shift my concentration. 'Tell me why you're here in Venice – *now*, Father!'

'We were approaching Marseilles.' The retired soldier's lips pressed momentarily together. That thin line altered all the other lines of his face. 'The weather was bad enough that I'd decided to give up and take a ship the remainder of the way home, rather than continue riding west on the Via Augusta. While we waited for the tide, a messenger caught up with the Egyptian's letter for me. And while I was pondering *that*, one of the men brought me news of another large party of travellers, this time coming up from Iberia and riding east.' He shrugged. 'I've learned to follow instinct – I decided to wait a day or so. As soon as I saw them, I recognised them from your drawing-book in Rome.'

Honorius's expression abruptly reflected the fear that he might have committed an intrusion.

'I forgot I drew them,' I mused, and added, amiably, 'I didn't know you were so interested in my notebooks.'

'Oh. Well. My son-daughter's work . . . You know.' He collected himself. Giving me a look of surprising self-deprecation, he continued. 'So I established the travellers' names – and struck up an acquaintance. Two noblemen from Taraconensis, meeting abroad – I behaved like a garrulous retired soldier. You wouldn't *believe* how amiable I can be! Talked about campaigns in Navarra. Bored them rigid. *But* – they took me for no more than a busybody and a fool. Evidently, there are no rumours about me being your natural father, yet.'

The soldiers' boots echoed loudly against the walls of a small paved square. Ropes strung between upper windows held frost-stiffened shirts, hung out to dry. The succession of white shapes receded above our heads. Momentarily I missed the *Iskander*'s sails.

'I discovered their proposed route. Florence, Venice – and Rome. That was suspicion enough for me. Your Aldra Federico told me he was looking for painters of the New Art, to hire and take back to Taraco, to work for the King. I thought he must be looking for one artist in particular . . . ' Honorius's eyelids lowered in covert amusement. '*I* said to Federico, what a coincidence, *I* was going to buy art for my new estates; why didn't we travel together . . . '

Honorius spoke as briskly as we walked. I noted him not out of breath, despite our pace and the cold air. My own chest hurt. Five weeks idle on a boat helps no one.

'So, all of us ride back towards Italy, up the Via Augusta – if I'm correct, Aldra Videric sent three murderers after you. I've some experience with spies in the Crusader camps,' Honorius added, before I might interrupt. 'I had my sergeants drink with Federico's servants. Then at Genoa, there was an unfortunate brawl between my soldiers and some of Federico's men. You know what soldiers are like.'

His look of innocence would have deceived no man in the court of Taraco. I thought it not intended to. Only to impress on his son-daughter the depth of his concern.

'Honorius – Father—'

He gave a deprecating wave of his hand. 'Federico put two of his men on a ship back to Taraconensis, since they were too injured to perform their duties. I suppose they may report to Videric. But deaths would have looked suspicious.' He made a face of self-disgust. 'Ramon the cook, and the big mule-handler; they were no more than petty paid spies. Probably Videric keeping an eye on his own hired killer. The third man – this Ramiro Carrasco – we failed to entice into a fight.'

Honorius glanced down at me.

'I left Federico where the road to Venezia turns east. They were going on towards Rome, and *that* was safe enough, because I knew from the Egyptian's letter that you'd left the Empty Chair. But damned if they didn't turn up again, here, three weeks later! Rome didn't have what they wanted, maybe Venice has better artists, *ad nauseam* . . . I've been hinting that they should leave, try Florence; but no.'

'They may have heard rumours in Rome.' I saw him catch something in my tone. 'I . . . will have explanations of my own to make.'

Honorius glanced about with eyes that seemed permanently narrowed against sunlight, even in such cavernous streets as these. The houses rose six storeys above us.

'I hope that damned Egyptian spy knows where he's going – if this *is* a short cut to the Campo S. Barnaba—'

He broke off, and stared at me closely.

'*That's what it is!* Ilario! You're not wearing a collar!'

'I'm not a slave now.'

A broad slow beam spread over his face. '*Good!* How did Messer Rekhmire' finally persuade you?'

One of the men-at-arms ran back out of an alley ahead of us, swung around, saw Honorius, and began shouting. His voice shrilled high and urgent. Berenguer: a corporal – I recognised him by the glint of sunlight on a Frankish-style sallet, rather than his face.

He urgently pointed at the buildings on the far side of the narrow canal. The Navarrese-accented words went straight past me, my ear not attuned.

'*Hackbuts!* Ambush!'

I stepped forward.

Hard arms caught me around the waist.

The world lifted up beneath me in tongues of fire and flame.

In the same moment, a body struck me hard between the bones of my shoulders, sending my head flying back against an armoured chest. I cracked my skull against the metal, hearing a muffled thud. Disoriented, I felt the world tumble—

The tackle bowled me over, face-down and flat.

Hard, damp earth slammed against my hip and elbow and knee: I made a vain attempt to brace myself, terror stabbing instantly through me, every instinct trying to protect my belly.

Stone hit the knuckles of my out-flung hand.

Mail-clad arms buffered me painfully across one breast and my hip, preventing my belly from striking the ground.

Honorius's tall, narrow body wrapped around mine.

Noise fractured the world, loud enough that my teeth snapped together, catching my tongue; my skull jolting on cervical vertebrae. Not one noise, but a dozen in succession, and then more: a row of explosions, stabbing my ears. Concussion snatched the breath out of my lungs. Heat swirled in the air.

A hail of bits, rubbish and trash, fell down across me.

'*Charge!*' Honorius's voice rang through my head. Deafened, I barely heard him shouting military instructions. If I could have clawed myself beneath the cobblestones, I would have.

I stared at masonry, pale as honey. It was a wall that I had been borne painfully down behind. The stout curved parapet of a hump-backed bridge. Canal-water a yard away from my left hand.

Shock fractured images. Armoured men running past; sun on sallets and axe-blades. One man – Aznar? – his arm upraised and mouth open, shouting orders. Splinters of black wood fountaining down from above, against a blue sky. Doors and shutters slamming.

Mud and stones were cold under my body. The heels of my hands bled, gashed. Honorius's knee pressed down, planted in the small of my back: he yelled incomprehensible commands.

'Get – off—'

Hands turned me. Honorius's anxious face peered down into my face. '*Are you hurt?*'

The winter cold bit me: I stared down the length of my body as if I could not own it again until I saw it unhurt. No limbs missing, no parts mutilated.

'Not hurt. I— What are "hackbuts"?'

'Guns!' Honorius's crouched figure lifted; he stood and waved his arm, calling three curt directions. Fists on hips, he stared breathlessly over the bridge and canal. 'Frankish for "arquebus". They're running! No balls, these hired bravos!'

His exalted grin gave way to a frown.

'I half expected an ambush – should have thought of emplaced guns.'

A brilliant silver-grey smear caught the sun beside me, on the masonry of the bridge wall.

Lead, I realised.

The mark left by a flattened bullet, made of lead poured into a mould in a craftsman's manner that is very like the acts of craft in a painter's workshop.

I couldn't help but mutter my thoughts aloud. 'Jesú! I may have been in danger from the golem, but when I was working for Masaccio no one was *shooting* at me!'

'Golem?' Honorius sounded startled.

A shrill whistle cracked the air. I jerked round.

Sergeant Orazi strode back towards us, lowering his fingers from his lips. A heavy falchion gleamed in his other hand. I've sketched similar blades in butcher's shops. His had the same webs of red liquid across the flat of the steel, as if he had been unjointing animals.

The rest of the escort re-formed with him, sending insults and crossbow bolts after what must be running attackers. Honorius's curt unintelligible snarl brought them to order.

A few yards away from me, in the middle of the bridge, the young ensign Saverico sat up, felt his head, winced, and blushed as he climbed back up onto his feet.

Hoarsely, Sergeant Orazi shouted, 'That's right, Ensign, fall over at them – that'll scare any enemy!'

The little man shot a keen glance from one man to the other. Checking, I realised. They chuckled at his caustic remark. One of the older men ruffled Saverico's hair, where he had lost his helmet in the melee. The younger man glanced about and winced as he bent over to retrieve it.

Honorius snapped his fingers. 'Don't drop your guard!'

Two soldiers trotted up and knelt down beside me, one with a shield and the other with a crossbow, both scanning the canal path and open alley entrances all around. The shield-man couched his sword as if he were a hunter about to receive boar. The building on the far side of the canal was a warehouse: I could see under its eaves and into the empty arcades where our attackers must have hidden.

'Are you hurt?' Honorius took hold of me by the shoulders, eyes narrowing intently against the light as he studied me with a battlefield gaze. 'Can you *move*?'

Too loud, because deafened, I bellowed, 'Yes!'

I have only bruises. Surrounded by soldiers in mail and plate armour, it is not the time to mention nightmares that my hands will suffer an accident; dreams that wake me from sleep in the cold-sweats. Or the past fear that any slave-owner will realise my dread of being mutilated.

I flexed my fingers, and pried gravel out of the heel of my right hand, watching the slow welling-up of blood.

Aiming at a normal level of sound, I muttered, 'Unless this festers, it's nothing to worry about.'

Honorius tilted his head towards Sergeant Orazi.

'We hurt 'em,' the small man observed. 'Hit right after the first volley. Piled straight in, went right through 'em! They can run better than they can shoot. Four blood-trails leading off. No bodies. They may have taken their own. Whoever was in charge . . . ' He shrugged.

Honorius helped me onto my feet, demanding, 'A feint? Are they estimating our strength first?'

'Looks more like they thought they'd take us all out first time. They put everything they'd got into that.' The Armenian sergeant shrugged again. 'If they'd hit us without Berenguer's warning, we'd all be dead.'

Saverico scratched in his dusty curls and added something under his breath.

I could swear he just said: 'Lucky hermaphrodite or not!'

'"Lucky"?' I blurted out, staring down at the ensign who seemed barely old enough to be a page.

'We're alive.' Honorius chuckled. 'That's always lucky . . . '

I opened my mouth to make a comment about superstitions, and shut it again.

Honorius felt in his leather draw-purse, and handed me a white silk handkerchief, indicating I should bind my hand up with it. After a moment, seeing I couldn't tie a knot one-handed, he took over. The two pairs of armsmen he had sent out into the immediate area trotted back, faces red despite the winter chill, shaking their heads at the officers' questions.

'*This*,' Honorius observed, with some self-satisfaction, 'is why I bothered to send scouts out in front of us . . . In front, to the flanks, and behind! So far as that's possible with less than a dozen men here.'

I said, 'This Carrasco – is serious.'

Wisps of smoke drifted up from the colonnades of the warehouse, blue in the still air and sunlight over the canal.

Abandoned slow-match. The smell caught in my throat.

My ears still whined from the volley of shots.

Honorius, reaching down to the bridge coping, fingered a demi-sphere blown out of the sandstone. The inner surface showed perfectly smooth.

'I didn't expect hackbutters. But I was watched. If they weren't fools, there'd be *something*. Even if they can't know of Master Rekhmire', or what way he'd direct us to go.'

The excitement attendant on survival burned through me: I turned to look for Rekhmire', to share it with him.

His tall, bald figure wasn't among Honorius's soldiers.

Honorius glanced up, his expression faintly questioning.

At the same moment, the other one of the large, silent Germanic bodyguards, Attila, muttered, 'Aldra Honorius?' and pointed.

3

Honorius swore.

Rekhmire' lay face-down a few yards away on the slope of the bridge, in shadow, slumped at the foot of the parapet wall.

A snub-nosed trickle of liquid ran out from under his legs. Black, as I stared at it – turning bright scarlet in seconds.

The colour of blood when it meets the air.

Pooling under him—

'*Rekhmire'?*'

With no consciousness of moving, I was on my knees on the cobbles beside the large Egyptian. Reaching out—

'No.' Honorius's grip on my shoulder stopped me dead. 'Sergeant?'

The Armenian squatted between me and the sun, and felt with startlingly delicate fingers under Rekhmire''s tilted head.

An aeon later, he said, 'Be all right to move him, I reckon. Carefully. Caught his head on the stonework here, see?'

Blood on the gritty masonry. Rekhmire''s shaven head had a reddened, bleeding patch just below the crown. Honorius's hand ceased to hold me back. Fear choked me; I didn't reach again to touch Rekhmire'. I have seen men die of a snapped neck in such a way.

His eyelids creased without opening. His face formed a scowl. Still unconscious, he whined in the back of his throat.

The Armenian looked up from where he lifted the hem of the linen kilt, and soundlessly exposed the Egyptian's knee to his commander, and incidentally to me.

Jagged black skin and red flesh bulged open on the cap of Rekhmire''s right knee.

Something white showed in the depths, like meat chopped to the bone for cooking. Crisp black patches stank of burned hair. In the wreckage of the knee-joint, I saw a translucent carmine washing over broken shards of bone.

We could all be dead, here, now—

Honorius's harsh voice cracked out above me. 'You men. Carry him. *Don't* drop your guard because you think they won't be back!'

Two of the soldiers dropped bill-hooks to the earth, knelt and swiftly knotted a cloak between the shafts

Frightening: how often they must have done this, to be so proficient—

Stooping, the two men seized the unconscious Egyptian under his arms and one knee.

Rekhmire''s monumental features convulsed: he screamed. The shriek cut through the officers' orders; men talking loudly in the exhilaration of having survived an attack. A cautiously opened door banged shut, with the sound of bars slotting into iron brackets; no chance of calling on any of Dorsodura's inhabitants for a surgeon—

Rekhmire''s scream cut off.

I sprang up beside the bodyguards hoisting him onto the makeshift stretcher, grabbed at the Alexandrine's damp, cold hand, and found him limply unconscious.

Eight protect him! I wish I knew the proper prayers—

Pain cut deep lines even into his unconscious face. Breath hissed between his rounded lips. Blood on his chin— Where he bit through his lip, I realised. Not wounded in the lungs. Oh, Jesú, but suppose the wound turns poison?

Blood soaked through the green wool cloak under Rekhmire''s shattered leg, spattered to the earth, and marked the dust.

'Bind that up as we go!' Honorius harshly ordered.

Saverico obeyed, his helmet still off, his brown curls seeming shockingly unprotected. He crammed cloth against the bleeding knee and yanked it tight, and Rekhmire' did not cry out, did not move—

Breathing. The lift and fall of Rekhmire''s dust-marked chest was just perceptible, to my eye and to the hand that I rested down on his sternum as we moved off. Breathing with an erratic jerk and fall.

'This needs a physician right now!'

'The embassy. The Campo San Barnaba. That way.' Honorius signalled. '*Go.*'

Rekhmire' became conscious before we had staggered a mile through the Dorsodura quarter.

I realised it only as his fingers closed about mine, where I gripped his hand as I walked beside the makeshift stretcher. Large, powerful, the skin oddly smooth for such a masculine hand – it clenched tightly enough around my right hand to make me yelp.

'*Ke'et*—' He slurred the word, rolling his head in the dip of the woollen cloak, and opened clear eyes to stare at the sky. Roofs would be passing him, I realised, glancing up to follow his gaze.

His eyes clenched shut: he screamed, and swallowed the noise into his throat.

'Can I help?' I let Honorius and the soldiers make our way, concentrating only on the man bundled between the staff-weapons. 'What can we do?'

A wavering, high-pitched noise came out between his gritted teeth. It put the hairs on my neck upright. His free hand clawed at his waist – at his belt and purse, I realised. *Does he have something in his purse?*

I freed my hand from his, yanked his belt-buckle open, took the leather strings of his purse and snapped them apart.

The purse fell into the crease of cloth at his hip. Rekhmire' hauled up the leather belt from around his waist, doubled it over, and thrust the leather between his teeth. The hinge of his jaw moved as he bit down.

Berenguer staggered; Rekhmire''s uninjured leg knocked against my side; he made a stifled whinny, like a horse in pain, that turned into a high muffled scream.

The bundle of linen around his leg blotted red, dark red, and clotted black. Blood dripped, leaving a trail down the road. A pair of wild dogs took up following us, thirty yards distant. We crossed another canal bridge. I looked back. The dogs licked the cobblestones on the path behind us.

'Are we close? Is this it?' I hated to demand anything of him in his agony. 'Rekhmire'?'

The whine in his throat cut off.

White showed under his eyelids – only white, in a fish-belly curve that made me shudder, even while I thought it best thing for him.

Honorius argued with his scouts. I took another cloth from Saverico, and tied it as tightly as I could around Rekhmire''s knee. Blood made my hands all the red earth colours. It dried itchily. My head swum with dizziness; I felt cold to my fingertips.

I have seen worse on the field of tourney. Have seen men crippled there. Have fought.

But this is Rekhmire'.

His jaw clenched again, the pain visibly bringing him back to consciousness. Bone moved under the skin. His teeth sheared into the belt-leather. He rasped out a noise of agony.

Sick and cold, I looked away from the jolting cloak, swinging under its heavy burden.

The alley opened onto a deserted campo, and a barred-up church.

'This should be San Barnaba,' Honorius announced, looking around.

A high wall took up all one side of the square, broken only by a single gateway.

All of that gateway, from the bell-tower occupying the tiny arch above, to the narrow gate itself, was closed up with interlocking wrought iron.

4

The bars had been rubbed down to be re-painted. Rusting a perceptible orange now, they were still solidly set into the stonework. No entry by climbing, or pulling a bar loose.

I seized the embassy's rope bell-pull, jangling the bell that hung inaccessibly high. '*Alexandrines!*'

No answer. Honorius stood head-to-head in a muttered conference with his soldiers. I peered through the iron gate into a disused garden, cypress trees growing like tall, skinny black quill-pens.

No, not disused – a garden that some man had marked out around a central well, and then it had never been planted. The dead Pakharu? Nothing more surrounded the Roman-brick well-coping than bare earth, empty tubs, abandoned stepladders, rakes, shovels, wicker baskets.

I got out, 'He said the place is shut up – but there's a caretaker.'

My father bellowed, stentorian. 'Hello the house!'

Humped Roman roof-tiles and small grilled windows made it look like any other of the rare Classical houses in Venice. All the walls were whitewashed plaster, except on the frontage, where a fine pattern of lines and diamonds showed the unplastered areas prepared.

How long has the work been left like this?

'Should we go looking for a barber-surgeon?' I gripped the rails. Winter made them burning cold. 'But these Franks can't doctor—'

A woman in Egyptian dress and Frankish cloak came out of the cloister forming the front of the embassy building.

Her steps caught and faltered, seeing us. I saw her look past me.

She ran towards us, twisted a key in the squealing iron lock, and flung the gates wide open.

'We need a physician—' Honorius began.

The tall, elegant woman in Alexandrine silks fell on her knees in the mud, seizing Rekhmire''s large hands in her own.

He groaned, eyelids moving.

'No!' I squatted and grasped her surprisingly strong wrists, pulling her hands away from his. 'Is there an Alexandrine doctor here?'

Rekhmire''s long lashes flickered. The book-buyer opened his eyes and frowned, evidently confused to find his ex-slave and a woman apparently holding hands across his supine body.

'Ilario?' His eyes moved away from me, the lines deepening in the skin, showing pain and confusion. '*Jahar* . . . ?'

'Neferet.' The woman emphasised the Alexandrine word, an odd long-suffering quality in her voice. She looked up. 'Is any other man of you hurt?'

Honorius shook his head. 'No worse than we can deal with.'

Rekhmire' shifted and stiffened. The cloak and weapon-shafts supporting his sagging body gave him increasing pain, I could see it. His teeth clacked together; he shivered as he spoke. 'Jahar – Neferet – we should – out of sight, quickly—'

'Rest.' The woman pulled her hands out of mine, and stroked a gentle finger along Rekhmire''s brow. She stood. I copied her, as she glanced at us, and then back at the Alexandrine House.

'Inside!' The tall woman ushered us quickly into the embassy grounds, her large hands clasped in front of her. She glanced down at Rekhmire' as she walked. She had the oval eyelids and grave long upper lip of a pharaoh.

'My name is Neferet.' She spoke to Honorius, his armour marking him out as a knight and man of rank. 'I'm a book-buyer for the Royal Library . . . '

She guided the soldiers under the cloisters; I saw we had arrived at the house's main door.

' . . . There *is* no physician here. Ours returned home after Ambassa-dor Pakharu died. I'll . . . find you the best Frankish doctor I can.'

Without opening his eyes, the supine Rekhmire' gritted out, 'Butchers!'

It was clearly a known macabre joke between them: the tall Alexandrine woman smiled at it with long acquaintance.

The house's interior hall was all carved beams and painted brickwork, ceilings higher than I had imagined. Frankish rather than Alexandrine style. I blinked, to become accustomed faster to the dim light. Neferet glided forward, issuing a stream of orders to Honorius's soldiers – I saw no house-slaves – my father merely catching Sergeant Orazi's glance and nodding consent. Boots clattered: I made out a wide staircase as Honorius's men carried Rekhmire' up it.

Saverico, his helmet discarded, had his head bent around so far he might have been trying to see his own spine. His fingers wrenched at the buckles down the front of his brigandine. One of the older men, Aznar, came forward and took the weight of the steel-plate jacket, while Sergeant Orazi brushed the boy's hands aside and undid the buckles.

They unpeeled him out of the brigandine like a clam out of its shell. Something fell to the tiles with a hard clatter.

Saverico, seeming uneven on his feet, nonetheless bent and snatched it up, and held it triumphantly.

A deformed, flat ovoid of metal – *of lead!*

Saverico cheerfully waved the bullet that had flattened itself against a back-plate of his brigandine. '*Told* you I didn't fall over!'

Orazi ruffled his hair affectionately. 'So you didn't. Keep that one to show your grandchildren. Of course, if you get one eight inches lower, you won't *have* grandchildren . . . '

I lost the noise of their affectionate insults, my hand stealing to the high curve of my belly. Barely less than flat, but under it . . .

One of the oak doors across the hall opened; a man came out, calling to the Egyptian woman.

Much my age, I thought. Four- or five-and-twenty. An Italian of some well-born variety; dark-haired, well-dressed.

His gaze swept the jabbering hall, past Honorius making rapid ceremonious and chivalric introductions to the Alexandrine Neferet, and his eyes locked with mine.

He stepped forward, an expression of shock on his face. 'But – I *recognise* you! Master Ilario!'

5

'It's possible that I've had entirely too many surprises for one morning!' I muttered.

Honorius hadn't noticed. He had his head bent – not so far down – talking to the Egyptian woman, evidently conferring about doctors. I heard the shouts of the soldiers upstairs, sorting out a sick-bed. My impulse was to push the Italian man out of my path to Rekhmire'.

But he knows Ilario!

I don't know him.

There is a dagger on his hip, but no sword.

Assassin? If this man knows my face and name—

The Italian gave me a smile replete with self-confidence. 'You're *Judas!*'

It took my breath. I stepped back, accidentally, into the light streaming in through the still-open main door. The Italian man gained a clear look at me.

A blush like a fourteen-year-old page-boy's went up his face, reddening him from his round doublet collar to his brown curls.

'How rude of me!' His words tumbled over each other on their way out, as if he had once stuttered, and trained himself out of it. 'I apologise! That must be your . . . brother? You are Messer Ilario's sister?'

Presumably he apologises for mistaking me for a man.

I had a momentary, slightly hysterical, desire to assure him that the reverse error is no improvement.

He wore Florentine fashion, I realised, as Masaccio often had. Striped parti-coloured hose and skin-tight doublet, the shirt itself of better quality than I could afford. Likewise his shoes, and the small brimless felt hat. I didn't recognise him. And I would at least have remembered that nose, I thought. Which he would need to grow into, like a puppy growing into its paws.

He may have been one of the visitors to the workshop in Rome: there were many. That might be how he knows me.

'Excuse me,' I said steadily, keeping a grim hold on emotion, 'my friend is hurt; I have to go.'

Honorius, passing me on his way to the stairs, gripped my elbow once and tightly. 'Come up in a minute, when we've got him settled in a bed! The damn spy won't want *you* seeing him in pain.'

He was gone before I could question or object.

He gave no glance to the Florentine man.

The Alexandrine woman's husky, pleasantly-musical voice interrupted as I stared after my father. 'Dear Leon!'

I turned to find her giving the Florentine man a look I've rarely seen bettered by Iberian chatelaines with eight hundred years of the blood of Castile and Aragon in their veins.

'Make our friend feel at home; she'll wish to be with her sick friend here – won't you—?' She left the questioning gap with which polite people demand one's name.

We didn't discuss this, I realised; hearing by the evidence of his bellows that Honorius had reached the first floor of the Alexandrine house.

Names are fiercely gendered in the Italian languages. With this belly, I felt inclined to thank Christ Imperator that my saint's day is that of St Hillary – a name which has so many variations, both male and female.

'I'm Ilaria.'

And I must tell Honorius and Rekhmire' that.

'Neferet,' the Alexandrine woman returned, as if I hadn't retained her earlier, less-formal introduction. 'And this is Messer Leon Battista, of the Alberti family; a lawyer, newly returned graduated from Bologna.'

She stood an inch or so taller than the Italian; her gown and layered petticoats (in a dozen consecutive shades of blue) shone with gold thread, her hair was caught up away from her ears with pearl combs, and kohl lined her eyes. The gauze scarf wound around her neck and pinned up to the pearl combs just about resembled the hair-covering that Venice requires of modest women.

Reminded of that, I put my cloak hood back, feeling myself shabby in water-faded silks.

Leon Battista stared the more keenly, making no apology for it. Something about his gaze struck a note of recognition in me.

'I see the differences now,' he announced. 'Are you and your brother twins?'

I smiled amiably, not lying in speech, but allowing him to draw the wrong conclusion. Faces do differ in context. The jolt of meeting someone who recognised me reverberated through my body. Outside of Taraco, it's not something I have been used to.

Leon beamed at me. 'Tommaso never mentioned his Ilario had a sister. But then, I don't suppose he ever noticed anything but his paints!'

Pain showed abruptly and incongruously on his youth-plump face.

News will have had time to travel here by land, while we were on board ship. And if this man was Masaccio's client, or friend . . .

'I must tell you, Madonna Ilaria – no,' the Florentine interrupted himself. 'Let it wait: you have more important matters. But may I beg a word, soon? And I have some thoughts about the art of painting . . . Perhaps we could discuss them, at a later time?'

A painter, yes – that's why I recognise that weighing stare.

A slave learns to intimate the slightest sign of jealousy; however, I had no need for the talent. Neferet put her hand very firmly over Leon Battista's arm and showed me all her white teeth.

Moved by sheer contrariness – and a wish to delay feeling helpless in the presence of Rekhmire''s sickening pain – I nodded at Leon Battista. Who I suspected Honorius would assure me was no potential murderer. 'Would it surprise you to learn that I also paint, sir?'

He shook his head, beaming under that great hawk-nose that went so incongruously with his boyish curls. 'The skill should be accounted a mark of honour in a woman, as it was in ancient times. Wasn't Martia, Varro's daughter, celebrated for her painting?'

I felt unaccountably warmed, despite not knowing either name.

'Painting shows the noble intellect in a man,' Leon continued, somewhat earnestly, over the clatter of soldiers' sandals, and the outer door banging shut and open again. I heard men bawling addresses, where possible surgeons and doctors might reside.

The Florentine added, 'Why not also in a remarkable woman? The only true requirement is nobility of mind – the ancient Greeks knew this: this is why it was forbidden by law among them for a slave to learn to paint. To be worthy of painting, a man must have a free mind.'

The darkness and the sepia horizons of Carthage come back to me, and the heat of encaustic wax. I do not forget the weight of a collar about my throat. Or the man who removed it.

'Nobility of mind occurs in the strangest places,' I offered. Neferet stretched her lips; the Florentine Leon Battista coloured again, seemingly susceptible to blushing.

Rekhmire''s voice cried out, muffled, somewhere above my head.

Why should I care if my father thinks the book-buyer's pride will be damaged by me seeing him in pain? Why am I standing down here as if I were a respectable unmarried Venetian female? Is the compulsion of mere clothing so compelling?

'You'll excuse me; I'm needed.' I smiled apologies to Neferet.

Messer Battista bowed lithely enough to convince me he might be Florentine or Venetian nobility by birth.

I grabbed at my skirts so as not to tread on the hems as I strode up the stairs.

Honorius clattered down towards me, Orazi at his heels, and brushed his hand over my shoulder as we passed, as he might have done to a mercenary recruit. 'Look after him, will you? I've told Attila to give him a little of the woman's poppy-juice—'

There was something more – *'I don't like to without a sawbones' word'?* – but he was across the hall and out of the Alexandrine house by then, massive wooden door slamming behind him.

If the assassin's attack was disrupted sufficiently well, no man will have watched to see where we went. No man will be watching my father now.

If not . . .

Rekhmire' lay sprawled on his back, on a low bed that had evidently been hastily dragged closer to the small room's window, for the better light. I would have walked softly to avoid disturbing him – but the soldiers, briskly moving about and making a field-hospital of the place, shook the floorboards with their tread. I saw him wincing each time, no matter that his eyes were closed.

Seeing how he sweated, I went into the room and sat down on the edge of the bed, and wiped his forehead with a clean kerchief.

'How badly does it hurt?'

He blinked, black pupils widening under the poppy elixir's influence. '*Fuck* . . . '

'That's much as I imagined.'

If there was anything to be said for the flat and doubtless flea-ridden Frankish pallet acting as his mattress, it was that it didn't dip under my weight and shift his wounded leg. Rekhmire' bore my ministrations with immense dignity.

'This Neferet. You know her? Can we trust her?'

I asked to distract him, more than anything; his hips moved against the bed, as if he continually shifted to find some comfortable position on the linen sheets, and as continually failed. And because I did not want to say, *Are you going to die?* or hear his answer.

'Neferet is – an old friend – a cousin—'

The room's door banged open: Rekhmire' winced. Honorius, in a swirl of cold air from outdoors, cursed and caught hold of the door's edge before the wood could reverberate back into the doorway.

'Got you a doctor!' He beamed, reaching up to unbuckle his sallet, scratching his fingers through his cropped grey hair as if the helmet-lining irritated him. He bent to cast a knowledgeable eye at the blood seeping through Rekhmire''s bandages. 'Found him by a Free Company man's word. He's from Edirne. He's a Turk. He'll be here inside the hour.'

6

Each minute took days to pass, even if I counted their number on my racing pulse.

'Inside the hour' – it's close on midday! *What's the delay?*

Rekhmire''s forehead grew hotter under my fingers. He lay in a rigidly tense stillness, flinching as men clumped across the house's uneven floor-boards, on this and the ground floor.

I wiped his sweat away. The thought of what any physician might say made me sweat, also.

Suppose the physician wants to butcher the leg off?

Or says *Nothing can be done: he'll die?*

'By the Eight!' Rekhmire''s voice sounded thin. He slitted his eyes weakly against the winter light flooding in through the leaded window. 'Turkish physician. Slaughter me anyway, I'd think!'

'Just because Alexandria and the Turkish Empire share a border?' I forced a smile. 'He'll make you suffer first. Maybe poison.'

The corner of Rekhmire''s mouth twitched, recognisably a smile of his own.

Dare I give him more of the poppy elixir?

I dared not look at the knotted bandage over his wound. The sheets were sodden now, under his leg.

'Rekhmire'!' Neferet's husky feminine voice sounded. 'I have your physician.'

She entered the room after Honorius, together with a tall, spare man in robes and trousers; all of them followed by another man in Turkish dress, who stood a head taller than Attila behind him, and must duck under the ceiling's exposed oak beams.

'This is . . . Bariş, I believe.' Neferet gave me the look that, when I was a slave, I would have taken as a cue to leave the room.

Being freed, I merely continued to sit, and looked up at the thin Turkish doctor. He appeared to be in his middle years. His head was swathed in scarlet cloth, not unlike the rolled hats of the Franks.

'Bariş.' He pointed at himself. And at his companion, who was setting down a large ash-wood box with a leather carry-strap. 'Balaban.'

It might have been the giant's name; it might have been a description of medical tools. I bit the skin at the corner of my fingernail, worrying at it.

There was a brief interchange that I thought included Visigoth and Alexandrine Latin, as well as medical Greek; Honorius jerked a thumb at where the small man Orazi stood by the door, and added, 'My sergeant speaks most of the Turkish languages . . . '

'That may help.' Bariş looked down, his knife-nosed face in profile, and gave Rekhmire' a polite nod. He stumbled, evidently not familiar with the language. 'Master . . . Rekhmire'? My commanding officer is here, Venezia, recovering from a wound and sea-sickness, or we would have left for Edirne before now. Your good luck, I hope.'

Rekhmire''s hooded lids came down over his eyes for a moment. 'You're from a Janissary regiment.'

The Turk nodded, his teeth white as he smiled. '"Bariş" is not my given name! The soldiers call me that. It means "peace". Either because I refuse to take up weapons and fight, or because I bring peace to many as a doctor . . . '

My father was smiling, I saw, and Orazi and Attila; Neferet looked blank and slightly upset.

With a ghost of his normal demure irony, Rekhmire' said, 'I hope your patients don't *all* die . . . '

'Do I look that poor?' The Turk signalled and his servant brought the wooden case forward.

'The Janissaries are soldiers?' I queried, and at Honorius's nod, couldn't help a sigh of relief. 'Good! This is a gun-shot wound. Madama Neferet had to send away the Frankish doctor she found about two hours back. He said gunshot wounds are poisoned—'

The tall Turk snorted, his face becoming lively. '*Poisoned!* Astarte's bloody hand! You'd think the Franks never saw a wound made by anything that burned before. If they'd seen a man left black by Greek Fire . . . '

Rekhmire' barely managed to lift his finger, but it stopped the physician's enthusiasm.

The Egyptian raised an eyebrow at me, dignified despite laying flat on his back. I swayed a little where I sat on the side of the bed. I suspect I was much of his own colour.

Rekhmire' murmured, 'It's not the moment for that discussion, I think. One forgets how clearly you painters see in your mind's eye . . . '

I know the techniques to make size and gesso and pigment mimic flesh blackened at the edge and red-raw underneath. Masaccio was teaching me them for the Church martyrs. I just have no desire to think of them while the bundle of linen around Rekhmire''s leg weeps blood and yellow matter onto the sheets.

'Balaban, go and boil water; bring it when it's just warm.' The Turk bent over Rekhmire''s leg, not touching the rough bandaging. 'Master Honorius, I will work easier if you take most of your men away. Leave me a servant.'

The Turk Bariş nodded in my direction; clearly judging Rekhmire'
content to have me there.

The other Janissary, Balaban, returned with water while Neferet was
still arguing; both my father and the doctor capped her protests with the
unsuitability of a woman being present at the physician's work, and the
door closed on her voice arguing, 'But *Ilaria*—'

Honorius walked back from the door, the window light illuminating his
face, shaking his head. '"Ilaria".'

With the Turks present, I would say nothing. I found my fists
clenching while the physician and Balaban, between them, carefully
soaked the bandages around Rekhmire''s leg and eased them off, crusted
with congealed blood as they were.

Fresh blood stained the sheets. Bariş bent over and peered, his ship's-
prow nose barely an inch from the Egyptian's flesh.

'You were lucky.' He straightened, pushing his hand against the small
of his back. 'The shot was below your garment. If it had gone through
your clothes, it might have carried street-filth into the wound and
poisoned it. I would say it was a shot from long range—'

Honorius, dragging up a joint-stool and sitting at the foot of the bed,
shook his head. 'Emplaced ambush, close range. I think they botched the
second volley through haste – my lads were bearing down on them.'

Bariş gave him a look which spoke of more kinship between mercenary
and Janissary than there was foreignness between Iberian and Turk.
'How did you know, Captain, they were a small enough number to be
overwhelmed?'

Honorius's smile was frightening. 'We didn't.'

The physician harrumphed a little. He leaned down again to study the
wound. 'You see, the cap of the knee is broke with a crack? This was
almost a spent round. I say the man panicks, perhaps double-charges his
arquebus.'

'*Double?*' Rekhmire''s voice echoed mine as I exclaimed.

Honorius shrugged, chin on the heels of his hands, as if his poring over
the Egyptian's wound would tell him as much as the physician's.

'It's not difficult. You panic, you forget there's a charge in the gun,
you load another ball and powder – the second charge goes *phut!*, at the
front end, with a lot of smoke, and very little power.'

'Balaban.' The Turkish doctor signalled. His servant took one tray out
of the wooden box and offered up the second one underneath.

The light gleamed on a metal instrument, not so unlike a stylus. I saw
Physician Bariş dipping his hands in a second bowl of water, muttering a
prayer to Astarte. Immediately after, he began to probe into the wound.

'It struck at the side, see?' His spoke loudly enough to conceal
Rekhmire''s gasp and cry. 'A very small wound, here, and then a large
one, where part of the lead ball has torn free. Stone shot would have been
better, but . . . here. Hold out your hand, Master Alexandrine.'

Droplets of sweat ran down Rekhmire''s face. His whole body felt hot, radiating against me where I sat next to him. He opened his fingers as if obedience were automatic.

The Turkish doctor dropped a ragged dark shape onto his hand.

'A keepsake!' Bariş smirked. 'Your bullet. There. Now . . . there are pieces that splash off. Can't have that . . . That *will* poison the wound . . . '

He pulled out five or six smaller bits of lead, no larger than orange-pips, and added the hardened droplets to the collection in Rekhmire''s palm. The Egyptian closed his hand convulsively.

'Think of it as dropping an egg . . . ' Physician Bariş's voice sounded absent with concentration. 'Most sits as a mess in the middle, some bits spatter. Lead ball is no different. And some of the bits are embedded in your *other* leg. Hold still!'

Rekhmire' reached across his body with his free hand. Belatedly, I realised what he wanted, and put my hand into his. He squeezed hard enough that only experience as a slave enabled me to conceal the pain. *But I would not show it, now, and not for fear of a beating.*

'You are lucky,' Bariş repeated. 'A professional soldier would have kept his presence of mind, and re-loaded properly; I'd be sawing off your leg, and not hoping to patch it. An underloaded lead ball is not the worst wound in the— *Ah.* That, I think, is the last piece. Now let me look at what we have. Balaban, more water.'

Rekhmire' swore in a whisper so quiet that I could make out none of the words. It was a continuous stream of sound. The Turk took other instruments from his box, delving into the bloody wound, prodding at bone and muscle. Rekhmire''s ruined knee appeared swollen, now, white at the edges, as if the meat were too large for taut skin to contain it.

I could not look, despite how much professional curiosity might oblige me to. Much as I might want to attend an autopsy, to know what it is under a man's skin that affects what a painter shows . . . this is in no way how I wished to come by the knowledge.

Rekhmire''s forehead glistened, hot to the touch. 'Well?'

'Hmm?' The physician Bariş straightened up. 'Oh – I've seen misload injuries before. This, not enough to kill or amputate, enough to put you out of commission for a few months. But the operation will be difficult. The bones need to be put in their proper places, to knit, but then it must also move, afterwards, as a joint. I think it probable you will limp, after this.'

Rekhmire''s hooded lids blinked. 'Badly?'

Not a question I had expected the Egyptian to ask. *He's not so vain as to care about that—*

But he's a book-buyer: he's in the habit of travelling.

Rekhmire''s frown turned into a wince as the Turk began to re-dress his knee. I thought it brutal handling, to my eye, but I may have been prejudiced.

'This is the worse break.' The Turk stood back, finally, and illustratively rapped the front of his own knee, in his worn woollen trousers. 'Once the operation is done, you spend six weeks with your leg tied to a plank while you lay in bed. Or you get used to being a cripple. I'll attend you, all the while my captain's here. And I regret, the operation will cost; I must buy supplies, and in winter that's difficult.'

I spoke to Honorius before the Egyptian could. 'You're always saying you want me to take some of your money – I will. For this. I can owe you, and pay you back as soon as I get a commission.'

Rekhmire' opened his mouth: Honorius glared him into silence and turned back to me.

'Of course.' Honorius's rapid agreement came in the dialect of Taraconensis. 'Let's hope it isn't more than I have with me. If I visit a banker, every man in Europe will know where I am.'

'Captain-General,' Rekhmire' began stiffly.

'Shut *up*, Egyptian.' It was the same tone he addressed to his men-at-arms. And the same smile.

Rekhmire' hissed in pain and reluctantly nodded.

I spoke across them, to Physician Bariş. 'Doctor. This operation needs to happen as soon as possible.'

'Clearly. Now—'

I couldn't identify my father's expression while we debated, but it came to me as we made final arrangements for Rekhmire' to be operated on. *Honorius looks proud.*

There was a back-and-forth of words as the doctor packed away his urine flask and probes, and stood back for his large companion to pick up the box. The Turk measured Rekhmire' with an eye I thought not unfriendly, given the long-standing rivalry between Constantinople and the Turkish Empire.

'I will come early tomorrow, when I have collected supplies, and we have all the morning's light.'

It was more than I could do not to speak up. 'Doctor Bariş. What are the chances of a full recovery?'

'If not dead of a sickness after the operation?' He spoke as bluntly as any military man. 'Half and half. If it doesn't go bad, it will take long to finally heal.'

Lines showed around his narrowing eyes; he shot an uncomfortable look at Honorius and – to my surprise – at me.

'The Egyptian's got an equal chance of being crippled. But I don't like the look of how you're carrying your belly at all – your chances are maybe worse.'

7

I gave them all the coldest look possible, which, after nine years in King Rodrigo's court, I had perfected. '*I* don't need to see a doctor.'

Honorius's expression clearly weighed up Rekhmire''s immediate need against my later one.

The white of his eyes showed momentarily all around his irises.

I believe he's just realised what childbirth may mean for me.

'We'll talk,' Honorius said, his tone both commanding and noncommittal, and meant for me as much as for Physician Bariş.

Honorius needs to catch his breath as much as all of us.

And to prepare to be one of those who holds down Rekhmire' during the mending of his knee.

At the Alexandrine house door, Bariş gave an apologetic shrug. 'I had thought this house was shut up after the foreigner died. It was said you had your own physician here. If he's gone, will you also need a midwife found?'

Honorius held the door for him. Neferet and I gave identical shrugs, I was annoyed to note; she as unwilling to talk about her nesting in the closed embassy as I was about my belly.

Immediately after the morning's ambush, with Rekhmire''s agony echoing off the walls of endless squares and across innumerable bridges, my back had prickled with apprehension. Every tendon in my body pulled taut – as it now did again. Can we trust this Bariş not to gossip?

I thought of mimicking a forgettable, skulking, idle slave, but that might not work as well in Frankish or Turk lands as it does around the Mediterranean.

Honorius inclined his head, every inch the Iberian knight. 'Master Bariş, you'll be well paid for your trouble.'

For your silence, I translated.

Honorius accompanied Bariş and the giant Balaban as far as the iron gate, while I stood watching from the door, and returned looking satisfied with himself.

'We'll stay holed up here.' He took my arm, escorting me in as a man does a woman. 'I doubt the Aldra's man will try ambush again on the streets, and this house is defensible. Most criminals, banditti, hired thugs; they don't want to take on soldiers. Word will get around. If our "friend" gets to hire a second gang of ambushers, I'll eat my gauntlets . . . '

His effort to put me at ease made me smile, and then sober. 'Do you think he was at the ambush – this Ramiro Carrasco?'

'I couldn't make out their captain's face. But we can hope!' Honorius glanced around the Alexandrine house, or all that could be seen from this entrance hall. 'It took me long enough to find the Janissary doctor, and I was visible on the streets. While we were searching – this is the first time in three weeks that I haven't caught sight of some bastard skulking about behind me. Either Ramiro Carrasco can't find a man willing to play spy, or, God grant it, we hacked his head off in the confusion of the fight.'

I understood, belatedly, why men might carry their dead away from an ambush. It leaves us uncertain.

The shock of the attack still made my heart shake. The bruises Honorius's armour left in my flesh showed now, coming out green and black. I clenched my fists, and unclenched them, forcing the tendons and muscles to relax.

'This.' Honorius put his fingertips gently on the swell of my belly. 'We must speak of this.'

A muffled cry upstairs made me look in that direction.

'Yes. Not yet.'

The lean man frowned, but he allowed me to walk away from him and climb the stairs.

'I have my own decoction of poppy,' Bariş observed, the day following. 'It's stronger than you Franks use. It should make the surgery on your knee less of a painful butchery than you would otherwise find it.'

I found I felt sick.

'We use straps,' the Turk added, setting out his sharpening stone and instruments in the lid of his case, 'and you have three men to hold the leg still. Balaban, and those two of your soldiers like him in size.'

Honorius nodded, calling for Tottola and Attila without arguing about it.

As preparations began, Honorius stabbed his finger at me. '*You* don't get to do this. Belly! God He knows what it would do to a child in the womb, to witness blood like this!'

'That is *nothing* but superstition—'

He seized me by the scruff of my silk bodice. I dug my heels in, so he should not thrust me out and bar the door behind me.

'I'll go if Rekhmire' wants me to, not otherwise!'

A sensible interior voice asked what a slightly-built man-woman with no medical training might do, apart from witness Rekhmire' humiliated by his lack of control over his own pain. Stubbornly, I reminded myself: It's not my decision to take.

'You will leave when *I* say.' It evidently defeated Honorius that he could neither make himself use force on a pregnant daughter, nor beat the obstinacy out of his son. He fumed. 'I have no *idea* how I'm supposed to keep you safe!'

Rekhmire''s voice interrupted from the bed. 'I want Ilario here.'

Honorius turned his head and stared at him.

My bowels twisted, as if I would need to run to the necessary-house before long.

'You do?' I sounded startled, I realised.

Rekhmire' met my gaze. His eyes were bloodshot, but the irises still glowed the colour of old brandy where the light through the window caught him. He gave a pained, gentle smile.

'You've got a cool head.' He made a movement of his lips that would have been a wry shrug of the body, could he have moved that. 'I want to know what's done to me. Even if I weren't out of my mind with poppy-juice, I wouldn't be capable of seeing it. You sit here, right here next to me, and draw it. Then I can look, when I'm recovered.'

I held out both hands to him.

'And your fingers will stop shaking as soon as you sit down with a drawing-board.' There was a hint of the brusque master I had met in Carthage, offset by the deprecating humour in his gaze. 'Will you do this?'

I didn't hesitate.

'Of course I'll do it if you want me to.'

I drew with charcoal, so that when my hand shook, it was easy to erase the mistake. I copied the shapes of bone and gristle and stitches, in the clear north light, highlighting with good quality white chalk. I shut my ears to his howling pain.

8

I have never been so glad in my life as when his skin was sewn up and the surgery was over.

Over the next few hours of the morning, I sat anxiously, dreading that Rekhmire' would wake up a different man than before the poppy had stupefied him.

Making copies of the surgical drawings occupied my hands. I drew them out with pen and lamp-black ink, with a spare copy also for Physician Bariş. (At which he smiled, and remitted ten per cent of his fee.) And then I had nothing to do but sit beside the sick-bed.

As the largely silent Attila dosed out smaller and smaller amounts of tincture of poppy, Rekhmire' ceased to wake and slip into drugged sleep at regular intervals, and woke fully.

At midday, becoming conscious, he snarled at me to help prop him up against the low bed's headboard. I had sent the men-at-arms away, seeing how he flinched as their heavy tread on the floorboards jarred his leg, even bandaged and bound securely as it was between wooden planks. It occurred to me that I should call them back to restrain him.

But he'll be quieter if allowed some part of his own way.

I put my drawing-board and ink-pot down. Eventually, Rekhmire' sat white-faced and sweating, supported by bolsters.

'Cursed, stuffed, *moth*-eaten Frankish furniture!' he snarled, staring at the hangings of the bed. He shifted uncomfortably on the mattress, and made disgusted attempts at removing the blankets. I wasn't sure of the wisdom of it, but I helped him anyway.

Tottola had come in earlier, deftly lifting the woollen blankets and putting down a framework woven of willow-branches, that held the covers suspended up over the Egyptian's right leg. Head down and muttering almost inaudibly, he confessed the weaving skill was his own.

Rekhmire' now sniffed, grabbed at the wooden frame, and attempted to push his large and now ungainly body out and off the side of the bed.

'*Not a chance!*' I grabbed his wrists; each muscular enough that I could barely close a hand around it, as long as my fingers are.

'Copulation!' Rekhmire' spat out, in a pure Alexandrine accent, and shifted his hands to grip me, instead, while I eased him back onto the mattress. 'I intend to get up— Copulating diseased male dogs!'

'Don't move your leg, damn it—'

'Go bugger a bastard mule!'

'I can see this is going to be an educational experience. Learning a lot of useful Egyptian phrases . . . ' I attempted to stifle a grin, and found myself needing to wipe wet eyelids. I rubbed my face on the shoulder of my dress.

'You're not hurt.' Rekhmire''s taut tone kept it from being a question. 'I didn't ask before – was any other man . . . ?'

'No, no injuries. We're all well.' I let go, and went to push back the shutters, allowing more light into the dark Frankish room, and giving myself a clearer view of the Egyptian's worrying pallor.

'There was a doctor? A Frank?'

'That's the one your cousin Neferet threw off the premises . . . ' Momentarily, I recalled the face of the Egyptian doctor in Rome – Siamun. For all his ability to see me as an interesting set of organs, and lack of tact, I would have trusted him more with Rekhmire''s injury than the Sorbonne-trained Burgundian that Neferet had thrown out.

' . . . Then Honorius found a Janissary. He's good. And coming to check on you again this evening.'

The human body breathes, moves, speaks. As a slave at sick-beds, I have seen how very easily it falls prey to hot infection, thickened lungs, brain-spasms, and inexplicable deaths in sleep. *I do not want to see the Egyptian die.*

The clouds outside the window shutters shifted, winter sunlight brightening as if a shutter had been opened in a lamp.

Rekhmire' pushed himself further upright, his colour changing. 'Find me something I can use as a crutch.'

'You can't get up!' I spoke with no more patience than was to be expected under the circumstances. 'You've just had your leg blown open and sewn closed!'

'I need to talk to Neferet!'

'However important it is, it can wait!' I sat down heavily on the edge of the bed. So what if it makes the Egyptian wince? That in itself should tell him to *stay still!*

'When did you start work as a book-buyer?' I demanded.

Rekhmire' gazed at me with dark pupils reduced to pin-points, every line denoting stubbornness showing clearly in his face. Both his eyebrows shot up.

He answered the question, to my surprise.

'Sixteen. I was apprenticed to old Nebwy.'

People moved about in the house below. Nothing sounded urgent. I continued: 'What else have you done?'

'Ilario—'

'What trades? Occupations?' I didn't move from the bed, despite Rekhmire''s continual fidgeting to shift the covers, since I didn't trust him not to attempt to leave it again. 'Nothing, am I correct?'

His mouth set in a familiar obdurate line.

'So,' I said, 'that would mean that for, what, half your life, you've been wandering around the Mediterranean lands. And Asia. And the Frankish countries. And Christus Imperator knows where else!'

Rekhmire''s glare was less impressive when delivered sitting up in bed.

'Oh, but I'm sorry I took your collar off you! What's your point, Ilario?'

'"Ilaria",' I corrected, and saw I wouldn't need to further explain that. 'Rekhmire' – when did you last stay *anywhere* longer than a few months?'

He frowned thunderously. In the voice of a man running out of his store of patience, and not much inclined to look for replenishment, he demanded, 'What precisely do you mean by that?'

I reached forward and shoved a supporting bolster more firmly against the side of his ribs. 'I *mean* that you're going to be a God-awful invalid!'

It reassured him, so much was immediately visible.

I could all but see his thoughts on his face – 'Ilario would not joke with me in this particular manner if I were dying.'

The Alexandrine eunuch, well aware of his build and six-foot height, imitated the pout of a small boy. Clearly it was designed to make me laugh in turn. Regrettably, I couldn't help a spluttering giggle.

'You look ridiculous!'

'You'll be sorry when you have to nurse me.' He beamed, glancing about the room. 'I believe I shall ask Neferet to bring in a truckle-bed, so that you can sleep here – in case I need a drink of water during the night.'

'There's a canal outside your window,' I assured him. 'Although if you drink from it, I think all your troubles might be ended, judging from the smell.'

Rekhmire' grinned. '*Ilaria*. Listen. If you let me lean on your shoulder, I can very likely walk—'

'*No!*'

The Alexandrine woman Neferet glided into the room as I gave vent to a bellow entirely too rough to be female.

She raised a brow in a manner that left me in no doubt she and Rekhmire' were fellow countrymen. And fellow bureaucrats. She swept her robes about her with one long-fingered hand, and seated herself gracefully on a linen-oak chest near the head of the bed.

As if I were no more present than a slave, she addressed Rekhmire'. 'How are you, now the surgery's over?'

Rekhmire' grunted.

Brightly social, the woman persisted, 'And how is Lord Menmet-Ra?'

She did not call the plump ambassador to Rome *old Pamiu*, I noted. Or not in front of me.

'He's trying to avoid promotion to here!' Rekhmire' snapped testily. 'Ty-ameny wants him to take over in Pakharu's place. The last thing Pamiu wants is an ambassador's place where he'll have to *work*. I imagine he thinks it was overwork caused Pakharu to drop dead at his desk, and not the fever!'

Neferet chuckled. Her behaviour seemed more free than a Frankish woman of Venice: I wondered if this was always so in Constantinople.

And wondered also whether Rekhmire' might like me to interrupt this conversation. *Since she's plainly come up to get whatever she can while pain and the poppy makes his tongue unguarded!*

Standing and passing behind the woman to close the room door, I gave him a questioning look.

Timed while Neferet poured him water, he returned the weak ghost of a wink.

Neferet helped him to sip, and then clasped her hands under the folds of robes in her lap. 'Rome may be a backwater, but I understand the food is good there. Menmet-Ra would like that.'

The line of Rekhmire''s shoulders altered enough to tell me his pain was increasing.

Bluntly, he demanded, 'Where's your guest? The German Guildsman?'

A memory of ship-board conversation on the *Iskander* came back to me. I watched Neferet's large, long fingers creep out and play with the string of faience beads that hung from her belt. 'Guildsman?'

Rekhmire''s normal equable expression dissolved into a scowl, either provoked by the pain of his wound or using it as a credible excuse.

'Yes, the man who claims to have invented a writing-*machina*! This "Herr Mainz" from the Germanies! The man Pamiu wishes me to see. The man your *employer* Ty-ameny urgently wishes to speak with!'

He struck the side of the bed in exasperation, and with worryingly little impact.

'You must have seen the messages, Neferet! I know that the Queen wrote to Ambassador Pakharu before he died; it will have been in the papers you cleared up and sent home—'

'Did she send you to check up on me?'

Neferet's expression held shrewdness and some dislike, but I had no idea what to attribute to the situation, and what to past interaction between them.

With the silent deference of a slave, I went to make up the fire in the hearth, relying on those movements to make the woman, at least, automatically forget that I was present. Lumps of sea-coal dirtied my fingers; I wondered what nature of marks one might make on paper or wood using it.

My back was to the bed. I heard it creak as Rekhmire' leaned against the headboard.

'The embassy mail hasn't had time to catch up with me, these last few months. What I know, I know from Menmet-Ra. He asked if I would come here—'

'To check up on me.' She re-emphasised the words.

I turned my head to watch covertly, and saw that her every limb was stiff.

'I didn't ask for Pakharu's job! I didn't ask to be here when he died! Sacred Eight, I'm a book-buyer, not a diplomat! All I've been able to do is shut the embassy down, and tell the Venetians that the Queen-Goddess will send a replacement when the weather allows travelling. And deal with some minor essential matters myself. I'll be *happy* to hand over to Pakharu's replacement – whether that's Menmet-Ra, or any other man, or you—'

'Me?' Rekhmire''s voice was a dry squeak. 'I've no desire for an ambassador's post!'

'Really?' The Alexandrine woman leaned forward, sitting right on the edge of the linen-chest. 'Is that why you're here before Pakharu's sandals are cold? Travelling in *winter*? Because you're not looking for a promotion into the diplomatic service, and out of book-buying?'

Her pronounced features were all drawn up in concentration as she studied him: the light from the window would have made her a wonderful study to draw. Kohl emphasised the narrowing of her eyes as she searched his face.

Some kind of conclusion came to her; the moment of decision was obvious.

She rose to her feet with fluid grace. 'I'm sorry; I shouldn't speak to you like this while you're injured—'

'Neferet! I really have *no* interest—'

'You sleep, if you can; I'll come up again later.'

Her sandals clacked across the oak floorboards. The door shut behind her.

I poured a mug of Frankish small beer and moved to offer it to Rekhmire'. The brightness of the sun showed me droplets of sweat coalescing on the skin of his forehead, trickling down his temples.

'She's not going to tell you about this Herr Mainz,' I observed. 'Whoever he is. Who *is* he? Is it the man you mentioned while we were on the *Iskander*?'

He drank, and closed his eyes briefly. 'Is that an effort to take my mind off pain? Or merely vulgar curiosity?'

'Both,' I admitted. I added, to make him laugh, 'But mostly, vulgar curiosity.'

The Egyptian smiled faintly, opening his eyes. He shook his head when I offered to help him hold the drink; the pitch-lined leather cup shaking dangerously in his hands, liquid all but slopping onto the sheets.

'Apparently—' Rekhmire''s voice sounded weak, but familiarly acerbic. 'According to Menmet-Ra, all the Eight bless his name and loins—'

I couldn't help a snicker, even if he hadn't been trying to provoke it.

Rekhmire' continued dryly: 'According to him, as I mentioned on the

Iskander, there's a man here in Venice who claims to have a *machina* that will print out written books, as easily and as clearly as woodcuts. This German Guildsman, Herr Mainz, is that man.'

Most of the picture-dealers I'd been to in Rome kept a stock of several thousand woodcuts ready to sell, since they were so popular and so cheap. The idea of a *book* being so available ... I blinked, dazed, wondering how sick I must have been aboard ship not to hear this when Rekhmire' told me.

I reached out to take the Egyptian's tipping cup, and Rekhmire' blinked himself back to awareness.

'Naturally, Ty-ameny of the Five Great Names wants Herr Mainz to come to Alexandria. Think of such a print-making *machina* at the Royal Library! Ambassador Pakharu died before it could be arranged. Menmet-Ra told me Neferet hasn't answered messages he sent in the autumn, but she *is* only a book-purchaser, and not a member of the diplomatic service; she can do no more than be a caretaker. Menmet-Ra is clearly hoping someone else will be posted ambassador to Venice if he delays long enough in Rome ... '

I must have looked blank.

'Ensuring the golem is sent to Alexandria.'

'Of course. You said: I remember.' I would not bring it to my mind's eye, I swore. And found myself vividly conscious of every delicate cog and piece of gearing in those polished marble and bronze fingers. Marble slick with scuffs of drying blood.

'This Herr Mainz may be a charlatan.'

Rekhmire' evidently sought to use the subject in turn to distract both me and himself from our different pains.

'I've seen men who claimed to set letters in the same way a woodcut can be printed off, but never one that wasn't slower than a good copyist, or more likely illegible after the tenth copy.'

I smiled. 'My job's safe, then.'

Rekhmire' punched at his pillow. 'The *profession* of scribe is safe. The chance of anyone ever employing *you*, with your habit of annoying marginalia ... '

'My ambitions are crushed.'

It made him smile, but with more lines of pain in it than I wanted to see.

'The Janissary says some men stop breathing if they take too much poppy,' I said apologetically.

He nodded, the scored lines in his rounded face not diminishing. 'True. Or else they're left buying poppy to take for the rest of their lives. The pain is not as bad as it was.'

The spots of dampness on his brow, and spotting his stubbled scalp, called him *liar*. I kept my mouth shut.

Rekhmire' switched the direction of his thought with no apparent warning. 'You should show yourself here in Venice. Go to the squares, the palazzos, the markets. Let Neferet take you to the salons. Show yourself alive – as soon as possible. It puts a small obstacle that any of Videric's murderers will need to avoid.'

'It's the Council of Ten who rule here, isn't it?' I took over Neferet's linen-chest to sit down. 'If they ever catch and question the men who ambushed us, I suppose Videric's name would eventually come up?'

Rekhmire' narrowed his eyes, looking slightly impressed. 'Which is what we have to thank for the *Iskander* not being boarded as soon as we docked, and our throats slashed there and then.'

I found I was resting my hand on my belly and the salt-stained silk skirts. 'I'll go out. If I must. But we can discuss this later—'

'You need Frankish woman's dress. My purse is on the chest, there. The Merceria will have tailors and cloth: buy clothing.'

I pointed at the wooden framework over his leg, half-uncovered with sheets and blankets as it now was.

'That evidently affects the memory,' I explained.

Rekhmire' looked bewildered. 'What?'

'*I'm not your slave any more!*'

The lines of pain on his face were cut by the creases of a deep, appreciative smile. 'A little louder, please – there may be some man on the mainland who didn't hear you!'

'Just so I'm heard in this room!' Restless, I got up to walk from door to window, and window to door again. 'I don't have money to waste on Frankish women's clothes!'

He gave up the argument too easily. 'You might see if Neferet has anything she'll loan; she dresses in Frankish fashion when she has to.'

I had made a sketch or two of the exotically foreign woman, during Rekhmire''s restless periods of sleep, marking her deeply reddish-tan skin, satin black hair, and large eyes. Generously built, with a high brow and flawless carriage, she carried herself regally enough that I felt short, mannish, and laughable in her presence.

Somewhat satirically, I said, 'I don't think her gowns are going to fit me.'

'Pin up the hems. I see you haven't been looking with an artist's eye.'

'No, I doubt I *am* looking with an artist's eye! Consider yourself lucky I'm looking at all!'

Rekhmire' grinned, seeming unoffended.

I demanded, 'What am I missing?'

Despite pain and dishevelment, he looked infuriatingly smug. If I hadn't known it another of the Egyptian's attempts to cheer me, I would have quarrelled with him there and then.

'Listen.' He held up one long, spatulate finger.

Voices came in through the open window. I leaned out a little, between the shutters. In fact we were overlooking the walled garden, and not the canal directly, I found. Neferet was speaking with the Florentine lawyer Battista, and one of Honorius's men-at-arms.

I stared at her, and then back into this room, dim by contrast. Her national kinship with Rekhmire' was immediately apparent; even if he was all curves, and she all angles. It spoke itself in the tint of her skin, the long-lashed dark eyes, the large and elegant hands—

Large hands.

My head whipped around: I stared out of the window.

Rekhmire'. Neferet. Rekhmire'.

I stared from the one to the other, comparing this line with that.

'*But!*' I protested.

Rekhmire' threw his head back and laughed out loud, even as he clutched at himself in pain.

'*But* – she's the perfect woman!' I protested. 'I could paint her so!'

'She ... doesn't have anything of what you have,' Rekhmire' said mildly, rubbing long fingers into the top of his thigh, massaging bruised flesh. He showed me all his teeth in a smile. 'Or, indeed, what I have. She was Jahar pa-sheri, when I knew my cousin first—'

He used the term as I'd heard him before, speaking of the Pharaoh-Queen Ty-ameny's bureaucrats.

'—and Neferet is a true eunuch.'

If I'd picked up anything about Alexandrine habits in Rekhmire''s company, and at the embassy in Rome, it was that it's common for Egyptians to take different names at different parts of their lives.

And that *pa-sheri* means 'son of'.

Rekhmire' added, 'Neferet chooses to dress as a woman in Venezia. And be one in all ways.'

Now that I looked, her softly plump shape had the appearance of being sleeked down under her robes by a corset. She was subtly too rounded at the shoulder and chest. The Egyptian woman stepped out of my view, under the colonnade at the front of the house; I heard the door open, and her voice and the soldier's diminish inside. If I listened with attention, her voice was low for a woman, and sensually husky: she might be a male alto.

'Christus Imperator!' I muttered, leaning back from the window ledge. 'Does *anybody* ever leave Egyptian Constantinople with their cock and balls intact!'

Rekhmire' choked.

I lurched to rescue the pitch-lined cup, taking it and setting it down on the chest. Rekhmire' wiped the back of his hand across his mouth, wincing between laughter and pain. His eyes spoke a volume or two.

'*Many* do!' he protested, when he had control of his voice. 'Neferet's an old friend as well as a cousin; she's not as intimidating as she seems, and she'll be happy to make you feel welcome in Venezia.'

'I suppose one of us should tell her about "Ilaria".' I managed a creditable imitation of his brow-raising. 'And as her old friend, "cousin", and my old master – that would be you.'

He thanked me, but not with the sincerity a man ought to use. I practised my sweetest feminine smile.

A thought intruded, pushing the mutual amusement aside. 'Is that why you never concerned yourself about my – condition?'

Rekhmire' laughed. It became a cough and a wince. The sweat of pain was back on his forehead; I regretted raising the matter. He snorted.

'Because my friend's made himself known as a girl since he was old enough to speak? As far as Neferet's concerned, she's been convinced since she was four that she has a woman's *ka* – a woman's soul. I've never doubted the strength of her opinion. And, truthfully, she lives a woman's life far more easily than a man's. But you – a matter of the body . . . and I would like to think that you and I get on rather more amiably than Neferet and I. Good a person as she is, we were jealous of each other as children, and it took some years to grow beyond that. It still comes out at times.'

He sweated. I sat on the edge of the bed again, to wipe his forehead with a clean kerchief.

'I don't know if it's a matter of the body.' I avoided meeting his eye as I spoke. 'It felt easy enough to live a man's life in Rome. Harder to be a woman here – but then, a woman's life *is* hard, almost everywhere. Restrictions are worse than obligations. What part of the soul is this *ka*?'

I doubted Father Felix, or any of the other clerks at the court of Taraco, would consider me competent to take part in a discussion concerning the soul. *But I'm willing to try, if it takes his mind from how he hurts.*

He fell asleep during his explanation.

The Janissary doctor Bariş came several times, twelve hours apart, worried for a time over the heat of the skin sewn over the wound, and then relieved. I let Honorius speak with him – he got more honesty, both being military men. After three days, he announced his visits could become less frequent.

He spoke with one eye in my general direction. I refrained from making myself scarce.

After a considerable pause for study, he observed, 'Five months, or a little more. Too late for measures of removal, without you die.'

I nodded, finding no voice.

Bariş gave me a smile strangely effective as reassurance. 'Then we concentrate on birth. Early or late.'

9

'*I don't care!*' I snapped, five days later. 'I'll move my bed in here and you'll have to watch me give birth! I'm *not* having you put any weight on that knee yet. You don't try to walk! Understand?'

'Yes, master . . . '

Rekhmire''s assumption of a slave's manner was too accurate for him to have been a freeman all his life, I thought, or even an Alexandrine bureaucrat-slave. He cocked an eyebrow at me. At my belly, in particular.

'I apologise,' he corrected himself. 'Yes, *mistress.*'

Since an appropriate insult eluded me, I reached down and ruffled the wheat-coloured bum-fluff that was growing on his scalp now he hadn't been able to get up and shave.

'That would carry much more weight,' I observed, 'if it didn't come from someone so closely resembling a dandelion!'

The Egyptian's eyes narrowed to slits, giving him the evil look of some ancient stone monument. 'Ask me if I wish to purchase you as a slave again – just *ask* me . . . '

'Not a chance!'

It made me grin to see him cheerful. Even if, to a degree, it sprang from being comfortably isolated in this sick-room from all responsibility.

'All those punishments you never subjected me to, *master*, and now it's too late . . . '

'Clearly.' He folded his arms and gave up the evil glare in favour of a blatant attempt to gain pity. 'But, as I recall, I never threatened *you* with anything so dire as being present at a childbirth. You're a cruel . . . '

'Yes?' I watched him trapped between gendered grammatical phrases, and was for the first time honestly amused.

' . . . I don't know. But whatever it is, you're a cruel one!'

I shifted my drawing-board to show him my work in silver-point. 'No, "cruel" would be drawing you when you're pouting.'

'Much as you may *think* you're amusing me,' Rekhmire''s smooth face might just have been concealing a grin, 'I assure you, I don't pout!'

'The silver-point drawing does not lie . . . This isn't bad. Of course, you don't have much choice about staying still for the modelling.'

'*Ha!*'

The sound of a book-buyer in full-throated outrage was something I'd missed. I grinned, and watched him fail to suppress a snicker.

'I can tell you're feeling better,' I added. 'So can everybody else. But you're still getting your food on wooden plates . . . '

And his drink in turned wooden drinking bowls, too; well-made Frankish ware. The beautiful grain of the wood was hardly the point, however, and by the Egyptian's shame-faced look I guessed he knew that.

'I only threw a bowl at you once, yesterday,' he protested. 'And it was completely called for!'

'Because I called you a bad invalid? You *are*—'

The drinking-bowl was at least empty when it bounced off the low ceiling-beam.

We sniggered like small children for a while.

I welcomed that, too. After the third and fourth days of his incapacity none of the Frankish servants would enter the room. Honorius's soldiers had had plates thrown at their heads with a frequency that frankly amused them, and caused them to openly admire the book-buyer.

But since I knew by now how little Rekhmire' likes to display temper, I could estimate the fear and fury that must be driving him.

'I assume you'll be walking before the birth . . . ' I added cross-hatched shadows that failed entirely to round out the drawing of his hand. 'I wouldn't mind if you were there.'

I looked up at Rekhmire'.

'I . . . hadn't intended to say that.'

The Egyptian briefly nodded. 'I'll be there.'

It had become second nature by now, I realised, to push the ballooning fear away, before it robbed me of all breath, and to assume a fatalistic stance.

My body will dictate when I deal with this. There's nothing I can do.

Close my mind firmly to the future as I might, I couldn't ignore a dislike of spending Honorius's money and living on the Alexandrine house's charity.

I doubt any workshop master would hire me for a job. But that doesn't mean I won't try to find one.

It surprised me that Honorius didn't attempt to stop my search.

'No man's seen Carrasco, or any other man watching us.' He shrugged. 'And besides, the lads and I will be going with you . . . '

I thought he preferred to see me outside the sick-room from time to time. The weather remained a dry cold without snow. I was willing to go out only because Rekhmire''s wound appeared to be mending both faster and better than even Bariş had anticipated.

No man in Venice appeared to teach the New Art. Which was no surprise, but no less infuriating.

On the next failed attempt to find employment, I thought it no coincidence that Honorius and I and a dozen of the men-at-arms ended up going back to the Dorsodura quarter by way of a campo that held pigment shops. I feasted my eyes on the rows of wooden boxes full of colour, and the small amount of unearthly and glowing four-ducat blue.

'I *would* go for a job picking the ashes for lapis lazuli.' I displayed my palms to my father, and we matched finger against finger. 'Women have small hands; they tend to be employed at it. But it's a job that goes nowhere in the industry, and my hands are in any case suspiciously large for a woman.'

I bought red chalk with Honorius's money and came away.

'I won't be a parasite.' I could not sufficiently voice my frustration. 'I don't have enough money left from Rome to support myself. And I owe Rekhmire' for the sea-voyage, leave aside what I owe you. Yes, you'd pay to have me apprenticed to a master here, if it could be managed safely, but this is a backwater – there's no one here who can teach me anything.'

Honorius pushed his lips together in a silent whistle.

I snapped, '*What?*'

'I like a man who's determined in her opinions!' Honorius grinned. 'But leaving aside the hypothetical genius we'd evidently have to find as your workshop master—'

One of the older men, Fulka, chuckled. I sneered at Honorius, since he evidently invited it. The Lion of Castile beamed warmly at me.

'I don't want you in a workshop.' He sobered. 'Even if any man would hire a pregnant widow—'

I winced, both at the necessary public pretence, and the brutal but true statement.

'—how would you explain the dozen or more soldiers there *with* you? You'd be too open to attack in a workshop—'

'I won't be locked up in the embassy!'

'No.' Lines wrinkled at the outer corners of his eyes. 'I see a lot of you in me. I'd hate Sergeant Orazi to be continually hunting you down after you climb out of windows.'

The Armenian grinned at me with his remaining teeth.

'As if I'd do a thing like that.'

'Trust me, you'd do a thing like that.' Stopping at a chestnut vendor, Honorius rubbed his palms and held them out to the iron brazier while his men bargained.

The roast nuts burned my fingertips and mouth, peeling and eating, but were worth it for the hot, dry taste.

Walking on, Honorius observed, 'Remember you're not the only one in danger. That whoreson Videric will bear a grudge. He will have heard the part played in all this by Master Rekhmire'. I'd as soon the Egyptian was tended by someone I implicitly trust.'

Is it too early for this untried trust between Honorius and I?

I can feel in flesh and bone the tension of his body covering mine, while the flames of arquebuses blasted over our heads.

Honorius's sand-coloured brows lifted in faux-innocence. 'And ask yourself who you think Master Rekhmire' would prefer as a nurse – you, or a bunch of hairy thugs from Castile?'

The eponymous hairy thugs grinned their agreement.

'I *could* ask. And he'd probably go for your crusader veterans!' My basic knowledge of nursing extends no further than patching up a beaten slave.

Honorius had an air of being much pleased with himself.

'Which of us can ensure the book-buyer doesn't make a cripple of himself, by assuming he's fit enough to get up and wander around Venice tomorrow? *And* the day after. And the day after *that*.'

There was enough nodding and murmured agreement among the men eating their roasted chestnuts that I realised, *They've adopted the royal book-buyer as a mascot. Along with the 'lucky hermaphrodite'* . . .

'Rekhmire''s got enough common sense to stay off his feet while it's necessary.'

'While there's spies in the city, and he's looking for this German Guildsman he keeps yelling at the Egyptian woman about, and he knows you've been ambushed once already?'

I settled for an irritated grunt.

Honorius said, 'You have the best chance of keeping him from crippling himself. And, while I want you under my eyes until we've removed this spy of Videric's, I think also that you feel you owe the Egyptian a debt, and would like a chance to repay it.'

I found myself giving Honorius a startled look.

Begin with the fact that Rekhmire' bought me, and never treated me as slaves are treated in Iberia. And that, even if he upset my life like an overturned cart, he intended well. He took me out of Rome when he had no reason to; when any other man would have abandoned me to my own business. But, more to the point, he is a friend who lifts my heart. If he cheers me whenever I see him, it only seems reasonable that I would want to do the same in return.

'I'll do what I can,' I said. 'Maybe I can sell some of my sketches while I'm here, though. There ought to be some money I can bring in.'

'I'll give you a commission.' Honorius held up both hands, palms out, as if to forestall an explosion. 'No, listen to me! The chapel at home needs rebuilding; I'd have to bring somebody in to fresco it. I've seen your work books. If you're not good enough now, you soon will be. And if what you paint is amateur—'

'You won't pay me?'

'I'll pay you half, for the time and work. But – worse, to you – if it's rubbish, I'll have another artist in to rip it out, and re-do the plaster and fresco. Do me a proper one.'

Fresco has to be done right the first time: there are no second chances. For all Masaccio's teaching, I'm nowhere near practised enough.

I wondered if I could talk my father into painted wood panelling without him realising that. *Probably not. So I must merely be honest.*

'It need not be fresco,' Honorius added. 'I'm open-minded on the medium.'

I suppose a man does get to be a reasonable judge of character when taking on soldiers for his companies. Or else my father is coming to know me.

'What subject do you want for the painting?'

'One of the soldier-saints. To be honest, I'd like it focused around St Gaius. A triptych, maybe. That would give you the joining, the betrayal, and the exile to the East.'

He seemed certain enough, which is a bonus in a client.

I could have wished my first patron not to come from nepotism, but I'll hardly be the first artist to begin that way. And I detected the steel under his surface – if his son-daughter produced anything inferior, no man would ever see it.

I'll make it good enough to take his breath away!

'There's no hurry,' I said, 'but I'll start some compositional drawings, so you can be thinking about them. What?'

My father stopped grinning like an idiot, said, 'Nothing,' and began grinning again.

Good enough that when he sees my work, he won't even be able to *speak*, never mind laugh.

'Ilario?' Honorius didn't correct himself, either because it would draw attention to my gender, or because he hadn't noticed.

'What? Oh.' I was walking with my hand high on my belly again, I realised, although it was scarcely less flat than before. The archetypal pose in which to paint the Mother of Christ Imperator. If without the toga and tiara.

With resolute optimism, Honorius said, 'I acknowledge you. I'll acknowledge my grandchild when it's born. If you want to claim the father in Carthage, I'll help—'

It must have been clear on my face that I pictured him and his household guard breaking down the doors of Donata's rooming-house, and beating Marcomir senseless.

'I have enough money even to hire lawyers,' he said mildly.

I smiled.

'I don't want Carthage involved,' I said, after a moment. 'They're too interested in me as it is . . . But thank you.'

Honorius patted my shoulder. 'One day you'll realise that you don't have to thank me for anything. I'm your *father*.'

I wasn't in a bad enough mood to mention Videric and Federico, my other experiences of paternal affection.

'I'll nurse Rekhmire',' I said, affecting a sigh.

Honorius smiled. Our gondola waited at the edge of steps, by the arc of a bridge leading over an ice-fringed canal. Honorius's men occupied both it and the wider oared boat beside it. I allowed my father to help me in.

Sitting, I hauled my skirts into some semblance of tidiness, arranging myself on the padded velvet seat in the stern; looked up, and saw Sergeant Orazi go down with a feathered shaft hanging out of his back.

'*All'arme!*' Honorius bellowed in the local dialect. '*To arms!*'

A flood of men – twenty, thirty, more – poured out of the nearby alleys, splitting into plainly practised groups. One group pushed the boat containing the majority of Honorius's men out into the centre of the canal, where it circled aimlessly for all one of the men attempted to paddle, and another to rack his crossbow.

I had only time to see senior Ensign Viscardo leap into the black water and start swimming grimly towards us. Honorius scooped me up off the seat with a powerful tug unexpected in a lean man, and dropped me in the bottom of our boat, turning back to command the brawl. Sparks shot into the air where two blade-edges slid down each other. Windows flew open overhead; banged shut again.

I managed to crawl forward, the skirts an intolerable obstacle where I kept kneeling on them.

One of our oars had fallen in-board. It was solid hard wood, perhaps twelve feet long, with the blade painted indigo and white on either side; far too cumbrous to wield as a staff-weapon, as I had with the iron candle-stand in Carthage.

Kneeling up, I squinted, spotting which man on the canal-path was plainly directing the operation.

A cloaked man wearing a Venetian white half-mask that covered him down to his lower lip. A plain expressionless mask-face . . .

Blank as a golem, I thought, as he loped towards the edge of the canal, calling out brusque orders.

I hefted the oar, found its point of balance, stood straight up in the rocking gondola, and cast the oar as a man casts the javelin in Taraco's Roman games.

The man turned, just as I fell forward from the impetus and landed on my hands and knees in the boat.

His movement shifted him enough that only the edge of the oar's end caught him – but the blow was to his temple. I heard the *thuck!* clearly over men shouting and metal scraping against metal.

The man's legs went out from under him: he dropped like a sack of meal.

'*That* one!' I yelled to Honorius, pointing. '*There!*'

A scuffle of swinging blades intervened. Men in blue livery with Honorius's badge swayed past me, in a rough and tumble that was more

235

beer-house brawl than battle-line. Honorius's voice rose up from the back, shouting as much. The hired assassins fell back, routing into alleys and across the square

I stared along the edge of the canal.

Bare. No fallen man

I don't suppose he fell in and drowned.

No, that would be too easy. Either he recovered, or some of the men abandoning the fight piecemeal dragged him with them when they ran.

'Was that your Ramiro Carrasco de Luis?' I demanded as Honorius jogged up, calling his own men back.

'Couldn't tell. Didn't get a good look at him.' He panted, scowling at me. 'You shouldn't be doing things like that!'

'Why not? Oh.' I found myself with my hand resting on my belly. *Again.* I felt no different to how I ever have. 'It . . . doesn't seem to have done any harm.'

Or any good, depending on how you look at it.

'Has to have been Carrasco,' Honorius grunted. 'If the Council was letting thieves' bands get *that* big, we'd have heard gossip about it – Ilario, where do you think you're going?'

Sergeant Orazi swore as one of his men extracted an arrow-head from between the plates of his brigandine. Orazi didn't seem hurt; more embarrassed. Viscardo was probably in worse case, on hands and knees on the path, puking up dirty water.

Making my way with care down the rocking boat to the padded seat, I lifted my gaze to Honorius.

'This has gone on long enough! You know the way to Aldra Federico's palazzo, don't you? We're going there. *Now.*'

Honorius and his sergeant, who had been exchanging glances with far too much exaggerated tolerance in them for my liking, both looked disconcerted.

'Or,' I remarked into his silence, 'I can find the way on my own.'

If I were wholly woman, the words *crazy pregnant girl* would have passed Honorius's lips. But he and his soldiers sensed also the knight's training I have had in King Rodrigo's court, and that confused them.

Honorius grumbled, signalling to the gondola oarsmen.

'And *what* do you propose to do when we get there!'

10

Travelling along the Canal Grande, I failed at memorising details of the facades, for Honorius's protests. He had a look on his face which I suspected his officers must have seen, in a command tent, on crusade.

'It's too dangerous for you. You can't go anywhere *near*—' He broke off. 'Damn, that was stupid. Whatever you had in mind, you'll do now, won't you? Those skirts are deceptive.'

His sergeant smirked.

'I don't know what *you're* so happy about,' my father muttered, 'since I happen to know you owe Attila twenty ducats!'

'A bet?' I didn't know whether to be offended or amused.

'Orazi here bet you'd go haring off after Carrasco on your own. Attila—' Honorius nodded towards the large man at his oar. 'He wagered you'd want an escort.'

'They both bet I'd follow him?'

Honorius gave me the 'raw recruit, you don't know enough to lace up your own sandals!' look.

I huddled back into my cloak, uncertain how I felt about Honorius's men-at-arms knowing me well. On balance, I found it reassuring.

'This Ramiro Carrasco de Luis,' I offered. 'You have to have some sympathy for the man.'

Honorius choked. '*What!*'

I smiled sunnily at my father. 'You say Carrasco's hired by Videric. He thinks all he has to do is assassinate some young man. What could be easier? Take a young man out drinking and whoring, stick a knife in him when he's dead drunk, and there he is – dead. Only now Ramiro Carrasco finds out that reputable young *widows* tend not to go out whoring and drinking . . . '

The youngest officer, Ensign Saverico, snickered. Since I was facing forwards, I saw the other soldiers grinning. Honorius very wisely didn't turn around in the gondola to castigate them. He knows a losing battle when confronted with one.

'If Rekhmire' weren't recovering so well,' I added, 'I doubt I'd be so sanguine about chasing down the man who attacked him.'

'Attacked *us*.' Honorius humphed. 'What's to stop Ramiro Carrasco sticking a dagger in you as soon as you walk up to him?'

'Six heavily-armed men with more axes than sense?' I made a show of counting heads. 'I beg your pardon. Eight. Oh, except you don't have an axe . . . '

Ensign Saverico apparently choked on something. Sergeant Orazi whacked him hard in the middle of his back-plate.

' . . . Besides which, I don't know what the Doge's Council do when they catch public murderers, but *I'd* bet it's painful and disgusting and better avoided.'

Honorius shook his head, but whether in agreement with that statement, or despair over my attitude, I didn't know. Long ago, I discovered that a minor joy of wearing skirts is baiting respectable men. I wasn't sure if I was amused or annoyed that it worked with my father.

'That's Federico's house.' Honorius pointed towards a landing stage, over the pale green ripples of the canal. 'Be careful—'

Having gathered up my skirts beforehand, I was able to step ashore the moment the gondola touched the canal-side, before Ensign Viscardo could throw a line around the mooring-post.

The impetus of my foot pushed the boat. It drifted back away from the quay.

I heard Orazi curse behind me. And the slap of rope falling onto water.

Pole-axes and crossbows aren't the way to solve this.

We had turned into a small side-canal – the access to this five-storey building for tradesmen and others who wouldn't disembark at the main jetty. I found myself on a paved quay with Gothic-arched windows in front of me.

Ignoring the shout from behind, I walked towards the narrow door, approached by six or seven stone steps.

On the top step, a dark-haired man in a cloak sat with his head resting down on one hand.

He looked up as I approached. A red and rapidly-darkening swollen lump showed on the left side of his forehead, bleeding from a narrow split in the skin. He blinked, his gaze glassy.

I walked up the flaking steps and smiled at him. 'That looks as though it hurts.'

I pulled a linen kerchief out of my sleeve.

The man sat and stared up at me.

I licked the kerchief and reached down to dab it carefully against his swelling flesh.

He hissed a breath, blinking, eyes focusing.

I showed him pink stains on the yellow cloth. 'Not so good. You may need a physician. Although it seems Venetian doctors are usually worse than the disease.'

'Indeed.' The man plainly agreed by reflex and instinct, not conscious thought. He had the curly black hair of Taraconensis, and skin the colour of old ivory, where it wasn't swelling and turning bruise-blue. Brown eyes showed so dark that pupil was barely distinguishable from iris. Under his cloak, the plain red doublet and hose he wore were servant's quality, not fitting him well; I concluded they were not his.

He didn't desire to come out dressed as Federico's family secretary.

'Who are you?' He struggled to get words out, squinting up from the steps. The sun must be at my back. He could see even less of me than I anticipated. 'What are you *doing?*'

'Don't be foolish. You know who I am.' I licked my kerchief again and gently cleaned around what looked like a splinter, driven shallowly under the skin of his forehead. 'This is going to hurt: hold still . . . Got it! You, your name is Ramiro Carrasco de Luis, and you – work for my mother's husband.'

He winced under my hands, wide-eyed.

I saw him visibly think to use the pain of the splinter's removal as an excuse – and then dismiss the idea.

'You're . . . '

'Ilaria.'

'Ilaria.' He emphasised the feminine ending very slightly.

'That's right.' I could hear voices, not far behind, on the quay; evidently my father and his men had achieved a landing, and were disagreeing over something.

Whether or not to interrupt the mad hermaphrodite, probably.

Ramiro Carrasco de Luis flushed darkly, high on his cheeks. He glanced dazedly at the armed men. I was uncertain whether or not he registered their significance.

'Madonna Ilaria . . . sorry . . . I'm – only a servant; I'm secretary to Aldra Federico's daughter—'

I managed an expression that stopped him stumbling out with a false story. He looked at me foolishly, his mouth open.

'You have an interesting face,' I said. 'Who should I ask for permission to draw you?'

Carrasco appeared thoroughly flustered. '*Draw* me?'

'I'm sure you were told I'm a painter . . . '

It isn't easy to exert any impression of authority sitting on your arse on a doorstep. I could have told him that myself. Every time he attempted to rise, I pressed down on the bruised flesh of his brow with fingers and kerchief.

He caught his lip between his teeth, bit down, and failed to suppress a yelp.

'Madonna Sunilda!' he managed to get out. 'Would give any permission. Or her father! Madonna, I don't understand what – why—'

'You should use witch-hazel for that bruise.' I straightened up, folding my kerchief neatly, and put it away under the bronze silk and brown velvet of my sleeve. Borrowing clothes from Neferet had its advantages. I reached up and put my large, lined cloak-hood back.

'It's nice to see a face from home.' I grinned at him amiably. 'Even if it does belong to someone who's been sent to kill me. I'm sure we're going to be *great* friends, you and I!'

It took me a minute, perhaps two, to wave and get Honorius to stop grousing at Sergeant Orazi and approach.

In that time, Ramiro Carrasco de Luis sat with his mouth open and couldn't seem to speak a word.

Other servants showed us inside.

The palazzo's tall rooms were decorated in the Classical style, ceilings plastered so that the structural beams didn't show through. I had no eye for the decorative work, or the carved ash-wood door frames and wall panelling.

After going so long without speaking to my foster father – *What am I to say to Aldra Federico, now?* And if Valdamerca's with him, or my sisters . . .

The servants threw open the doors to a great gallery overlooking the Canal Grande.

It was full of people.

11

Most were middle-aged men; most were in Frankish gowns and hose. Rich Venetians.

Honorius muttered, '*Fuck,*' under his breath, and straightened his shoulders. 'You do pick your moments.'

I looked for the horse-face and dark hair of Valdamerca, for the fiend-sisters of my childhood, and saw none of them. *Only a male gathering,* I realised, as Aldra Federico looked up from the servant who directed his attention to us.

He hadn't changed – still a good-looking middle-aged man, as curl-haired as Carrasco. He washed his hair in henna, I suspected. He must be in his middle sixties by now, but seemed fifteen years younger.

Federico stepped out of the crowd with a formal smile. 'Welcome! Ilaria!'

The smile took on an avid edge, that he must imagine he was keeping concealed.

'My dear! When I invited Venezia's artists, I'd no idea you'd hear of it! But welcome! I had no idea you were in the Serene Republic!' Federico waved a careless hand. Following his gesture led my eye across the throng.

I glimpsed the Florentine lawyer Leon Battista, talking to soberly-dressed older men. No Neferet, that I could see. No other man I recognised.

How do I broach the subject of Videric sending a paid murderer to kill me?

I caught the moment that Federico's pupils widened.

Rosamunda's voice sounded in my memory. '*As soon as you stand in a room together.*'

I saw by Federico's open stare at Honorius that at least one secret was now out in the open, to be gossiped about.

Best court manners returned as if I'd never left Taraco. 'You know Captain-General Honorius, he tells me. I was certain, sir, you wouldn't mind him accompanying me; he's a fellow art-enthusiast.'

'Not at all . . . ' Federico spoke absently, his deceptively sharp gaze still anatomising Honorius's features.

Is Federico interested for any other reason than gossip and scandal? Is he Videric's man, now? Useless to guess. He *would* be interested in scandal, in any case; I'd known that since he took me to court at fifteen.

As to whether he now reports back to Aldra Videric . . .

'*Honorius!*' A large, floridly blond man lurched between the conversing groups of Venetian men, rolling up with a blast of brandy on his breath. He slammed a hand on my father's shoulder, which somewhat to my surprise didn't knock Honorius over.

'Had no idea you were down this way! Not looking for a job, are you?'

The retired Captain-General of Castile and Leon smirked, looking down at the Frank. The fair-skinned man was in his late thirties, I estimated. Both men allowed themselves to be served wine, in Venetian-made glasses. Both looking as if they shouldn't be holding the delicate spiral parti-coloured glass stems. And for the same reason, I realised. *They're both soldiers.*

'Ilario.' Honorius didn't correct his suffix. 'This is Messer Carmagnola. We commanded troops together up in Aragon. He's running Venice's land forces now – isn't that right? Carmagnola, my daughter Ilaria.'

The piggy red eyes of the Captain-General of Venice surveyed me with subdued lust. Subdued out of deference to Honorius, I realised.

'I'm a mercenary; I do what I'm paid to do.' Carmagnola grinned, took my hand, and kissed it. He wavered, falling-down drunk.

Honorius slapped him on the shoulder in return. 'You beat the Milanese!' He spoke expansively to me. 'The current Doge has been in power these five years: he wants a mainland empire. I think our Carmagnola's going to give it to him. Are you being treated all right here, boy?'

My father gave an expert demonstration of a man concealing that he is not entirely sober – which, since he hadn't yet drunk from his Venetian-made glass, would give this Carmagnola and my foster father Federico the reassuring idea that Honorius had been apprehensive before he arrived. And so more likely to put a word wrong, here and there.

'Doge Foscari's very good to me,' Carmagnola slurred. 'Everybody is.'

The law I learned a long time ago in Rodrigo's court – *always* speak as if you are overheard – seemed to apply here, despite the talk around us being philosophy and the arts, rather than politics, or anything else the authorities might not like. I glanced about, uneasy.

The Frankish man Carmagnola leaned forward and prodded Honorius's shoulder with a weather-beaten finger. His nails had been chewed down so much, and plainly so consistently, that they had grown back a little deformed.

'Is it true Carthage is sending the legions into the Iberian coast? You know – where you always said you came from. Taraconensis.' He stumbled badly over the name.

Legions!

242

Social mores dictate downcast eyes for women; I was glad enough of it then, or else I would have given away my shock. If this man is a captain for Venice's Council of Ten, he's involved deep in Frankish politics, and North African affairs too. And what he says is a confirmation of all Rekhmire''s concerns over Carthage.

'Legions?' Honorius spoke mildly enough to rouse my suspicions, if not the drunken mercenary's.

'Lord God, *you* know Carthage! They've got to have their import grain! Give 'em half an excuse and they'll take over any farmland outside the Penitence—' Carmagnola waved the hand that held his fragile glass; expensive wine slopped on his doublet's velvet cuff, and the so-fine flax linen of his shirt under it. I wondered numbly if I could accurately reproduce that stained translucent effect in oils.

'Didn't the government in Taraco fall?' Carmagnola added, visibly pulling himself together, glancing over at Federico. 'Or a king die? Or *something*? Honorius, I know you always said there was no career for you there – no wars.'

My foster father Federico shrugged, at his most diplomatic. 'There haven't been wars in Taraconensis – wars *involving* Taraconensis – in twenty-five years. Our noble Honorius needed to travel north as far as Castile and Leon to make his name.'

Honorius bowed with the lack of subtlety of a blunt soldier. I doubted Federico would believe that role now, with me standing beside a visible blood-father.

Carmagnola, apparently as if he forced his senses to obey him through the wine-haze, said, 'Taraconensis has a border with the Franks, doesn't it? Only a short one, where the Via Augusta runs between the mountains and the sea, but still a border. Carthage would love a land-route into Europe.'

I assumed the stupefied expression of a woman confronted with politics.

Given that Federico still thought of me as a King's amusing freak, he might credit my lack of interest, too.

I took a polite step back. A woman on the edge of any group is easily ignored; I wondered if I could use that to avoid the urgent questions Federico would doubtless have for me.

Bad weather will have delayed messages. How recent will this Carmagnola's news about Taraco be? Do mercenary commanders have better means of communication, even in the months when war is impossible?

Lost in deliberation, I missed my moment – Leon Battista appeared at my elbow without sufficient warning for me to avoid him.

'When may I see your brother?'

Whenever you like!

I managed not to smirk at my thoughts. If I did, Leon would put it down to feminine frivolity.

'He, ah, went into Dalmatia for the winter. Can I help?'

If one ignored his boat-prow of a nose, it was possible to note that Leon Battista had small, keen eyes. He studied me for a longer moment than was polite, and steered me a step aside from the crowd.

'It was you, madonna, wasn't it?'

'Me?'

With all else – with not being able to step outside the Campo San Barnaba without expecting an ambush – I have forgotten to think up a plausible tale for Neferet's Florentine.

'You.' Leon's hazel eyes shone bright with two catch-lights from the sunny window. 'There is no "brother". You disguised yourself as a man to work in Masaccio's workshop, didn't you?'

I managed to reply without hesitation. 'I wore men's clothing in Masaccio's workshop, yes.'

That much is certainly true . . .

'You will excuse me.' Leon's voice held subdued excitement. 'I'm here on business, but I saw you, and was suddenly sure . . . '

He had a roll of papers clasped in one hand. He noticed my interest, glanced about, and on a sudden pushed them into my grasp.

'These are common enough in Venice.'

The top one was a manuscript news-letter – composed of foreign news, propaganda both political and military, and stories of horrid crimes and murders, and the state executions they inevitably led to, all described in minute detail. Murders of husbands by wives appeared especially popular.

'I brought them to circulate, useless as they are. All bell-tower politics,' Leon Battista sneered. 'No Italian city-state ever cares about matters further away than the ringing of their own *campanile* can be heard! But I pass them privately because the Council of Ten would ban them if they could,' he added. 'The Doge thinks it's only one step from circulating manuscript news to having women preaching, pagans in the Senate, and the baptism of cats and horses!'

Most of the letters purported to have been written by some 'foreign visitor' to Venice. I turned my head sideways to squint at the penmanship, recognising the Venetian style.

'This is something I never considered when I was looking for employment! Although I suppose they hang the scribes, as well as whoever dictates the news-letters?'

Leon narrowed his hazel eyes, evidently not decided on whether I had a morbid sense of humour, or whether I made some attempt to feel out his political stance. Before I could add a joke to push his mind in the one direction, he reached out to extract one sheet of paper from the sheaf in my hands.

I held on to it, having a better grip than a woman.

'What's this?' I turned it about in my hand, adding, not too quickly, 'I don't speak your Florentine Italian.'

The relief in his expression was brief, but I caught it.

'This? Oh – I have bought some foreign letters to circulate, also. This is a similar letter of news, but for Florence.'

It's true I don't speak the Italian language of Florence. However, months in Masaccio's workshop, puzzling out the notes Tommaso Cassai left me, mean that I read a little of it.

Enough to enable me to make out 'Cast down the blood of the Medici Duke!' and 'Make this a true republic!'

Dangerous, I reflected.

I wondered who he had come here to meet, and pass these papers on to. *Not that it matters.* If I know little about Venice's politics, I know even less about those of Florence, but any invitation to depose a duke is rarely welcomed by a ruler.

It was not that which made me retain the paper.

This one was not written by a scribe.

The letters showed round, black, even, and as clear-edged as oak-gall ink and the sharpest quill could make a line. No smudging – I pushed the pad of my thumb across the page.

'How long did this take to make?'

Leon Battista's wariness vanished, seeing me involved in the manufacture of the news-sheet rather than its contents.

'As long as it would take a man to count to thirty.' He grinned at my expression. Relief may have moved him to speak out more than he intended. 'The setting up of the letters takes longer, to begin with.'

'Like a woodcut.' Masaccio had talked a little to me of that, and engraving.

Leon nodded. 'But then . . . this is neither the first nor the five hundredth sheet made.'

Which makes the sharp clarity of the edges more than remarkable.

'How many in Florence can read?' I mused aloud.

Leon Battista shrugged. 'Enough that if you nail a news-letter to a door, one man can read it aloud to a dozen before the Duke's guards arrive.'

Too much of a coincidence, that Leon Battista would have something printed of such quality, and that Neferet knows of the existence of the Herr Mainz that the Pharaoh-Queen wishes to see.

'Can I keep this?'

Because I know Rekhmire' will want to see it!

Leon shook his head. 'I'm truly sorry, madonna, but you know what the authorities are like about news. I take enough of a risk conveying letters myself; I wouldn't forgive myself if I put you in danger of being thought a spy.'

A flicker of movement in my peripheral vision: Ramiro Carrasco de Luis.

The sleekly muscular dark man made an unobtrusive presence in Federico's apartments, acting as major-domo to pass on orders to the lower servants. He had taken a necessary handful of minutes to change out of his muddied and blood-stained clothes, reappearing in a charcoal-black Italian doublet and hose, of a quality remarkably good for a servant. But then again, it would be like Sunilda to want her secretary to appear smart.

The secretary rolled his eyes, evidently overhearing Leon Battista.

I said amiably, and a little loudly, 'True. Venice can be full of dangers.'

Leon frowned. If not for Carrasco being a servant, and therefore invisible, the Florentine might have noticed him flush, and deduced that I'd landed a dart in a vulnerable place. Which might lead to further undesirable conclusions.

Without showing haste, I changed the subject back. 'The printing is very fine.'

'Yes.' Leon didn't look guilty, which gave me some hopes for him as a conspirator or insurrectionist, or whatever he was to Florence.

He did bite at his lip, as he looked down at me. Momentarily, his gaze was distant, as if he could not help where his mind turned.

'Masaccio . . . Tommaso . . . ' He spoke in a sudden rush. *Is the child his?*

I might burst into laughter, or tears, or punch the Florentine.

The moment of decision must have given him the impression I was distressed.

'Madonna, I'm sorry! Forgive me for hoping that there was at least something left of my friend.'

I smiled forgiveness, as women do, and sought a way to distract him. 'How did you know that "Ilario" was not a man?'

His lips quirked in a very small smile. 'You know too much about painting for a normal woman, Madonna Ilaria. I doubt that comes from talking to a brother – you're too passionate about it, and you use Masaccio's very phrases. He must have been the master you learned from.'

Leon's expression was so seriously intent that I again desired to laugh. The thought of eavesdroppers sobered me. It was difficult not to stare around at the nobles of Venice that Federico had gathered under his roof.

What Leon evidently thinks a romantic, adventurous tale will be looked on as criminal by the Council of Ten, especially if they find out the whole of the matter.

A movement signalled Honorius's approach.

I looked Leon Battista in the eye, with what I thought he would read as defiance and shame. Speaking in an undertone, I said, 'Master Leon . . .

246

I can only ask you not to reveal what I've done. The child isn't Masaccio's. He never knew I was with child. I went through a marriage ceremony in Rome. Then . . . then the bride was deserted by her groom.'

My father hung back until Leon Battista had finished his apologies, protestations, reassurances, and promises that he would come to the Alexandria House in the near future, to further put my mind at rest.

Arm linked implacably through mine, Honorius steered me steadily towards the doors.

'And you say *I've* been too much under the Egyptian's influence!'

'I said nothing to Leon that wasn't true!'

'But you said it so he'd hear a lie!'

'You recognised that,' I said mildly, 'so I blame Rekhmire', because mercenary commanders are blunt, unsubtle, unpolitical animals . . . '

He laughed, hard enough that he choked. 'Ah, you *have* been talking to Carmagnola. The man's as much a conspirator as any damn courtier – we're better off out of here!'

I could only agree.

'Ilaria!' My foster father Federico reappeared. 'You're not leaving?'

'I have business elsewhere.' Honorius's smile was amiable and intractable in equal measure.

Nothing need be said out loud, I realised. Here I am. Here is my face on an older version of myself. If Federico's a pawn of Videric, he has scandal to pass on; if he's an ally, then Honorius's men-at-arms downstairs are adequate warning.

And as for Aldra Videric's assassin . . .

I glimpsed Ramiro Carrasco de Luis behind Aldra Federico, and guessed it to be the secretary who had prevented us slipping away unnoticed. He gave me a very swift, covert stare.

'Foster father.' I confined myself to a modest female's demeanour. 'I know you'll understand that, for my work, I have need of a trustworthy and discreet artist's model. May I borrow Secretary Carrasco from you?'

Federico put his hand through his curly hair, dishevelling it enough that the baldness of his crown became visible. His expression was extraordinary.

'You don't need to worry about disgrace,' I added. 'While I'm dressed as a woman, I have a duenna at all times – Madonna Neferet, the Egyptian representative in Venice. Well, her, or her women-servants. And Master Honorius loans me his honour guard when I go out.'

Seeing neither of the men with me react to 'dressed as a woman', Federico demanded bluntly, 'What about when you dress as a man?'

Either he's unobservant, or I don't show as much as I feel I do.

Valdamerca, he said, was out at the Merceria with my foster sisters. She was always the more intelligent one in the family. And she has a woman's eye for such things. One look at my very minutely larger breasts . . . *Thank God it's just Federico!*

'I don't dress as a man in Venezia.' I met Federico's suspicious gaze. 'For a while, it's easier to be a woman.'

He snorted. 'Oh, well, it would be! No need to work for a living, or defend yourself, or trouble your head with business.'

Work for a living? What do you think your household's women servants do?

'This drawing, though . . . '

'I have a commission.' I need not even lie about it. 'I need to make sketches for a chapel fresco. I haven't yet decided on the treatment of the subject, but the Franks seem to have a certain attitude to Judas – St Gaius – that I'd like to explore.'

Ramiro Carrasco had evidently been educated well enough, or been around enough Franks, to pick up the reference. His face was as blank as the wooden panelling on the walls.

'Tomorrow will do, to start,' I said briskly. 'If you don't need him, foster father?'

It occurred to me that the difficulty with Aldra Federico always seeming a little shifty is that it made it impossible to know if he was being more so, now.

'Oh, you can take him – you and Sunilda always did squabble over your toys.' Federico managed an unpleasant smirk. 'I'll have her send him over.'

Departing publicly enough that Federico couldn't ply me with questions, I promised to come again when my foster mother and sisters should be present, and allowed the Aldra's servants to show us out to the canal jetty. The salt wind off the lagoon caught me with a razor-edged chill.

Ramiro Carrasco de Luis, as my father and I passed him on the way out, turned his head away, incidentally giving me his best profile. Which was, at this moment, quite definitely not the left.

12

Knowing how little Rekhmire' liked his mind unoccupied, I gave him the story while I unpacked my chalk.

'Messer Leon Battista has letters not written by a scribe's hands . . . ' Rekhmire' tapped his thumbnail against his teeth.

His bed had the occupied air of the long-sick. Rumpled sheets and blankets were covered in scrolls, among which I saw the accounts of the Alexandrine House, as well as several military treatises loaned him by my father. He snarled absently at the willow-withy cage supporting sheets over his strapped leg.

'You're certain?' he queried.

'There was a nick in the "e".' So small as to be all but invisible, except to an eye used to drawing letters. 'That made me think of woodcuts, where an error's repeated in every printing. These letters were printed that way, I think. Every "e" had the nick.'

'And Messer Leon is Neferet's . . . lover, one assumes.' Rekhmire''s eyebrows lifted, which together with his unshaven skull gave him the air of a ruffled buzzard-chick. 'If Leon Battista of the Alberti family has found a man who prints letters, and it's *not* the German Guildsman that Menmet-Ra is after, then that is a remarkable coincidence.'

'Surely Leon wouldn't have let me look at the letter if he'd known his printer is wanted here?'

'It may *be* such a coincidence. In which case he wouldn't know.' The rounded brows snapped down. 'Or he may not have been told all by Neferet. I'll keep an eye on her. Matters may be opposite – you say Leon Battista was unwilling to let you see what is, after all, seditious writing. He may feel he needs to keep Neferet safe in ignorance.'

'Or Neferet provided him with this German Herr Mainz.' If Neferet was Rekhmire''s friend, it was up to me to state the obvious, and save him sounding as if he condemned her. 'It's not possible to travel anywhere in this weather. She may think the German can't go to Alexandria yet in any case, so he may as well help Leon.'

'By getting embroiled in Italian Peninsula politics!' Rekhmire''s fist came down too weakly on the bed-frame. 'They *burn* the authors of sedition here!'

He heaved a sigh, his body slumping at the end of it.

'We therefore proceed with great caution. If anything should come to you, be certain to tell me. If this is *not* the trail of Herr Mainz . . . then I have nothing at all to follow.'

'I'll listen out,' I promised.

His gaze through the leaded window at the cold sky became distant. 'You will not have seen the Great Library. Walking past mile on *mile* of scroll-cases . . . Do you know what there is, every few yards, on every floor in the Library?'

I shook my head.

'Sand buckets. Blankets. Against fire. So many of those scrolls are the sole copy. Our scriptoria work through the night as well as the day, but . . . can you imagine? To have as many copies as a printer's *machina* could make?' His voice took on a pained quality. 'And then – never to lose the last copy of a book, ever again?'

Ramiro Carrasco de Luis arrived at the Alexandrine House the following day, in a fine wool cloak against the winter rain, under which he wore a charcoal doublet so dark as to be almost black, the metal tags of his points all silvered. His shoes had small fashionable points, and his hose fitted his legs as close as another skin.

Not the clothes in which to control an ambush, I reflected, and put up with half an hour of the man preening when I ordered him to sit on an upright wooden chair and lift his head, as if he gazed up at the Tree.

Finally, I abandoned coal and chalk and tinted paper. 'Remorse.'

Ramiro Carrasco's head snapped down. He gave me a startled look. '*What?* Madonna,' he added hastily.

This was in part a response to the glare from the duenna whom Neferet had provided: a round, elderly Venetian woman who evidently didn't hold with handsome young foreign men. And in part a certain natural sense of self-preservation, since Honorius detailed off-shifts of his more intimidating household guard to sit in my room as I sketched.

Over the last weeks, the soldiers had dragged home a few unfortunate men they suspected of being spies for Lord Videric. 'In the way that a cat brings dead birds home to its master,' Rekhmire' commented, although these men tended to be only half-dead. After questioning them, Honorius donated the wounded men to the city's charitable hospices, where they could be more easily watched.

If what he learned is true, Aldra Videric might have more men than Ramiro Carrasco in Venice.

Or Ramiro Carrasco might hire men in order to give us that impression.

'You're St Gaius.' The white chalk had managed to mark not only my hand and my cuff, but the front of my bodice, and my lap. I shifted the drawing-board, and thought it just as well I'd borrowed old clothes from one of Neferet's Frankish servants. 'St Gaius – *Judas*, according to the people who pray at the local chapels here. You're looking up at the man you betrayed. Whether it's Christus Viridianus on the Green Tree, or

Christ the Imperator, it's all one. He's been hung up and broken, on your word; bones broken but no blood spilled; he's *dead* – and it's your doing. So stop looking as if you're wondering how many girls are staring at you . . . '

Ramiro Carrasco de Luis blinked, and then essayed a small smile. 'As far as I know, just the one, madonna.'

I let his smile die in the coldness of my reaction, and under the granite looks of the duenna and soldiers.

'There's a difference between staring and studying,' I said.

He appeared bewildered, and put out.

I added, 'And I'm not sure you'd like *me* staring at you . . . '

Carrasco opened his mouth to make some gallant protest, evidently recalled I was not entirely a woman – *or* a man – and blushed like a court page of fourteen or so.

I told Rekhmire' I could keep him off-balance. So far, I'm right.

'Studying close enough to draw detail,' I mused aloud, 'tells me things. You may dress well, but you didn't start in the literate class of servants. Your bones say you were hungry as a child. You're very clean: that means you'd like to keep the position you've earned. And then there's that nasty lump on your head. Somebody seems to have hit you, perhaps as you turned towards them, but clearly not with a fist . . . '

My hand moved as I watched him; I couldn't help making the briefest line sketches, trying to capture his successive expressions.

I can see why Videric would choose him as a spy; he barely gives away anything.

But a spy doesn't normally suffer the close inspection of an artist's model, and I could see every minute flinch, and tiny sheen of sweat under his hairline. At my last comment, his large, limpid brown eyes met mine – and I had been right to want to paint them.

'*Somebody* hit me?' His tone struggled with incredulity, and with outraged dignity, also; which is not what one usually sees in a servant. Someone has praised him above his merits, and he's wanted to believe them.

'A regrettable accident,' I said briskly. 'It would have to be, wouldn't it, messer? Anything else would mean reporting to the Council of Ten that I have my suspicions about who headed the gang of brigands that attacked the representative of Alexandria-in-Exile, and the noble retired Captain-General from Taraco.'

I had thought he would give away annoyance, if anything got through his poker face. Instead, I found my chalk and coal giving shadows and highlights to eyelids and pupils that showed, as they went down on paper, an expression somewhere close to desperation.

Now *why* would he . . .

'Isn't that appropriate for the nobility?' Ramiro Carrasco's tone sounded acid, although he returned to the pose of staring up at a hypothetical Tree of Grace. 'The merchant-princes of Venice are entirely happy to look after the interests of the landed princes of Iberia.'

'You ought to talk to a friend of mine, a lawyer . . . ' I rubbed at coaldust with the pad of my thumb, and achieved a gradation of tone so impressive I abandoned it for fear of ruining it. 'He's all for containing the power of princes. He wants to do it with law . . . '

'The law's nothing beside armed power.'

'That depends on how many people agree to behave as if the law were a real thing.'

Carrasco's face had changed yet again when I looked up to take the line of his jaw.

Is he amused?

As if he spoke to an equal in status – and I suppose he did, if you rank 'King's Freak' against 'paid assassin of Aldra Videric' – Ramiro Carrasco explained, 'I thought *I* was a cynic.'

'Oh.' I smiled. 'For all I know, you may be. I prefer to think of it as recognising how the world really functions. You see a lot of that, as court fool.'

He blinked, fractionally fast, as he did every time I spoke with blatant honesty and appeared not to care I had an audience. I suspected he had realised that the old woman was very deaf. And that Honorius keeps his trusted soldiers well informed.

'Really,' I said. 'What would be the point of me pretending you haven't been told these things?'

'I, ah—'

'In the same way that I know you've tried to have me killed twice.'

I nodded at the ugly lump on his forehead, turning purple-black and green in about equal parts, with a scab beginning to form on the cut.

'I don't know whether or not you know *why* you have those orders. If it's assumed that I've told you . . . well, it probably will be assumed I've told you *all* I know. That puts you under a death sentence, if you weren't before.'

The same over-rapid blink was all that gave him away.

'Madonna . . . ' His shoulders, in the Italian-fashion doublet that showed every broad muscle, relaxed a very little. 'What comes next? The bribe? After the threat? You *are* attempting to get me to change sides?'

I found I was biting at the end of my tongue, while I took the shape of his short hair, tapering back to the nape of his neck in a servant's crop. Even the shortest hairs still had a curl.

'No, Messer Ramiro . . . that would just be silly. No one trusts you, and you must have realised at the beginning of this that you'd be wanted dead at the end. By your employer, if no other man. For some reason, you must think that's worth it . . . Or that you can escape. You can't.'

I flicked up a gaze and caught him staring at me with absolute fury. It was gone in a second, but I held it in my memory long enough to put it on paper. Staring down at the constellation of heads and facial features on the *caput mortuum* tinted surface, I wondered where his ferocious outrage stemmed from, what it meant.

How I might use it.

'Don't blame me,' I said quietly. 'I certainly don't blame *you*. I'm sure you have your reasons.'

Ramiro Carrasco looked completely bemused; whip-lashed back and forth.

'The Franks revile Gaius as Judas,' I added. 'He betrayed their Green Christ with a kiss, and they say he'll be the last man still in Hell, when all the other damned have been redeemed and released. But you and I know the story goes differently. *Someone* had to make the betrayal, because He needed it. The world needed that act, for Him to redeem them. And Gaius was the only man with courage enough to do it – *because* it was necessary.'

Carrasco closed his hands on the chair, knuckles shining white through tension-stretched skin.

'Don't move.' I smiled at him. 'I've got you exactly where I want you.'

The expression I managed to get down on my sketch paper was notable.

A thunderous knock sounded on the outer door. One of Neferet's other servants got up from where she had been sitting by the fire in the antechamber – able to observe us through the doorway, not close enough to overhear, and in any case chatting with two more heavily-built soldiers in brigandines that Honorius had insisted also be present. She padded across the chill floorboards to answer the knocking.

'Madonna!' she called. 'It's Messer Leon.'

I had no chance to say I was busy; Leon Battista of the Alberti family bustled in, brandishing a sheaf of papers in one hand, smiling broadly at me, and ignoring the duenna and the Iberian men completely – both soldiers and assassin.

Leon must assume Carrasco is another Venetian I've called in as a model; obviously not one of freeman status – no, what do the Franks call it? 'Yeoman'?

While I tried to remember how the Franks divided up their society, the artist-lawyer walked up and laid the papers beside me. Hand-written, I saw; covered with diagrams. I picked the bound sheets up, turning them to look at one of the drawings.

'I invented that.' Leon Battista sounded proud. 'Did Masaccio use one in his workshop? Or outside?'

A drawing of a frame of wood, with lines crossing it.

Cloth, I realised. But spun with a heavy thread at every inch-mark, so that the translucent linen was crossed with a grid.

'See.' Leon held his fingers as if they framed a square, absent-mindedly putting a startled Ramiro Carrasco in the centre of his view.

'Now imagine you have it held still, by some means, and that you see all against these lines. How much *easier* is it, to see where your perspective must be drawn?'

I glanced from the papers to his hands, visualised – and wondered if one might use drawn wire, as the men-at-arms used to repair their mail. A wooden frame, strung with taut wires laterally and vertically, like the strangest of musical instruments.

I realised that I was now taking no more notice of the assassin than Leon had.

I shot Ramiro Carrasco a womanly flirtatious grin, that I thought might unsettle him, and added, 'I wonder how long it would take to build one of these?'

'Your "brother",' Leon prompted.

'Masaccio never mentioned it, that I knew,' I said honestly. 'You knew Masaccio . . . '

'I'm his executor.' Leon drew himself up a little; I could see the pride in him. And also see why Masaccio would choose a friend who was both a lawyer and an artist to draw up his last testament.

I said all I could think of. 'You will not have expected it to happen so soon.'

'No. Nor he.' Leon lifted his head, with a little shrug. 'He was often used to add to his will, or take things out . . . He wrote me a letter, and asked me to bring this to Ilario if the man was still living then.'

At *this*, he indicated the bound sheets.

'They're mine, in fact,' he added, almost shyly.

'What is it?'

'A draft of something I was working on. Masaccio was to read through it, and tell me what he thought should be added, but I don't know if he did before . . . ' Leon Battista picked up the papers and smoothed them, looking at the writing. Which must be his, I realised.

Leon Battista said, 'I follow the ancient scholars on how it is that the eye sees things. I'm trying to devise a way for the New Art, for the artist's eye to truly see what is there.'

Ramiro Carrasco chuckled.

I looked up. The Iberian man might never have made a sound. His expression was as demure as any servant in the presence of a master.

'*Truly see what is there.*'

He thinks Leon takes me for a woman.

If I had not been used to such conundrums in Taraco, I suppose I might have blushed.

Leon Battista looked irritated at the interruption.

I said carefully, 'Masaccio wanted my brother to have this?'

It was painful to have to lie, even though Leon Battista insisted on keeping my 'secret', as he conceived it.

More painful to think that Masaccio never knew who he had in his workshop as his apprentice.

'Tommaso wrote to me that Ilario might benefit from reading it. Might learn.' Leon looked embarrassed. 'He also wrote that Ilario would benefit from meeting *me*, but . . . that was mere kindness on his part.'

Having the assassin present at that moment of humility was awkward, although Leon Battista took no more notice of Carrasco than if he had been furniture.

'I wouldn't object to sketching outside,' I said, standing, and looked back at Ramiro Carrasco. 'Are you permitted to come tomorrow?'

The Iberian secretary-assassin spoke demurely. 'Aldra Federico permits it.'

And what am I to make of that? Aldra Federico would happily see his foster son-daughter dead in a backwater canal? Aldra Federico is too stupid to know why one of Videric's men is travelling with him? Or why Videric wants the King's Freak found? Not after the scandal when the Carthaginian envoy arrived – and now he's seen Honorius and I together.

Leon held the door open for me to leave with him.

Glancing back, I caught an expression on Ramiro Carrasco's face.

The assassin, now realising what he has been looking at without seeing. The gentle curve of a pregnant belly . . .

Ramiro Carrasco looked deeply confused.

He's not the only one, I reflected, resting my fingers on Leon's arm as the lawyer led me out towards the campo.

I wonder if he will succeed in getting this news back to Lord Videric?

And if it will make Videric willing to let Nature assassinate me, rather than his paid murderer?

13

It may have stemmed from having a killer in the house. Dawn light reflected up onto the room's ceiling from the canal, making bright fractured crescents on the plaster, and I woke from a vivid dream of Rosamunda.

Rosamunda, much younger, with her womb full of her child; giving birth, and then – what? – being forced up from child-bed, still bleeding, to be wrapped in a cloak and led out into the snow, and told to leave the new-born on the chapel steps?

Or was that a lie? Did the midwife show her what was between my legs and did she turn away? Did she hide her face and let Videric give the orders to dispose of the thing as a foundling? Knowing all the same, by the snow and the winter cold, that it would die before being found?

I lay listening to Rekhmire' grunt in pain as he slept. My body stayed motionless under the flat of my hand.

If anything quickens in my belly, it's too faint for me to feel.

And I can hate Rosamunda, since she had every reason to expect to get up out of child-bed.

As a slave, being a shameless snoop aids survival at court, and indeed anywhere else. Privacy is for freemen. The absence of a collar, I found, couldn't convince me differently.

Rekhmire''s voice echoed out of his partly-open door:

'You will not walk out of this room!'

I winced, because as statements go, that one is so easily proved untrue.

Since it was Neferet who'd come upstairs earlier, I expected Neferet to come striding out of Rekhmire''s room. I froze to the spot at the head of the stairs, unable to decide whether it would be ruder to enter and demonstrate I'd overheard them quarrelling, or to appear as if I was eavesdropping.

'What in the Eight's name are you doing keeping the Queen's offer away from him!' Rekhmire''s voice sounded high, cracked – as out of control as I'd ever heard him. 'It's there in the ambassador's papers! "Bring him to the Library; Ty-ameny will give him all the funds he wants." You couldn't miss seeing it!'

Impetus carried me on until I stood in the open doorway.

I might have been modelling nude for both roles of the Whore of Babylon's seduction-dance, and neither one would have looked at me.

Rekhmire' sat just on the bed still, his strapped-up leg dangerously close to teetering off the edge of it. Neferet had her back to the window, so he must squint against the light. Her arms were folded tightly across her just-too-wide-for-proportion chest.

'I need Herr Mainz!' Her heel dug at the floorboards. 'He can go home in a month or two—'

'He can end up in the Council of Ten's dungeons in a week or two!' Rekhmire' hit his fist against the feather-stuffed pillows. 'You've got him printing sedition for that boy of yours—'

'My "boy" is the man who'll bring the Alberti family back to power in Florence.' Lines dug in beside her mouth and nose, and I saw how she would look when she was fifty. 'As opposed to your *pregnant* boy, who does nothing to earn her money except scribble drawings!'

Rekhmire' pushed forward, missed his grip, and the plank on which his leg was bound slid forward and cracked one end down on the floorboards. I winced, automatically inclining forward, and then stopped as Rekhmire' slapped Neferet's offered hand aside.

He leaned, both hands on the splint, not touching anywhere on his bandaged leg, never mind his knee.

'If Ilario is in trouble, it's my fault.' His voice was stiff. 'I did something ill-advised in Carthage—'

Neferet snickered.

Rekhmire''s scalp and face turned a dull plum-red.

Dropping her hands to her hips, Neferet drew herself up, still smiling. 'I'm not that stupid – the day *you* sire a child is the day *I* give birth to one!'

The line of Rekhmire''s body folded forward from the hip, losing tension. He sighed. 'Whatever it is you're mixed up in, it must be bad. You used to do this when you were a boy – pick a quarrel until everyone else had forgotten the question. You've just grown better at picking tender spots.'

'I was never a boy.'

Rekhmire' corrected himself without the shadow of malice or contempt. 'When you were a girl with prick and balls.'

The older Egyptian nodded. She sat down on the oak chest under the window, with the graceful movements that it occurred to me she would have had to learn. Just as I was trained in them.

I was trained to move as a woman does, *and* as a man does. The difference between myself and Neferet being that neither one of them seems natural to me. A woman's movements are restricted, a man's exaggerated.

Neferet sighed and rubbed the heel of one hand into her eye. 'Talking of women born into the wrong bodies – will the scribe survive child-bed?

Should I keep the Turkish physician on retainer? Or are you just making her comfortable until the time comes?'

I couldn't see Rekhmire''s face. Mine felt numb and swollen, as if any expression would emerge caricatured.

'Neferet . . . ' Rekhmire' straightened, leaving his leg propped between himself and the floor as if it were not part of him. 'Stop this. Ilario is with me because I took an ill-advised action in Carthage. Cousin Ty-ameny will be happy to rip me open for the wider political aspects. Don't *you* start on anything else.'

'Ill-advised' – the politics of the matter? Or buying me?

Nothing stopped either of them seeing me in the doorway, except that I was so still. Hearing these things, I couldn't move. Only the blood went to my cheeks, knowing that within moments I would be mortified by discovery.

'You have the apparent right to question what I do with Leon.' Neferet's voice took on an ugly, uncontrolled rasp. 'But you think – *Cousin Ty-ameny* will think – that it's acceptable for you to abduct a boy-girl she-male, who's a magnet for Carthage and Iberia.'

'*Jahar*.' Rekhmire' used the male name as if it were both challenge and appeal.

'Why did you have to follow me here? What business is it of yours!'

'You're right: it's *not* my business. I'm here as a favour—' Rekhmire' grunted emphatically, trying to shift his leg. 'A favour to Menmet-Ra—'

'Oh, I might have known! Fat old Tom-Cat doesn't want to leave Rome, so he twists you around his little finger until you come nosing in here!' Neferet grinned triumphantly. 'And another report goes back to Ty-ameny and your name gets written up in phoenix gilding! Great Sekhmet, don't you ever get tired of creeping around the Pharaoh-Queen?'

The strain of the tilted plank obviously hurt him: I was frozen between helping him and hearing Neferet's words spill out. Lines cut deep on Rekhmire''s face.

Neferet turned back to the window, the morning's light showing gold thread in the weave of her linen over-dress. It was not true gold, I thought.

'Just because you're happy to run around doing favours for an old friend from the *scholarium* . . . ' Neferet unlatched the shutters, opening them to the winter air. I could hear the tolling of church bells, deep in the mist; the sound of a passing bell, for some man drowned or dead of plague.

'You'll run anybody's errands, Little Dog. What I'm doing here is *important*. In Florence they have laws to permit the burning alive of men who copulate with other men – twenty years ago they burned hundreds, under this Duke's father. And *they* decide who is a man.'

'And your Leon has of course told the Alberti family here in Venice

258

that you have a woman's soul, but not the womb to give the family an heir . . . '

Neferet spat out a piece of fishwife-Greek and I couldn't blame her; if Rekhmire' had spoken to me in that self-satisfied tone, I would have punched him.

'Leon loves me!' Neferet finished. 'Barbarian Frank he may be, but I had to come a hundred leagues from Alexandria to find a man who sees I am the woman for him!'

Her cry was equal parts pain and pride. In the same way, I didn't know whether to shed tears, or take up the refuge that cruel laughter would be.

Rekhmire' stubbornly dropped his chin down. 'Yes, I would happily see the Inquisition out of Fiorenza. And every other Frankish city! But Alexandria carries no weight against the believers in the Green Christ, or any man who chooses to speak for him. You of anybody ought to know that it's essential for Ty-ameny to have this German Guildsman. If he can do what he says he can do – and he won't have written it down, will he? There won't be more than sketch-plans; the secret of it will be inside the man's skull!'

He waved a hand, as if he indicated the passing bell.

'So easy to lose everything! It need not even be a competitor who wants him out of the way. An accident, a brush with cholera . . . Then it's *gone*, can't you see that?'

'I need him.' Neferet's voice was flatly stubborn as she stared down at the canal, three floors below. 'Leon needs him.'

'And why could this not happen next year? Let Herr Mainz come to Alexandria *first*.'

I was fascinated enough to breathe; shift, as men do when not sitting for painters or sculptors – and immediately both their heads turned.

Not next year, I realised, seeing her undefended face. Because for all Neferet says he loves her, she doesn't believe Leon will be here in twelve months' time. Not without the scribe-*machina*. She thinks he only stays because of that.

I don't know Leon well enough to know whether that's true or false. I know Neferet just well enough to be sure she'll hate me if I speak my guess.

'How long have you been spying there?' Neferet turned from me before I could answer, spitefully prodding at Rekhmire'. 'Training her up, are you? To listen at doors?'

Rekhmire' gave me the look of a disappointed pedagogue. As if, for a few denarii, he'd demand I stand up straight and apologise politely.

They reminded me so much of Sunilda and Reinalda before their coming-of-age feasts that I had to stifle a smile.

Stepping inside the room, I said equably, 'If you don't want people to know these things, I advise not quarrelling at the top of your voices with the door open.'

The Alexandrine woman looked taken aback. The same expression showed on Rekhmire''s face.

Her voice hostile, but subdued, Neferet demanded, 'What did you hear?'

'Nothing that was my business. A lot that wasn't. You can probably be heard as far as the *kitchens*.' I exaggerated. 'And Visigoth Latin and Alexandrine Latin aren't that different. I'd have a word with Honorius about his guard, if I were you – you know how soldiers gossip.'

Rekhmire' and Neferet exchanged the kind of look that only a childhood spent quarrelling over the same toys will give you. I suppressed a smug grin at successfully uniting them against a common outsider. That doesn't come from Rodrigo's court, but from thirteen years of scrambling for a place with 'Nilda and 'Nalda.

'Pushy little thing, isn't she?' Neferet's long upper lip quivered, in the way that Rekhmire''s does when he suppresses a smile.

'Ilario, pushy? What would give you an idea like that?' He turned a pitch-coal eye on me. 'Help me up with this leg.'

'Your will is mine, O master.'

'One can only live in hope that some day that will be the case . . . ' Rekhmire' looked pious enough to make Neferet and I grin; she less willingly than I.

I slipped into the room past Neferet, and studied the position the book-buyer had got himself into. He abandoned the pose, braced himself on his hands, and shifted his backside towards the headboard as I lifted the plank and splints, taking care not to touch his leg at any point.

'Fornicating Carthaginian goats . . . ' He used the cuff of his Frankish morning-gown to wipe his forehead, immediately darkening the blue velvet with sweat. Without a word, Neferet poured him a drink from the pottery jug and passed it over.

I had a moment to wonder how the green glaze was done on the jug, and whether it was possible to reproduce the room's curved and monochrome reflection. Rekhmire' and Neferet spoke at once.

Neferet gestured elegantly, ceding. 'I'll leave you to talk to her.'

'I thought you might!'

The Alexandrine woman avoided the *sotto voce* comment, gliding out of the room with an elegance I envied now that all my weight was high and forward.

'I won't insult you by asking for secrecy.' Rekhmire' cradled the cup on the blankets in his lap. 'The Hermopolitan Eight know, we're aware enough of each other's lives. I *will* ask you to curb your immediate indiscreet tendency to leap astride the nearest horse and gallop off in all directions . . . '

'You have an over-inflated idea of your skills as a judge of character.'

I imitated him as closely as I could, and was rewarded by one of those quaking giggles that robbed his monumental gravity of all dignity.

'I wonder,' he said, regaining composure, 'whether it's too late to return to that Carthaginian slave-dealer and ask for a refund?'

'Much too late.'

It's a narrow step from macabre humour to thoughts that make me shudder – that Rekhmire' was in Carthage by the merest chance, and might never have bought me, is one of those things.

The Egyptian said quietly, 'You should never have been sold before. By your Aldra Federico, I mean. You were *freeborn*. Of two freeborn parents, even if not legitimate – but your father would have acknowledged you. Granted that was unknown then, but the sale itself is invalid. If you are ever back at the court of Taraco in anything like peace, you might ask Honorius to have lawyers look into that and void the original bill of sale to Rodrigo Sanguerra.'

Ever since I realised that Rodrigo's manumission documents burned in Donata's fire, there has been a nudging discomfort at the back of my mind – that even Rekhmire''s manumission of me in Rome was not valid, because it did not cover the years before he bought me.

'I take it back,' I said. 'You're a reasonable judge of character.'

He snickered and patted my shoulder; it might have been friendly mockery, or consolation, or – knowing Rekhmire' – both. He gazed levelly at me.

'Are you prepared to have a look around on my behalf? If you'd stayed my scribe, I would have begun this with you. Now you get a choice. I hear you keep your escort busy enough, taking your drawing-pad out. I swear I heard *Tottola* yesterday talking about "egg tempera fresco" . . . '

'He *asked*.' I may have sounded injured.

'And now he knows. Quite a lot, apparently, for a man I've never been convinced grew up knowing how to cook his food . . . '

The picture of Tottola and Attila in the depths of some German forest untouched since Varus's legions went missing, growing up on raw rabbit and fish, was all too easy to bring to mind.

'They'd like you thinking that,' I said, sitting carefully on the edge of the bed. 'They cultivate the reputation. People think if they don't speak, that means they must be stupid.'

'Not a mistake any man will make with you, scribe . . . '

The combination of Pharaonic dignity and angelic innocence was a sure indicator of whether he meant a compliment or insult.

'If *I* were about to ask someone a favour, *I* wouldn't insult that someone . . . '

'No, indeed.' The innocence increased.

'So what am I about to do?'

'Take your drawing materials out. You have an excuse to go

anywhere. The soldiers will doubtless complain about this cold, but you do Honorius a favour by keeping them keen-edged.'

'Oh, I'm sure I do . . . '

And I'd hear all about it, too, now that the variegated group of men – all of whom had been with Honorius a decade and more – had got over their shyness at the General's son or daughter turning out to be a son-daughter. It had been easier, or at least *quieter*, in Rome, when they'd been in awe of the phenomenon of the hermaphrodite. Familiarity had now brought matters down to, *Oh, it's just Ilario.*

Which I supposed has its own comfort.

I gave Rekhmire' a hard stare. 'It's not like I know how to do any of this . . . stuff . . . that comes with being a book-buyer. What am I looking for?'

Rekhmire' smiled. 'Listen. Watch. Don't ask questions, if you can avoid it; they *will* always sound awkward. If nothing shows up, that's what sometimes happens. And—'

'And?'

'And,' Rekhmire' said, 'if you can find the German Guildsman Herr Mainz, you can tell him I'd very much like a word with him.'

My freedom in Venice lasted ten more days.

14

It was Leon Battista who ended it.

Departing from one of our discussions while drawing Ramiro Carrasco, Leon remarked, 'I know your father is careful of you, in your state of health – but will you come to any of the Carnival festivities, with Madonna Neferet and myself? It would be my honour to show you how we do these things in Venezia.'

Wisdom fought desire. I could hear the arguments before Honorius voiced them. And I thought Carrasco's ears were keen enough to have overheard Leon.

'I think,' I said, 'that my father will say that Carnival is too dangerous a time for me to go out of the house.'

My guess proved accurate.

I argued only half-heartedly with Licinus Honorius. Part of me, at least, agreed with him. *I have taken my pitcher to the well twice already in the Most Serene Republic . . .*

The Alexandria House immediately felt as if it became a cramped prison.

Granted, there was no room to set up a full painter's workshop – but I could still work. I found myself missing the space in Masaccio's workshop . . . even missing the stench of fish glue being rendered down for size, and the permeating odour of varnish. Or in Tommaso Cassai's case, fifty different experiments with varnishes, to see which did not blue or yellow the pigments in his tempera painting.

'I've given up colour, for now,' I observed to Rekhmire', speeding my pen to try and catch his features before the angle of the light changed.

If I flicked through this particular work-book, I could see him become less gaunt, less pained, more himself, over the past weeks.

'Colour's a snare and a delusion.'

The Egyptian smiled. 'If not colour, what's left?'

I glared at him. 'Tone. Value. Perspective. The proportion of one part – every part – to every *other* part. How things grow short and fat when you foreshorten them—'

Rekhmire' felt at his nose.

'I even gave up drypoint,' I said, ignoring the implicit joke. 'I've been using a reed pen, so that I don't get trapped into fine detail. I do what

263

Masaccio said: observe, observe, observe . . . But it's knowing what I'm looking at.'

I was beginning to accept Masaccio's death. Or at least, I could bear to recall his precepts, and speak of them without tears or shudders.

Honorius entered, and stood behind my back for some time, observing me draw.

'Isn't he supposed to be smiling? He looks more like he's bawling his head off!'

'Since when did I ask for your opinion?' I blotted the reed pen dry, so I might cut it to a sharper point, and gave my father a frustrated smile. 'I'm still planning compositions for yours. I take it you want the donor's right of appearing in the picture?'

'He does,' Rekhmire' put in hastily. 'Sit down, Captain-General – it's the Lion of Castile's turn to be told off every fifty heartbeats for fidgeting!'

They continued somewhat in this manner while Honorius called for a drink, and Ensign Saverico bought a jug and drinking bowls. My father sat on the wooden settle facing the window, light falling on him unobstructed, and I began to draw.

The results were beyond bad.

I stared at my fingers, flexing them. I couldn't blame the black chalk, even if this batch *was* too hard and somewhat particulate, making for scratchy drawing. Sometimes the closer the subject is to the artist's heart, the less well it is painted.

I need to direct that artist's eye that Rekhmire' had me point at Neferet, and turn it on *il leone di Castiglia*.

Changing black chalk for willow charcoal, I smudged the paper where there were shadows on Honorius's face, and lifted part of it off again with rolled bread-crumbs, to lighten it. The shift in values was pleasingly gradual.

'Have you thought more about how you want to see St Gaius?' And then, particularly because my father must have spent so much time close to the Frankish border, 'Why St Gaius, *Judas*, of all the soldier saints? Why not Michael, or S. Bellona?'

He pushed his fingers through his hair. His nails were not bitten like Carmagnola's, but pared neatly down.

'I wanted something . . . ' He struggled for words. 'When you're fighting . . . Men die. That simple. And if you're giving the orders, they die because of you. You send men out to fight as a feint or diversion, when you know that, even though we'll win, these men will all die . . . All, to a man.'

Tottola came in with more wine at that point, and lifted his thick brows, and nodded to show assent.

'That's what soldiering is,' Honorius said. 'Who dies last. And someone has to give those necessary orders.'

He paused. I began a new drawing.

'St Gaius didn't kill himself,' he added softly. 'After the Lord-Emperor was dead, he went East, to the Turks and Persians and Indians, and beyond. Could you paint him when he's deciding that?'

'No.' I didn't hesitate. 'No. Not yet. I've had to forget every way of painting that I knew, and learn again. Ask me in a year. Better – in a year I'll make an altar board of St Gaius for your chapel, and you tell *me* if I can do it.'

My father slowly nodded.

He set his drinking bowl down and came to look over my shoulder again, effectively cutting off the drawing, but he spent long minutes studying what lines there were.

'I wish I could call up faces as you do.' His fingertip moved high above the paper's surface, mirroring the line of his jaw and ear. 'I made good friends when I first went north. Many of them. I can see them, in the eye of my mind; men I fought beside. We loved each other like brothers; *died* for each other. The last of them was killed at Candlemass, last year, and I decided I was done with fighting.'

He removed his hand, staring at what I had drawn of his face as if it could tell him something.

'I felt no grief when Antonio died. *None*. A man I knew for twenty-five years . . . Nothing. Then I knew I could either continue as a successful captain, and never mourn any butchered man of mine, or I must *stop*. I told King Juan the following day that I would be returning to Taraconensis.'

I rubbed my charcoal-black fingers on a rag, turning my skin grey. 'How can you command for all that time and still grieve when men die? How could you bear it?'

'War is horror. Let no man tell you otherwise. But if this is war, then at least it can be prosecuted with the least possible waste. I did not desire to turn into one of those commanders who gets their troops killed carelessly, and then hires more and does it again.'

After a moment, when I saw he wouldn't say more, I remarked, 'And I thought St Gaius was going to be easy!'

Honorius chuckled, as I thought he would, and leaned his arm across my shoulders. 'I mean to get my money's worth out of you, son-daughter!'

The desire to urinate thirty times a day, along with aches in joints and a general feeling that my body was becoming unfamiliar to me – and God He knows, it was unfamiliar enough as a human body before this! – left me in a foul temper.

'*Out!*' Honorius bellowed, on the second morning of Carnival season, when my ill-temper rubbed up against Rekhmire''s until the Egyptian so far forgot himself as to quarrel violently with me.

'Tell *him* to stop shouting!' I snarled.

'*I did not shout!*' Rekhmire', loudly indignant, slammed his hand down on the side of the bed and flinched. 'I may have raised my voice. I do not "shout"!'

'Then *I'll* leave!' Honorius snarled, and stalked out, slamming the door hard enough to rattle the scroll cases, pestles and mortars that stood on the shelves.

Silenced, I looked at Rekhmire' in embarrassment.

The book-buyer huffed out his breath, and looked at me from the corners of his eyes.

'He's a lot like you,' Rekhmire' said after a moment.

'Ha!' I was torn between the compliment and insult, both implicit in the Egyptian's words. I waddled over to sit in the wooden armed chair by the fire.

'I wish I thought I'd do half as much with my life as he has. Do you want to play another game of chess?'

'Not until you learn enough skill at it that the whole experience isn't a worse tedium than this!'

I left it a minute, and looked at him from the corners of *my* eyes. An unfamiliar eye wouldn't have seen it, but I read a degree of contrition on his face.

'Suppose you teach me chess,' I offered, 'so that I get better at it.'

Rekhmire' shrugged and nodded. It was an attempt to indicate that he didn't care either way, and a not hugely successful one.

'That might be better.' He waited for me to edge the chair over to the bed, and set the chessboard up on the cover. 'Thank you.'

'You're welcome.'

He smiled, almost shyly. One of the soldiers, Vasev, I think, currently shaved him in the morning, so he was back to his neat self. You would not have known he stayed in bed for any other reason than apparent idleness.

Which means he must be good at concealing pain. Considerable amounts of pain.

I wondered where and why he had learned it. Which for some reason turned my mind to Taraco's court, and I turned it resolutely away.

Sixteen moves into the game – with Rekhmire' explaining extensively at each where I might have done better – Honorius stomped back into the room. Evidently his body-servant had only got his cloak from him; his boots tracked slush across the floorboards and old dried rushes.

'Strange pick-pockets they have in Venice!' Honorius snorted. 'Most thieves cut your purse to take something *out* . . . '

I must have looked bewildered.

'Here!' He tossed his leather purse to Rekhmire', who caught it out of the air with a wince. 'See what you make of that.'

I eased my belly by leaning back from the chessboard. 'What's happened?'

My father looked down at his leaking muddy boots as if surprised to see them. 'Saverico!'

With one hand resting down on Saverico's shoulder as the man drew each boot off in turn, Honorius went on:

'The usual thing in the Mercaria, I thought – knocked aside by one man, purse cut off my belt and passed to a second. I chased them into the back alleys, thought I'd lose them; my fault for not taking one of the lads at my back. Then I saw the purse by the first bridge, where they'd dropped it. The money was gone . . . There's now a letter in it.'

Rekhmire' lifted his head from peering at the unfolded sheet of paper. 'This is an approach from Carthage!'

'That's what I thought, yes.' Honorius dropped down onto the hard wooden settle and wriggled his feet in front of the fire, as if that would dry his hose faster. He shot me a sharp look. 'You may have been right back in Rome. The King-Caliph thinks I'm interested in betraying King Rodrigo.'

'Or he'd like to have evidence that you would.' Rekhmire' carefully re-folded the paper along exactly the same lines. 'Either would help Carthage. You'd make an equally good figurehead governor, or distressing evidence of further internal dissent in Taraco.'

'The King-Caliph can sodomise a male goat!' Honorius said, in passable Carthaginian Latin. 'But that isn't the point!'

'Ask the goat!' Rekhmire' surprised the life out of me by murmuring. He nickered almost precisely like a horse when he stifled his laughter. It was silly enough that amusement bubbled up irresistibly in me, and I had to put both hands over my mouth.

'This is the subtle wit of the Alexandrines, evidently,' Honorius muttered, and tried hard to look as if he were not pleased to have reduced the large Egyptian to a quaking mass.

Honorius looked back at me, after a moment or two, and the laughter left his face.

'The point,' he said, 'is that this message has been delivered to me *here*. There are agents of Carthage in Venice. They must have arrived a month or more ago – travel's impossible now. If they know where I am, they know where *you* are, Ilario.'

Rekhmire' looked annoyed, plainly feeling that he should have been the one to say this.

'Carthage has no reason to hurt me,' I pointed out. 'The reverse, if anything. They need their witness alive and well.'

'That's as may be, but I don't fancy hiring a pirate fleet or a company of mercenaries to haul your backside out from under the Penitence!'

I smiled. He stopped glaring and looked embarrassed.

'Rescuing the maiden in distress?' I raised a brow at him, as much in Rekhmire''s manner as I could imitate.

'Carthage can have you!' Honorius snorted. 'In fact, I have a better idea – when I offer my services as local Carthaginian Governor of Taraconensis, I'll offer to sell them my son-daughter at a very reasonable price! Then there'll be no North African interference in my government, because you will have driven them all mad . . . '

I whispered solemnly to Rekhmire', 'You can see he *is* cut out to be a tyrant.'

The book-buyer, having been perilously near a sulk, abandoned it and gave me a smile; perfectly well aware that I attempted to entertain him into a better humour.

'That will stem from commanding armies,' he said as if Honorius were not in the room. His gaze grew sharper, directed at me. 'And your peace-making talents come from your years as Court Fool.'

If anybody would know that there's more to the position of Royal Freak than a quick tongue and a dual set of genitalia, it would be Rekhmire'.

'Rodrigo didn't like his nobles to kill each other – well, more than was absolutely necessary. And not at court.'

'Ilario!' Honorius rapped his knuckles against the wooden seat of the settle, as if he called a meeting to order. 'This settles it. You don't go outside at any time with fewer than two guards – and Lady Neferet can get used to my men doing guard duty in this building.'

Rekhmire' rested his fingers on the folded letter. 'What will you do with this?'

Honorius grunted, stood up, and slipped the paper out from under the Alexandrine's hand. 'You reminded me – I was on the way to the privy!'

Rekhmire' gazed at the door as it shut behind Honorius.

'And this is the man the Carthaginians wish to make Governor of Taraco . . . '

He gave the particular secretive smile he had when something amused him, and directed it at me.

'Not that I say the people of Taraconensis wouldn't benefit from being ruled as if they were a company of mercenaries.'

'I could say the same about the book-buyers of Alexandria!'

We went back to chess. In the short intervals while Rekhmire' considered his moves, I regarded the world beyond the leaded glass window, where the rain had now turned to sleet.

Videric's spies. And now spies from Carthage.

I said nothing of Rekhmire''s injured leg, in the same way that he made no reference to my swelling abdomen.

Neither of us debated the possibility of a winter voyage to Alexandrine Constantinople. Between storms by sea, and washed-out roads, mud, flooding rivers, avalanches, and landslides, there's little enough travelling done in this quarter of the year. Which should have comforted me – if we couldn't move, neither could any other man. But it persisted in seeming to me that things weren't as simple as that.

Rekhmire', being as keen a reader of expressions as drawing was making me, echoed my thoughts aloud. 'Likely we have trouble enough already here in Venice.'

Honorius, re-entering the room in time to hear it, scowled at the Egyptian, and then at me as he squatted to warm his whitened fingers at the hearth fire.

Abruptly, he said, 'Let me adopt you.'

'Will that make me safer? Or merely give you the illusion of having authority over me?' I grinned at his expression. 'I'm half inclined to think life was easier as a slave.' I looked at Rekhmire'. 'You wouldn't buy me again, would you?'

'Sun-god's egg, no! You were far too much trouble!'

If there had been anything breakable and moderately inexpensive to hand, I would have thrown it at him. Neferet stored only expensive knick-knacks in the embassy, and art that she said would repay the investment within a few years (which I personally doubted). I was reduced to glaring at the Egyptian.

'I was a better slave than you were a master!'

Rekhmire' and Honorius swapped looks. They had the effect of making me feel closer to fifteen than twenty-five.

'You see?' the Egyptian remarked. 'Nothing but trouble. And insolent, too.'

I grinned at him, and ambled to the window. If I could, I would paint the darkening sleet-streaked sky, with the serried ranks of wide-capped chimneys spouting smoke bent over by the wind.

'*And* you two gang up on me,' I added.

'Self-defence!' Honorius.

'Self-preservation!' Rekhmire'.

I snorted. 'If I had a *job*, I wouldn't have to sit here and listen to you two old codgers every day . . . '

Rekhmire' sounded offended. 'I'm not old!'

The retired Captain-General of Castile and Leon distinctly snickered.

'Isn't it Carnival?' I said sourly. 'You two should take that act on a *commedia* stage.'

Rekhmire' pointed a large, blunt finger at me, his expression changing. 'Yes. Carnival. Masks. Parties. Riots in the streets. Boats overturned. Could anything make life easier for an assassin?'

'Well, I'm already making it as easy as I *can* . . . '

I grinned at the Alexandrine's expression.

'They say "keep your friends close and your enemies closer", don't they? Ramiro Carrasco can sit next to me any day he pleases. He knows that. He just can't kill me. He knows that, too. It may,' I speculated, 'be driving him slowly insane.'

'I sympathise!' Honorius rumbled, but I could see that he was suppressing a smile. He had confidence in his men-at-arms.

As a slave, one grows used to living with no privacy. I had envisaged life as a freeman or freewoman significantly differently: plainly that was an error. It had taken a distinctly female fit of hysterics to keep Sergeant Orazi out of the garderobe with me. Two men slept in my room at night; one across the door, and one under the window.

'Federico will assume I'm only to be kidnapped.'

Honorius frowned. 'He must know that's ridiculous!'

'He'll know nothing he doesn't want to!' I snorted. 'There are plenty of pleasant lies Federico can tell himself, if he wants to. That Videric merely wants me kidnapped, not killed, say. He's capable of believing Videric only wants to lock me up in some back-country fortress, like an errant daughter.'

I wiped my hands free of charcoal on a rag, and realised it was a lost cause. My oatmeal-coloured woollen bodice and skirts were comprehensively smudged with black.

I got a look from both of them that silently informed me it was a penalty of wearing skirts.

I know that.

'If I don't get out of this house, I'll go mad! I know where Ramiro Carrasco is—'

'You don't know where every thug he's hired is!'

Honorius straightened up and looked at me with a hurt expression. 'I've told you, you can go anywhere you want to—'

'If I don't mind taking six hulking great Taraconian farm-boys with armour on their backs, and a Venetian woman with a face like a *prune*!'

The retired Captain-General put his hand over his mouth. I realised he was hiding a grin.

'*What?*'

'You really do sound like a woman when you put skirts on.'

Rekhmire', appearing to study the chessboard, grinned.

Honorius's gaze went up and down me, in a way that I am used to.

More soberly, he said, 'You don't walk in Venice on your own. Not dressed as a woman. And not because of Carrasco. You *know* what cities are like, for a woman—'

'Why do you think I dress as a man in Frankish countries!'

'—and if you're hurt when you're alone, every man will say that you *deserved* it. Do you understand me?'

My hand rested on my abdomen again, I found. The obstruction to me wearing doublet and hose here in Venice, because my body has so evidently the shape of a womb, and not a man's belly.

As if we were alone in the room – which spoke volumes for his trust of the Egyptian – Honorius asked, 'Has it kicked yet?'

I shook my head. *It may be dead*, I thought but didn't say.

The lean ex-soldier drew in a breath, and stared into the low flames of the hearth-fire.

'My wives – both of them lost children early on. I suppose I know the signs. I don't . . . I don't know whether to hope to see them, with you, or hope not to.'

He shot me a look that, after a moment, I realised was to see whether he was hurting or offending me.

'The Egyptian says you could die of the birth,' he added.

I glared at Rekhmire', where he sat with his leg strapped uncomfortably to the ash-wood plank. 'The Egyptian should keep his damn mouth *shut!*'

'You weren't going to tell me?'

I faced both men. 'It hasn't quickened. It's more than five months. I don't feel anything. Except fatter and off balance. It's not a baby to me – and it might not be a baby,' I added. 'It might be a monster. Look who it's been fathered on.'

Honorius stood up and put his arm around my shoulder. Which I would have shaken off, had I not found it unexpectedly comforting.

'Skirts make you want to weep more,' I said, pulling out Neferet's kerchief, and dusting my nose hard. '*I* blame skirts.'

'Oh, so do I.' His grip tightened.

'Will *you* get a bad name if I go walking around on my own?'

'Yes. Of course.' He looked as hangdog as a man used to commanding armies can. 'But I worry about your safety, not that.'

'I'll take the Eight-gods-damn-them escort, then!'

I suspected I would narrowly escape being dragged back by the men-at-arms themselves, none too keen on being reprimanded by Honorius in the mood he would have been in.

Honorius steered me to sit down beside him on the settle, the hard wood not comfortable under my aching joints. Rekhmire' looked up from under his eyebrows, tipped his king over, and began to set up a new game.

'What I need to do,' I sighed, 'is talk to someone about what happened in Rome.'

Honorius gave me a look and a nod, both straightforward and accepting. Rekhmire' placed a row of pawns. He has heard this before, or most of it. My father . . .

I leaned my shoulder against the shoulder of Honorius. 'It involves more than you think. More than you'll be able to repeat. But I trust you. And I need to tell someone how it is that Masaccio died.'

I stayed indoors throughout Carnival.

Leon and Neferet came in after midnight every night, flushed with wine, and shaking gold-tissue streamers out of their hair. I tried not to sound as bad-tempered about it as I felt. Each campo had its own particular festivities, and a *commedia dell'arte* team set up in the square by the Alexandrine House for several days in succession.

'In Taraco, I would have been allowed to watch *that*,' I muttered at Honorius. 'Even if the King's Freak were dressed in skirts on that day.'

'Ilario—'

'You want to know where the assassin is?' I demanded of Honorius. 'I'll send a message and invite my foster father here, with Sunilda and Reinalda, and I'll make sure Ramiro Carrasco is with them. If he's here, nothing's going to happen!'

Rekhmire' began an objection.

'Nothing will happen,' I repeated, 'because Sergeant Orazi and the other men will happen to *him*. If he so much as looks at me funny. Am I right, Father?'

Honorius matched the Egyptian for gravity, clasping his hands lightly behind him, and rocking on his toes. 'She's right.'

'She's always right,' Rekhmire' muttered. 'Ilario, I suppose you want to draw the actors?'

'That too.'

I did draw them. The swaggering captain who played up to that portion of his audience consisting of the Iberian military, and won himself a great success, with Honorius slapping at his thigh and laughing until the tears came. The wily thieving servant, smarter than his masters – at whose appearance I shot a look at Carrasco, and was rewarded by something very like a blush. The woman—

There *is* only one woman in the *commedia*, and unlike the others she goes bare-faced. Except that her uncovered face represents Young Girl, and is as much of a mask as the others.

And the plague doctor, with his long-beaked leather mask, pretending to drink all of his urine flask at some turn of the plot that depends on the Girl's pregnancy.

Rekhmire' saw me put my chalk down. Barely audible over the shrieking, guffawing crowd, he queried, 'Ilario?'

I put my mouth close to his ear. 'Nothing. Lend me a cloak. It's cold.'

It *was* cold – a white rime of frost outlined the bricks, carved wooden house-beams, and well-trodden earth, and gave the *commedia* artists more pratfalls than they planned for. But it wasn't the winter that chilled me.

Mummers came next, from some northern country. From the Alexandrine House's upper windows, by torch-light, I watched them play the Frankish Sacred Boar's ceremony.

No one played the aulos flute.

The day after that, we were back to masked revellers; and so it went on, for what seemed like weeks, and was in fact nearly a month, until Ash Wednesday cut all short, and there was only a sludge of papier-mâché masks left floating in gutters and canals.

Frankish Lent being a time for austerity, I was glad to be in Neferet's house. She muttered something unusually low-voiced about 'superstitious Europeans!' when an official from the Council of Ten called to ask why the household didn't attend church. She told him that the servants certainly did attend, she and her colleague Rekhmire' were preparing to sacrifice to the gods of darkness and invisibility, and didn't mention my name at all.

'We need a young man and a young woman to eviscerate on the altar, for the requisite entrails,' Rekhmire' said, far too mildly. 'Thinking about that, *you* . . . '

'Could do both?' I threw an old paint-sponge at him. 'Have I mentioned how *very* much I dislike you?'

'Daily. Hourly.' He grinned, which was a startling expression on that monumental face. It turned rueful. 'If that young officer was as devoid of humour as he seemed, I may have to spend some time explaining to Doge Foscari that Alexandrines don't, in fact, practise sacrificial rites . . . '

'Wouldn't it be easier just to eviscerate someone?'

The knock on the door came with such fortuitousness that I couldn't help remarking, 'Ah. Carrasco. Come in . . . '

Ramiro Carrasco de Luis was shown in by Sergeant Orazi. Carrasco looked at Rekhmire', clearly more than a little bewildered by the Egyptian greeting him with a snort of amusement.

I smiled. Videric's man had been far too close to recovering his mental balance, now he was used to sitting as my model.

'Come in,' I repeated. 'Sit down, Ramiro. Take your hose off.'

'I *beg* your pardon!' he yelped.

Rekhmire', who had been rising to his feet, exchanged a glance with the sergeant and the other soldier, Aznar, and sat back down on the settle. 'I'll stay for this session, shall I?'

Ramiro Carrasco was looking satisfactorily aghast.

I beamed at him. 'Judas – St Gaius, rather – should be in Roman legionary uniform. I need to make some studies of your legs and feet. Do you have suitable legs?'

Carrasco muttered something unintelligible, and glanced around the room as if he would much rather not have been under the eye of the Egyptian and two of Honorius's crack troops. He shot me a glance in which I thought I discerned some unflattering disgust. As if this might have been titillating if I were a woman, but a man-woman was merely revolting.

'Stand there.' More harshly, I pointed. When he had rid himself of boots and hose, and wrapped around himself the cloak that I had put out

273

for him, he stood not far from the fire, pale-skinned muscular legs on show. He was moderately hairy, but his feet were well-shaped – few people have actually well-shaped feet – and I lost myself in capturing their dimensions from various angles.

Not every man can retain his self-possession when bare from the thigh down. Ramiro Carrasco held his cloak around him with one hand, and stroked the narrow, clipped beard that he had taken to growing in this Frankish city, and eventually looked perfectly at ease.

Rekhmire' stirred, and departed to check Neferet's current stock of imported scrolls, and advise her on what should be sent back to Alexandria when the ships could sail again – not that he needed to give the advice, or she to hear it, but it gave them an excuse to pore over the finer points of papyrus, ink, ancient treatises, and rare finds with which they could make each other jealous.

Consequently, Leon Battista stepped in for some moments, on his way back from visiting Neferet, and studied the wood-and-linen frame I'd made up from his plans, scribbling some alterations down on a scrap of paper as he watched how I used it.

Without giving away my small reading vocabulary of the Florentine language, I had to think carefully how I would phrase it when I asked.

As he put the perspective frame down, I said, 'This is hardly my business, except for living here in this house – is it really wise, to be passing around letters that the Council of Ten have banned?'

'Some things have to be done.' Leon looked intensely at me. 'As for Florence – my family has been so long exiled from it . . . If Taraco were— If Carthage sent legions in and occupied your homeland, would you not do the same thing?'

'No.' I rubbed my thumb over the line of Carrasco's thigh, hopelessly botched, and began again. 'It's different for a slave. But you're not occupied – *Florence* isn't occupied. It's a quarrel between rich families—'

Leon crumpled the paper he wrote on, glared, and the door slammed behind him before I could find anything to say.

I found Sergeant Orazi and the soldier Aznar, and Ramiro Carrasco, looking at me with identical expressions.

'That . . . could have gone better.'

I ended the day's session because I tired of Ramiro Carrasco's grin. Which was not unlike that of Aznar, or Orazi.

The sergeant murmured, 'Could have told *you* that! Ma'am . . . '

'Suppose we go for a nice walk?' I muttered. 'All six of us?'

I managed to see quite an area of Venezia in what fine winter weather there was, by walking to places in which Honorius's soldiers might take an interest. This covered areas from Dorsodura to the shipyards – the Venetian Arsenale being the fifth largest in Frankish territory, as Aznar decided I needed to be extensively informed – where I decided it wouldn't be wise to sketch, given the number of guard-towers. And back, past the Doge's palace, to an area containing a number of commercial armouries.

By way of a fair return, Honorius's household guard were possibly the most well-educated soldiers in respect of church frescoes that you could find in a hundred-mile radius. I suspect they were pleased when my sixth month made me tire more easily, and desire to stand for shorter amounts of time gazing up at paintings.

It was the first time I had spent a period in close contact with men who were very much of an age with me (the sergeant excepting), and who were prepared to treat me as Honorius's son-daughter without anything in the way of questions. Berenguer was loud-mouthed and lectured me on the way I ought to behave as a man who was 'handicapped by being partly a woman'. Viscardo and Fulka and the others treated me as I was dressed, but with much less of that attitude common in Rodrigo's court: that a woman who can talk like a man is as amazing as a trained jackdaw – or that a man who can speak as a woman must be an effeminate catamite.

True, the same loud-mouthed Berenguer made a comment or two about 'men with no balls'. But a single look from Rekhmire' taught him an instant lesson in tact. The Egyptian pretended to no skill with a sword, but he didn't need to – it was an article of faith among Honorius's soldiers that he could break most of them in two with his bare hands.

'Torcello,' I remarked, on a morning in February when the first stirrings of spring were perceptible on the wind, and put my hand on my curved stomach, looking up at Honorius. 'I want to see the frescos on the island of Torcello. Before I can't walk more than fifty yards at a time!'

15

'Frescoes—' Honorius glanced over his shoulder at the bare garden in front of the Alexandrine house, where his guards had been a moment before. 'Look at that. Not a man in sight!'

Neferet, walking outside at that moment, smiled down at me. 'Ilaria, Leon will act as your escort, if you like. And I'll come with you. I like the idea of being out of the house.'

'So do I.' Honorius put his hand under my elbow as we walked back into the house to prepare. 'I'll detail off men to go with you. I suppose you want *me* to keep Aldra Federico and the damned assassin busy?'

'Ramiro Carrasco's useful. The longer we keep him writing messages to be sent back to Videric, the longer it'll be before Videric sends more men here.'

Honorius harrumphed under his breath about how many others we might not know of – though they would likely be hired men, by his opinion, and worth little without Carrasco's motivating presence.

Rekhmire' stumbled off the last stair as we came in, one crutch firmly under his arm as a support, and the other skidding on the oak floorboards. Honorius steadied him with one hand, at the same time notifying him of the proposed visits.

I picked up the dropped scroll Rekhmire' had been carrying under his arm. 'I wish you could come with us.'

The Egyptian cocked an eyebrow at me. 'Torcello?'

'Island. On the far side of Murano and Burano.'

He snorted, amused, hobbling towards the warmest downstairs room – which in the Alexandrine House is the kitchen.

'Is it a monastery?' He answered his own question before I could. 'No. Does it have old scrolls or books? *No*. Does any man live there now the bad air brings plague? No—'

'It's winter! There's no plague in cold air. Besides which . . . ' I adjusted my pace to keep level with him, avoiding his crutch impaling my foot. 'You could hold my hand, while Neferet holds Leon's. So I don't feel so – superfluous.'

'Not even for that.' Rekhmire' smiled. 'Charming as the thought is. *I* intend to stay here, and check over this stock that Neferet is so slow in sending back to Alexandria. By a brazier. With wine. In a room that's warm.'

'Coward!'

'At your service.' His round features curved into a grin.

But he was persuaded to leave the vast inglenook fireplace in the kitchens to bid us farewell, and my last sight was of him swinging his immobilised leg between the two crutches, and with difficulty waving a hand.

Leon Battista helped Neferet down into the low, wide boat that was to take us across the lagoon to the island of Torcello. His smile was brighter than the winter sun, and Neferet smoothed her white-and-lapis Alexandrine robes around her, gazing up at him with an affection that held no cynicism at all.

'Careful!' She caught my hands in hers as I sat down on the stern seat beside her. 'Ilaria, you really should take more care. The baby . . . '

This 'baby' is likely a dead stone within me.

Sergeant Orazi, at the prow, gave the order to cast off and row. I adjusted my borrowed bronze and gold robes around my shoulders, and the thick winter cloak over them. Neferet brushed my fingers aside to assist. Of all of them, she never had any hesitation in calling me 'Ilaria'.

I muttered, 'The baby will kill me. Or die at birth. Or turn out to be a monster. Rekhmire' must have told you what I am.'

She looked at me less coolly than I expected. 'You're a woman, Ilaria. Oh, I know, you may have a vestigial penis – but you're a woman, truly.'

Ensign Saverico, who happened to be sitting on the bench in front of me, coloured a bright red all up the back of his neck. Somebody choked; I thought it might have been Orazi. Certainly the sergeant looked back with an expression that spoke a desire to have the Alexandrine under his orders.

'Neferet – I'm not a woman!' I held up my hand, as she started to object. 'Yes, I'm woman enough to have conceived from some man's seed. But I'm also a man. I stand up to piss!'

Her calm demeanour didn't crack. Berenguer's neck went purple: he leaned forward and put his head into his hands, despite the rocking boat, *I don't want to be here!* written clearly in his posture, for all I couldn't see his face.

That made me grin. 'Believe me both. Not one; not the other. I'm – Honorius's son-daughter.'

'You behave like a woman,' Neferet contradicted. 'I've seen you.'

'I'm not permitted to behave like anything else here!'

'You couldn't if you tried!'

I felt a desire to smack her. And to take her around Rome, to the places I frequented as Masaccio's apprentice.

'Your body doesn't matter.' Neferet peered intently into my face. 'The spirit matters. The *ka*. The soul. What you truly are. Your *ka* is female. Like mine.'

I opened my mouth, and shut it again. Who knows how many of Honorius's men know that Neferet is the same as Rekhmire'? This is not the moment to educate them.

My drawing skills had improved enough that I'd borrowed a mirror from Neferet and achieved several charcoal and red chalk self-portraits. Drawn as a woman, you could see the male in my bones. Drawn male, I looked too effeminate. I drew as I saw myself in the mirror, and came back to my sketchbook to find Sergeant Orazi and Attila arguing over whether I'd drawn a man or a woman. Both their arguments seemed to come down to 'But it's *obvious!*'

Neferet, tall and elegant as she was, made a better woman than I. With her throat covered – since her male shape there was noticeable – and ignoring her too-large hands, she showed in my drawings much more of a female than I ever did.

'You won't be able to avoid the matter, once you've had the baby,' Neferet added. 'I know a Green priest, Father Azadanes, who's very adept. You could think about having your vestigial – *organs* – removed.'

Saverico put both hands over the cod-flap of his hose and crossed his legs.

It was unkind but I howled with laughter, slumping back against the padded stern seat and ignoring how both of them – for different reasons – glared ferociously at me.

'I need nothing removed!' I stated. 'It's not a matter of being one thing or the other.'

'Your *ka* is female.' Neferet sounded utterly stubborn.

'Fine,' I grumbled. 'My *ka* is female. My cock is male!'

If she had ever been inclined to abandon female decorum and punch me in the eye, I thought that was the moment.

I took the moment to be one in which shivering, huddling down in my cloak, and asking Saverico if I could borrow *his* cloak, too, to put over my knees against the spray, was a good idea.

Torcello had a thousand-year-old church, the stone throne of the Emperor Attila, a fresco which even I had to grant wouldn't teach me anything, and broken capitals from Roman pillars, scattered in the grass down by the landing place.

'The style is nothing new.' Leon Battista straightened up from studying the church's fresco 'torment of the damned', completely unmoved by their pain. 'The architecture – this is the old Roman style . . . '

I abandoned Neferet to be lectured on architecture, taking my sketchbook out of the church and back towards the boat. Ruins covered the sparse turf, embedded in the earth. I crossed my legs and sat on one fallen pillar, drawing another; the layers of petticoats doing something to keep out the cold.

Under the petticoats, I had put on and pinned up an old pair of countryman's breeches, mostly unbuttoned. It might make me look fatter than my pregnancy, but it was, thank Rekhmire''s Eight, *warm*.

I grinned to myself, thinking of the Egyptian's firm refusal to be rowed out to the island of Torcello. *He's not wrong*, I acknowledged, squiggling a line that was more acknowledgement of the acanthus leaves in ancient marble than an actual drawing. Notes for a drawing, perhaps.

My fingertips, where they protruded from the gloves I had trimmed for the purpose, were a whitish-blue that didn't argue well for control of red chalk, or charcoal.

'Learn all about naves and pediments?' I remarked as Neferet and Leon walked back down the slipway towards me, she with her hand tucked into his arm, and both of them flushed more than the winter chill would account for. 'Barrel vaults? Apses?'

Leon gave me the look a man would give a cheeky younger sister. 'Your appetite for knowledge being so inexhaustible, of course?'

'I needed to sit.' I tapped the front of my cloak. 'You don't want knowledge of swelling ankles . . . '

He agreed with unflattering haste.

It was a spring day come unexpectedly in the latter stages of winter, the sky a deep blue, and the sun warm when the wind fell, and if one did not discard a cloak too hurriedly. Even the lapping water looked deceptively blue, and not so bitterly cold.

'It's past three. We should think of going back.' Neferet shaded her eyes with one gloved hand, looking down the strand to where our soldiers and oarsmen were squatting around a driftwood fire and cracking obscene jokes in a dialect I hoped she would not understand. Leon caught my eye.

Much speculating about who does what and to whom, I attempted to put into a look. Leon nodded, fractionally.

His glance went past me, to the lagoon.

The creak of oars, that had been present in the back of my mind for uncounted minutes while I drew, became louder.

I scrambled down off the fallen Roman pillar, feet numb and prickling, and grabbed onto the carved marble to avoid falling over.

Orazi appeared at my elbow. I realised he must have been no more than fifteen feet away from me, he and his men watching the island with care.

A large shallow-draft row-boat grounded on the strand, and a man leaped ashore, waving towards us what I suspected he intended to be a reassuring dismissal.

His hat was a Venetian version of a Phrygian cap, banded with embroidery in the same blue and white as his tabard. I registered the blue tabards of his oarsmen, and the blue-and-white painting on the blades of their oars as they lifted them from the water.

He's an official of some kind—

Six armed men jumped onto the slick beach behind him. In the Doge's livery.

'In the name of the Council of Ten and Doge Foscari!'

I glimpsed in peripheral vision our own oarsmen, and the rest of Honorius's men, jogging towards us. I looked at Neferet. Her reddish-brown face was grey.

We are short in numbers – Attila must have left with Tottola and Fulka again, patrolling the grounds of the ancient church.

Leon Battista took a step forward, as if he were the only man present and therefore ought to control the situation.

I spoke before he could. The cold air made my voice harsh and much too low. 'What do you want?'

The Venetian in the Phrygian cap raised his eyebrows. 'Not you.' A pause. 'Madonna. Now—'

His head turned as he looked from me to Neferet, back to me, and then at the Alexandrine again. I felt my face growing hot. The official said nothing, but I considered what I might use in the way that I had used the oar with Ramiro Carrasco.

'Leon Battista Alberti.' The man's voice grew confident as he looked at the obvious man amongst us. 'By order of the Council of Ten, you're under arrest.'

'I'm *what?*' Leon sounded stunned.

'You're coming back with me now.' The official lifted his arm in what must be a pre-arranged signal.

I started to walk forward – Viscardo caught my arm, and Saverico stepped in on my other side – and the six men split up.

Two walked to Leon, and took him by each of his arms. The other four trotted to our boat, leaned over the side, and thrust with iron spikes – spikes long as a man's arm; a tool used for something, but I couldn't tell what.

They smashed through the bottom of the boat in seconds.

The oarsmen running up halted as if a wall had appeared in front of them. One small, spare-bodied man swore and spat, railing furiously against the Venetian official.

'*Council of Ten!*' the official repeated.

The two of the official's men that held Leon thrust him forward, towards their boat. I wrenched free, pushed past Orazi, and Neferet's long-fingered, broad hand closed over my elbow:

'You don't argue with the Council of Ten! *They'll take you too!*'

Leon sat down in the prow of the boat. His gaze rested on Neferet. He did not call out. Not a word.

The official stepped aboard. The men who had wrecked our boat thrust theirs into the lagoon, lurching up over the side and onto their rowing benches as the water deepened under their hull.

I looked at Neferet. At our broken boat.

'They can't just—!'

'They *can*. This is Venice. If someone's denounced him . . . ' She blinked, blind gaze turned in the direction of the boat. 'I don't have enough influence. Not for this.'

Squinting at the lagoon around Torcello, I saw no other craft. The blue-and-white-painted boat receded into the haze, oars delicately picking at the surface of the water like a skating-insect.

'Is there . . . anything we can do?'

'Appeal to the Doge.' Her eyes showed hazy, like the distance. 'But, foreigners. The Doge doesn't like . . . '

'My father knows the mercenary Captain-General of Venezia. He can probably kick Carmagnola into supporting us. What—' I wondered if she would tell me what I thought was the truth. 'What did they arrest Leon *for?*'

Neferet shook her head, gazing in the direction of the city of Venice. 'It really doesn't matter, you know.'

Attila's and Tottola's boots hit the soil hard enough to kick up divots as they pounded around the church's end-wall, and out onto the strand, outpacing Fulka and the few other men-at-arms who trailed panting behind. Orazi signalled his men into a defensive circle around us. I saw the oarsmen clustered, complaining vividly in low growls.

Orazi stared at the smashed hull on the island's beach.

'They can't . . . ' the Armenian sergeant began.

Neferet spoke as if he should already know what she said. 'They're the Council of Ten. They can do anything they like. *Foscari* can do anything he likes.'

'We,' Orazi scowled, narrowing his eyes against the last of the winter sun off the water, 'can see if the boat is capable of being mended. You were right, madonna,' he added, to me. 'No one lives here or comes here now. Not even peasants. There's no help to be had.'

Pain crunched the muscles of my belly.

A streak of something piercingly hot and wet ran down the inside of my leg. An almost-welcome warmth flooded my thighs and breeches and petticoats. Steam went up white into the winter air.

I had a moment to think in agonised embarrassment that I had pissed myself through fear – and another roll of muscle-pain all but closed over my head.

I grabbed Neferet's arm, shaking in panic. A snap of Orazi's fingers sent the men into armed stance: swords and bows at the ready to face whatever might be approaching. Neferet winced: my fingers dug into her arm, clenching the wool of her cloak.

Another cramp creased down my belly, following the wet and heat, sharp enough to make me gasp.

I don't bleed upwards of twice a year, and sometimes not that. This is different from women's cramps – but only in intensity, not in kind.

Orazi's blue-grey eyes opened in frank amazement.

'Jesu Christus!' I prised my fingers out of Neferet's arm. 'My waters broke!'

Pain washed over me; I lost long moments to it. My vision blurred, I thought – and I realised that it was mist on the late afternoon surface of the lagoon.

'Use the wreckage of the boat,' Orazi bellowed. 'If we can't row it, we can set it on fire as a beacon! Someone'll come.'

Specks moved in my field of vision.

It took me sluggishly long to decipher what it meant.

I pointed, and dug my other fist into the side of my body, against the dragging, grinding pain that washed through me.

'Someone *has* come.'

Light-headed and sweating, I watched a long shallow boat streak towards us, propelled by four standing men with oars. The failing light didn't let me accurately count the number of men in the main body of the boat. *I would be surprised if it were less than a dozen.*

Help or harm?

'I thought,' Neferet stuttered. 'Rekhmire' *said.*'

'Carrasco's out of town with Honorius and Federico.' Narrowing my eyes didn't bring me a clearer view. The oars knocked up foam from the lagoon water. Ramiro Carrasco might be being dragged round a mainland villa in Sunilda's wake, or he might be sitting fifty yards away from me in the boat.

I blinked. 'The light's bad. We could run.' Nothing I'd seen on Torcello made me think that would last long. *But –* 'Orazi, could we shut the doors of the church? Stand a siege inside? The windows are small, and those doors are solid oak—'

'Yeah. Best option.' He turned and gave quick orders. There was no milling about as men obeyed him; Honorius impelled his men to discipline even in his absence. I saw our oarsmen had vanished. Run. *I wish I might do the same!*

Hobbling with the pain, holding Neferet's arm, I let her inch me away up the foreshore. She glanced impatiently about; frightened, angry, frustrated. If I'd been shorter, or not pregnant, I think she would have picked me up and run.

But she doesn't seem to think of doing anything that a woman of her height and build can't, despite her male aspects.

Neferet peered back towards the lagoon, and slowed her steps. 'We're too late.'

The boat altered course, hissed up the pebbles on the foreshore and disgorged a band of men who pelted up the bank in a straggle.

Running to get between us and the church.

I stopped, legs aching, leaning one hand against a fallen marble pillar. No use in trying to race. Thirty heartbeats and they had us out-manoeuvred.

Orazi and Saverico and Tottola dropped back, swords out, yelling orders to the other men-at-arms – who spread far enough apart that their line would block attackers without bringing them close enough to cut each other.

The lessons of the Sanguerra sergeant-at-arms came back to me. *If a sword falls, I will pick it up.* Some acts stay bred into the muscle and bone. Even if that muscle is cramping so that the watercoloured late afternoon whites out into encompassing pain.

There will be swords falling, I thought grimly, counting the men now spreading out in a loose line before the church. Blocking us from refuge.

Thirty, at least. And we are, what, ten? A dozen with Neferet and I.

I suspected the men had known who they followed and how we were guarded: three against one are the preferred odds for beginning battle. If four against, or five to one, are impossible.

'All right.' Orazi's voice lifted a little. 'Here's what we're going to do. Vazev, Tottola, Saverico; you're going to feint like you're trying to break through to the church. The rest of you, we'll cut down to the beach and take *their* boat.'

I all but choked. I saw grins among his soldiers, too.

Orazi pulled the falchion from Attila's belt while the German furiously racked his crossbow, and pushed the sword's hilt at me. 'You can use a weapon.'

The weight of the blade-heavy cleaver pulled against my wrist.

He barked at Neferet. 'You?'

Even with the murderers closing in, she looked affronted at the insinuation that she might not be a woman. 'Give me a knife.'

Someone had a heavy, single-edged dagger with a bollock-hilt in ivory and brass, a souvenir of the Frankish Crusades, and a hand appeared and shoved it at the Alexandrine. I suspected whoever offered that particular weapon was entirely aware of why Frankish men wear it at their crotch, scabbard pointing down, the jutting two-lobed hilt blatant in its symbolism.

Neferet took the dagger, and I had a moment to look at each of the faces I now knew by name; to realise *they may end here, and so may I*, and to feel a burning fierce rush of fear and anger.

'I can't run.' I looked at Orazi. 'I'll move as fast as I can.'

There was a glimmer of contempt in his gaze, that I recognised as *Not a proper man*, before it vanished. The worst of it was that it was kind. Sympathetic.

'If it comes to it, we'll carry you.' His hand shot out and closed like a vice on my elbow, crushing muscle and nerve against bone, holding me bodily upright, ignoring my wet skirts. He abruptly glanced up the slope. '*Shit.* We've left this too late!'

The silhouettes of shoulders bobbed as armed men jogged down the slope from the church. Towards us. Attila let a bolt loose. Judging the range.

We shouldn't see silhouettes, I thought numbly.

The light's wrong!

The other half of the church's huge oak door banged open, and the light brightened still further from candles within.

A throng of men charged out of the church, and piled into the back of our first attackers.

Tottola said, 'What the *fuck?*' in pure Visigoth Latin.

Neferet raised her dagger.

Orazi yelled with the voice of a brazen trumpet, '*A Honorius! A leone di Castiglia! All of you, follow me!*'

Pain twisted my womb. Twilight blurred my vision. Orders, shouts, cries: all went up from the scrum of men desperately fighting on the turf in front of the church. In the light from the open door, I saw one man trip back over a half-buried Roman statue of a lion's head.

A sword caught the last true daylight, cold and blue. The man wielding it pushed it into the fallen man's throat, just into the soft part under the chin.

A hand went under my arms from either side.

My toes hit the earth. I tried to move enough to run, even to walk, but the two Germans Attila and Tottola lifted me higher and ran as if I were a sack of meal between them, sprinting down towards the beach. The pain in my shoulder-joints almost overwhelmed the pain between my hips.

'*Fuck.*' Orazi swung around.

My feet hit the sand by the lagoon. I staggered, taking my own weight on my feet again.

I smelled pitch burning. The boat the men had arrived in sent up flames too fierce to come from an accidental torch-fire. Coughing rasped the tender inside of my throat, and filled my eyes with water. *Our last chance, gone!*

The contraction buckled my knees.

Limp, I slid down through Attila and Tottola's grasp. Instinct wanted me up and pacing, but I couldn't force myself to my feet. Could only think *Pain, Jesu!*, as the waves of it bit down on me, burning into the pit of my belly.

On my knees on the fine sand and shells, I stared back at the ancient round roof of the monastery. Below that perfect curve, torch-light poured out of the doors, and fell like honey.

It fell on grass turned black by twilight, fell glistening on spreading blood, shone impartially on men huddled dead, and men shrieking and sobbing at mutilation and amputation, and men fighting who trampled over them all.

Pain made me weak-stomached. I vomited over the beach and my skirts, wet strings of mucus dependent from my fingers.

With so much death, I should think of the life I'm carrying under my heart, that I'm to give birth to. Except that it's never stirred, and the birth will kill me as dead as these men.

Five men ran shouting towards us, swords in hand.

Attila, crossbow racked again, shot the first one through the stomach.

The unwounded men skidded on the wet ground, boot-soles locking in the clinging sand – stared with doubtful expressions, in the light of the burning boat – and turned around and ran, so fast it resembled the acts of clowns in the *commedia*.

Attila raised his voice over the sick grunts of the shot man.

'Bugger's not dead.' He looked over at me. 'Did you drop my falchion?'

There was vomit on my right hand. The reason the fingers of my left hand hurt so much was that they were locked by cramp around the hilt of his sword.

I looked at it mutely. Attila squatted down and began to gently move each finger from the leather-bound grip, pushing his fingertips into my muscles and knuckle-joints, surprisingly gently. The cramp eased away.

Orazi prompted the men-at-arms in front of us into a loose half-circle, their backs to the burning boat and facing the church. 'What they doing up there?'

'Dead, hurt, or run.' Vasez grunted. 'Far too many of 'em run. If they get their shit together and come back, we're fucked.'

'That's "we're fucked, *Sergeant*",' Orazi rasped, and got the expected rawly-tense ripple of laughter from all. He shook his head. 'Now if we had *one* fucking boat in *one* fucking piece—'

A voice spoke up out of the twilight.

'There's a boat. Hidden thirty yards south. In the stand of willow.'

A convulsion pulled at my womb. The hairs on my neck shivered. *I have never heard a human voice sound like that in my life.*

After an appalling sound, the voice finished, 'But I don't know – when my men will come back for it.'

Orazi made a silent gesture, two soldiers picked up burning planks as makeshift torches, and he stepped forward with Saverico and Berenguer, all with naked blades in their hands. The small Armenian swore as his foot skidded.

The flickering light showed clearly what lay ten feet in front of me.

A man with fair hair and trimmed fair beard sprawled on the slope. He would have been flat on his back, but his face pointed directly towards me – because of the acanthus-flower capital of the fallen pillar behind him, propping up his head. A dark smear marked the marble. *Skull smashed?* I wondered, and then—

This is the man Attila's bolt hit.

I met the shining, too-bright eyes in his wet grey face.

I had not considered the kinetic force of a crossbow bolt, though I could tell you that of the stones from a trebuchet.

Chunks of bone scattered around him, as if his pelvic bone had not merely been pierced, but exploded. I thought at first the debris was stone, rubble, where the bolt had gone through him and struck the pillar. But the pieces showed white and scarlet, chopped like bones at a butcher's stall.

It was too cold to smell more than the throat-closing thickness of blood. Torn chunks shone, glistening like a display. His intestines bulged out under his ribs on one side; the same side that a leg lay motionless beside him.

It is his own leg, I realised. I had thought it could not be, because it lay in an impossible position. But it was not connected to his body. The rounded knob of a hip-bone glistened, exposed in the dim light.

Movement caught my eye – blood, bubbling up through the grass like water from a spring.

He can have only moments more—

'Ilario.'

The man's eyes caught the light of makeshift torches. He stared directly at me. His voice was numbed, and polite.

'Ilario . . . '

It felt as nightmares do: frozen, implacable.

I pushed myself forward on hands and knees, no man breaking his own shock to help me. Wet skirts rucked under me. I stopped, crouched, a yard from that appalling face, and stench of shit.

He moved nothing but his eyes and his mouth. 'You, Ilario.'

'Yes.'

The fair hair and the breadth of his shoulders gave him something of a resemblance to Videric. I might have wished just this on Videric.

I spat out sour liquid. 'You were trying to kill me!'

He actually smiled.

If I prayed, it was to Rekhmire''s Eight. I want only a small miracle. Let him stay numb with shock. Let him feel nothing of what's been done to him.

Attila bent down, his mail sleeve flashing in the twilight, and stuffed a bundled-up mass of rags into the man's groin. The German's hand closed over the injured man's shoulder, and I saw the line of his back tense with the pressure he put into blocking the artery.

The dying man whispered, 'I stopped them killing you.'

The men who came running out of the church.

Attacking those who attacked us.

286

Led by this man?

His eyes showed pale. I saw the black gauze rag knotted around his neck. Men from under the Penitence often bandage their eyes when they first travel in lands outside the Darkness, because of the intense sunlight.

Under the mess of blood, his drenched clothing was Carthaginian.

He spoke again. *'Take the boat.'*

There are an unknown number of armed men in the dark winter twilight of Torcello. This man's. Videric's paid criminals. No man knowing who his enemy or friend is. Yes, we need the boat; we need to leave—

I bit back a groan as my belly contracted. It will be a ghost of pain beside his. I can control it.

I blurted, 'We can't just leave you here!'

By the burning spar's light, as Saverico held it lower, I could see that the man's eyebrows were blond, too. His lashes a dark sand colour. Laughter-lines on his face now cut too deep, in the intensity of agony.

'I was to take you to Carthage.' His voice faded to thread-thin. 'Your Alexandrine spy. Tell him he succeeded. All the way to Florence. And then I hit the ghetto walls . . . Your Etruscan wife – is lovely.'

Saverico all but dropped the makeshift torch; Orazi swore. Fear turned my guts liquid. 'Have you hurt her?'

'Not even – speak to her. They don't let New Races in.' His eyes glistened. 'It took me too long to realise you . . . Then, here . . . Go . . . so I know you live.'

I was to take you to Carthage. Kidnap me; my guess was correct.

Coming to Torcello with so few soldiers – I didn't realise how many people would find that irresistible bait.

Orazi gripped my shoulder. 'We're going.'

'What about him!'

He gave the Carthaginian a professional glance. Speaking directly to him, Orazi said, 'You can live two or three hours – but you probably don't want to. Want one of my lads to help?'

Attila shifted, where he gripped the man, but looked determined.

The Carthaginian agent looked as if he attempted to shake his head. An odd shudder went through him.

'No.' There was no resonance in his voice. 'You never know – what will happen.'

Orazi's expression was clear in the light of the burning boat. If he'd spoken, he clearly would have said he knew precisely what will happen. The numbness wears off and you die screaming.

'Every man should have his choice.' Orazi dusted his knees and got up, stooped to grab under my arm, and I gripped the hard edges of his brigandine as he pulled me onto my feet and I towered over him.

He jerked his head at Attila. 'Up.' Orazi widened his tone to include the rest. 'Find these fucking willow trees! Find the boat!'

Attila stood up, his arms soaked red beyond the elbows. I looked down. The Carthaginian agent paused, I thought, to gather his strength before speaking.

His face was utterly still. His chest didn't move.

His eyelids drifted down a little, leaving only a curved line of white visible.

The welling wetness at his hips no longer attracted the eye with its movement.

There must have been some moisture rising from the hot shining tissue, distinct in the cold air. It was gone now, all his exposed viscera dull. His ribs had barely moved in the shallow breathing of shock; now they did not move at all. My eye insisted that the rise and fall of his chest continued; my ear, that I could detect the hiss of his breath. *All illusion.*

There is no lack of motion, no silence, that is like death.

'Just as well.' Orazi jerked his head to call Tottola in on the other side of me. 'I would have had to tell somebody to do it. Couldn't have him telling those other fuckers where we've gone.'

He sounded faintly apologetic. I identified what else was in his tone after a moment. Gratitude.

Because this man attacked for his own reasons, to abduct me – but he kept us all alive. He must have secreted his men in the church crypt. And without that attack in the rear of Videric's other agents . . .

I crested another burn of the pain, and wondered if his sacrifice was useless.

'He may have papers.' It occurred to me in Rekhmire''s voice.

Evidently this was not unusual to Orazi in my father's service. He nodded, and gave Fulka brief instructions.

'He's painstaking,' Orazi said aloud. 'If there's anything, he'll find it. Are you all right?'

'It – hurts a little.' I couldn't decide if the surges came more frequently now.

Neferet jogged back, skirts held up, large bare feet muddy where she had kicked off her shoes to run in the winter mud. Fire and flame shone back from her black hair.

'There *is* a boat! We found it!'

'Thank Christ for that!' I looked wanly at her as another pang went through me. 'I don't want to give birth on this damned island!'

Neferet's eyes rounded, as if she hadn't realised until now. 'You're two months early!'

'I know!'

The death of the Carthaginian agent swept over me with an absolute horror. He had known what had happened to him; he knew what *was* happening as he died. But the knowledge had not helped him. His heart is cool and still in his chest even now.

Every word I had ever heard or read, between the Penitence and

Rome and the Most Serene city; every warning from Rekhmire' or physicians or Neferet's tame Green priest that she had brought into the Alexandrine House – all of it closed down on me like the metal jaws of a trap.

My body *will* do this. No matter what I want, or what I do. My body will labour and try for birth, and if common opinion's right, in a few hours I'll find out what the Carthaginian now knows.

The Carthaginian, and whoever else of these men lies back there in the darkness, not wounded, not hurt, not 'in danger, but may heal' – *dead*. Dead, and there has never been any appeal against it.

Orazi gave a sharp nod, and Tottola and Attila linked hands and wrists and scooped my body up between them, carrying me out to the boat. Neferet splashed heedlessly through the rippling water and climbed into the bows, so that she could help me in, and seat me among cushions and half a dozen cloaks on the stern bench.

Saverico wrapped a blanket around my shoulders; he shook as badly as I. He took up one of the oars and smiled – or I assume his grimace was intended to be a reassuring smile.

'You did well,' I said aloud – startled, because I am not the person who knows how to encourage others. 'You've known Honorius longer than I have – but I know he'll be pleased with what you did here. All of you.'

Orazi's callused hand closed briefly on my shoulder as he scrambled forward in the boat, past me.

'Which is *why*,' he said generally and aloud, 'you idle buggers are going to row like *fuck*! Because you all know what the Lion's going to be like if we lose his son-daughter now . . . '

It was a reminder of warmth, more than the thing itself, but I saw Attila wryly grinning, and Vasev reach enthusiastically for his oar. The Carthaginian agent's boat had been intended for three or four lances of men, and what is heavy enough to carry thirty is a bitch for ten or a dozen to row.

We have no dead or wounded, I realised, breathless with relief, as the last man-at-arms shoved the boat into deeper water and scrambled in. Brushwood burned as makeshift torches, winter-dry gorse popping and crackling, and smelling acrid.

My stomach turned.

The child didn't quicken – and it's been barely six months—

I must have said at least the last words aloud. Neferet corrected me: 'Seven.'

I tried to count up the time lapsed since Carthage, and doubled forward again, lost in a red haze.

If there's a time for womanly fainting, I reflected, this would be it.

The birthing pangs had the contrary effect of making me wide awake.

Conscious for every lift and fall of the oars, every spatter of cold water coming inboard as we were rowed past the cypress island, past the merchant ships, and after what felt like aeons, past the Arsenale, and towards the Piazza San Marco. The last light in the west showed silhouettes of Venice's roofs and funnel-shaped chimneys, black against the sky.

Neferet told me to count breaths between the pains.

I used what vocabulary I remembered from being trained as a knight in Rodrigo's court. No man has quite such a hand with an insult as a sergeant at arms.

'Not long,' Neferet said. And, 'Not long now,' Sergeant Orazi said, as the boat rowed what felt like infinitesimally slowly up the Canal Grande, and entered the side canals of Dorsodura.

Saverico began, 'Not lo—', and cut himself off in mid-word, at least giving me a smile as he did it.

The boat grated against the side of our campo, and Neferet leaped ashore in the dark like an Alexandrine eunuch, not a Venetian lady.

16

I could hear her screaming for assistance even as Honorius pelted out of the iron gate, and knelt down to help me from the wide stern bench. Between the cold, and stiffening against the pain, I could barely manage to stand on feet that were like blocks of wood. I flinched against the light of the soldiers' torches; held onto my father as he supported me in through the bare garden and oak door.

'Call the midwife!' Honorius bellowed at one of the ensigns, who left at a run.

'And Bariş!' Rekhmire', clinging to his crutch and the door-frame, shuffled with difficulty backwards into the hall. 'Go to the Janissary captain's lodgings. I've paid a retainer fee; Bariş will come! Ilario, you should do well enough, between the Turk and a midwife.'

The warmth of the Alexandrine House made me shudder after the night's biting chill. My cloak and sleeves glistened, sticky with half-dried blood. The Egyptian shifted his weight onto one crutch, and seized my shoulder with the other. I was used enough to obeying him as his slave that I inadvertently closed my mouth on what I had been going to say.

'Ilario. Whether the child is coming too soon or not – *you* will do well enough.'

His tone was firm and confident. If, as he met Honorius's gaze where my father supported me, it did not quite match what I saw in his eyes, I wouldn't question him. As full of fear as of pain, I only want to hear reassurance.

Neferet brought me to the room that was Rekhmire''s and mine, undoing every latch and lock in it, and let me sit on the larger wooden bed that was the Egyptian's, loosing the draperies. I sat with my back against the bolster, and gripped my bare ankles, and swore. The hearth fire spread heat; extra charcoal-braziers made the room warm – too warm, I might have thought, if, with the blissful sensation of heat soaking into my body, I could have considered anything as *too* warm.

The Alexandrine and her women changed me out of my waters-soiled clothing, into a voluminous light cotton shift. They undid my hair. It was not truly long enough to braid up, but they let it down in any case, and it hung around my face, turning into rat's-tails as I sweated.

'Where's Rekhmire'? Where's my father?'

Neferet frowned. 'Allowing men in—'

'Don't be ridiculous!' I barked the deep order. 'Do it!'

Honorius walked through the door with his hand on the shoulder of a Venetian: a rosy woman who looked somewhere between fifty and sixty. One of those midwives who has birthed thousands of babies and borne none. Rekhmire' followed, swinging himself adeptly on his crutches, in turn followed by the Turkish physician Bariş, who nodded a cheerful greeting.

Dual examinations stopped me from realising, until it was too late, that a green-robed and black-bearded Frankish priest also entered – Neferet's Father Azadanes. He and the Alexandrine women removed the chess-board from the table by the hearth, and set up a Frankish prayer-box.

'Son of a bitch!' Waves of pain rolled through me. The professional hands of Bariş and the Venetian midwife seemed unbearably clammy on my skin.

She and he stepped back to confer. Possibly to argue, from their lowered, intense tones.

'Closer together?' Rekhmire' eased himself carefully onto the side of the mattress, sitting with his crutches resting between his knees. 'Your pains, I mean.'

'Yes.' I gritted my teeth. 'No. I don't know. Perhaps. This will be over soon, won't it?'

'All I've read of first labours—'

'I can do without hearing that!'

The retired Captain-General of Castile sat down on the other side of the bed. 'How many of these people do you want here, Ilario? I can throw the rest out.'

My instinct is to hide in a dark place, like a beast wounded during a hunt. *Send them all away!*

I looked from him to Rekhmire', and back. 'You don't have to be here. You forget, I *do* know what men think about child-bed. If you wait outside, that won't distress me.'

The two of them exchanged a glance across the top of my head.

'I want to watch the midwife,' Rekhmire' observed in an undertone.

Honorius echoed: 'And the priest.'

They turned their heads in unison, looking at the dark, full-bearded man in the green cowl and habit, who was picking over the midwife's herb basket with her. Every so often the Venetian woman's gaze would stray towards me, but she never looked above the line of my now slightly swollen breasts.

The hours went past, as they do even when it seems impossible they will.

The warmth made me dizzy, I found.

'Could I have something to eat?'

The midwife immediately came forward. 'That can't be permitted.'

Bariş frowned. 'It's not uncommon, in my country.'

The argument went on long enough that, between the fierce pains of the contractions, my head sank back against the bolster, and I found myself all but falling asleep.

I closed my eyes until I could see only a line of the fire's golden flickering light. *My body should have expelled this in Rome.* Or before. To carry it so long, and now have it die – if it was ever alive . . .

Pain tires. I have found this from injuries, before now. I debated requesting my sketch-paper, to while away the time, but the warmth sank deeper into me, and I began to doze. It was not unpleasant, except where I would find myself riding up the crest of the pain, until it burst in a cramping wrench that felt as if it would tear my body open.

I did sleep a little. When I was next fairly awake, Rekhmire' had swapped to sitting on the other side of the bed, Honorius was deep in reminiscences of battlefield doctoring with Neferet's Father Azadanes, and the midwife was having what looked like a sulky argument with the Turk. I couldn't see Neferet. The clock's single hand showed it gone midnight.

'Eight hours . . . !' I sat up, appalled.

Rekhmire' propped more bolsters under me. 'In the courts of the Pharaoh, women walk about for their birth. Neferet's gone looking to see if anyone has a birthing stool, if you wish to try it.'

'Walk!' I snorted, and then squinted across the room at the midwife. 'What's the argument there?'

'She wants to give herbs to hasten the birth on. Or to stop it, in case this isn't time.' The Egyptian curved a large hand and rested it on my abdomen. The touch felt reassuring. 'Physician Bariş says you've dropped down; it's time.'

Whether the child can survive this or not.

Or I.

'I just want this over! And in God's name get them to stop treating me like an invalid!' I pushed myself more upright in the bed. 'Maybe your "pacing" has something to be said for it!'

Rekhmire''s solemn face split in a grin. 'I'm told that, after my mother birthed me, she got up and cleaned the house from top to bottom. My father aided her. You're just such another as she.'

I smiled. The mental image came to me of what she would have been cleaning. I stopped smiling.

'Gah!' A jolt of pain made me grunt. 'Teach me more of the eight gods' names, will you? I think I may need to blaspheme very loudly before long.'

In the warmth of the panelled dark room, Rekhmire' amused me by teaching me how one properly addresses all four duads of the Hermopolitan Ogdoad, under all circumstances, and Honorius went irritably in and out of the door until the midwife tried to banish him. He clearly had no intention of obeying, and took one of the clay lamps to the

293

embrasure of the oriel window, where he sat and stared out at the Venetian night.

The Green priest's prayer-box was somewhat like Rekhmire''s own, but this one had in it a model of Christus Viridianus's mother at the foot of the Leafless Tree, the blood of the birthing red between her thighs, and the Eagle above and the Boar beside her. Father Azadanes set the female doll's legs wide apart. It seemed oddly obscene, even if she was wearing a minutely-sewn silk birthing robe. (Which I don't for one moment suppose the Mother of God had with her in the German forests.)

'It's – the superstition of sympathy—' Pain made me slow with words. 'That like can affect like. Rekhmire'—'

He shot a glance up at me from where he bent over, pressing his fingers into his healing knee. 'Less trouble to let him pray than to throw him out and have Neferet bellowing at us.'

'You are sure he's safe? Nothing to do with Videric?'

The Egyptian shook his head. 'Nothing. But if it eases your mind, Honorius will call the soldiers back. You couldn't be safer.'

'Draw the curtains.' I pointed up at the tester bed curtains, and realised my hand shook. *The enemy is not outside this bed, not tonight.* 'I don't think anything's going to happen for a while.'

I was accurate, and I could wish not to have been.

The hours of darkness went by. For some reason I expected to pass the child's dead flesh in the small hours of three or four in the morning, but all that happened was that the long cramps continued. Indeed, they began to lessen in frequency. I saw, between the curtains, Rekhmire' and the midwife speaking to one another. I was too tired to wonder what they said.

The slow grey light of pre-dawn illuminated in the sky.

Coal braziers burned black and scarlet, their scent contending with the winter air. I could not tell whether I was warm or cold. Neferet's insistence on having the shutters undone meant I could lay back in bed and look at the sky.

There is nothing left to do.

The long, slow, rolling waves of pain lifted me up, dropped me down, ebbed away, and slowly gathered again. It might have been a tide. I felt heat between my legs, and the midwife took soaked cloths away, but there was nothing else. When her fingers felt my belly again, she set her mouth into a hard and inexpressive line.

Bariş frowned, also, but at her.

Back at Federico's estate, much younger, I would sometimes aid with the lambing or the calving. It always frightened me to see beasts with bodies so different to my own. The weatherbeaten farm slaves handled their ewes and cattle much as the midwife offered to handle me, grease-slicked fingers poised to slide up the birth canal.

If her fingers were hesitant, I realised, it was because of the hermaphrodite organs she found when she raised my linen gown.

The Turkish physician Bariş caught my gaze and came over, shifting a bunch of cloth to cover my penis, and steered the midwife away with a hand to her elbow. I noted that this led to him sending Balaban for more water, and washing, even though the last of the dead Carthaginian agent's blood was long gone from my cuffs and his own hands.

'Ilario?'

Honorius's voice, I realised.

I had slid down the bolster. Trying to hitch myself back up, I caught a stench of human scent released by the movement. Sweat. Rank sweat. And blood of my own.

The pain didn't stop. I tried to concentrate on his words. 'Are they arguing *again*?'

Honorius smoothed black strands of hair from my eyes and forehead. 'You may have to choose. The midwife can give you herbs to bring on the birthing. But that will endanger the child, if . . . '

'If it isn't already dead?'

He held a wooden water-bowl to my mouth, and I sipped gratefully. 'I don't think it can ever have been alive. I've felt nothing.'

The herbs tasted bitter.

They did no good.

I lived through every hour between dawn and early afternoon, but have no great wish to recall them. They say the pain of child-bed is forgotten. This is a lie.

At one point, when the midwife and Neferet and Bariş and the priest were all screaming at each other – and I was too breathless to scream any more – I reached down, but could feel nothing different between my legs. It all stayed resolutely in my belly.

The memory of lambing returned. Dizzy, I wondered if they would try to pull the infant out bodily, which would fail as that always does, and if I would look white and blue and greasy, as dead ewes do when they die with their litter still in the womb.

'Remind me to have a word with your foster father.'

Honorius's voice sounded rusty and grim. I opened my eyes, realising I must have muttered aloud.

'Lambing,' Honorius added, with revulsion that sat oddly on a veteran of battlefields.

'Not my fault!' The midwife's voice rose self-righteously high. 'How can I help a monster give birth!'

Honorius's weight left the bed in a rush. By the time I had myself as upright as I could manage – leaning on my elbows – I glimpsed him hauling the woman out through the door. It slammed. Voices rose from the hall.

'"Monster".' I shrugged. 'She's not wrong.'

Neferet's Frankish priest, Father Azadanes, peered myopically at me from where he stood on the other side of the bed. 'Madonna Ilario, shall you and I pray for this child? And for you?'

I had not sufficient concentration to be rude to him. 'If you wish.'

For all the pain, I felt as if I were being kept from a job I badly needed to do – manual work, like a slave in a mine or on a farm. I could feel it in every sinew, every muscle: *I need to get up* now *and work!*

Pain rushed through me, hard enough that I crested it yelling, as I was taught to yell on the impact of my sword or axe in knightly training. Once: once more: once again—

'Nothing!' I snarled, frustrated. Looking up at Honorius and Rekhmire', I asked, 'What's Physician Bariş's advice?'

Honorius was white to his mouth. 'That he should act as a surgeon.'

I think I have known since Rome that it would come to this.

I saw Father Azadanes praying by the hearth.

'I don't care what the Church says about the pains of sinful Eve in child-bed . . . If you cut me open, I want poppy.'

Pain and poppy together made me hallucinate a Carnival mask on Bariş's face. The long-beaked leather mask of the Plague Doctor, in lapidary detail. If I could only see so well when I draw with a silver rod . . .

I must have struggled to get out of the bed. Hands pushed me down. I stared; felt myself writhing, sweating—

Honorius held my right shoulder in an immovable grip; nothing to suggest him fifty years old. Decades of soldiering have worn him to rawhide strength. Rekhmire''s hands pressed less heavily down on my left arm, where he sat on the bed, and I felt it when his own pain made him shift.

Each time the poppy took hold, I dropped into intricate, lengthy, narrative dreams, that took years to pass in my mind, and only moments by the burning-down of the marked candles.

Bariş set up a sheet that draped my knees.

I almost laughed out loud. I have *no* desire to see what's going on! And, for the others here – what do they not already know about me?

Another rolling wave of pain made me grunt, biting down until I drew blood from my lip; the small pain lost in the arid, scraping, swollen agony in my womb.

The poppy made clear in my mind the paper on which I drew Rekhmire''s flayed knee. Every fibre, tendon, shard of bone; and rivulet of blood among the so-fine hairs on his skin. There is no one present who can draw me. And no one who can draw these images from my mind.

Time slipped, as it does in high fever or pain; I caught myself cursing, and then lost interest and energy in it. The Frankish priest stood by the physician's shoulder, I saw, but I was not sure that Bariş knew it. All his attention fixed on something below my line of sight.

Below the raised flax-linen sheet – spattered with perfect ovals of blood.

I opened my mouth to ask how he did, and a constricting pain shattered my pelvic bones, and tumbled me into a state where time didn't exist.

Father Azadanes' bushy black beard moved. Anger boiled through me.

'No prayers!' *I want no final rites from a Frankish priest! I don't want the rites at all—*

Bariş straightened up, wiping a bloody hand across his forehead. His dark skin smeared brilliant red in the sunlight that shone in through the window. *Is it afternoon? Another morning?* I did not know.

The Turkish Janissary's eyes narrowed. He didn't look down at me, but at the two men either side of me. 'If it comes to a choice, which shall I save? The baby or the – mother?'

Honorius and Rekhmire' spoke together, both in the same breath: 'The mother!'

I saw Honorius give the Egyptian a look, to which Rekhmire' remained oblivious.

The mother. A faint feeling grew in me that I ought to protest that. I ought.

The obligation seemed no more and no less than that: obligation.

A dribble of water ran down my forehead, narrowly avoiding running into my eyes. The stench of some herb or other startled me into jerking my head back against the bolster. The cuff of a green habit brushed my chin as the hand drew back. Azadanes' deep bass rumbled, 'Blessed mother, blessed infant, *Mater dolorosa, Sancta Mater—*'

I growled a protest, and a grinding pain sliced at my body; took me enough by surprise that I could only reach up and grab wildly – catching my father's arm, and Rekhmire''s shoulder – and grunt as something was lifted out of the cavity of my body.

The physicality of the sensation so amazed me that I had no memory of the physician's actions after that. Something seemed flaccid; moved. The Janissary physician reached down, I speculated, *How many times on campaign does he deal with childbirth!*, and there was a great gush. His hands as he lifted them were vermilion.

'Gahh!' I said, or thought I said.

Honorius chuckled and ruffled at my hair.

Rekhmire' squeezed my fingers.

I snarled weakly, 'I'll never lie with any man again! And if I ever see Marcomir, I'll *geld* him!'

A face leaned into my field of view. Neferet's reddish-tan profile. She peered down behind the sheet, where I couldn't see, and then looked back at me. 'Ilaria, shall I have Father Azadanes also pray to remove those vestigial organs you don't need?'

'*No!*'

Someone yanked Neferet aside. *Rekhmire'*, I thought; since I could no longer feel the warmth of a body on that side of me. Chill struck on the other side, too, as Honorius leaned away from me, intently staring at something.

'Father . . . '

His lean, muscled frame sat back. His hands were cupped.

It must be something to do with me, I thought, or he would not be offering it. Am I to say farewell to my dead child? My chest was hollow, blown up suddenly with a grief that choked me.

'*Take* her!' Honorius whispered.

But I saw nothing, felt nothing!

I looked into Honorius's cupped hands. She was tiny. It took the breath out of me with a fierce tug, how very small she was. A miniature screwed-up face, pink and bloody and greyish-white, as if she had been lightly rubbed over with clay. I touched my thumb-tip to her face, before I knew I would do it.

Her small and perfect lips reflexively moved.

'It's alive!' I wondered instantly how long this would last.

'Look,' Honorius breathed.

The scrunched blue-purple-and-red face wrinkled itself up further under my gaze. She yawped, yawned, and settled into an undramatic breathy grizzle. A person, there before me.

'She's *alive*.' I put my hand out again, touching my fingers to her slick greasy-grey belly, where the swollen cord still lay. '*I'm* alive. What—?'

She lay on Honorius's brown hand, barely long enough to cover him from wrist to fingertip. If she weighed two Frankish pounds I would be surprised.

The priest's deep voice rumbled at my shoulder. 'Thanks be to God Himself for this miracle!'

Barış muttered something under his breath in Turkish. I didn't think it was devout. My body moved with the tug and rip of stitches being put into my skin, but the poppy kept the pain at a distance, even though I felt it.

I let him move my hands when he came to tidy up the birth-cord. I could not stop looking.

'She can't live, surely?' I measured my thumb against her minuscule hand, and jolted with shock as her fingers momentarily closed on me. 'It's too soon. She wasn't due for two months.'

Honorius's hand began to shake: he steadied it by gripping his wrist with his other hand.

'Your midwife keeps saying "seven-month babies live all the time"!'
His voice was ragged, and his eyes ran over with sudden bright water.

The sheet shifted. I glimpsed a dark scarlet mess in the bed, that was
either afterbirth or my inner organs. I thought I would feel considerably
less well if it were the latter.

'She has black hair. Like mine.'

'The first hair is always black.' Rekhmire''s weight came down on the
mattress, pressing against my ribs. He sat holding a clean cloth in his
hands, dampened with Balaban's tepid water, and as Honorius continued to support her, the Egyptian began very delicately to clean the
new-born.

He glanced at me. 'Do you want to do this?'

'It's . . . She's so *small*!' Her arm, as he lifted it to wipe the skin, was
no bigger around than my finger.

Bariş reached over with a dry cloth, tucking it around the minute
body. He scooped her from Honorius's callused palm, and put her
against my chest. 'Sorry, madonna, it's a girl.'

I did not note the apology.

'Are you sure?' I stared down. It took no more than one of my hands
to keep the new-born weight tucked against the warmth of my naked
skin, on the slope of my breast. '*Are you sure?*'

'Of course. Ah.' Bariş nodded.

With Rekhmire''s help, and Honorius's hindrance, the Janissary doctor
re-examined the child's nether end. I thought about long campaigns, and
soldiers' wives and whores.

I do not care if the child is female or male: only let her not be like me!

'Girl.' The physician tucked the cloth napkin back, his fingers
extraordinarily gentle. 'Very small. There is sometimes trouble with small
and—' He tapped his chest. 'The breath?'

Fascinated, I nodded, and rubbed the very tip of my finger over her
lower lip. '*Look* at her.'

The little mouth made a sucking noise.

Panic washed me hot and cold in one second. I saw in my mind the
Carthaginian agent: how his chest stopped moving, how breath just –
ceased.

'We have to find it a tit to feed from! We have to put it to one; it'll die!'

Bariş smiled at me. 'What? No. She doesn't need to eat until she shows
she wants to. You think you won't be able to feed her?'

Seizing authority, he sent the priest out of the room, and directed
Honorius and Rekhmire' to the fireside, since they wouldn't go further
from me. Bariş set himself to examine my small breasts that, while
painful, were no larger than before the pregnancy.

'Sometimes milk, this takes time coming in,' Bariş said finally,
frowning. 'I can find you a wet-nurse? If you haven't one?'

Numbly, I nodded assent. The damp, warm weight in my palm

wriggled faintly – *so small!* – and settled her head back against my useless breast.

As Physician Bariş began to speak to Honorius about wet-nurses, Rekhmire' limped over from the room's door, propped himself upright on his crutches, and pulled the bed drapes fully back.

The child in my hand wailed faintly, rolling her head away from the bright day. Hastily, I shaded her with the fingers of my other hand.

Rekhmire''s brows dipped down.

'I know,' I said, dizzy with wonder. 'The chances of her living are . . . If she makes two months, I'll name her.'

Her hair was soft and dry now under my thumb, and I smoothed it down.

Rekhmire''s frown didn't lift. 'Azadanes wants to go through some Frankish Christian rite. To clean her soul?'

That would have been his business at the door, I realised. Throwing the Frankish priest out.

I shook my head, bemused. 'How can she have done anything wrong yet? An hour ago, she wasn't *here*.'

'Don't ask a man who worships the Eight . . . '

The small lashes on her cheek were perfect. As they lifted, I saw she had deep blue baby's eyes. *If she lives, they might be any colour.*

'You hold her, Rekhmire'.' I scooped both hands about her, supporting every part, waiting until the Egyptian settled himself on the bed. I placed her gently in Rekhmire''s large hands.

'It's strange.' I couldn't take my gaze from her. 'She never moved inside me. I never felt I was with child. She wasn't born to me in the normal way. She . . . Is she really from me?'

Rekhmire' smiled. He stroked his fingertip in her tiny lined palm. Her fingers could not grasp all his finger's circumference, but I saw her try.

'No one else here was with child. The evidence suggests she's from your womb. Or was that howling merely to entertain us?'

'I can't feed her.'

'You don't know that yet.'

'I know.' My conviction was irrational but strong. I took her back into the crook of my arm. 'See if they have a wet-nurse yet? Or at least if the kitchens would have any goat's or cow's milk?'

The door openly, briskly; I saw every man in the room startle. Ensign Viscardo's dark face made me sigh in relief. We are all as tight as an overwound harp-string here—

'What?' Honorius snapped, ferocious at an interruption.

Viscardo's eyes showed wide.

'Sir – it's Ilario's family!'

My heart physically jerked in my chest.

Which family?

The minuscule new-born let out a breath of a wail.

Viscardo's eyes opened wider, seeing me; he suddenly grinned like a boy, and as abruptly collected himself – although his gaze kept sliding sideways to the new-born child.

'Sir, it's Signor Federico, and his wife, and his daughters. They're here! They heard about the labour. They want to see Messer Ilario!'

Honorius looked completely blank.

Venetian servants, I thought. Since here it isn't slaves. The rumour-mill grinds just as efficiently. Federico and Valdamerca . . .

An ominous set of rising voices came from downstairs.

I pushed the sweat-darkened sheets into a nest on my chest, and settled the new-born where she could feel my heat and heartbeat. I looked up at Honorius and Rekhmire'.

'Can I have these sheets changed? Then, let them in.'

Viscardo nodded acknowledgement, barely waiting for Honorius's signal, and ran out.

'Ilario,' Rekhmire' warned.

'They can see me and *go away*.' I snorted. 'I'll be asleep in a quarter-hour! I'm exhausted. But I know Federico – he won't go away until he does see me.'

Tired as I was, I made the shift to the Iberian of Taraconensis, speaking both to Honorius and Rekhmire'.

'You know he won't go! Federico has come here to find out whether or not he can send a message to – to my mother's husband . . . telling him that I'm dying or dead.'

17

Neferet's servants worked around me, replacing the dirty sheets with clean cool linen that soothed my skin. The child lay in a makeshift wooden cradle – in fact, originally a small oak linen-chest – by the fire, with both my father and the Egyptian blocking all access to her.

Reclining up against the bolsters, I found myself unable to settle. Without that steadily pinkening small figure under my eye, how can I believe in a baby's existence?

Poppy-extract kept my scurrying mind numbed, as well as my body. I barely heard the shuffle of feet outside, that I knew must be Honorius's men-at-arms moving into position.

As the door opened to let in Federico, the invisible child proved itself far from inaudible. She sent up a hunger-wail that made my throat thicken and my eyes prick with tears.

'Ilario!' Federico bustled up to the foot of the bed, gesturing for the others with him to stand back.

I saw Valdamerca's long-nosed equine features at the back of the group; she caught my eye and gave me a grim smile. Reinalda's look was softer. She stood with her sister, her arm linked through Sunilda's, and had the same look as her mother. *Welcome to the sisterhood.*

That's right, I thought groggily. Carrasco told me. Reinalda married, a year back; she has a baby. Sunilda, no, she's not . . .

Bariş's voice came from the far side of the bed. 'Don't trouble her long, sir. I've given her a drink for the pain, and she'll sleep now.'

Federico waved an impatient hand. He frowned a little, looking down at me.

'If I'd known . . . ' he began slowly.

'If you'd known I could be put to stud,' I said acerbically, 'you would have included that when you sold me to King Rodrigo. Right?'

'You do me very ill.' He made a gesture, as if he would reach out to me, but didn't complete it.

'Signor Federico.' Honorius's brusque tones came from the hearth. He interrupted a minute or two before I had told him he should, but I was grateful all the same.

Jesu! I can't breathe!

With the servants of Aldra Federico, and the retinue attending

Valdamerca and her daughters, and Neferet's women acting as chaperones, as well as at least four of Honorius's soldiers, armed in mail, and lining the walls, I found the room very much too crowded. Polite words were spoken, the dozen or so people in the room congregating at the foot of my bed, and then moving towards the cradle. I wondered if I could pull the bed-curtains and fall asleep without anyone noticing.

As I thought of it, a figure stepped alongside the bed, running the curtain soundlessly along and blocking off much of the view of the rest of the room.

Sunlight shone in on Ramiro Carrasco's black curls. He gave me a strained smile, reached for one of the loose pillows that lay on the bed, and pushed it down over my face.

Ilario has started on a precarious path towards freedom, but
many challenges lie ahead, not the least of which include art, intrigue
and destiny itself. Not to mention assassination attempts, double crosses,
cross-dressing. And that's just the beginning. . . .

Turn the page for an excerpt from

ILARIO: THE STONE GOLEM

A Story of the First History, Book Two

To be published in September 2007.

An Imprint of HarperCollins*Publishers*

www.outofthiseos.com

www.myspace.com/eosbooks

From *Ilario: The Stone Golem*

Ramiro Carrasco has not seen me as a man!

It was the only thought in my head.

I couldn't breathe. His hands pressed cloth and a bulk of goose-down feathers into my mouth and nose. My vision blacked into sparkles.

My chest hurt as I tried and failed to pull in air.

It can happen just this easily! – because people are busy for a few minutes looking at the baby, because these curtains are drawn—

'Ilario's heart stopped.' Even Physician Bariş will say so. The labour of having the baby. Too much for a hermaphrodite body. Even Rekhmire' will believe it. The midwife will confirm it. Ramiro Carrasco has nothing to do now but wait until my face is blue and then scream out an alarm that I'm not breathing—

And Ramiro Carrasco has never seen me dressed as a man.

The pillow blinded me towards the left field of my vision, but left a sliver of my right eye clear. Carrasco stared down at me, his expression curiously desperate as he bore down with his full weight.

I had time to think *Shouldn't I be the desperate one?* and ceased to claw at the pillow, and at his rock-hard muscles.

I let my arm fall out loosely to the side, over the edge of the bed.

Hard ceramic clipped the tips of my fingers.

My heart thudded hard enough to take the remaining air out of my lungs. My ribs ached with trying to breathe. And— Yes, this is where I saw one of the servants set down a water-jug. A brown-glazed pint jug, with a narrow neck, and two moulded loops for lifting.

My head throbbed under the pressure of his hands. I slid my fingers through the glazed loops at the jug's neck, gripped tightly, and locked my elbow. The weight pulling on tendon and muscle told me it was still completely full.

Lifting pottery and the weight of water together, barely able to see where I aimed past the pillow and his arm, I brought the jug round in a hard arc. And crashed it into the side of Ramiro Carrasco's head.

MARY GENTLE published her first novel at the age of eighteen, and has a master's degree in Seventeenth Century Studies and another in War Studies. The author of several novels, including *A Sundial in a Grave: 1610,* she lives in Stevenage, England, with her partner Dean Wayland.

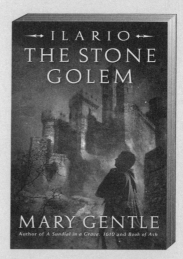